A riveting read. **The Last Moon** is a novel set against the 1902 eruption of Mount Peleé on the West Indies island of Martinique that resulted in the death of some thirty thousand people and the seaport town of St. Pierre consumed by fire—an impressive historical novel, author DeAnn Lubell has paid careful attention to detail and accuracy with respect to historical facts including the Creole language spoken there, the culture, lifestyles, geography, and the geological phenomena that occur with respect to the eruption of a volcano. Deftly written from beginning to end. **The Last Moon** is very highly recommended for community library historical fiction collection. *Midwest Book Review*

❏ **Andrew Neiderman**, the international best-selling author of *The Dark, The Devil's Advocate, In Double Jeopardy, The Curse,* and *The Magic Bullet* to name a few, as well as the highly acclaimed writer of the V.C. Andrews series. The 2010 novel *Guardian Angel* by Andrew Neiderman celebrates his 100th published book.

"The authenticity with which DeAnn Lubell fictionalizes the actual events in her novel *The Last Moon* gives the reader the sense of being an eyewitness to historical events, but the manner in which she captures the real character of the people, their struggles, the political intrigues, and betrayals makes this a truly riveting dramatic read with the added bonus of all the history and culture. Her graphic depiction of St. Pierre, down to the smell of Mt. Pelée's white ash, the Creole rhythms of the inhabitant's speech, the rich colors of the vegetation and flowers, and the vivid pain of the people who trusted their government, makes this all a roller-coaster ride. You can't come away from this book without feeling this is an author who is passionate about her story."

❏ **Barbara Seranella**, national best-selling mystery writer of *No Human Involved, No Offense Intended,* and *Unwanted Company.*

"DeAnn Lubell has done a wonderful justice to the people who perished in the 1902 eruption of Mt. Pelée. She has successfully recorded in (almost too) vivid detail the events surrounding the tragedy of St. Pierre. She does so many things well—painting the gay atmosphere of turn-of-the-century Martinique, catching the flavor of the West Indies, as well as faithfully recreating the horror of natural and man-made disaster alike. *The Last Moon* is a wonderful, sad history lesson wrapped in a beautifully wrought epic romantic novel."

❑ **Tish Martinson**, French West Indies born and raised, and the author of *The Last Lover*.

"Having been born in the French West Indies and the niece of the island's mayor, I found DeAnn Lubell's gripping tale of Martinique's mysterious characters and intriguing, eruptive society most compelling. Not unlike what I at times experienced as a child in the islands, such as the undertow of social racism and the overflow of selfish hypocrisies, the political power struggle between blacks and whites, and then again, between those of island birth versus the newcomers, all very familiar, yet told here with new spice. This story brought to surface a well of vivid memories and information passed on to me during my youth by my elders, black and white alike. A road taken, a sight described, a food eaten, a mood felt through DeAnn's descriptions took me back on a well-known journey through my own past while still enticing me onward with its intricate plot and building mood of doom to come. Albeit we know, through recorded history, of the story's inevitable outcome—the eruption and devastation of the Mont Pelée volcano—we are, nonetheless, swept on into the story, transported especially by the vivid characters. *The Last Moon* is a delightful novel told by an artful storyteller, DeAnn Lubell. Once started, it is a compelling read."

❑ **Barbara McClure**, former publisher/owner of the *Desert Woman*.

"DeAnn Lubell's new novel *The Last Moon* is a fascinating, beautifully told story, meticulously researched for historical accuracy and integrity. The reader will be captivated by the colorful history and locale intertwined with the play of human emotions leading to the devastating volcanic eruption on the island of Martinique in 1902. No less intriguing are the author's own synchronistic experiences, which led her to chronicle this little-known tragedy."

❑ **Fred W. Renker**, author of *Conversations in the Lobby*.

"DeAnn Lubell's *The Last Moon* is a fictionalized account of the actual 1902 eruption of Mt. Pelée on the Caribbean island of Martinique. It is wonderfully written—filled with period detail and characters that truly come to life. The vivid descriptions of lives forever altered by this historic story draw the reader into a story that is both suspenseful and heartbreaking."

The Last Moon

DeAnn Lubell

To order additional copies of this book, contact:
Xlibris Corporation
1-888-795-4274
www.Xlibris.com
Orders@Xlibris.com
68637

MARTINIQUE

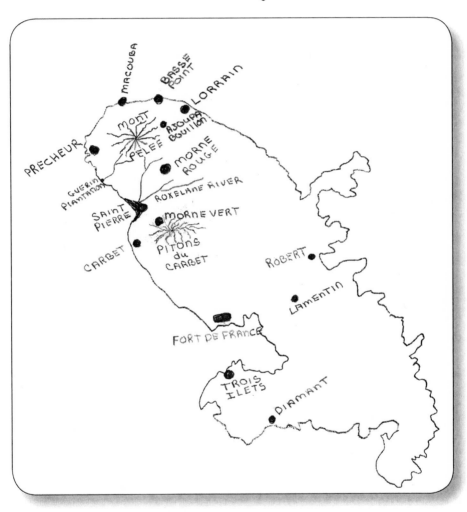

WEST INDIES

To the memory of

Joseph Lubell, who patiently supported my efforts and believed in me

Jackie Lee Houston, friend and champion

Yves Clerc, who opened the doors to my dream

Barbara Seranella, friend and author

Fred Renker, friend and author

ACKNOWLEDGMENTS

I must extend my deepest appreciation to historian, artist, and friend Marie Chomereau-Lamotte of Le Robert, Martinique, for the contribution of her vast knowledge of St. Pierre's colorful history and for her exquisite detailed drawings of that enchanting time.

Special thanks to the following people for their help, support, and dedication:

- Alain and Catherine Clerc, of St. Pierre for their tours and history lessons
- Marthe Hayot, of Fort-de-France, Martinique, for her outstanding hospitality
- Lyne-Rose Beuze, of the Fort-de-France Bureau of Patrimoine
- Judith Johnson, editor and friend, who dedicated long hours of editorial skills
- The McAllister brothers, friends and believers
- Publisher/editor Barbara McClure, friend and editor
- Andrew Neiderman, friend and author
- Tish Williams, Caribbean born, for edifying my limited French and Creole

PROLOGUE

The West Indies, May 8, 1902

Clear blue skies, a windless afternoon, and the gentle lapping of the sea against the hull of the steamship *Silver Eagle* should have guaranteed trouble-free sailing to the French-owned island of Martinique less than an hour away. The American captain of the *Silver Eagle*, David Cabot, had just departed the island of Dominica, where solemn English officials issued warnings that the volcano Soufrière on the island of St. Vincent was in full eruption. All vessels traveling the trade wind route along the curvature of the Lesser Antilles islands were advised to stay clear of the disaster area.

Leaning over a vellum map of the West Indies, David manipulated a magnetic compass and nautical divider to chart a new course a good distance from St. Vincent in hopes of reaching Martinique by sunset. Four months had passed since his last port of call to this island paradise and its coastal town, St. Pierre, often referred to as the Little Paris of the West. It was of no wonder that foreign ship crews and sightseers sailing in from all over the world rejoiced when setting anchor in its scenic crescent-shaped roadstead. Intoxicating to the senses, St. Pierre's colonial charm, mystical culture, and forbidden offerings were irresistible.

Five years ago, during the *Silver Eagle's* inaugural voyage, David, upon first sight of the pretty seaport town, fell under its enchanting spell. Yellow stone buildings, red tile roofs, and wrought iron adornments provided a dramatic contrast to the adjacent rolling lime green hills and picture-perfect azure blue harbor. Waterfront bars, brothels, and back alleys enticed lonely sailors seeking lustful favors. Centuries of interracial one-night stands and love affairs produced a mixed-blood race of stunning mulatto women with skin of white, cocoa, orange, and black;

eyes of emerald, sapphire, citrine, and amethyst; and athletic bodies, tall, strong, and sexy. These intelligent, bewitching females knew how to calculate every sensual move for maximum allure.

One such mulatto, Yvette Chevalier, the tenacious, well-educated daughter of a banana plantation owner, had captivated David with her green eyes, copper hair, honey skin, long legs, and irresistible beauty. He adored his island goddess like no other port of call woman he had ever experienced in his seafaring life.

There was a dangerous and ugly side to St. Pierre that David respected and feared. His breathing quickened with thoughts of the inactive volcano, Mont Pelée, rich with dense green jungles and mineral-healing waters. Observed from the sea, the formidable mountain appears as a gigantic octopus with thick tentacles wrapping around the northern tip of the long, kidney-shaped island in one solid hold. Innocent in appearance and unpredictable in nature, its capability for thermal-combustion energy was mighty enough to annihilate plant, animal, and human life within minutes. Fifty years earlier, Mont Pelée briefly awoke to spew ash about the land long enough to remind those living and working within its umbra of its supremacy; then, just as fast, it returned to its slumber.

David was more wary of a second threat to St. Pierre, not as prevailing as the omnipresent volcano, but just as deadly. For decades, corrupt white French officials and men of business had placed politics, greed, and racial intolerance above the welfare of the island people. In many ways, St. Pierre was utopia; and in many ways, it was purgatory. A presentation of refinement and loveliness on the outside, but upon closer look, behind the cloak of its dazzling facade, the dark, invisible world of crime and injustice was not so different from the unseen molten lava bubbling deep within the magna chamber of the serene mountain overshadowing the vulnerable city and harbor area.

The map before David detailed familiar bodies of land and waterways along shipping routes that formed a chain all the way from the eastern coastline of the United States through the Caribbean down to the northern tip of South America. Three to four times a year, he navigated his steamship between the port of New York to Venezuela, loading and unloading passengers and cargoes at various stops.

David was in the middle of calculating the suggested detour route when a chorus of terrified screams shattered the tranquility. Startled by the unexpected commotion, he dropped the magnetic compass. Turning away from the charting table, he faced his first mate, Nathan Smith, who stood nearby behind the pilot wheel. Nathan's eyes were transfixed on the bow.

"Sir, look ahead," instructed Nathan.

David aimed his mahogany and brass pocket telescope in the direction of the starboard railing, where he spotted three hysterical female travelers, silk bonnets askew, pointing white-gloved fingers toward the open sea. As the southern horizon sharpened into focus, his knees buckled. Human and animal carcasses littered the ocean currents, their bloated remains burnt beyond recognition. Stomach bile rose to his throat. He stared in disbelief as frenzied sharks fought over charred flesh of the dead. This carnage could only be the consequence of a disaster of unimaginable magnitude. One passenger pressed a lace handkerchief to her lips and fainted.

"Nathan, do you not remember being advised in Dominica of volcanic eruptions currently taking place on the island of St. Vincent?" asked David. "This volume of destruction could not derive solely from the activities of its volcano Soufrière. St. Vincent lies too far away."

"Aye, sir," agreed Nathan. "St. Vincent is almost one hundred knots from our current bearing of fifteen degrees latitude north and sixty degrees longitude west. There should be no signs of a volcanic aftermath from Soufrière in this area."

"What can this mean?"

"I can think of only one answer, sir," said Nathan. "Another volcano on another island has erupted at the same time. Begging your pardon, sir, but you must take into consideration that Martinique is less than twenty knots away. It could be Mont Pelée."

"It surely cannot be Mont Pelée," snapped David in nervous response to such an unthinkable notion. He removed his captain's hat and, with the sleeve of his jacket, wiped away droplets of perspiration forming along his hairline. "Please, God, don't let it be so."

PART I

1

Marcel and Eveline—Tragedy and Destiny
1874

In late March of 1874, feeling the luckiest man alive, Marcel Chevalier, an established plantation owner from St. Pierre, Martinique, set sail on a British steamer headed for Europe to visit his parents and sister in Arles, France. Unlike his two younger married brothers, Bernard and Grégoire, Marcel was a bachelor. His refined good looks, thick auburn hair, and charismatic demeanor kept his genitalia in high demand with a smorgasbord of island women: rich, poor, prostitute, black, mulatto, and white. A lifestyle that he would not trade for anything in the world—it suited him perfectly.

Marcel, relaxing with a glass of cognac in a quiet corner of the ship's great, elegant smoke-filled saloon, exchanged news and anecdotes with two prominent businessmen—a textile and weaponry exporter from Liverpool and a Wall Street financier from New York. This marked the third evening in a row on the transatlantic voyage that the three men had met to engage in predinner drinks, cigars, and conversation, hardly noticing the other first-class passengers, who played cards, read books, and occupied themselves in idle hobbies of art, music, and knitting to stave off travel boredom.

"My great-grandfather started a lucrative Liverpool company in 1791, trading goods in exchange for African slaves to sell to Americans from the lower states," remarked the exporter, his belt-busting belly rubbing against the edge of the table. "After the abolishment of slavery a few years ago, our bills of lading changed, but not for the worst. Transcontinental traffic of goods in demand is flourishing. Now then, Mr. Chevalier, please tell us about your business."

"Yes, Marcel, I too would like to know what led you to become a plantation owner," chimed the American financier, toying with his goatee. "The port of call that we made in Martinique was just long enough for me to develop much curiosity about your island."

Marcel selected a cigar from a humidor, snipped off the end, and brought the flame of a kerosene lantern to the tip. After the first intake of the aromatic smoke, he sighed, satisfied with the flavor, and spoke. "My grandfather and grandmother—Leon and Amy—and their twin five-year-old sons—my father, Jacques, and his brother, Edward—relocated from France to settle on the island of Martinique in 1830. Leon began operating trading posts in the major port cities along both coasts. Within a decade, he had earned the trust and respect from both the natives and the whites. It was his hopes that his sons would follow in his footsteps. Edward demonstrated great interest in the family business. However, by the age of twenty, my father was clearly more interested in the magical growing powers of the fertile, mineral-rich volcanic soil than peddling merchandise. A man of uncanny insight, and opportunity, Grandfather Leon purchased three parcels of land on the northern end of Martinique and presented my father with the opportunity to grow island produce. It didn't take long for my father to acquire success. He married my mother, Liliane, the daughter of a prominent St. Pierre esquire, in 1847, and within eight years, they had four children—myself, Bernard, Grégoire, and E'laine. By the time my father was forty-three, in 1868, he had become one of the largest producers of bananas, tobacco, and sugarcane in Martinique, if not the world."

"Why is Jacques now living in France?" asked the American.

"Shortly before his forty-fifth birthday, four years ago," continued Marcel, "my father developed a respiratory disorder, forcing him to depart the tropical dampness and move to the South of France with my mother and E'laine for a more tempered climate. They purchased a charming two-story château in the countryside of Arles, France, overlooking the Rhône River on three hundred acres of grassy knolls, fishing ponds, and gardens. My youngest brother, Bernard, acquired the sugarcane plantation in Le Robert on the east coast of the Martinique. Grégoire, the middle sibling, received the smaller tobacco plantation in Basse-Pointe. And I acquired the main banana plantation near St.

Pierre. My brothers and I were well trained in plantation management, ensuring an easy transition. We were sad to see our parents and sister depart, however, I must say, thrilled to remain behind to continue our father's work with the soil."

Their conversation was interrupted when, at precisely six o'clock, an ear-piercing screech resonated from the steam-whistle, signaling passengers that it was now time for dinner service.

Seven days later, Marcel found himself in Liverpool and, forty-eight hours after that, the South of France, where the reunion with his parents and sister commenced. On his third morning in Arles, he was enjoying a quiet breakfast and reading the Sunday newspaper at an outdoor café near the popular Hôtel du Forum in Arles. The air was cool and foggy, a nice change from the suppressed heat of the Caribbean.

A petite, attractive woman with an air of supremacy strolled by his table with a feisty poodle pulling on the end of a leash in front of her. Marcel peeked over his newspaper, taking note of the woman's small oval face and prominent yet regal nose. Round dark eyes sparked like burning embers. The tiny raven pin curls framing her delicate face from beneath a lace-trimmed bonnet had him squinting for a closer view. She was young, maybe eighteen years old, and quite different from the women he knew in Martinique, not an exotic beauty, more European delicate. Her alabaster, fine Grecian appearance captivated him. Marcel was most intrigued.

Much to the woman's chagrin, the poodle stopped to sniff bread crumbs on the ground at an unoccupied table not far from where Marcel continued his observation. Annoyed by the delay, the dog's mistress stomped her foot. "Mauvais chien," she demanded, "allons!" It yipped once when the tip of an umbrella poked its wooly backside and then again when a high-top boot caught the side of its head in one swift kick. The startled animal broke free from its leash and fled to the other side of the public square, where it sat down in defiance.

"Je ne sais pas quoi faire avec lui," the woman complained with a gloved hand dramatically hitting her chest. (I don't know what to do with him.)

Marcel dashed across the rough-edged cobblestone avenue, retrieved the nervous bundle, and handed it back to its stewing mistress. Within those few seconds of chivalry, the course of his life would be changed forever.

"Merci beaucoup, Monsieur . . . ?"

"Marcel Chevalier," he replied with a bow. "And what is your name, lovely lady?"

"Eveline Madeleline Montcalm."

The blossoming of their romance was swift. Never were two human beings so different in beliefs, backgrounds, and upbringing. Marcel was gentle, easygoing, and a country boy at heart while Eveline was tempestuous, moody, and schooled in blue-blood tradition. The old saying that opposites attract proved true in this case. The new lovers saw what they wanted to see in each other at the moment of their passion. The weekend before departing for Martinique, Marcel married the French socialite in an elegant ceremony at the Montcalm estate. During the long honeymoon voyage back to Martinique, Marcel's impressionable young bride possessed the stamina of a sex-starved tigress. Their amorous journey, however, ended as soon as they reached the threshold of the plantation house in St. Pierre.

St. Pierre Market Place

On May 5, 1874, Eveline, almost one month to the day after her arrival to Martinique, wrote the first of a series of letters to her mother documenting her new life on the island.

Dearest Maman,

I am sorry that my first correspondence to you is not of a happier note. I have made a very bad mistake by marrying Marcel and coming to Martinique. It is not what I had expected. It turns out that my premarital fantasies about life on an island were not realistic. Yes, the estate home is very beautiful and grand; however, that is where paradise ends for me. There are too many of the dark-skinned people here. They outnumber the whites four to one. The servants are slow and unskilled in accordance to our standards of domestic service in France. A constant stench of mold and mildew fills the nostrils, as it is very damp and humid. The food is awful. The juice of the fruit sweetens everything. You cannot imagine the bugs and spiders. Oh, they are most dreadful. I search my nightclothes every evening for these devils. Once I discovered a giant centipede hidden in one of my shoes. I thought my heart would stop. Ants are everywhere and in everything. Marcel and I have a net over our bed at night to prevent the mosquitoes from eating us up alive. I feel that one day I shall die from the bite of the spider. And every morning, for the past few days, my stomach ails me terribly.

A nightmare has surely befallen me, Maman.

Je t'embrasse bien fort, Eveline

Le 25 1874 Mai

Dear Maman,

I write to you a quick note. I have wonderful news. I am with child. Life seems a bit bearable now. The doctor tells me that the baby will arrive around Christmas time. It will be my best holiday gift ever. I still deplore this dreadful place, but at least now, a child might fill my lonely life. My husband certainly does not. It saddens me to learn that you and Papa are having health issues

with the gout and shingles and unable to travel here. It is just as
well, you would be miserable.

With joyous heart, Eveline

le 15 1874 Juin
Dear Maman,

I cannot stop thinking about the baby inside me—my child.
It makes me feel in charge of my life. Marcel seems very pleased
about my condition. He tends to me unlike before. I can tell he does
not love me so much, but he does exhibit some feelings for me and
our unborn child. It is a wonder that my belly does not show this
pregnancy as yet. I asked Marcel if perhaps we can give a party of
celebration in late July to announce our blessing. Planning for it
would occupy my mind. He told me that come October, after the
rainy season, there would be many parties, operas, and plays at
the Grand Theatre in St. Pierre that we may attend. I explain that
by then I will be the size of a bloated pig and in no mood nor shape
to be seen in public. He said whatever will please me. At least,
planning for this event shall keep me occupied in this hellhole.

My love, Eveline

le 5 1874 Septembre
Dear Maman,

I had hoped that my party would be one of the grandest that
the upper white class, including the island's elite Families of Ten,
would have ever experienced on the island, thanks to the social
training you provided me. Oh, but it was to be a notable social
affair. Two days before the party, Marcel's brothers and their
families arrived from the east-coast plantations. I had a special
dinner prepared in their honor. It went well. On the morning before
the party, dark clouds rolled in from the southeast. By the following
morning, the winds were howling with great force. By noontime,
a powerful storm slammed into the island. Flash flooding washed
out many roads. No one was able to travel to the plantation. We
had no choice but to cancel the affair. That night I overheard my
sisters-in-law talking in excited whispers in the library. Maman,

they actually pitied me. They said Marcel should have known better than to allow me to schedule a major social event this time of year. They said that we would be the laughing stock of St. Pierre. They called me the naive city girl from France trying to fit in where she didn't belong. Who are these people to pass judgment on me? I am a Montcalm, for the love of God. I fear, Maman, travel to the continent will be impossible until after the baby is born. Then, as soon as I can, I am returning to Arles.

Your daughter Eveline

le 15 1874 Novembre
Dearest Maman,

André was born premature two weeks ago. He is no bigger than a sparrow. The doctor said that my son could not tolerate a lengthy voyage overseas to Europe for several years, if he survives. He is a frail infant with a weak heart. My husband is back to his old routine and is gone most of the time. He claims that nothing he does makes me happy. I loathe the man. We sleep in separate rooms. I shall never allow Marcel to touch me again. He will be shot by my own hand if he tries. Rumors have it that he spends his free time at a brothel in St. Pierre called Maison Des Chats. Let him be with his filthy whores. Of course, we put on proper social appearances and act the perfect couple when out in public. Rarely do we speak. I am a prisoner now. There is no escape at this time, as I would never leave my dear son. My decision is to stay here and suffer this wretched lifestyle no matter how long it takes. When André is strong enough, we will leave together. Oh, how I long for the cool breezes of home.

I do hope you and Papa are fine, Eveline

2

Eveline and André—Tortured Souls
December 1882

Marcel may or may not have recognized Eveline's fragile emotional imbalance and her steady indulgence of apple brandy, nor cared. He opted to look the other way and spend the majority of his spare time absent from the rambling, loveless plantation house, his undesirable wife, and his strange, sickly eight-year-old son. He was freer and happier residing at the tiny bungalow located five miles away in the mountain village of Morne Rouge along the south slope of Mont Pelée with his handsome mulatto mistress, Nicole, and their giggly green-eyed, redheaded one-year-old daughter, Yvette.

Perhaps if Marcel had known the disturbing, twisted acts taking place within his wife's chambers at the plantation house during his retreats, he would have dealt with Eveline in a different manner, kindly sparing his pliable son irreparable emotional damage spawned by a despondent mother consumed with isolation lunacy.

Eveline, incapacitated by a broken ankle caused by a drunken fall and suffering in a bottomless abyss of self-pity, languished her time within the confines of her private suite. Her only obtainable pleasure was the peculiar games she played with André. Games a mother should not be carrying on with an impressionable young boy who had no social interaction with other children and who knew nothing more than a secluded life with his Maman, whom he adored.

André possessed no barometer for normalcy. His father dropped by the plantation house once or twice a week to check his mail and collect his record books, long enough to briefly tussle with his son's long, thin black hair and then disappear as fast as he came. André was an angry, confused child, who, when not getting his way, flew into uncontrollable rages lashing out at the nearest object, animal, or person. Only his mother could control him, and Henrillia, the black plantation housekeeper. Henrillia, wide at the hips with an engaging smile and loving heart, had nurtured Chevaliers for decades. Her cooking and nursing skills were legendary. She was the only person of color whom Eveline ever practiced any tolerance and patience toward.

Henrillia had cared for André since the day Eveline gave birth. This was the newborn baby that none of the other servants would go near because of his unsightly appearance and constant wailing. Superstitious beliefs prompted rumors that the wee creature was an incarnation of something evil. Henrillia right away felt sorry for the odd-looking infant no bigger in size than a large rat. In fact, the tiny baby resembled a rodent with its strange black eyes and hawkish nose dominating the entire upper portion of its face. Henrillia did what she could to humanize André's atypical existence by providing an essence of the affection that he craved, despite the restraints that had been placed upon her from Eveline. Henrillia was clueless as to what went on behind the locked doors of her mistress's bedroom with André. Her sixth sense told her that these "games" they played were in nature disquieting. As a dutiful servant, she decided that it was best to mind her own business and ignore any curiosities about abnormal behavior.

One of these clandestine games was called Ladies Teatime.

Eveline donned a long green silk kimono, her favorite lounging costume. In her drunken stupor, she granted André permission to investigate her armoire and select whatever outfit appealed to him to put on during game time. The boy took pleasure in the feel of the expensive fabrics brushing against his cheek as he searched for his favorite selection—either the pink negligee edged with black feathers or the red satin day dress. André had fun playing dress-up in her gowns, jewelry, wigs, and makeup. Like a peacock, he pranced back and forth in front of the mirror while cups filled with his mother's mixture of black China tea and fresh goats' milk steeped to perfection. Mother and son would then pretend they were best friends in Arles having afternoon tea at one of the upscale restaurants. Eveline often addressed André by the name of Nanette. He did not think that anything they did together was out of the ordinary; he was too naive to know any difference.

Eveline kept a silver flask hidden away in her lingerie drawer. André's nostrils flared at the strong aroma of apple brandy that his mother generously added to her own tea. She told enchanting stories about growing up in Arles. "André, my darling," said Eveline, her breath reeking of alcohol, "one day you must go to Arles. There you will find much happiness with your grandparents Montcalm. It is my wish that you are educated in fine arts as you demonstrate a talent for painting. Take a look at this petite masterpiece, for example, my love." She held up a sheet of paper. An image of a long-stemmed black rose oozed blood from the tips of its thorns. The crude rendering was obviously executed by the hand of a child, not by a professional; yet in his mother's eyes, it was quite good for a youngster. "This drawing shows much promise. I predict that you, my son, will be a famous artist one day. Yes?"

The mending of Eveline's ankle was slow in progression; in fact, the doctor ascertained that the bone was not knitting properly and suggested surgery. This unexpected prognosis sent Eveline's mental health into a radical decline, her marathon bouts with alcohol worsening.

Soon after the doctor's visit, she held yet another tea party with her son. André reacted in fear to the uncontrolled rage reflected in his mother's swollen red eyes. For the first time ever, he did not feel like participating in their afternoon games, and he did not want to be alone with her. Calling him by his pretend name of "Nanette," Eveline forced him to dress in a black linen mourning dress and a black veil. She shoved a bottle of champagne in his hand and invited him to celebrate the unfairness of life and the virtue of death.

"Your father, he prefers his voodoo whore to your Maman," said Eveline, tipping her bottle of champagne and gulping. It spilled onto her green kimono. "Nicole seduced your father with black magic. She is powerful. Do not trust those of dark skin as they worship Satan."

Eveline coaxed André to consume the whole bottle of champagne—a deadly amount for a child. He somehow managed to unlock the bedroom door as soon as his mother drifted off to sleep. Staggering in a zigzag line down to the end of the hallway, he whimpered for Henrillia before collapsing. By the time the servant reached him, he was barely breathing.

André spent a week in the hospital in an alcohol-induced coma. Meanwhile, Eveline, under house arrest, was secured in her room with a twenty-four-hour nurse at her bedside. By the time she had sobered up and realized what she had done to her son and to her reputation, she refused to eat or speak. Marcel paid off the local law enforcement to avoid her arrest and ultimate public ridicule. The doctor suggested that she be institutionalized. Marcel thought it best for everyone to send Eveline back to Arles into the care of her parents. Meanwhile, he would undertake the job of raising the boy himself. His guilt was enormous.

Calm and subdued, the night before Eveline was to leave for France, she asked permission to say good-bye to André, who was now home from the hospital recovering in the comfort of his own bed. Marcel refused.

"He is my son," she pleaded. "I will not hurt the boy. Surely, a few minutes alone with him, while you stand just outside the door, will cause no harm. I do not know when I shall see him again, Marcel. Please, I am begging you." Marcel relented.

Eveline entered her son's room fully clad as if she were going to a gala. She hobbled on crutches. She was elegantly dressed in an ivory brocade gown from Paris; it matched her skin tone. Tendrils of coiffed black curls fell in dainty swirls alongside her temples. Multistrings of iridescent pearls draped her long neck. But for the crutches and the splinted ankle, she was a picture of perfection. André was stunned by her presence and grateful to have his mother as she should be. Eveline stood by his side and held his hand. The pain in her eyes gave away the enormous grief that filled her soul. For a long time, she didn't speak; and when she did, her voice was low and graveled with resentment. His eyes widened.

"My darling little boy, your father either wants to lock me up like a lunatic in the asylum or send me far, far away from you. This breaks my heart and robs my spirit. You must be strong and sensible and never forget that your father is a very weak man who is possessed by an evil woman. Hold your father and his concubine accountable for my departure. I count on you to one day make them pay for what they have done to us. Do you hear? Make them pay. Promise me you will seek revenge against this woman of voodoo and their she-devil child. And never forget how much I love you. You are the only thing in my life to ever give me joy."

She bent down, kissed him on the lips, stood up, and removed a concealed pistol from within the cuff of her sleeve. Squaring her shoulders, she placed the weapon to her bosom and pulled the trigger. André watched in horror and disbelief as a bullet ripped through the fabric of her dress and exploded in her chest. A steady fountain of blood erupted from the wound, soaking everything in sight, including the traumatized boy. Eveline's dying words were but a whisper. "Maman, finally I am free of this ghastly place."

André tried to breathe. His lungs tightened up until no air would come in or out. In his weakened state, he nearly died. His recovery in the hospital from shock and the asthma attack was long and slow. Days turned into weeks. As soon as he was released and back home again, Henrillia rarely let him out of her sight. She nurtured the gaunt, vacant-eyed boy as she would nurture an abused puppy, knowing that he, like that puppy, could grow up to have one nasty bite.

Three months later, Marcel married Nicole and moved her and their toddler, Yvette, from the Morne Rouge bungalow into the Chevalier plantation. It didn't take long for André to feel like the outsider. His deep-seated hate toward this perfect family only intensified as his cherub half sister with the big green eyes, deep dimples, and red curls won over the hearts of everyone she encountered. On the other hand, when most people met the irritable, pouty boy, they shied away, repulsed by his standoffish personality and disturbing odd appearance.

3

Five Years Later
A Happy Family Minus One
August 1887

The stone tiles in the kitchen felt cool beneath the tapping feet of five-year-old Yvette sitting at the table near the stove where her mother, Nicole, was making callaloo soup, an island favorite. Nicole hummed a native song. Yvette's toes kept up with the rhythm of the melodic tune. A golden retriever slept near an open door. It was a sultry summer day. Soon, her father, Marcel, would be arriving for his noonday meal. The three of them would dine together. She never quite understood why her half brother, André, chose to eat alone in his room, as was his routine. In a way, she was glad. He was cruel, and she preferred distance between them.

"Maman."

"Yes, Yvette?"

"Why is André so mean?"

"Beware of this boy," warned Nicole. "He blames us for the death of his mother, and there isn't anything going to take that notion out of his head. His grandparents on his mother's side have petitioned for him to come live with them in France. Your Papa fights this request, as he wants the boy here with us. Your Papa feels much guilt, I fear. Of course, child, this is all too complicated for you to understand. Someday you will."

"He shoots rocks at me with his slingshot, pulls my hair, breaks my toys; and the other night, he put a mountain crab in my bedsheets. I am afraid of him."

"You best learn to defend yourself, my daughter," said Nicole in a stern voice while waggling her soup ladle and spraying broth in the air about the kitchen. "When I was your age, I was taught the art of carrying objects upon my head. I began my apprenticeship by balancing a simple jar of water. After a while, I could run and play without spilling a drop. This prepared me to become one of the *les porteuses*, carrier women, who possessed great strength and stamina. They work the toughest, most grueling jobs on the entire island. I am happy, my child, that you will never know this labor. However, I feel it necessary that you learn skills to defend yourself."

Yvette had a vague idea as to what Nicole was talking about. By chance, a few months earlier, she was granted permission by her mother to spend a rare day with her father, Marcel, accompanying him into town to meet with a newly arrived importer from San Francisco, who was a potential buyer of Chevalier bananas. They picked the man up from the dock area and transported him by carriage to one of the fields. Yvette sat alone in the backseat while her father and the American sat up front talking business. Marcel yanked the reigns and brought the carriage to a stop. He was explaining the potential crop yield when a group of stately barefoot women passed by on a narrow mountain road heading in the direction of St. Pierre. They carried upon their heads heavy baskets of produce and goods. Quiet as a mouse, Yvette listened to the conversation between her father and the visitor.

"Who are they?" asked the American.

"They are island porters," said Marcel. "We call them les porteuses."

"They are incredibly beautiful."

"There isn't a man alive who will argue that point with you," laughed Marcel. "Les porteuses represent more than two hundred years of inbreeding with black African slaves and the native Carib Indians, French, Italian, English, and Dutch. When slavery was still in force and ownership of another being in fashion, these females were so beguiling that the masters virtually became slaves of the slaves. Mulatto women held in bondage in the late sixteen hundreds often bought their freedom and the freedom of family members with the gold beads and favors acquired from admirers. Today's porteuses, and other mulatto women on the island, still cast the same kind of deviltry over the male species."

The American watched the women with great interest.

"By the age of ten they can accompany one of the older carriers on shorter excursions, sometimes up to fifteen miles a day," continued Marcel. "The professionals are capable of sustaining more than a hundred and fifty pounds of wares or produce on their heads. It takes two people to lift the bundle to the head of the carrier. If the carrier dares to sit down with this burden, it could break her neck. Concentration and balance are weapons against injury. Most of these women travel west from St. Pierre across the mountains to the port city of Basse-Pointe on the east coast and return to their starting point on the west coast. They make this fifty-mile journey between sunrise and sunset every day."

"And they go barefoot? No shoes?"

"Shoes would hamper the long journey, producing bunions and cripple feet. By going barefoot, the soles of their feet harden to padded skin tough enough to withstand rocks without pain. This is the fastest and best method of inner-island cargo transport available. A horse and buggy could never do what these amazing women accomplish in a mere ten to twelve hours of walking under pounding sun or rain. The threat of poisonous snakes and murderous bandits is constant. It is uncommon to see a carrier over the age of thirty. On the average, they can earn about six dollars a month."

"Six dollars?"

"Some can do better than that if they are young, strong, and fast. Compared to the average twenty dollars a month that a white male clerk can make in town, it is an excellent source of income for a woman of color."

A graceful sixteen-year-old walked by the idle carriage. The teen kept her upper body rigid while her hips swayed from side to side. Pressed against the thin material of the carrier's dress were firm round breasts. The American moved his gaze up from the girl's chest to focus on her face. High cheekbones, square jaw, upturned nose, and intense hazel eyes rattled his manly senses. Her skin was as radiant as the oranges she supported upon her head. Unlike her companions, who looped their hair into chignons, this girl allowed her black tresses to hang loose over a long, narrow, muscular neck. Her delicate hands swung freely by her side.

The carrier girl caught the eye of the stranger, and a slight smile touched her lips. Sensing his desire, she sashayed her backside while humming a sensuous tune. Her companions called out in complaint, "Cendreine, dépéchez vous. The day is ending, and we will be late. We are tired and the merchant, Philippe, will be most angry at our delay."

Cendreine fluttered her cat's-eyes at the American. Yvette suppressed a giggle as the man twisted around in the buggy and ogled the carrier girl for as long as he could before she disappeared out of sight.

"Don't get any ideas, my friend," warned Yvette's father. "These carrier women are only free from their merchants when they are financially able to buy their independence or when a suitor does his bidding. Until then, it is hands-off for most men. A romantic encounter would require too much energy for the carrier woman. None of which she can afford to lose. It is hard on the men who fall in love with these women, especially if work is the porter's first priority over the love of a man. They are exceptional females. Les porteuses innately know how to make a man feel like a man. I should know as I was one of the lucky fellows who married one."

With the side of her face pressed against the warm burgundy leather of the carriage seat, in those few minutes of eavesdropping, Yvette acquired the information about the origins of her magnificent mother. She decided that she would try to be just like Nicole—stately and strong.

Nicole placed the wooden ladle back into the kettle.

"Yvette, go upstairs and watch for your father."

The girl sprang to her feet with the dog barking at her heels and flew up the staircase to the second-story balcony. She stretched up high on her tippy toes, peeking over the railing in anticipation for that magical moment. Then, right on time, her father and his white stallion broke through the banana plants and galloped to the back of the house.

Yvette ran down the steps and out the front door like a small bird in flight with arms spread wide as he dismounted. She nearly knocked him off his feet with her powerful hug around his knees. He bent down and kissed her forehead. "Bébé," he cooed, kneeling eye level with his daughter, "for such a petite one, you are very strong." He took her by the hand, and they skipped into the kitchen, where Nicole greeted him with a kiss. Yvette giggled as he picked Nicole up by the waist and twirled her high above the terra-cotta stone floor. He shouted to the top of his lungs how much he loved her—how much he loved them both. The golden retriever barked in a gleeful reaction to the affectionate family display.

These sounds of tenderness did not go unnoticed by André, secluded in his room, where he slouched over a table, drawing morbid pictures in a notebook near an opened window. The noise of laughter and happiness nauseated him. He narrowed his eyes and gritted his teeth.

Later that day, André's only friend from school, Louis, stopped by from a nearby plantation to play. Louis, a bully, was from an all-white family. He too disliked those of color and was not afraid of anything or anyone. They were two peas in a pod and took delight in teasing and tormenting five-year-old Yvette. The two boys were in the middle of a chess game in the library when Yvette and her dog scampered through the room accidentally toppling over the chessboard, sending pieces rolling across the floor.

"Get your black ass out of here, you stupid nigger brat," screeched André.

Yvette fled to her room. She stood before a mirror and studied her features. She was not as white as the whitest cloud, more like caramel candy, but certainly not as black as licorice. What had André meant?

Seconds later, Nicole rushed into the room, scooped Yvette into her arms, and headed for the veranda overlooking the front grounds and the stables. She sat down in a big rocking chair. Yvette felt secure nestled in her mother's lap. The dog placed his chin upon Nicole's knee and whipped its tail against the floor. Yvette asked her mother why André had said those things. Nicole explained that Yvette's maternal grandmother was a black woman from Africa and her grandfather a white man from Ireland. With the bloodline of these diverse ethnic backgrounds, along with that of her white father, Yvette had inherited the best of everyone.

"Now you listen to me, girl," instructed Nicole. "I want you to remember my words for the rest of your life. It is not the color of one's skin that makes one special, but the kindness of one's heart and the wisdom of one's mind. It does not matter that you have light skin. Being one of mixed blood can bring out the ignorance and cruelty in some people. Promise me that you strive to be the best at whatever you do whatever that may be. Be the bravest, the strongest, the funniest, and most important of all, the smartest human being possible. Allow no one to take away your self-esteem. Stand up for yourself. Be proud of who you are."

Yvette nodded, not quite grasping the lecture, but memorizing the words.

That evening, Marcel, in a rare rage, took a belt to André for saying such horrible things to his half sister. It was the first time that Marcel had ever really punished André. Caught up in culpability, he always excused the boy's behavior. Yvette felt relief that André got in trouble, and she hoped that he was hurting from the whipping. Knowing this, she slipped into a deep, content sleep with her dog curled up at the foot of the bed. About three in the morning, Yvette rolled to her side. As she reached out, her hand landed on something soft, warm, and gooey. In the light of the full moon illuminating her chambers, she tried focusing on the glistening pile next to her. Leaning in to take a closer look, she discovered clumps of yellow hair, blood, and a dislodged eyeball—pieces of her dog with the scent of animal death. Screams bounded through the house.

It took less than a week to book overseas passage on a cargo clipper ship for André to be exiled to France. After a short rail ride from Paris, he arrived at the train station in Arles, where he was delivered into the open arms of his maternal grandparents.

At least, for a while, there would be peace and harmony at the Chevalier plantation.

PART II
Eight Years Later

4

St. Pierre, Martinique
Yvette, Paul, and Maxi—the Hunt
August 8, 1895

As the soft golden light of dawn signaled a new day, it also signaled the arrival of the fishermen in the bay, the laborers in the fields, and the washerwomen in the river. It was a humid West Indies morning, and the Caribbean island of Martinique was stirring to life. A few miles inland from the turquoise coastline, four colossal black men, one fidgety sixteen-year-old boy, and one sure-footed thirteen-year-old girl, forged their way up the western slope of Mont Pelée in search of wild boar.

The girl, straight and tall as a palm tree, was sturdy for her age and gender. Apple green eyes reflected a zest for adventure. Unruly hair popped out like copper coils from beneath her ragged hat. She was island born and island raised. When allowed the freedom to be her unpretentious self, exploring the rawness of the mountain or the endless vistas of the banana plantation where she lived, she was her happiest. Earlier that morning, she had stuffed her pant legs into a pair of scuffed riding boots encrusted with dried mud from hunts of the past. Most often than not, the young teen shunned the stiff, fancy clothes of her father's social class; she preferred work shirts and khaki pants, which were more reflective of her own style of comfort.

In high contrast to the girl, the boy, a visiting relative from France, the son of a wealthy banker, wore pressed Bermuda shorts, starched white shirt, and safari jacket. His scrubbed pale face hosted a roadmap of freckles, and his nervous brown eyes were framed by thick glasses. Not one slicked-back hair on his head was out of place. His schoolboy appearance seemed more suited for the study halls and libraries at his private school in Paris.

The leader of the hunting party brandished his machete and cleared away the rope-thick lianas and mold-encrusted tree roots blocking the path to the low woods. Naked from the waist up, he wore baggy, lightweight burlap pants cropped off just above his mud-covered ankles and bare feet. Blue-black skin stretched tightly over his well-defined muscles. Like most of the population on the island, he was a direct descendant of African slaves. He slowed his pace and focused on the girl, who was in close step behind his callused heels.

"Tell me now, Mademoiselle Yvette Chevalier," he said in a sonorous island accent, "how you *be* on this most glorious day?"

"I'm okay, Maxi," she said. Her answer lacked conviction. "My summer at Uncle Gregoire's plantation was excellent even though I missed my home and you all. Paul taught me how to play chess," she pointed to the scrawny lad behind her.

Maxi glanced back at the boy and rolled his eyes. He was not happy to be saddled with someone as inexperienced as Yvette's cousin from the continent. Maxi's main concern was for Yvette, knowing that she grieved deeply from the loss of her beloved mother, Nicole, who had died a few months earlier of smallpox. To make matters worse, Nicole's death had prompted the unexpected reappearance of Yvette's half brother, André. This was bad news. Maxi's frown shifted to a grin as he surveyed his tomboy mistress.

"Maxi, what is so amusing?" asked Yvette.

"I was recalling that time when your aunt gives to you the fancy bonnet with the bird feathers and all those little white pearls. What a lot of bother you caused. You only wanted your old Panama. You say it *be* your lucky hat, that the fancy hats *be* silly."

"Poor Auntie was never quite the same after I insisted that feathers should be left on the wings of the birds rather than on obnoxious Paris creations."

"Oh, dear girl, it is so good that you have returned home," said Maxi as his machete cleared away a patch of forest reeds. "You have always been like the daughter to me."

"And you, a father to me," Yvette answered with love in her voice.

"Prenez garde!" shouted Maxi. "It is the tree of the tarantula ten paces ahead."

From a distance, the tree looked quite harmless. Maxi knocked the base of its trunk with his machete and vaulted back. A few seconds later, it was raining hairy spiders as big as Maxi's fist. Paul started squealing. He frantically waved his hands over his head and ran in nonsensical circles. Yvette broke into wild giggles at the reaction of her sissy cousin as dozens of startled tarantulas scattered into the safety of the woods.

"Mademoiselle Yvette, let us go forward now," said Maxi, laughing at the trick. "The *matoutou-falaise* will most likely not bother us now. They be very fast on the run, I think."

After several minutes of silent walking, Yvette spoke, "Maxi?"

"Oui, Mademoiselle Chevalier."

"Would you please tell Paul about what happened to your family in Africa?"

"Very well, we will take a short break, and I will tell Paul this story," said Maxi. The group stopped and sat down on the path. "Two lifetimes ago," Maxi began his tale with sorrow in his eyes, "my honored ancestors were very important members of the Senegambian tribe in Africa. My grandfather, father, and his brothers were great hunters—very proud men. White foreigners invaded their villages, enslaved them, and brought them to live and work the land of this island. My grandparents were separated and auctioned off to plantation owners, including the Chevalier families. Then the time comes when no more slaves live in Martinique."

"Why did your family stay on the plantation, Maxi?" asked Paul, swatting at a mutant mosquito flying near his head. "Weren't they free to go anywhere they pleased after the law against slavery was instituted?"

"The Chevaliers *be* very good to their slaves," answered Maxi. "Your uncle Marcel and me, we *be* the same age, and we grew up together on the plantation like brothers. Always I am treated like a member of the Chevalier family. Marcel gives me much respect and friendship. It has been an honor to work with him as his meat purveyor. It has been an honor to be his friend."

Yvette shifted her boar rifle. "How can you stand André? He is unkind to you too."

"Let us not talk of this person and spoil the pleasant day," said Maxi firmly. "Come, we return to the walk. We have a long ways to go yet."

Not paying close attention to where he was walking, Paul tripped over a long vine and knocked his rifle against the trunk of a tree. One round misfired into the ground. The tranquility of the dense forest shattered from the echoing explosion. Startled birds took flight in a fury of beating wings and screeching. Maxi's deep voice carried over the complaints of the birds. "I do not want to advance with the hunt today if you not watch where you go, Paul. Mont Pelée is no place to be careless. It is too dangerous."

"I'm sorry, Maxi," whispered Paul, chagrined.

"Very well, then," said Maxi, "I believe we had better keep our eyes and ears alert and be mindful of the hunt and not of old stories."

By the time the sun was directly overhead, they reached a break in the forest where the path ran twenty feet along the rocky lip of a thousand-foot cliff. Maxi motioned for them to stop for their noontime meal. Sitting in a circle upon mats, the hunting party dined on salt bread, cheese, and sweetened tea. They were ready for a respite.

With tea in hand, Yvette and Paul left the group and stood near the edge of the cliff to admire the unusual crystal-clear panorama of the coast. Rarely did cloud-shrouded Mont Pelée throw aside her foggy cloak to allow such views. Paul marveled at the magnificence of the land that stretched out as far as his eyes could see. Directly below were thick canopies of emerald-colored jungles, endless webs of white cascading rivers, and rich checkerboard carpets of sugar and banana fields. In the distance, four miles away, nestled along the gentle green hills of the aquamarine coastline, were the yellow and red buildings of the seaport town of St. Pierre.

"I am looking forward to meeting your friend Indigo in the next day or two," said Paul, breaking the silence.

Yvette smiled at the thought of her dear friend. "I've missed her a lot. You two will get along splendidly, Paul. You are the same age, and you have similar interests. Indigo is beautiful, smart, and very funny. I am scheduled to meet with her later this afternoon at the botanical gardens located at the edge of St. Pierre. The park is one of our favorite places to visit. There is a magnificent waterfall there. It is breathtaking. We made this arrangement a few weeks ago."

"How did it come about for Indigo to live with your family?"

"Like so many of the women of color on the island, Indigo's mother, a washerwoman, Honorine, had entered into a three-day affair with one of the foreign sailors who frequented St. Pierre's roadstead," said Yvette, recalling tales of Indigo's early childhood. "According to Indigo's mother, the sailor was a slightly built man from Denmark with sandy hair and the deepest blue eyes. Honorine was smitten with this likable fellow who treated her to sweets, a strand of gold beads, and a new straw mattress. She gave herself to him willingly in gratitude for his kindness. The result of this union was a baby girl with cinnamon skin and azure eyes named Indigo. The washerwomen who worked alongside Honorine would often tease her, saying that her baby would one day be a lady of means as she already processed priceless jewels. Honorine knew that this prophecy was most unlikely as daughters of washerwomen were destined to become washerwomen themselves as soon as they reached the age of twelve or thirteen. That was the order of things. River work is difficult, requiring these women to stand knee-deep in frigid waters from dawn until dusk under the relentless tropical sun. Garments and linen have to be smacked over and over against the rocks. Before the age of forty, most women contract a common river ailment and die.

"By the time Indigo neared the working age of twelve, it was evident that her petite size made her an unlikely candidate for the rigors of river work. This created a great burden for Honorine, who, in her midthirties, experienced severe weakness in her legs and pleurisy in her chest. She had hoped that her daughter would take her place in the river so she could retire and recover from her river ills. It would be too much to expect Honorine's husband of nine years to support the three of them on his meager dock salary.

"What happened?" asked Paul, intrigued.

"Honorine took in laundry for my mother," stated Yvette. "As soon as my parents learned of Honorine's economic plight and physical hardships, they invited Indigo to join our family. This is a common practice in Martinique. Mulatto girls and boys are often reared as members of prominent families. Indigo was clothed, fed, and even sent to private school with me. She was given her own room with a canopy bed and a valley view. I was so happy to have a sister in my life, even though at first she was shy and hesitant. Later, I found out that moving away from her home offered her the opportunity to break away from the advances of her flirtatious stepfather and the poverty of their humble surroundings. It was a dream come true to Indigo to have a real bed with real sheets instead of the thin ripped mattress and flour bags she normally slept on in their two-room shack near the west end of the Roxelane River."

"Why didn't she join you on vacation in Basse-Pointe?" asked Paul.

"Honorine's condition worsened, and that, along with the fact that my half brother, André, returned to the plantation after the death of my mother, caused Indigo to go back home to help out the best she could. I don't blame Indigo. André was suggestive and aggressive toward her when my father wasn't around. Taunting and flirting with Indigo gave him great pleasure."

"I feel I shall have to have a serious talk with cousin André about his inexcusable behavior," declared Paul, already smitten with a mulatto girl he had yet to meet.

Yvette sipped her beverage and grimaced. "Stay away from him, Paul. He's dangerous and he won't care what he does to you. Please do not challenge him."

Thoughts of André stirred up hurtful memories from that summer eight years earlier when her twelve-year-old half brother made his decision to terrorize her. The resulting brutality of the death of her dog inspired Yvette to develop survival skills not normally considered a part of an island girl's education. Maxi showed her at age eight how to throw a knife. Soon she was hitting her mark twenty feet away. On her ninth birthday, she pleaded for a target rifle. Maxi taught her how to stalk small game in the fields near her home. She was so unrelenting about her desire to hunt quarries of a larger size that by age eleven, her reluctant parents granted her permission to go on a mountain hunting expedition with Maxi. A natural-born hunter, Yvette easily bagged her first boar. She reminded Maxi many times that if she could kill an attacking boar, she could kill an attacking André.

"Is he really that bad?" commented Paul, almost reading her mind.

"Yes, he is really that bad," growled Yvette. "Be careful. André will only hurt you. I am afraid that you are too nice of a guy, Paul. Let's just get you back to Paris in one piece."

Maxi joined his young charges. "Our city is calm in this light of the morning. Now then, it is time for us to go on."

The hunters gathered their belongings and continued the difficult climb. As soon as they reached an elevation of two thousand feet, they entered the high woods called *grand bois*. Dense vegetation blocked the sun. The tiny hunting group quietly followed the narrow trail. Damp, stagnant air hung heavy with pungent smells of mold and decomposing vegetation.

Paul struggled up the steep, narrow path; he was tired and out of breath.

Brackish gel from slippery roots and wet moss oozed up like jelly and flowed between the toes of the men. Prickly vines, hidden in the green depths, grabbed and clawed at their ankles like spirals of barbed wire. The light of their torches exposed a variety of gnarled vegetation, enhancing the eeriness of the shadowy surroundings. Paddle-shaped palms formed thick overhead ceilings. Giant bamboos reached out with thin feathery leaves. Hidden in this impenetrable green fortress was deadly foliage armed with flesh-tearing thorns, numbing perfumes, and burning glazes.

The experienced hunters were solemn. They walked with great care. Their biggest fear was the bite of the fer-de-lance lurking within the dark shadows of the grand bois. The memory of fallen comrades who had died horrible deaths weighed heavy on their minds. Maxi first witnessed the death of someone from the poison of this snake when he was nine years old. He and his young friend had been walking through the jungle. The snake slithered out unnoticed from the dense underbrush. It happened fast. Fangs latched to the ankle of Maxi's friend. The boy dropped to the ground with icy chills followed by the paralyzing of nerves. His wound quickly blackened and softened as gangrene manifested with rapid speed that spread throughout the dying tissues of his ravaged body. Skin, muscle, and fat peeled away from the boy's skeleton in corroded ribbons. Within hours, the remains of Maxi's companion were no more recognizable than a piece of sun-rotted fruit with the stench of decay attracting swarms of flies.

The hunting party emerged from the jungle onto a rocky path reaching an altitude of 3,500 feet above sea level. Only pygmy trees, low-growing bushes, and miniature ferns could survive here. The air was thin and cold. Less than a thousand feet away was the summit of the volcano. The town of St. Pierre, in the distance, came into view as a yellow-and-red caterpillar trapped between the blue of the sea and the green of the land. A fine mist chilled their faces.

Maxi pushed Paul to safety behind him, tapped Yvette on the shoulder, and pressed a finger to his lips. He pointed to a line of bushes thirty feet away from where they stood. He winked. Yvette raised her weapon, and Maxi raised his.

The boar rushed from its hiding spot, stopped short, and surveyed its domain. Two huge tusks pushed out from a wrinkled snout. The enormous creature prompted gasps. Picking up the scent of humans, it furiously pawed the ground.

"Can you handle this one?" Maxi asked Yvette.

"Oui, Maxi," answered Yvette.

"Then it is all yours, mademoiselle."

Blowing puffs of vapor into the chilly air, the boar charged.

Yvette's closed her left eye and twisted her mouth as she lined up the animal within the crosshairs of her scope. It was an ugly, menacing, and hateful beast. In her mind, it was André.

"Ugly," she whispered as anger coursed down her fingers.

"Menacing," she murmured as she slowly squeezed the trigger.

"Hateful," she yelled as the rifle fired.

The boar dropped to the ground with Yvette's bullet lodged between its eyes.

The men and Paul danced and laughed around the fallen beast.

"Très bien. What a grand boar you have killed," they shouted in unison.

A faint smile moved Yvette's stiff upper lip.

"Oui, I have killed him."

5

St. Pierre, Martinique
August 8, 1895
Indigo and André—the Proposition

Dressed in a long white sheer dress made of the finest silk and embellished down the front with genuine pearl buttons, sixteen-year-old Indigo watched the rising sun through the brothel window and cursed her fate.

It had been two long months since she had last seen her close friend, Yvette. Indigo had been a happy part of the Chevalier family from the time she was twelve years old. She had her own room, she went to school, and she shared their meals. Indigo recalled how Yvette's mother, Nicole, had taught her the proper way to walk with an erect posture and a tilted chin. Indigo had spent hours in the plantation's rose garden reading and writing poetry or absorbing fashion magazines from France. In an old storage trunk in the attic, Indigo discovered expensive fabrics from Paris imported by André's mother, Eveline. Nicole granted Indigo permission to do what she pleased with the material. Indigo designed the most exquisite robes and dresses. Yvette clapped in celebration over each one of the fancy creations.

"Where in the world, my dear Indigo, are you ever going to wear such costumes?"

"Someday I shall be a respected lady of means living in the best section of Paris in a noble brick manor. I'll own an ivory carriage with grand horses. You'll see."

"I believe you will," Yvette had declared.

Now in the glow of dawn, on this eighth day of August, Indigo's dreams had been shattered as part of an intricate plan of André to wreak vengeance against the Chevalier family by first going after and humiliating Indigo, who was near and dear to them all. As soon as Yvette left for her uncle's in June, he approached Indigo's mother, Honorine, with the plan to put Indigo to work at the waterfront whorehouse Les Chats in exchange for many francs. Honorine was infuriated by this insult. She refused his offers even though her family was in financial ruins due to the costliness of her illness. Not giving up, André went back to offer Honorine a better deal only to find her sick in bed and unable to speak. Indigo's stepfather, Michael, however, was interested in André's offer. In exchange for Indigo, there would be a nice cottage in the better part of town, a lifetime allowance, and payment for all of Honorine's medical expenses. One stipulation, not one word of this deal was ever to be mentioned to anyone associated with the Chevalier family, not one word. Michael agreed. How could a man refuse such an opportunity? He would never have to work again. All of this wealth for the loss of his stepdaughter's virginity was a minor sacrifice. Honorine was too sick and weak to understand. Her input didn't matter to him anyway. Indigo dare not refuse this arrangement for the sake of her ailing mother, reasoned Michael. After all, they needed the money. End of story, no harm done. Michael suspected that Indigo's good looks would insure a good income as a whore, and she would be no worse off for it. He could care less what happens to her as long as he received his cut of the bargain.

In less than forty-eight hours, shortly after the deal was made, Indigo was delivered to Les Chats by her stepfather and placed into the care of Madame Rose. Indigo decided not to contact Yvette or Marcel for help. It was not protocol. She lived in an era when women had few rights, especially a teenager of color. Her usually sharp mind was clouded, and she felt powerless.

Upon arrival, she was examined by one of the brothel's seedy doctors, assuring virginal status. André was scheduled to be her first customer, and the time had come; today was the day. The thought of him touching her made her sick to her stomach. She had never met a more offensive man. It would be as if the devil himself took her to his bed.

Nineteen-year-old Luci Fetussie, a seasoned prostitute, received assignment to care for the "new girl" called Indigo. Luci had been a brothel whore at Les Chats since the age of thirteen and, therefore, considered one of the "old-timers" at the brothel. She was neither beautiful nor ugly, comme si, comme ça, yet blessed with a marvelous sense of humor, a kind heart, and a sensuous touch. It was up to Luci to make sure that all of André's bedding requirements were met. It did not take long for her to pity her new charge. She listened to Indigo's sad tale with keen interest and realized that the lovely girl did not belong in a brothel and certainly was not destined to be defiled by the likes of André. Luci's outrage escalated the more she thought about this unfair twist of life.

Earlier that morning, in the dark before the first rays of the sun, while the rest of the whores slept, Luci escorted Indigo to a large bathing room. Lilac oil scented the tepid water that filled a claw-foot tub. Indigo allowed Luci to help ease her naked body into the vat of bubbles.

"I cannot allow this crime to happen to you, and you cannot allow it to happen to yourself," announced Luci, sponging Indigo's back. "You are a special human being and too fine a young lady for a place like this. It is wrong and I must do something."

Luci towel-dried Indigo's damp skin, dusted rose-scented talcum powder about Indigo's neck, shoulders, and tied a white ribbon around her mane of sleek black hair. Pink rouge was then sponged onto Indigo's full lips. "You are utterly exquisite, dear Indigo. You are too perfect to be wasted on the worm André Chevalier. He is unsympathetic and brutal. His harsh lovemaking tactics will surely cause you unmentionable harm."

Luci retrieved a tiny pistol that she had hidden earlier between a stack of towels on a lower shelf and handed the weapon to Indigo.

Indigo eyed the weapon with puzzlement. "What is this for?"

"I have been doing a lot of thinking," said Luci. "Is it not true that your mother has acquired a new house, a paid doctor, and some of the money promised by André, yes?"

"Yes."

"If anything happens to him, no one is going to take that away from her. So kill him, Indigo. The worst that will happen is that they may send you away, but you won't go to jail for the murder of someone no one on the island can tolerate. It happens all of the time. No one wants the scandal. Then you would be free."

"Are you serious?"

"Oui. Kill him dead. Mort!"

"I couldn't."

"Yes, you can."

"No!"

"Listen to me, *ma chèri*, do you wish him dead?"

"I just want him to leave me alone."

"There is only one way for that to happen. Go ahead and keep the pistol. You will certainly change your mind. This I know."

6

St. Pierre, Martinique
August 8, 1895
Marcel—the Burden

Marcel had been up since four that morning, reviewing an export contract arranged between his St. Pierre shipping broker, Laurant Montour, and an Italian firm out of Lisbon. It was a lucrative deal representing the sale of tons of green bananas. The Chevalier banana plantation was having a busy, bountiful year, which was a good thing as it distracted him from brooding thoughts over the abrupt loss of his darling Nicole—at least, during daytime hours.

Marcel reached across his desk and unlocked an elaborately cut glass humidor. His nimble fingers danced over a row of highly prized cigars before selecting an expensive import from Spain. Savoring the cigar's mellow berry flavors, he finished reading the contract. It seemed in order of their agreement. He placed the cigar in an ashtray and picked up an ink-dipped quill pen. He was in the middle of applying his signature when a servant knocked on the open door.

"Sir, the morning postings are here."

Two travel-worn letters had arrived from Arles, France. One letter was from his father and the other from the mother of his first wife, Eveline.

Saving the worse for last, he opened his father's letter first.

July 10, 1895
Mon Cher Marcel,

Your house will seem empty without the warmth of Nicole by your side. For my granddaughter's sake, please keep your grief private. She needs you strong and steady now.

Keep a close eye on André. I know he is your only son, and I know how much you love him, but he is one not to be trusted, even if he is blood related. When he was living here in Arles, certain actions gave your mother and me much trepidation about the positive development of his character. He clearly demonstrated heinous attitudes toward life. I find him as a young man no different from the cruel boy of eight years ago. If anything, he is worse than ever. His recent return to Martinique has given me great pause. I fear for Yvette. You must watch your son and guard your daughter.

Allow me now to relay news from Arles. Your mother is doing splendid. She is deeply devoted to France—including the cold weather. Of course, a family reunion here with you, your brothers, and loved ones would fill her heart with joy. Your sister will be arriving by train from Paris the day after tomorrow. I know it is difficult for her with such a busy schedule. E'laine's haute couture is quite the talk of the continent these days. She is almost ready to debut her line of designs in Paris. I occupy my time reading current works of literature and playing chess.

Son, I truly miss my beautiful island home. I will never love another land as I love Martinique. Embrace Yvette. Your Devoted Papa

"You pragmatic old bastard," said Marcel out loud. "What shall I do about André? I prayed his return would give me solace. He seems incapable of compassion. I love him as a son, but I dislike him as a person. He is as heartless as his mother was."

Marcel missed his parents and wished they were on the island to enjoy the wonders of his highly inquisitive teenage daughter. Just last night, shortly after dinner, Yvette bombarded him with questions about her grandparents in Arles. Since the death of her mother, she had been desperately seeking answers to her identity.

"Oh, Papa," declared Yvette one evening, "I do so love our home and our plantation. I would never want to *have* to leave here like Grandpa and Grandma did."

"I know, Yvette, your passion for the land is obvious. This is your home and this is your inheritance. Someday it will all be yours."

Marcel picked up his mother-in-law's letter from atop his desk and walked through a set of French doors that opened out onto a private red-tiled terrace. Facing northwest, he viewed Mont Pelée standing like a green empress in the distance. Without fail, every morning, like everyone else, he gave thanks that the dormant volcano still slept. It had been fifty years since its last eruption. Marcel respected Mont Pelée. It concerned him that his headstrong daughter was up there hunting boar with her inexperienced cousin Paul.

"Dear God in Heaven," prayed Marcel, "please watch over those two today."

Marcel sat down in a lounge chair to focus his attention on the sealed letter held tightly in his hand. He knew the contents of its message. It would be no different from all the other postings from the Montcalms that had periodically arrived every month or so for the last dozen years with the same communication blaming him for Eveline's misery and death. He reluctantly opened the envelope and unfolded the sheet. In red ink across the top of stark white paper, the accusatory word "MURDERER" was spelled in bold letters. Nothing else was on the page.

"Why can't you let it rest, Mrs. Montcalm?" he pleaded. "Why can't you let it rest?"

Marcel crushed the letter. Never would he accept responsibility for Eveline's demise.

"More coffee, sir?" asked a large black woman who appeared at his side with a carafe of freshly brewed java. Thankfully, his housekeeper had interrupted his bitter thoughts.

"Thank you, Henrillia. Is my son up yet? We must depart for St. Pierre in one hour."

"Yes, sir," she replied. "He *be* up since half past seven."

7

St. Pierre, Martinique
August 8, 1895
André—the Revenge

Applying a straight-edged razor to his uncomely face, André studied his reflection in the mirror and brooded. How did he end up with this ugly mask? With a handsome father and a beautiful mother, it made no sense. He resembled neither one. He slid the blade across his hollow cheek and mulled over the absence of Eveline. In many ways, he missed her; in others, he did not. She had been a delight when she was sober and a horror when she was inebriated such as the time when he was all but a toddler and she pinned him to the floor during one of her drunken stupors. He could still feel the pressure of her dead weight against his chest and smell the stench of her sour breath. "You, my son, are nothing more than a misfit conceived out of lust."

"You were right, Mother," agreed André, rinsing off the shaving cream with water from a ceramic bowl on a stand. "I am a misfit—in more ways than you could have ever imagined."

Before sitting down at a wicker desk located near an open window in his roomy bedroom suite, André changed into white pants and collarless shirt. A breakfast of fried fish and potatoes cooled on a plate next to the morning mail on a silver tray. He eyed a letter postmarked from Arles. A rare smile broke his scowl. It was a posting from his grandmother Montcalm. How grand. He pushed away his unwanted food and read the news from home.

André missed his mother's parents, and he missed his friends. Arles had been good to him. He paused to roll and light a cigarette. The melodic sounds of workers singing in the nearby banana fields filtered through the opened window. He thought of this island, this plantation, this house, this room, and his mother's suicide. He had thought nothing more than this for years. In agony, André placed tight fists to his temples. His memories of the tragedy had haunted him since he was eight years old. He often awoke drenched in sweat and trembling from recurring nightmares. Drinking was the only coping mechanism that helped him get by day after day. It was a habit that he had learned all too well from his alcoholic mother.

"I need a drink," André announced to the ghosts around him. He retrieved a bottle of whiskey from the stash he kept under his bed. Removing the cork, he proceeded to gulp down huge amounts of the alcohol. Soon his nerves steadied, and the memories began to fade.

A knock on the door forced him to hide the bottle. "Oui, what is it?" he barked.

"It *be* Henrillia."

"What do you want?"

Henrillia opened the door with unease. She never knew what to expect from André when he was in one of his moods. "Your father says to be ready to go to town in ten minutes," announced the servant. "The carriage will be waiting out front."

"Tell him I'll be there momentarily."

As soon as Henrillia left, André buried his head in his hands.

"I promise you, Maman," vowed André, "that your death will be avenged as you requested when you decided to take your own life before me. But first, I want those who are guilty to experience fear and pain. It will take more planning and time; then, I will destroy them all. My greatest weapon is patience. When the sins have been cleansed, I shall return to Arles."

8

St. Pierre, Martinique
August 8, 1895
David and Stefan—the Arrival

Passengers aboard the *Silver Eagle* cheered as their ship steamed south down the palm-fringed west coast of Martinique and into full view of the French seaport town of St. Pierre. This picture-perfect city had stood awash in vivid Caribbean colors for more than two hundred years. Weatherworn, the saffron yellow of the stone buildings cast a rich, inviting warmth above St. Pierre's coastline. Sweeping across the top of these sturdy structures were tomato red roofs and seventeenth-century dormers. Open windows adorned by winsome hurricane shutters called out in muted shades of blue or green. Black wrought iron lattices decorated balconies.

Several travelers gathered near the bow. Those who had visited here on previous trips eagerly expressed their fondness for St. Pierre. An outspoken teenage boy from Maine on holiday with his parents was asking anyone within hearing range a barrage of questions about the quaint town and its vibrant roadstead.

"St. Pierre, my dear lad," declared a wealthy Boston businessman holding on to his bowler against the strong Caribbean breeze, "is one of the most prosperous ports of call in the Western Hemisphere. She is a gold mine of valued produce and wares. Her busy docks overflow year-round with cargoes of local rum, sugar, coffee, bananas, wood, and dye—just to mention a few. That is what this town is all about."

Leaning against the railing, a comely woman raised her hand to speak. A wide-brimmed straw hat decorated with a red ribbon that tied beneath her chin prevented the tropical sun from blistering her fair complexion. Long skirts billowed out around her. This marked the third trip in six years to visit her brother, who ran a small but successful export business near the lighthouse.

"To be certain, young man," she addressed the inquisitive boy, "the bounties of St. Pierre have been most excellent for my brother's trade business. The city may be a little crude around the edges in some respects, but it does offer exciting cultural activities. I very much enjoy its wonderful theater, operas, and carnivals."

A traveling preacher stepped forward and put a hand on the shoulder of the teen. "These good people have missed the essence of this wicked, but wonderful, place. I have traveled and preached the Gospel throughout the Caribbean for thirty years. St. Pierre is an equivocal town faithful to the praises of the Almighty on Sunday mornings and devoted to the songs of its waterfront whores on Friday nights. This is where her true soul lies."

"Why, Reverend!" gasped the woman.

"I do beg your pardon, miss," beamed the preacher, tugging on his graying beard, "but that is the truth of the matter." He winked, tipped his stovetop hat, and moved away.

In the pilothouse, David Cabot, the twenty-eight-year-old captain of the *Silver Eagle*, steered his turbine-powered passenger and cargo ship toward St. Pierre's roadstead where he would drop anchor. This maiden voyage of the newly launched ship marked the beginning of his commission to deliver mail, freight, and passengers from New York and deposit them to various Caribbean island ports before returning along the same route to the United States with a new batch of travelers and the hold of his ship bursting with island exports.

Thus far, the voyage had been uneventful. The first five days out of New York Harbor were spent sailing. On the sixth day, the *Silver Eagle* docked in Frederiksted, St. Croix. It was here where David began to understand the diversity of the islands in the Lesser Antilles. He took pleasure in the Spanish-influenced city of Frederiksted and its delightful blue-green buildings and yellow arcades. On the seventh day of the voyage, the steamer arrived on the Dutch island of St. Kitts. Old windmills dotted the barren countryside. David discovered a friendly fair-haired population as his crew unloaded barrels of lard, beef jerky, kerosene, flour, and three bags of mail. On day eight, the steamer reached Montserrat, where the populace still spoke with an Irish brogue as thick as that of their forefathers, who had established the town of Plymouth back in 1632.

The last stop before reaching Martinique was the British island of Dominica located one hour away to the north. Its craggy mountain peak emerged like a mystical apparition before sunrise in the early morning darkness of their ninth day. In the capital city of Roseau, David unloaded five American-made carriages, a small steam generator, mail, and three passengers.

All was uneventful, until shortly after departing Dominica, when the ship's first mate, Nathan Smith, discovered a frightened twelve-year-old black boy hiding in the cargo hold.

"What is your name, son?" asked David kindly.

"Stefan, sir," he answered while eyeing in fascination the captain's golden blond hair tied into a ponytail below his captain's hat. Stefan had never seen hair of such color.

David was impressed by the lad's command of the English language.

As soon as Stefan realized that he was in safe hands, he relaxed and told his story. "I ran away from home to escape beatings from my father. He most favored the taste of rum day and night. My mother feared that one day he would kill me. A week ago, she bribed a dockworker with homemade trinkets to sneak me aboard your ship as she could not afford passage. She was in hopes that I would have a better life in St. Pierre with my grandmother. I am sorry if I have caused you any inconvenience, sir."

Crocodile tears spilled from the boy's black eyes.

"Don't you fret, young Stefan," said David. "We will find your grandmother. Why don't you stay with me here in the pilothouse? St. Pierre's roadstead is nearly in sight."

David and Stefan, standing side by side, entered St. Pierre's port.

"Sound the arrival," ordered David.

One of the ship's four cannons was fired. A resounding boom echoed loudly across the roadstead and over the rooftops of the town. Stefan giggled at the noise and fanfare. This was mighty grand treat for a poor stowaway with no future. David smiled at the boy's reaction.

Ship greeters in St. Pierre

Within minutes, a small armada of crudely fashioned canoes approached them from shore. Each tiny canoe held two boys. Excited first-time visitors learned that the tobacco-colored ship greeters were called *ti canoties*. The ti canoties laughed and shouted and shaped their hands into the universal sign for begging as they neared the ship. Their comical antics and pantomiming bemused the ship's passengers, who tossed coins into the pristine waters of the seaport. The boys dove in unison deep into the bay. Their lithe naked bodies could be seen beneath the surface. The first boy emerged victorious with a recovered American Indian head nickel glistening between his teeth. Like corks popping up out of the water, one after another, they were all soon showing off their prizes of bright coins.

David pointed to the city and remarked to his first mate. "She's a pretty town, Nathan."

"Aye, that she is, sir," answered the officer who had entered St. Pierre's harbor many times before. "Behind all that quaintness looms an ugly side."

"What do you mean?"

"The black and mulatto majority, who have served the white French minority for more than two hundred years, are becoming more aggressive in expressing their grievances. There is a new attitude among the men of color. Some of the more educated ones have even managed to seize a few important political seats. This has not set well with the French white elites who have enjoyed colonial rule for nearly two centuries."

"No matter to me, the city is still a pleasing sight."

"Aye."

David turned to Stefan. "Well, young man, are you ready to explore this new land with me? It is my first time here too. We shall be brave adventurers together. What do you say?"

Although a little apprehensive, Stefan smiled at his new guardian and nodded.

9

St. Pierre, Martinique
August 8, 1895
Maxi—the Bite of the Demon

Yvette and Paul helped the hunters roast the gutted boar, wrap it in banana leaves, and tether it to a long pole for transport. Afterward, tired and hungry, they rested on straw mats around the fire. Maxi handed his young charges bits of the cooked meat.

"Maxi," said Yvette with her mouth full of the juicy morsel.

"Oui?"

"Did André's mother really shoot herself in front of him?"

"It's not good to talk about these things, Yvette, especially in front of Paul."

"I want to know. Papa will not talk about it. I get little bits and pieces from Henrillia now and then. Maxi, I am thirteen years old, please, no more secrets. I *have* to know."

"I want to know too," said Paul sheepishly.

Maxi stuffed a piece of the roasted boar into his mouth, studied the teens, and shook his head. At this point, what did it matter? Someone was going to tell the story sooner or later, and it might as well be him. Yvette sat cross-legged with her ragged hat in her lap and her short copper curls in complete disarray. Maxi loved her like an uncle would love a niece. Perhaps Yvette should know about the night André's mother killed herself. Maybe it would help her understand his out-of-control rage toward them. Yvette and Paul listened as Maxi spoke. Her green eyes narrowed and widened in response. Paul's mouth hung open the entire time, the meat balancing in midchew between his teeth. Stunned by the details of Eveline's suicide, the cousins stared in disbelief, for this was a tale so horrible, the mightiest of men would cringe.

"I feel sorry that André witnessed such a thing," said Yvette solemnly, "but I shall never forgive him for what he did to me and my dog. I was only five years old!"

"I know. That *be* a very bad time for you."

Yvette glanced at her pocket watch. She had three hours before she was scheduled to meet Indigo at the botanical gardens that afternoon. André had caused so many people so much heartache. It infuriated her that his indecent behavior had frightened Indigo enough to flee the Chevalier plantation. Yvette could understand why André was the way he was, but she could not condone his malevolent behavior toward decent people.

Large drops of rain ricocheted off Yvette's hat. She stepped up her pace along with Paul, Maxi, and the hunters. They made haste to leave the mountain before the weather worsened. "We must hurry," shouted Maxi, "the hard rain is coming."

A bamboo pole holding the prized roasted boar rested on the shoulders of two men as the hunting party made its decent down the mountain trail. Rain plummeted from the sky. Pelée's summit storms struck swift and hard several times a week. Yvette pulled her hat farther down over her ears against the downpour. The agile and experienced hunters proved no match for the strength of this tempest turning the path into a small stream. They were trapped where they stood as the rain hammered for five long minutes. It was no good to move on until it stopped.

"Ah, at last the rain is leaving. It has had enough for one day and so have we," said Maxi.

Maxi changed their course, leading them in a direction that would take them north toward the village of Le Prêcheur and along the coastal road to Fond-Corre, where they had left Yvette's horse and small surrey. It would be a longer route to follow, but easier.

As Maxi bent down to remove a fallen branch blocking the trail, a snake latched its fangs onto his forearm. One of the men grabbed a stick, forced the release of the snake's jaws, and flung it to the side of the path where it slithered away. Maxi cursed his bad luck. He began to shiver. It was the first sign that venom was entering his bloodstream. A minute later, he fell to his knees.

Yvette took out a knife from her pack. If the snake hadn't pierced a vein, Maxi may have a chance. She plunged the sharp edge deep into the fang marks, forcing the poison out with the blood. The nearest physician was more than two hours away; by then it would be too late. Maxi would certainly be dead. She knew that the men would not like it, but there was only one option.

"We must take Maxi to the jungle dwelling of the old voodoo woman, Aza."

"*Mon Dieu*, Mademoiselle Yvette, please do not make us go to de house of de witch," the hunters begged in unison. "We shall all surely die."

"We are going to see a witch?" asked Paul, incredulous. Between the pounding of the rain and the fright over Maxi's snakebite, he felt as if he was going to pass out.

"We have no choice," said Yvette. "Paul, you have to be strong. Let's go now."

Reluctantly, Paul and the men followed Yvette.

Glancing from side to side, the hunters felt as if every zombie in the universe was going to jump out from behind the trees and rob them of their souls.

"It is said that Aza is de queen of de zombies."

"Is she not de friend of Mademoiselle Chevalier and Maxi?"

"This witch is not our friend. I heard that five hunters were never seen again, and those men now *be* the fat chickens living in her coop."

"Hush," scolded Yvette. "Those rumors are not at all true. Aza is a wise and kind woman. No harm will come to us. Hurry up your pace. Allez!"

Twenty minutes later, they came upon a lone bamboo shack planted squarely in the middle of a secluded clearing. A patchwork of rusted corrugated tin adorned the roof, and a small wood crate served as the front step. Lying in the front yard was a little dog. He jumped to his feet and barked as soon as he saw the approaching strangers. A very tall black woman appeared in the doorway, wearing a bright yellow handkerchief turban with all three of its ends pinched up through the top. Her pantaloons, fashioned out of a lightweight sky blue calico and hand-painted with green frogs and orange butterflies, fit loose about her wide hips. A red tunic concealed enormous breasts. Her feet were bare save for a plain gold ring on her little toe. Heavy ropes of golden chains and medallions looped her neck, wrists, and ankles, causing a cacophony of jingles whenever she moved.

"Who is there and what do you want?"

The hunters and Paul froze.

"Maxi has received the bite of the fer-de-lance," cried out Yvette. "Please help us. Au secours! Sil vous plaits."

Aza lowered her weapon in response to the familiar voice.

"Oui, enfant."

The men placed Maxi's bloated body on a straw mat inside the dark shack. Aza heated a cast-iron pot filled with rum upon a wood-burning stove. She dipped a clean rag into the boiling liquid and applied it to Maxi's arm. The rest of the rum sterilized her tools. A sharp piece of green bamboo sliced through the wound. Blood, poison, and pus erupted from the incision. Once sufficiently drained, a hot metal cup covered the infected area. Festering flesh popped and sizzled from the heat.

"Fetch me that jar of leeches," Aza ordered Paul.

There was no describing how ashen Paul was at this point. His knees were knocking, and his head was spinning as he wobbled over to a rickety old cabinet. The shelves held wild herbs, witchcraft materials, and a myriad of potions. He retrieved a jar of live leeches—something no city boy should ever have to do. His stomach lurched at the sight of the slimy creatures. He handed the jar to Aza and, trying to disappear, backed into a safe, dark corner.

Aza selected five of the leeches and placed them on the wound. The leeches wiggled and squirmed before taking hold with their powerful suckers. Within minutes, they had drained enough of Maxi's blood to expand their bodies to over three times their normal size. Aza spread a voodoo concoction of crushed garlic, pepper, cinnamon, cloves, and orange leaves upon Maxi's festering arm and covered it with strips of white cloth. Taking the crisply roasted head of a fer-de-lance, she pounded the charred lump into fine black dust and added it to a mixture of rum and orange juice. Maxi's mouth was forced open and the drink trickled down his throat. The crude homemade medicine was biting and strong. Maxi coughed and gagged from the putrid taste.

"If Maxi survives the night," said Aza, "then he have a good chance to live. He must receive the drink every day for a month to be completely free of the venom of the snake. I will keep him here for healing time. I do not want his wife to come. She *be* in my way. Yvette, you and your cousin stay put." Aza pointed to the startled hunters. "You men must leave now."

The hunters bolted out of the door and did not stop running until they had reached the bottom of the mountain. Aza scowled at their antics. She sank down wearily into her rocking chair, stuck a corncob pipe in her mouth, and lit it with burning straw from the fire. Rings of smoke encircled her head and floated to the ceiling.

"Sit down by my feet, children."

Yvette did as she was told. The dog jumped into her lap and rolled onto its back. Yvette rubbed its underbelly. Paul remained petrified in the corner.

"I said *sit* down, young man," ordered Aza, pointing to the floor.

Paul didn't sit; he dropped. His teeth chattered, and his body shook. His level of panic was building to a crescendo. He just knew that he would be boiled alive. Never again would he see the Eiffel Tower or the Champs Élysées, not to mention the Louvre. His life was over.

Aza puffed hard and long on her pipe, carefully studying the children. She frowned at the boy, finding him insubstantial. Turning her attention to Yvette, her eyes softened and her expression relaxed. "Three months have passed, my sweet," said Aza. "How you *be*?"

"It has been difficult without my Maman. If that isn't bad enough, I have to put up with André and his hatefulness. Did you know that he was so rude to Indigo that she was forced to leave our home? I hate him. Nothing is ever going to be the same again with him here."

"This *be* true. Minute by minute, nothing is never the same."

"Excuse me, please," asked Paul politely, trying to act friendly with small talk. Maybe if the old lady liked him, she would spare turning him into a toad or worse. "Just how do you two know one another so well?"

Aza knocked ashes from her pipe and broke into a bright smile. "It *be* quite the surprise to find an eleven-year-old girl out in my vegetable garden two years ago. No one ever came to visit my house on the mountain."

"As a little girl," added Yvette, turning to Paul, "I loved hearing the voodoo *tim-tims* about zombies and witches and sorcery. You know, the kind of stories told late at night by gossips, drunks, and children. One such legend was about this giant black woman who lived alone in the low jungle. It was said she stood more than nine feet tall and she was a sorceress."

"The people think that I stand this tall?"

"Rumors have it that you can transform yourself into any animal or demon at will. Some swear that you aren't a real person, but a ghost or zombie who walks the mountain roads late at night hunting for innocent souls to feed on." Yvette grinned.

"Good, I like that they think this," said Aza. "It keeps the curious away."

"Oh, Aza," said Yvette, clapping, "you are so funny."

Aza faced Paul and scrutinized him from head to toe. She knew his thoughts.

"You are too skinny to eat, young man, we need to fatten you up some."

"Eh, Yvette, please go on with your story," he suggested, trying to divert the voodoo woman's attention away from him. "What happened next?"

"I had to know more about Aza and voodoo," continued Yvette, glancing over to Maxi to make sure he was still breathing. She was terribly worried. "Well, Paul, I decided to visit the workers' compound on our plantation to seek the advice of the voodoo priest, Yébé."

"You have a voodoo priest at the plantation?" asked Paul.

"Oui," said Yvette, shifting the dog on her lap. "Yébé is an old friend of the family. He told me that voodoo is a religion observed by the Fon people who live in Nigeria. Those who believe in voodoo believe in a heavenly father, which is the same belief practiced in most all religions. In voodoo, the heavenly father is called the Gran Mèt, who is sometimes too busy to attend to the needs of all of his people and enlists the help of aides or spirits called *délégués* or *loa*. These spirits of the Gran Mèt ensure that the main forces in life—water and fire, love and death—are kept in harmony."

"This all be true," said Aza. "What did Yébé say about the zombies?"

"He said that there are many strange happenings in the world that have no reasonable explanation. The zombie can hide in the hearts of all humans, or it can be set free to walk on its own. It can be a way of thinking, and it can be a way of being. It can be real, and it cannot. It can be what one wishes it to be. I asked Yébé about witchcraft and black magic and the people on the island who call them *quimbosieures*. They abuse power for purposes of greed and revenge with black magic. Never look a zombie in the eye as it might be harmful to the soul."

"Yébé be right. These *be* very bad people."

"I had asked Yébé if you were a quimboiseur, and he told me that you were a good woman who used her magic to fight off the bad intentions of evil spirits and evildoers. He told me that you were once a high priestess, but when you could not save your husband and child from the smallpox epidemic in 1886, you fled to the mountain to live out your life alone. Yébé said that every month, he brings you supplies. I was excited to learn that he had actually met you in person. More than ever, I wanted to seek you out. And I did."

"Oui, you did."

"Wow," said Paul, trying to absorb everything.

Aza bent down and took one of Yvette's hands into her own. "The moment I looked into those green eyes, I could see deep into the future and knew that our meeting was no accident. It be fate. I have cherished our friendship ever since, and that of Maxi and Indigo as well. The four of us have had many wonderful times talking at the fireside."

Maxi moaned. They went to his side. Aza gave him more of the drink. His rapid breathing steadied, and his fever lowered. Aza, Yvette, and Paul watched over him in silence.

Paul finally relaxed. He realized that Aza was just a kind old lady. He couldn't wait to get back to school and tell his friends about his adventures in Martinique.

Yvette glanced at her gold chain watch. "Indigo must be wondering what has happened to me. We were supposed to meet at the botanical gardens an hour ago. I have exciting news for her. Uncle Gregoire has promised that she can live with his family and go to school with my cousins in Basse-Pointe when her mother, Honorine, is better. Isn't that wonderful?"

"Oui, it be wonderful, but it *be* too late," said Aza sadly.

"What do you mean?"

"You would not have found Indigo today. Her stepfather made other plans for her."

"What plans?"

"While you be away, many things happened," said Aza. "You must promise that if I tell you this unfortunate news, you will not blame your father. Marcel *be* a well-meaning man, but he cannot admit to the deep sickness of his son. His eyes *be* closed to the doings of André."

"Don't blame Papa for what?"

"You also must not blame Maxi for not telling you of this thing. Because of his black skin, he *be* forbidden to interfere in the private matters of the white man." Aza rushed her words. "And you must not blame Aza. My powers cannot combat what is meant to be. I could not do anything to help. Destiny commands this. C'est une punition du bon Dieu."

Yvette stood up. "What are you trying to tell me?"

Aza reported on the arrangement taking place at Les Chats that evening.

Yvette's cheeks burned with tears. "That is only one hour away," she yelled, tearing at her hair and heading for the door. "How could you allow this to happen, Aza? Why wasn't I told sooner?" Paul jumped to his feet, not understanding and not knowing what to do.

Aza tried to block Yvette. "There *be* nothing you can do, my child. This *be* something that Indigo must handle on her own, and she will. Trust me. She doesn't need your help or your interference. Things will work out for the best."

"When I find André, I will kill him," said Yvette, grabbing her rifle. She pushed Aza out of the way and ran out of the shack into the jungle.

Paul reached out blindly as if he were trapped in a nightmare with no escape.

10

St. Pierre, Martinique
August 8, 1895
The Waterfront

A flat-bottomed barge transferred the captain, stowaway, and disembarking passengers from the *Silver Eagle* to one of the landing piers a short distance from the old lighthouse that stood sentry. Nathan tapped David on the shoulder and pointed out the various landmarks along the south end of the waterfront district. Rue Bouillé, a busy cobblestone street, ran parallel with the curvature of the coastline. The eye-catching two-story Chamber of Commerce, with its wraparound veranda on a lower floor and its elegant diamond-shaped clock attached to the facade of the upper floor, dominated the street. The colossal roman numerals adorning the face of the clock were viewed from great distances. Saffron-colored trade buildings, hotels, taverns, and homes lined a narrow railroad track where a bored-looking mule towed a passenger trolley.

Nathan directed David's attention to the customhouse. The walls of this ancient building showed decay from age and weather; however, its upper-story addition appeared fairly new. This is where David was scheduled to meet with his shipping broker, Laurent Montour, to declare bills of lading including beans, potatoes, cheese, lard, garlic, salt meats, and flour.

Multiple stockpiles of tarp-covered barrels containing sugar, rum, syrup, and fruit stretched for blocks along a half-moon-shaped beach. Slothful dark-skinned dockworkers, laboring in long-sleeved shirts and long pants in the sweltering heat, went slowly about their daily business, singing upbeat Creole songs as they lifted, piled, and rolled the heavy barrels of freight set to be loaded within the cargo holds of the foreign ships sitting anchor in the bay.

"I like the pleasant sound of their voices," commented David.

"Aye, sir, it adds sweetness to one's soul."

"Would you look at that," commented David, pointing ahead.

The old landing pier that jutted out several hundred feet into the surf was a flurry of activity. Foreigners in white linen suits and straw hats or petticoats and bonnets—along with barefoot locals in vibrant costumes, colorful turbans, or casual tropic wear—jammed the pier's narrow boardwalk in a shoulder-to-shoulder confusion of parasols and canes, duffel bags and civilian trunks, hand fans and smoking pipes, hogs in crates and chickens in cages, not to mention the native women balancing bundles precariously atop their heads.

"That is *Tropaze* roped to the dock," said Nathan, climbing a wooden ladder lifted from the barge onto the pier with the stowaway and David not far behind. "The *Tropaze* is a busy interisland transfer vessel that moves islanders to and from the capital of Fort-de-France about fifteen miles away due south. Watch your step, the walkway is hectic today."

They pushed through congestion where the combined stench of sweat, perfume, animal odor, smoke, salt air, and freshly caught fish was overwhelming to their nostrils. A few minutes later, they reached the top of the pier where David spied two white men. One of the men was tall and rather handsome with a healthy tan. He appeared to be in his midforties. The other man, years younger than his companion, was of small girth and pallor skin. His beady, distrustful eyes and thin, unfriendly lips forced people to cautiously sidestep around him.

"Bonjour," greeted the older man, extending his hand. "Captain Cabot, I presume?"

"Yes."

"Bienvenu! Welcome to St. Pierre. I am Marcel, and this is my son, André."

They shook hands. "I have heard much about the Chevaliers of Martinique from my grandfather, the shipbuilder, John Cabot," said David. "It is a pleasure to meet you."

"I pray your grandfather is well. I remember him from his visits to our island when I was but a boy. He was a pleasant fellow. Your grandfather and my father, Jacques, spent hours drinking rum and always the better place, land or sea. They were wonderfully mischievous together. *Deux palisanteries*—two jokesters!"

"Grandfather has not changed."

Marcel looked behind David and raised a curious eyebrow. "Qu'est-ce que c'est?"

David retrieved the stowaway who had doggedly trailed behind him up the pier.

"This is Stefan. He is a young guest of mine from Dominica. We are in hopes to locate his grandmother who lives here. Is there any way you could help us find her?"

"*Mais oui*—but of course," said Marcel with a welcoming smile directed at the boy.

Stefan smiled back, but his smile was short-lived as soon as he took notice of André's hostile eyes burrowing down upon him. The boy took refuge behind David once again.

Marcel called over a burly white man, Felecien, the Chevalier plantation overseer, who stood waiting nearby. An exchange of French ensued. Marcel asked Felecien to try and locate the boy's grandmother. Felecien reached out his hand and led the apprehensive lad away.

"Don't worry about your young friend," assured Marcel. "Felecien may look ferocious, but he has a heart of gold and is gentle. Please come with us. Your shipping and receiving agent, Laurent Montour, is waiting for you at Customs. When your business is completed, my son will take you to Les Chats for a bite to eat and some light entertainment. I regret that I must attend a business meeting at the bank this afternoon. You should know that Montour has made arrangements for you to stay at a nice hotel very close to here. It would be my pleasure if you joined me tonight for dinner at the plantation. If that is in order, I will pick you up at your hotel around four o'clock and give you a quick tour of the town before we go on to my home."

"Thank you," said David. "I would enjoy that very much."

Marcel and André escorted David past the old lighthouse onto the public square La Place Bertin, where the core of all waterfront activities took place. Fontaine Agnès, the elaborate baroque-styled fountain, graced the middle of the plaza. Spring-fed water spilled from an urn held up by a bronze cupid while a quartet of bronze cherubs frolicked in its sprays.

Place Bertin and Fountain Agnes in St. Pierre

As the trio walked through the square, David observed the ever-steady parade of natives and tourists. Foreign sailors hastened to the nearest saloons and brothels as groups of black and mulatto workers meandered by at a more languorous pace.

"The natives act as if they have all the time in the world," commented David.

"Yet they seem to get done what has to get done," said Marcel.

David was escorted to the Customs House and introduced to Laurent Montour. An hour later, his business dealings had been secured. "Tomorrow morning, I will unload my cargo," announced David to Montour. "I estimate that the process will take a day and a half to complete before I leave to continue along the southern route all the way to South America. I expect to return to Martinique in four weeks, at which time I will pick up contracted island cargo on my way back to America."

Marcel departed by horse and buggy for his two o'clock meeting. David and André left the Customs House by foot and headed to a three-story stone house located about five minutes from the Chamber of Commerce. Painted in black script across the straw-colored facade of the house were the words "Maison de les Chats." Several white men, mostly sailors, were seated at outside tables in the company of wiggling and laughing prostitutes perched upon their laps.

"There is no better way to initiate newcomers to St. Pierre than by introducing them to Madame La Rose and her Maison de les Chats," announced André with a sly wink.

When David entered the front doors of Les Chats, he entered another world. A bamboo bar curved along one wall and halfway down another. The bartender, pushing up a red garter that had slipped down the sleeve of his white shirt, poured a shot of 100-proof rum into a small glass and slid it down the high-polished surface countertop into the anxious fingers of a drunken French sailor. The Frenchman tossed down the contents of the glass and escorted a giggling black whore up the center staircase to one of the brothel rooms located on the second level.

The saloon supported fourteen tables, a small stage, and a dance floor. Squeaking ceiling fans did their best to circulate the fog of cigar and cigarette smoke. Near the stage was a trio of white musicians wearing red-and-white striped jackets. Their spirited honky-tonk music created a merry din that spurred on the gaiety of the crowd. Loud voices and shrill laughter competed with the upbeat sounds of the piano, banjo, and drums.

"Bonjour, André," announced a chubby woman outfitted in a too-tight, low-cut red velvet dress. Painted red lips and cheeks clashed with frizzy orange hair. David took a guarded step back from this moving mountain of flesh. She planted a sloppy kiss upon André's pale, hollow cheek. For a moment, André's short bony body disappeared within the thick folds of her arms.

"Bless the gods, what prize have you brought Madame La Rose on this most glorious of days, André? Just look at this hair from the sun and these eyes from the sky. Ooh-la-la, what a sexy specimen," she purred at the newcomer.

David had encountered many madams during his worldwide travels as a sailor, but none quite as flamboyant as this one. Introductions were made, and he gallantly kissed her hand.

"Come, my elegant Captain Cabot," she commanded, "I will take you to your table."

They were led to a pleasant distance from the loud music. A black busboy broke all records wiping down the table and chairs before they were seated.

"Bring us a bottle of rum and the fresh catch of the morning," demanded André. "Don't forget the bread and goat cheese."

Madame La Rose bent close to André's ear and whispered in French. "Your special dessert is being readied for you upstairs. A mighty fine parfait, I must say."

"I have waited a long time for this sweet treat," he snickered with malice.

The winks between Madame La Rose and André indicated that this was no ordinary pleasure-seeking arrangement. David sensed something sinister in the works. Their round of drinks arrived. David took a sip of the warm golden liquid. As the rum slid down his throat, it left a cool burning path that was effective, but not harsh. He liked the taste.

"Very good," said David

"The best-made rum on the island," declared André.

A raucous scream startled David. He wheeled around to find a slender white woman running toward the stage. She wore a yellow skirt gathered over several layers of petticoats, black stockings, high-topped boots, and an off-the-shoulder blouse. A black velvet ribbon encircled her neck. Brassy hair had been severely slicked back and tucked into a topknot. The dancer picked up the front of her skirt, along with her petticoats, and held them high in the air, fanning the layers back and forth showing off faded white lace bloomers. Her long legs kicked out with the gusto of a bucking horse. Approving hoots and whistles echoed from the saloon's exuberant customers. David recalled having seen this same dance performed in a similar saloon while stationed in Marseilles only a few years before.

"Fifi is a Paris import," said André. "She is a little old and a little outdated, but the best dancer that St. Pierre has to offer. However, no dancer in the entire world can compare to a little hell-raiser from Paris by the name of Lillie Lodine."

"Who is Lillie Lodine?" asked David.

"She is a cancan performer from the Moulin Rouge club."

"Ah, yes, I have heard all about the Moulin Rouge," said David. "My grandfather was there in the early seventies during a visit to Paris. He once told me that it was the place to go for aristocrats and visiting dignitaries looking for an acceptable bourgeois atmosphere."

André laughed. "Your *grand-père* was right. It is still that way. It seems the more shocking the show the more it delights the elite. It was quite fun watching them watch the entertainment. I used to go there with my friend Toulouse-Lautrec."

Bread and cheese were brought to the table. The floorshow finally ended, and the band began playing music that was softer, more romantic. David could hear himself think again.

"Who is this Toulouse-Lautrec?"

André choked. "Henri is one of the greatest artists of all times. An accomplished genius trapped in the crippled body of a dwarf. My intellectual sessions with this man are what I miss most about Paris. We spent many nights drinking, telling jokes, and philosophizing at the Moulin Rouge with our friends. It is a wonderful place where fellow artists, poets, and intellects can comfortably gather and exchange ideas and works."

"You are an artist?"

André nodded. "Not as good as some, but not bad. My work is selling fairly well in Frankfurt, Amsterdam, Milan, and New York City. Funny enough, I have had little success in Paris. Come, I'll show you some of my paintings."

"How old are you?" asked David as he followed his host to one of the walls near the entrance of the saloon where several works of art were on display.

"I'll be twenty-one my next birthday."

David found the paintings disjointed and abstract with unfamiliar, eerie scenes of people, places, and things not in proper perspective. The subjects of his works radiated complexity in composition, and yet, they unleashed a powerful idiom of real life.

"What kind of art is this?" asked David.

"It is what some are calling expressionism. The artist tries to present an emotional experience in its most compelling form. I strive to capture the inner nature of my subjects."

David studied the works before him with much curiosity. Deep bright colors of square—and triangular-shaped men and women were caught in scenes of nature, in scenes of poverty, and in scenes of lust with overtones of torment, despair, and pain. David noted that the last painting was very different from the others, showing a more realistic portrait of a handsome young man with humbling brown eyes and a dazzling smile.

"Who is this?"

"Daniel Defarge," André's jaw tightened. "He was my best friend."

"Was?"

"Daniel was killed two years ago in a duel outside of Paris."

"Really? A duel? Why?"

"Are you asking why he was killed," snapped André, "or why he was in a duel?"

"The latter," answered David cautiously.

André's shoulders slumped. "Come, let us go back to the table, our meal is almost ready." Once seated, André ordered another bottle of rum and, in a sad low voice, continued his story. "I met Daniel five years ago at the Café Tamourin, where he was giving a reading from his best-selling book, *La Lumière*. He was a twenty-four-year-old revolutionist, and I, a very impressionable sixteen-year-old student of the Ecole des Beaux Arts."

"Sounds like a fine school."

"The instructors were rigid and archaic in ways of stylized painting. Too much time was spent on classical and sentimental subjects, although I did enjoy the works and techniques of the old masters. I left this school after two years to join a group of artists studying at Cormon's."

"Another art school?"

"Yes. However, I did not stay long there, as I soon became displeased with Félix Cormon's staid, conventional teachings. The impressionists concern themselves more with effect of natural light on a subject rather than its inner form or force. I then moved on to the Académie Julian, where I found my true home. This school was a bit unorthodox, a bit unruly, and, perhaps, a bit uncouth. But I loved it."

"Tell me more about Daniel," prompted David, not interested in André's schooling.

"I will never forget the night I met Daniel. It had been snowing for hours. The café was bitterly cold, and my group and I had been drinking black coffee spiked with absinthe to keep us warm. When Daniel began to read, the cold went away. His voice was the light of the sun. His ideologies ran true for me. He spoke words that expressed my thoughts and feelings. I had not felt the presence of someone so great since the time I was involved with Van Gogh and Gauguin in Arles in the late eighties."

David wrinkled his brow. "And they are?"

André was exasperated. "Artists! Vincent van Gogh is dead now. He shot himself in 1890. He was a true master of the style of art. The last I heard, Paul Gauguin was living in Tahiti and painting naked natives. Although I was not impressed with Gauguin's subject matter and political views, I admired his brilliance. I first heard about Paul when he came to Martinique in 1887. That was also the year I was sent to the South of France to live with my grandparents in Arles. A year later, when I turned thirteen, Vincent van Gogh arrived. I was completely in awe of this man and his funny carrot-colored beard and hair to match. He was deliciously odd. Some said he was mad. The townspeople were horrified when he decided to paint his house at 2 Place, Lamartine, a bright canary yellow inside and out. It was his favorite color. Rumor had it that he was preparing the house in hopes that Gauguin would soon join him."

"He sounds like an odd lot," said David.

"Yes, he was odd, but he fascinated me. I followed Vincent's every move and tried my best to copy his painting techniques, which were unconventional and bold. He was both flattered and annoyed. When I wasn't in school, I was with him. Gauguin arrived in October of 1888. Paul and Vincent were completely different personalities. Where Paul was neat and organized, Vincent was a hopeless pig. Yet they had an undying admiration for each other and each other's work. At first, I wasn't sure if I would be able to accept this stranger. I was still mystified why he had been so fascinated by Martinique and its people. I also got tired of Paul trying to compare Arles with Martinique. Except for the vividness of color in both locations, I could never see the connection. Anyway, if I wanted to hang around Vincent, I would have to accept Paul no matter how I felt. They were an inseparable couple. It was Paul who took me to one of the brothels where I had my first sexual experience at the age of fourteen with a less-than-attractive prostitute by the name of Mary."

David laughed. "That must have been an interesting evening for a young boy."

"Some months later," continued André, ignoring David's comment, "Vincent and Paul began to get on each other's nerves. Their arguing grew worse and worse. Vincent preferred painting real subjects out in the open air while Paul began staying indoors, creating from memory. Vincent's mental health rapidly declined, forcing Paul to leave for good."

André leaned forward and placed his hand on top of David's. "Do you know what Vincent did the night when Paul did not return?"

"I can't imagine," answered David, furrowing a brow at André's hand upon his own.

"To protest Paul," said André, his eyes widening in excitement, "he hacked off one of his ears, wrapped it up in a piece of cloth, and presented the bloodied part as a gift to one of the whores who had befriended him. Isn't that the most romantic gesture ever?"

David pulled his hand away. "I'm not so sure."

André eyed the disappearing hand and shrugged. He then ordered one of the waiters to fetch his sketchpad from behind the bar. "Allow me to do a sketch of you while we talk."

"Fine," said David, glad to have André's hands occupied. "Now then, getting back to your friend, Daniel, why was he killed in this duel? What prompted it?"

André picked up a piece of charcoal and began to sketch. "The night I met Daniel was the night of my rebirth. I went up to him after his reading and told him how much he had touched me with his magical words. I too believed in the natural order that placed white Christian males above all others. I believed we were far superior to women and to any other race on this planet. Daniel was flattered by my attention and equally impressed with my political convictions. He did not hesitate to invite me back that night to his grand apartment on the Boulevard Montmarte. We were never apart after that."

"Until the duel," said David. He was anxious to get to the end of this story.

André narrowed his eyes. "Oui, Captain, until the duel."

Lunch was served. David took a bite of the pan-fried fish covered in a delicate sweet sauce. It was delicious. André pushed his food away and continued to sketch as he spoke. "It is common to settle disputes by dueling in France. One night at a café, I forget which one, Daniel and another man got into a bitter argument about the anti-Semitic contents of Daniel's latest bestseller. The stranger would not let up on his idiotic liberal point of view. My Daniel had no choice but to take off his glove and slap the bastard's face. They decided to meet with pistols the following morning at sunrise. Daniel was not a marksman. He was an artist, a brilliant creator of words. He was dead within seconds."

"All this bloodshed over political differences," pondered David.

"Honor is very important to a Frenchman. I am strong in my beliefs, perhaps even more so since Daniel's death. When he died, a little of me died as well."

André handed David the finished sketch. It was a flattering likeness. David thanked his host, folded the piece of paper, and stuck it in his shirt pocket for safekeeping.

"You are a very good artist."

"Merci. Art is my life. Even though I have been back on the island three months now, I have found that I have little or no interest in my father's plantation business. Oh, I have helped out with some of the port business, but art is my true vocation. It is my salvation—that and my political involvements. I have joined the Progressive Party here. I am well-known and held in high regard, however, not by my father. Marcel and I don't see eye to eye on many subjects, particularly politics. My father is one of those liberals."

David took another bite of his fish. "What is this Progressive Party all about?"

André threw his chin high into the air and straightened his narrow shoulders. A peculiar intensity radiated from his eyes. "Total white supremacy!"

David stared back in total disbelief as André continued his platform.

"My party has controlled the island for years and years. Of late, too many radical men of color are forgetting their rightful places, especially a black bastard by the name of Amédee Knight. The son of a bitch thinks that just because he was educated at the École Centrale in Paris, he has the right to function as an equal with the whites in our government. Would you believe he has actually gotten himself elected assistant mayor of Fort-de-France? Now, I ask you, white man to white man, what is happening to our world? Negroes are good for two things and two things only—labor and bedding."

11

Racing nonstop from Aza's shack down a sheer rocky jungle path and through a field of sugarcane, Yvette finally reached the stables in the beach hamlet of Fond-Corre, where her horse and little white surrey had been quartered. She looked a mess covered in mud and blood.

"Mon Dieu, garçon," she pleaded with the stable boy, who had been hired for the day to tend her horse, "hâtez-vous!"

The young man eyed Yvette's enraged expression with apprehension. Her frenzied demeanor frightened him. He quickly hitched her golden stallion to the surrey. As soon as Yvette's whip stung the animal's backside, it broke into a run. Yvette's buggy swayed dangerously past a group of carrier women alongside a grove of trees near the edge of the road. Fists shook and Creole voices screeched at the insolent girl. The women came close to losing their perfectly balanced head cargo as they jumped out of the way of Yvette's racing horse. The law of Martinique mandates that all pedestrians, colored or white, have the right of way.

Yvette, in her crazed state, was not aware of her actions. Her mind spun with stomach-churning visions of André assaulting Indigo. How could this be allowed to happen? The surrey rolled by a line of field workers hewing sugarcane crops. Behind every two men ambled a brightly dressed female gathering the fallen cuttings, securing them sheaves and placing them on top of their heads. Behind this army of laborers were *crieurs* pounding a special drumbeat to the rising and falling cutlasses. The *commandeur* of the crew rode upon the back of a cream-colored stallion. He was willowy in stature with alert large eyes.

In one hand, he held the reins of the horse and in the other a loaded shotgun. Usually this sight would intrigue Yvette, but not today.

Yvette was forced to slow down the horse and surrey at the edge of the Fort Quartier. A new market had just been erected, and the pedestrian traffic in this area was extra heavy. Brightly painted fishing skiffs, carried in from the shore by jubilant fishermen, lined the sandy beach near the market stalls. The hulls of these skiffs displayed an abundance of fresh fish. It had been a fruitful day of fishing, and vendors were celebrating their good fortune with celebratory dancing and singing. Yvette was in no mood for this gaiety.

At the outer edge of the marketplace, old women with deep crevices in their faces gathered in small groups on handwoven mats, selling fresh flowers to citizens wishing to make peace offerings to the small roadside shrines of the Virgin Mary dotting the countryside.

Once past the market, Yvette lashed her horse with the whip. The steed, feeling the pain on its backside, broke into a full gallop, dangerously pulling the little surrey over the Roxelane bridge and down toward the waterfront. Spectators standing or driving along the road surmised that the girl was trapped in a runaway buggy. In bewilderment, when they saw her deliberately striking the horse, they realized that it was the child who was out of control and not the animal.

Yvette careened at such an alarming rate of speed down the steep grade heading toward La Place Bertin that her frothing horse barely missed sideswiping another buggy. The stallion, scared out of its wits, screeched to a defiant stop, teetering precariously near the edge of a cliff.

"Mademoiselle Chevalier," scolded the irate driver, jumping out of his buggy and grabbing her reins, "you could have killed us both."

"Monsieur Clerc, forgive me, a dire situation is occurring. This is a matter of life and death. Let me go," she cried out in frustration. *Of all people to run into, it had to be Fernand Clerc*, she bemoaned. He was a friend of the family, the largest planter and richest man on the island and one of the most popular commercial overlords and social leaders of Martinique.

Fernand's bushy mustache danced back and forth along the sides of his frown. "Where in the world are you going?" he asked, holding steadfast to Yvette's reins. "You nearly killed us both, child. I will have to report this accident to your father, you know."

Yvette managed to wiggle from his grasp. Taking in a deep breath, she raised her whip and, with all of her might, struck her exhausted horse. It whinnied in protest and bolted away.

Fernand Clerc was left in a cloud of dust.

12

The ceiling fan did little to relieve the oppressive tropical air trapped in David's bayside hotel suite. Apart from the stifling heat and little breeze this day, his accommodations were satisfactory; he had a decent bed, a panoramic view of the outlying harbor, and an easy walk to the customhouse and docking areas.

David treated himself to a sponge bath and changed his shirt. He went out onto the balcony, where he viewed his ship bobbing in waters of the roadstead about five hundred yards directly before him. Admiring the polished steel structure gleaming under the force of the tropical sun, enormous pride swelled in his chest. The *Silver Eagle* was by far the newest and most commanding craft in the harbor.

At four fifteen, Marcel arrived by carriage to pick up David for the scheduled tour of St. Pierre and the Chevalier plantation. Stefan, looking quite happy, was quietly sitting next to the carriage driver. David and Marcel climbed into the backseat. The driver tapped the rump of the dozing horse. Annoyed at the interruption, the animal snorted and stomped in protest before trotting off north along the bustling waterfront.

"We found Stefan's grandmother," announced Marcel. "She is a very old woman who is nearly blind. A twelve-year-old boy would be quite a burden for her. I did get her permission to let him live at my plantation. There is more than enough room and more than enough people to watch out for him. We will give him his own chambers, plenty of food, an education at one of our local schools. He is a fine lad and will be a welcome addition."

David nodded his approval and thanked Marcel for his kind consideration. He was a little concerned about the living arrangement for Stefan though. David thought Marcel to be a sympathetic gentleman with a good heart; however, his insensitive, racist son, André, was another story. Stefan would have to be warned to keep his distance from André.

The carriage turned left and headed east up a hill. The side street marked Rue de la Magdalene bustled with late-afternoon activities. On one corner, a French soldier in full military regalia conversed with a civilian fashionably outfitted in a checkered suit and straw hat. Both of these distinguished-looking men ogled an attractive, but tired-looking, woman sashaying by with an oversized fruit basket balanced on the top of her head. She was not amused.

Marcel initiated the tour by describing the different sections of town.

"St. Pierre is divided into three districts," explained Marcel. "The Fort Quartier lies to the north, the Centre Quartier in the middle, and the Mouillage Quartier to the south. We just left the waterfront and are now in the Mouillage Quartier approaching the Cathedral of St. Pierre. The original cathedral was built in 1654 with side towers added in 1885. Driver, please stop."

Marcel stepped out of the carriage with the others following him. They marveled at the life-size sculptures of four saints inside individual alcoves surrounding the main doors of the church. The holy sentries seemed to bestow blessings on each visitor entering the spacious prayer hall. Kaleidoscopic patterns danced on the ceilings and walls as shafts of afternoon sun pushed through the stained glass windows. The interior was ornate with crystal chandeliers, Greek-styled moldings, Roman columns, elaborate candelabras, and a gold coronal representing the sacred head of the Virgin Mary. At the back of the church was a semicircular dome, typical of early-seventeenth-century Baroque architecture. Painted on the ceiling was a massive mural of a divine female saint surrounded by devoted angels in heaven.

"Bonjour, Marcel," greeted the elder of two Jesuit priests.

Marcel clapped his hands in joyful reaction to the men. "Father d'Anjou and Father Roche, how are you, my friends? I would like you to meet David Cabot. He is the captain of a new steamer just arrived from

America. Captain Cabot is taking a tour of our fair town. But of course, I could not begin our journey without first stopping here."

Father d'Anjou replied in English. "You are in very good hands, Captain Cabot. Not only is Marcel one of our finest citizens, he knows the history of this island like no one else. He truly represents all the people. He is charitable and honest and—"

"Enough," shouted Marcel, raising his hands up in surrender. "This kind of testimony from the likes of you is most flattering." Marcel turned to the younger priest and folded his arms. "Well, Father Roche, I can see by the grime on your frock that you have been busy, once again, climbing to your mountaintop perch above the village of Morne Vert in the Pitons de Carbet to get a better look at our volcano."

Father Roche brushed off the dirt in vain. "Please don't make fun of me nor the volcano, dear Marcel. Mont Pelée appears innocent, but I can assure you, she is not. From my position in the Pitons de Carbet, I can better study the volcano, even though it is four miles across the valley."

"Let me explain," said Father d'Anjou to the American captain. "Father Roche fancies himself to be an amateur geologist and volcanologist. He owns volumes and volumes of books on the subject, and these wonderful little instruments for measuring seismographic activities. He is one of the island's unofficial overseers of Mont Pelée, along with our friend, Fernand Clerc."

Marcel and David bade their good-byes to Father d'Anjou and left in the company of Father Roche. The trio paused in the courtyard for a few seconds to cautiously eye the 4500 ft. green mountain that sloped down over hills and valleys and pushed under St. Pierre at sea level.

"Is there a threat?" asked David.

"Volcanoes are unpredictable," shrugged Father Roche. "Look at her now. See how peaceful she seems. But be warned, her thermal core is bursting with energy that sustains the very life of this island. Martinique's harvests are exceptional due to the valuable minerals and nutrients derived from Mont Pelée's endless supply of purified waters and fertile earth."

David grinned. "You still didn't answer my question. Is there a threat?"

"If she chooses," answered Father Roche seriously, "the volcano is apt to awaken at any moment and take away the bounty. It could happen today, tomorrow. Maybe never. My friends tease me about my doomsday attitude, Captain Cabot. I know for a fact that such a force is not to be taken for granted. However, to answer your question . . . yes, there is always a threat from the great mountain that dominates our island."

David whistled. "You must feel as if you are living on a keg of dynamite."

"Yes," agreed Father Roche, putting on his hat, "a keg of dynamite indeed." He warmly shook David's hand. "I must be off to my parish in the Centre Quartier. I do look forward to meeting you again soon, Captain Cabot."

Marcel directed his driver down St. Pierre's main thoroughfare, Rue Victor Hugo. The narrow cobblestone street curved through the middle of the town about a mile and a half from the south end to the north end. Black zinc awnings, wrought iron balconies, wooden shutters, and red tile roofs provided additional charisma to the architecture of the two—to three-story yellow stone structures lined up in a row and positioned in close proximity to one another.

Rue Victor Hugo—Main Street of St. Pierre

"The Mediterranean style of the buildings reminds me of the quintessential town of New Orleans in America," commented David. He tilted his nose up and inhaled deeply the delicious aromas of roasted sugar and garlic scenting the air. "It even smells like New Orleans. Creole cuisine happens to be a favorite of mine. I enjoy the spices."

Street vendors crowded the avenue on both sides, offering a pageant of touching and comical sights and sounds. Especially enjoyable to David were the sweet high-pitched accents of the brightly dressed women, young and old, who invited him to buy their products.

"Çé moune là ça qui le bel mango?" asked a delicate voice from the other side of the street. David was drawn to a pretty girl with a basket full of ripe mangos. She raised her eyebrows in question when asking if he would like to try her lovely fruit. He politely declined.

"Ça qui lè bel avocat?" pleaded an old woman with gray hair, missing teeth, and a crippled leg. The basket under her wrinkled outstretched arms contained oversized avocados.

"Ça qui lè bel es-cargot?" invited a vendor selling live snails under the shade of an awning. At her feet, a small dark child in a simple smock played with a black leather doll.

"Ça qui lè titiri?" inquired a teenage girl with skin the color of chili powder. She made good use of a cup to dip out teeny fish from a metal pail hooked over her arm.

"Creole is spoken like a melody. What are its origins?" asked David.

"It is a bastardized language borrowing words from Portuguese, English, Spanish, and Dutch with strange little terms thrown in from Africa and India. The hodgepodge dialects are woven into French. The way Creole is verbalized with much speed makes it very difficult to understand, but extremely lilting and poetic to the ear, especially coming from all these lovely ladies present here this afternoon on Rue Victor Hugo."

David nodded. The more attractive of the females selling goods were most pleasing to watch. They wore robes of varied patterns and jaunty plaids while others dressed in elaborate costumes dyed in an array of vibrant tints embroidered with flowers and animals. Under their loose bodice tunics flowed long, full skirts pulled up and in between the legs from the back and attached with brooches or tied to the waistbands in the front. All of them were barefoot.

"These are the traditional pet-slave costumes most likely handed down from their grandmothers who were once the celebrated *belle-affranchies* of slave holders," explained Marcel, noting David's curiosity. "Although these garments are a little threadbare, they are still popular apparel with the younger generation. There is an ancient rule of thumb that if one chooses to sport a scarf with their dress, it has to contrast sharply with the rest of the outfit, creating a harmony of colors like blue with yellow, green with red, and violet with orange."

The carriage rambled along the avenue at a slow pace. There was a vendor on the street for everything. Clay cooking pots, fruit, charcoal, clothes, sewing aids, vegetables, fish, poultry, and spices were all marketed from the heads or arms of these gregarious people. They jabbered at the same time enticing, cajoling, and begging the world to take note of their precious products.

David spotted an elderly man sitting cross-legged on the ground surrounded by dozens of baskets. Tufts of curly white hair framed his head. It was a mystery how his mustache grew as black as his hair was white. His frayed shirt was missing buttons, his patched jacket was three sizes too small, and his baggy pants were held up by a piece of fishing rope at his waist. Shreds of newspaper had been used to stuff the toes of his oversize shoes. He was poor and it showed.

"Please stop for a moment," asked David of the driver. "My mother collects baskets. I would like to buy a few to take back home to her." The American captain purchased six of the handmade baskets, paid the grateful vendor in francs, and returned to the carriage.

"The *merchand de vanneries* will be able to feed his family of ten for a month," remarked Marcel. "You have made a proud black man feel very rich today. This is a good thing."

"It was my pleasure," said David.

"Monsieur Chevalier," sang a deep baritone voice from the sidewalk. "Let me serve you only the freshest, the finest, and the tastiest of pies." Next to the carriage, a towering pastry seller—clad immaculately in white pants, shirt, and apron—stared at them with a well-trained smile upon his face. His chef's hat topped his spotless attire, and his black shoes were spit-polished.

"Ah, pastry man," teased Marcel, "how fresh can these pies of yours be by the end of this day? Have not the rays of the sun overbaked them a bit too much by now?"

"Monsieur," answered the wounded pastry seller, placing a hand over his heart, "surely you must know that mine are the best of sweets and never go stale." He diverted his attention to David sitting next to Marcel and spoke in English. "You are new face here, yes?"

"Yes."

"Ça qui lè di pain aubè? Perhaps you would like to sample one of these loaves shaped like cucumbers? Have you tried a *diri-doux*?"

"I can't say that I have. What is a *diri-doux*?

"For one penny you can find out!"

David and Marcel marveled over the man's bravado. "You might as well try something," suggested Marcel. "I fear he won't leave us be otherwise. The island's most popular sweet treat is a simple recipe of boiled rice with sugar rolled in a banana leaf. You may also want to try the *pain-mi*, a delicious sweet maize cake. I warn you, it is very rich."

The rice wraps were purchased for Marcel and his driver, and the cake wraps for David and Stefan. Once paid, the pastry seller theatrically bowed and tipped his hat. He then skipped down the cobblestone avenue, singing a love song to his sweet treats:

"Oh qu'ils sont bons!"

"Oh qu'ils sont doux!"

The rich sugary cakes triggered a terrible thirst from their sweetness. Marcel instructed the driver to pull the carriage over to the side of the street. There, mounted to the wall of a building, was an ornate drinking fountain in the shape of a lion's head. Cool mountain water spilled through its brass lips. David drew in a long refreshing sip of the delicious and refreshing ice-cold liquid. He pulled out a handkerchief, soaked it in the water, and chilled his face.

"Come here, my friends," instructed Marcel, bending down on one knee and placing an ear against the cobblestone pavement. "Try to tune out the street noises and listen carefully to what is taking place below." David and Stefan lowered their heads to the ground. A bit startled, they could hear the roar of what sounded like a powerful underground river echoing from beneath the street.

"What you are listening to is our water system," said Marcel after they stood back up and returned to the carriage. "It was engineered over two hundred and fifty years ago by some very clever fellows. To this day, our city is continually supplied with the purest and most delicious water in the world. All thanks to the generosity of Mont Pelée.

David could not wait to continue the tour of this most fascinating town.

13

St. Pierre, Martinique
August 8, 1895
The Conquest of Indigo

Les Chats was fairly quiet at the moment. Members of the band were taking a dinner break in the far corner of the room. The cleaning crew prepared for the evening crowd. Two sailors sat silently at the bar drinking warm beer. Five brooding patrons puffed cigars at one of the poker tables, sizing up their loosing hands while one beamed. Most of the whores were taking late-afternoon naps, resting up for the long night ahead; some were working regardless.

André Chevalier was alone at his table near the stairs. He moved a piece of charcoal across the paper, sketching a series of macabre drawings reflective of the psychotic thoughts running through his alcohol-soaked brain. He checked the clock. It was time. Drunk from drink and revenge, he staggered up the stairs bumping between the wall and the railing onto the second floor that housed the brothel rooms.

A few doors down, Indigo was savoring her last few minutes as a virgin. "Oh, Maman, you have no idea what I am about to do for you," she whimpered as she peered through the slats of the window. The golden globe of the setting sun was reaching the distant line between the sky and the ocean. Everything its rays touched reflected pinks, oranges, and reds. It was fairly quiet on the waterfront this time of day. Indigo blinked away her tears of regret. She realized that her dreams of becoming a fine lady living in a big house in a respectable Paris neighborhood would never be realized. "You bastard of bastards," she cursed André.

Indigo placed the cold steel of the palm-sized pistol against her forehead. It cooled her flushed skin. She knew that André would be brutalizing and torturous. He would take pleasure, not only in raping her body, but in raping her soul as well. She held the pistol up into the late-afternoon sun. The more she thought of André, the more resolved she became. With undue determination and mental conviction, Indigo decided that she could not allow this monster the satisfaction of breaking her pride. She would find a way to help her mother and her stepfather.

Suddenly the pistol felt like an old friend.

André stumbled down the hall to Indigo's room. The door swung open, his eyes menacing. The ocean breeze was moving her silk gown in little waves over the contour of her shapely body. He expected to see terror in her blue eyes. He expected her to drop to her knees and beg for mercy. He expected to smell her fear. Indigo turned. There was something defiant in her posture. Her irreverent stare alarmed him. Her lips parted and she dared to smile. At first, he was taken off guard and did not know how to react. It was hard to draw conclusions with the rum muddling his brain. The bitch defied him. This was all wrong.

André was three feet away when Indigo pointed a small object at his chest.

"Is that toy a pistol?" he laughed. "Yes, indeed, a toy pistol it is. You arm yourself with a weapon? Good, I very much like this kind of game."

Shouts of sexual pleasure reverberated through the wall from the prostitute in the next room. The noise distracted Indigo long enough for André to knock away her weapon, slam her against the wall, and place a large bowie knife to her throat. The tip of the blade nicked her skin; a tiny line of blood streamed down between her breasts and onto her white dress.

"Do you know what I once did to a woman who tried the same thing in Paris?" announced André to the trembling girl. "You remind me a lot of her. She too tried to take my life, although her weapon was much more substantial than this useless thing of yours. I made her perform tricks like an animal before we played a marvelous game of pain. It is amazing how many places there are to whittle away on a human body. Now, my dear, prepare yourself."

14

St. Pierre, Martinique
August 8, 1895
A History Lesson

"We are now approaching the Grand Théâtre," said Marcel to the American captain as the carriage came to a stop before an imposing Renaissance building. "It was built in 1786 as a replica of Le Grand Théâtre dé Bordeaux in France. Its three levels accommodate up to eight hundred patrons. Inadequate finances have hurt the quantity and quality of performances. Many years ago, notable entertainers, famous opera stars, and world-class acts performed here."

David and Stefan followed Marcel to the front of the imposing building. Two grand staircases positioned on the outer corners of the second-story mezzanine swept out and curved down to the cobblestone ground level where a deteriorating sphinx-shaped fountain teetered above weather-worn bronze dolphins. After a hearty climb up the stairs, the sightseers reached the mezzanine, which had been fortified with arched breezeways and massive columns.

"During its first fifty years," said Marcel, "the Grand Théâtre served as a venue for our balls and political meetings. We still use it, but not as much. Please come join me inside."

They passed through one of the arches into a small tiled vestibule. Several rows of seats angled down toward a large orchestra pit. Beyond this was a stage fitted with hundreds of yards of red drapery edged in golden tassels. Private opera booths, reserved for whites only, dotted the walls. Secondary seating on the second level accommodated mulattoes, blacks, and poor whites.

Ten minutes later, Marcel continued the tour along Rue Victor Hugo. Shop windows displayed expensive perfumes, premium silks, couture fashions, fine jewelry, souvenirs, dry goods, rosaries, hats, cigars, spirits, and stationery. David craned his neck upward in reaction to a cooing noise coming from the upper-level apartments. Bored teenage girls passing the afternoon away leaned out of wrought iron terraces, twisting and turning in seductive poses to flirt with off-duty soldiers, foreigners, locals, and every other male who came within their sight. An angry mother or two would scold and yank their naughty daughters inside; however, for the most part, the other fidgety girls were left alone to lift their skirts above their knees and blow sweet kisses to the street below. Sitting on front stoops were men of all ages and backgrounds playing chess, discussing politics, and watching the foreigners watch the coquettish girls.

Marcel brought David's attention to a group of children representing all skin tones who were playing games in one of the alleyways. "With their light hair, skin, and eyes, it is interesting to note that these children of color could easily pass for Caucasian," remarked Marcel. "Here in the city, the mulatto offspring are kept away from the pure-blood white children. The parents firmly enforce this segregation. Out on our more liberal self-governed plantations, and in the distant villages, the regulation of separatism is lenient."

The driver of Marcel's buggy jerked his horse to an abrupt stop as a nonplussed young white woman walked directly in their path attempting to cross the avenue. Not once did she take notice of whom she was interrupting with her rude behavior. Her long sleeved, high-necked rose-colored dress kept her properly concealed. She carried a pink parasol in one hand and a white Bible in the other. Her wide-brimmed hat was adorned in pink imitation roses. She ignored Marcel's complaining horse and marched steadily by.

"Who in the world is that?" asked David.

"She is a new citizen—the wife of one of the bankers. He married her in Paris three months ago and whisked her back to Martinique. It is the same old story over again—another Bible-thumping puritan attempting to save the souls of those of color in an amoral town. I don't give her a year before she gives up and flees the island or dies from disparage or malaria. I was once married to a woman just like her. Only, my first wife didn't want to save our people of color, she wanted to rid the island of them. My son is just like her."

"I got that impression about him when we had lunch at Les Chats today," noted David.

"Hopefully, he didn't bore you too much with his political convictions."

The carriage moved on. The more David saw of St. Pierre, the more enraptured he became; oddly, he felt as if he had visited the city before. He was told by Marcel that many first-time visitors experienced this feeling of déjà vu.

"St. Pierre is quite a town," said David.

"She is a unique town," agreed Marcel with a smile. "Fort-de-France may be the administrative capital of the island, but St. Pierre is the commercial capital. More than fifty million francs of business are exchanged on an annual basis here. We have six consulates, three newspapers, two hospitals, numerous distilleries, a foundry, a mechanic cooperage, dozens of butchers, as many bakers, fifteen doctors, and twelve chemists."

"It sounds like you are the island historian," said David.

"I fancy myself as one," said Marcel. "Columbus discovered us in 1502. One hundred and seventy-two years later, in 1674, the island was fought for and won by the French. The original people of Martinique were the Carib Indians. In 1658, most chose to commit suicide by throwing themselves off a mountain cliff rather than surrender to the French.

"They jumped?"

"Rather than be conquered, they jumped."

"Fascinating," said David.

"By 1736," continued Marcel, "seventy-two thousand African slaves populated the island. In 1762, the British seized Martinique. The following year, it was won back by the French. Then in 1789, Martinique experienced a revolt by its African slaves. A second revolt took place in 1831. Two years later, men of mixed color were given political rights."

At the end of Rue Victor Hugo, they came upon an ancient stone bridge.

"Shortly, we will be crossing the Roxelane River. We are now leaving the Centre Quartier where many blacks and mulattoes reside in poverty. And on the other side, we will be entering the Fort Quartier where the majority of the whites live in grandeur."

A mile out of town, they ventured upon a vast botanical park.

"Someday, my friend, you will have to visit these gardens," suggested Marcel. "Le Jardin des Plantes was established in 1803 here on the slopes of Morne Parnasse. Like everything else on this island, the park is not as spectacular as it once was nearly a hundred years ago. We don't have the upkeep monies from France anymore. This wonderful park is referred to as the eleventh wonder of the world as it contains an extensive variety of rare and exotic plant life. Many nations send us their young botanists to do internships. It is a place of natural wonder that fascinates and captivates not only the casual viewers, but scientists as well."

The steep incline of the road forced the carriage horse to wheeze. Beads of sweat soaked its hide. Flies teased its ears. After years of experience traveling these mountains, it knew that it would soon be back at the Chevalier plantation resting in the comforts of its stables.

Five minutes later, Marcel pointed south. "There's your new home, Stefan."

Stefan's brain could not comprehend what his eyes were seeing. There in the distance, a noble two-story manor dominated the entire top of an emerald green hill. It was the most glorious sight he had ever seen in his life.

15

Yvette's dust-covered surrey pulled up to the front of Les Chats. Her horse panted and foamed at the mouth. With rifle in hand, she dashed inside the brothel and up the stairs before anyone could stop her. She kicked open each closed door lining the hallway interrupting sexual encounters. The sudden appearance of a wild-eyed girl standing in the threshold with rifle pointed their way froze the naked women and their customers in creative positions.

Yvette hesitated at the last door before pushing it open with her foot. She came across André standing butt-naked with his trousers dropped down around his skinny ankles. Indigo was pinned against the wall. One of his hands held her wrists above her head while his other groped her breasts. Indigo's neck and chest were laced with cuts. Blood was everywhere.

André pushed Indigo to the floor before facing his half sister.

Yvette stared at his erection and grinned.

He followed her gaze to his private parts.

"What the hell are you up to, you half-breed daughter of a she-devil nigger?" His voice cracked as he realized his vulnerability.

Yvette steadied her rifle and fired.

16

St. Pierre, Martinique
August 8, 1895
The Plantation

The Chevalier plantation house reminded David of the fine old mansions he had seen during his travels to New Orleans, Charleston, and Atlanta. White Ionic and Corinthian columns adorned coral-colored walls. The wrought iron and brick balconies lining the upper and lower galleries of the house were not gaudy, but ornately classic in design.

A little room off the kitchen would be Stefan's quarters. The boy was giddy over his good fortune. A brass bed, a three-drawer dresser, and a window with a view of the vegetable gardens were all his. Henrillia, the cook and main housekeeper, brought Stefan a stack of old school clothes once belonging to André. Stefan had never seen such finery in all of his life. He was served a bowl of soup. The hearty flavors caressed his tongue. He ate with gusto.

That night David and Marcel enjoyed a meal of rice and chicken along with a cold white bean salad. They sat in the formal dining parlor, where a stone fireplace warmed the spacious room from the chilly mountain air. Paintings of exotic island scenes painted by Gauguin added gaiety and color to the room. Bowls and vases of freshly cut flowers provided fragrance. Havana cigars, potent local rum, and good conversation followed dinner. Topics included current market revelations to the latest news from abroad and, of course, women. They laughed at each other's harmless jokes. It was apparent that these two men would be great friends.

"It does the heart good," said Henrillia while clearing the dessert dishes, "to hear laughter in this old house once again. It *be* much too long."

"Marcel," cried out a voice belonging to a young man.

The men jumped to their feet.

It was Paul. He appeared haggard and out of breath from running. His normally groomed hair stood out in all directions, his white shirt was soiled, his knees were scraped, his eyes were the size of hen eggs, and his contorted face revealed recent horrors.

"Why, Paul, dear boy," asked Marcel, "whatever happened to you?"

"There was this rainstorm . . . so much rain . . . and slimy snake . . . eh . . . the big voodoo woman . . . her leeches . . . lots of leeches . . . and Maxi, he was bitten . . . and Yvette . . . eh . . . she ran . . . eh . . . to kill him . . . yes . . . to kill André."

"What are you trying to say, Paul?" demanded Marcel.

Paul, delirious from his experiences on the mountain, kept repeating the same thing over and over again, not making any sense. His eyes dilated, his breathing quickened, and his body started to shake. Tears rolled down his sunburned cheeks. He was going into shock.

About that same time, the front door banged open with the arrival of yelling men and wailing children. There was so much shouting and crying going on under the roof of the plantation house that David found it impossible to grasp what was happening. He was to find out later that it was Fernand Clerc and a brothel doctor from St. Pierre who escorted Marcel's sobbing daughter, Yvette, to a chair. The other two men—nervous workers from Fernand's waterfront warehouse—carried Indigo and placed her on the divan in front of the fireplace.

"What in the name of God is going on here?" Marcel asked.

"Take it easy, Marcel," said Fernand. "No physical harm has come to Yvette, but the poor dear has been emotionally traumatized. Indigo has suffered superficial knife wounds to her throat and breasts. The doctor and I brought them here as soon as we could get away from the military police. It seemed, under the circumstances, the best thing to do. The less the public knows about this situation, the better off you will be."

"Knows about what?" asked Marcel.

"Allow me to explain," said Fernand. "Earlier today, Yvette barely avoided colliding into my buggy with her surrey. She was hysterical and not making any sense at all. She got away from me, so I followed her directly to Les Chats. By the time these old bones got up the stairs, she was in one of the brothel rooms taking aim at André with her boar rifle. The weapon discharged just as I grabbed her arm. André was hit in the thigh and is at the hospital in St. Pierre undergoing surgery as we speak to save his leg. It is not known if he will survive."

"Why did this happen?" quavered Marcel.

"Yvette learned about André's plans to molest Indigo . . . something about a deal between Indigo's stepfather and your son. It's quite a simple situation, Marcel, your daughter was trying to protect the honor of her friend."

Marcel held out pleading hands to his daughter.

"Yvette, my darling, did you have to shoot him?"

Yvette gritted her teeth. "I hope he dies."

Marcel turned to Fernand. "I must get to my son now."

Yvette sprang from her chair and ran for the dining room door at the exact moment David moved forward to see if he could be of assistance. They collided. The sketch of David drawn by André earlier in the day fell from his pocket and fluttered through the air down to the floor, where it landed beneath the end table next to the divan.

David steadied the girl covered in mud and blood. Anger flashed from beautiful eyes the shade of apple green. She pushed him away and ran out of the room.

PART III

Six Years Later

17

St. Pierre, Martinique
December 15, 1901
The Return of Yvette

It was hot. Damn hot. Midday temperatures registered into the upper nineties with a humidity factor just as high. The overheated sailors, tourists, and merchants who crammed the busy docks grimaced in dismay against the glare of the unrelenting sun while barefoot, dark-skinned cargo loaders went about their daily chores, impervious to the assault of the brutal rays.

Captain David Cabot had yet to adapt to the tropical climate of the West Indies even after six years of trade winds travel. Wearily he leaned against a crate of avocados earmarked for France, batted an annoying cluster of sand flies attracted to the sweet scent of his sweat, and smiled despite his discomfort. He so enjoyed the ideology of the islands, especially Martinique.

"Easy does it! Easy does it," shouted a man at a pair of zealous cargo loaders who were piling rum barrels haphazardly onto a transfer lighter. David looked up to see his cargo foreman, Danny Sheehan, frantically waving his hands to catch the attention of the local negro *canotiers* hired for the job. Once the cargo was steadied and secured, the cargo foreman signaled the okay sign for the workers to transport the rum to the ship. The *canotiers*—clad in cropped white work pants, long-sleeved shirts, and straw hats—manipulated oar poles to launch the lighter away from shore and out into the harbor toward the *Silver Eagle*.

Since five o'clock that morning, Danny Sheehan had been directing *canotiers* in the loading of transfer lighters hauling outgoing goods to the American steamer anchored in the motionless waters of the bay. "We are finished for the afternoon, sir," he said to his captain.

"Good work, Danny," said David. "Like an arrow to the bull's-eye, you are always on target. Tomorrow morning we shall receive a quarter ton of refined sugar from the Gruenin plantation and five loads of green bananas from the Chevaliers. At sunup the following day, we gather our fifteen passengers and pull anchor."

"As you say, sir."

"I bid you leave."

It was three o'clock in the afternoon. David had just enough time to stop by his hotel, bathe, and change into clean clothes before heading into town to purchase a welcome-home gift for the daughter of Marcel Chevalier, Yvette. She had just returned from six years living in Europe. A formal reception was scheduled that evening at the Chevalier plantation. David recalled the angry, mud—and blood-covered thirteen-year-old girl he briefly encountered after the shooting of her brother in the St. Pierre brothel. Her beautiful, defiant green eyes still haunted him. What is she like now as a young woman? wondered David, departing the dock area.

For the ten-minute walk to his hotel, David chose a well-traveled cobblestone service road that separated the wide cargo beach from the tree-lined edge of La Place Bertin north of the lighthouse. His attention was drawn to stone benches beneath a line of mango trees allowing those who wished to watch the activities of the loading areas a place to sit in the shade. On one of the benches sat a shipping agent shouting profanities while brandishing sheets of contractual documents before an exasperated Italian captain, who shook his head expressing disappointment over the agreement. All around reverberated a symphony of French, English, Spanish, Dutch, Italian, and Creole, making it nearly impossible for David to tell who was saying what to whom in the chaotic hustle and bustle of daily St. Pierre seaside commerce. It was a small miracle that any business got done—but somehow it did, six days a week, all year round.

Dock area near Place Bertin

Other dockside sounds mingled with the foreign tongues: the banging of barrels and crates, the clicking of hoofs against cobblestones, the braying of mules and oxen, the cries of hungry seabirds, the clanging of hauling chains, the booms of unarmed canons, the shrill trill and rings of signal whistles and bells, the persistent meowing of hungry dock cats, the pounding of hammers, the sweet laughter of Creoles, the smacking of sea waves against piers, and the merciless squeaking of greaseless cart axles.

David spotted a group of high-ranking dark-skinned municipal soldiers anxiously pacing back and forth near the Fontaine Agnès in La Place Bertin. The discomfort of their stiff wool uniforms was obvious. They eyed him with contempt as he walked by. White males were not held in favor by privileged Negroes of elevated status.

Not wanting to be a target of the soldiers' irritability, David picked up his pace and headed down Rue Bouillé, passing houses of ill repute masquerading as quaint Victorian homes displaying an air of innocence to most newcomers and, to a certain degree, nobleness from the outside—houses very similar to the saloon and brothel known as Les Chats. If not for the stale cigar smoke, naughty laughter, and honky-tonk music wafting out from the opened doors, one would never suspect what was really going on behind those pale yellow walls.

It seemed a lifetime ago since David first met with André Chevalier at Les Chats. He hadn't liked André then, and he certainly didn't like him now. David surmised that the brothel shooting and resulting crippling of André Chevalier had only intensified the vile existence of a human being who sadly lacked common morals and decency. David's relationship with Marcel Chevalier, on the other hand, had developed into one between trusted friends and business associates.

"Bonjour, monsieur," greeted three street prostitutes who selected David as their latest prey in the *place des mosges*. The ringleader was no more than sixteen years old. "What a handsome canary you are," she cooed seductively in broken English while undoing the first few buttons of his white shirt and playfully running her dirty fingernails through his blond chest hairs before he could protest.

The second whore kicked the first one out of the way. In a theatrical sweep of her hand, she reached up, yanked off a bright yellow and blue madras scarf tied island style around her head, and proceeded to wipe David's damp brow with the fabric. "Mon Dieu," she lisped through missing teeth, "this tall banana is melting."

Not to be outdone, the third street urchin reached deep into the pocket of her soiled skirt and produced a flask of sugary *vonti ponch* liquor. "Gazelle and Bebé," she ordered, "restez tranquille! Keep quiet! This pretty man be no canary or fruit of the banana. He *be* a mighty fine palomino pony. Now then, my stallion, you tell Yzore what you want—a sip of fire?"

Bebé stepped back, waving her scarf in the air and happily twirling around on her bare toes in a comical dance. Gazelle made little kissing noises while plucking David's chest hairs. Yzore yanked out the cork from her canvas flask with her teeth and offered David a swig. Accustomed to frequent encounters with the local street whores, David removed the caressing hand from his chest, buttoned his shirt, pushed away the drink, and politely begged off their advances. In a swirl of crimson skirts, the bemused whores scampered off in a chorus of giggles to the other side of the avenue, where they lewdly propositioned a group of astonished Danish sailors.

18

St. Pierre, Martinique
December 19, 1901
The Anger Builds

André protectively touched his crotch and winced at the memory. Yvette had come very close to hitting her target six years ago—a deed that nearly killed him. The bullet ripped through the upper right thigh, shattering bone and shredding muscle. He didn't lose the leg; however, it left him crippled. A noticeable twist of his knee to the inside caused his foot to drag with each faltered step. He despised weakness; he despised his worthless leg.

It had been exhilarating when his father had sent Yvette away. It had been exhilarating to bask in the limelight while receiving undivided attention day and night in the hospital by a man who openly grieved at the thought of his son dying. It delighted him when his father built him a private cottage on the plantation near the west banana field where he could paint and recuperate in solitude. It gave him pleasure to enjoy the company of his father once a week for card night at the elite white-males-only Club del'Hermine. His life was almost bearable with Yvette away in Paris. He could fool himself that he was the special one in his father's eyes. Now that Papa's little darling was back and the center of his attention, André's indignation toward her fostered sheer lunacy. Life had gone back as before. It had all been an illusion—this desire for a normal father-son relationship.

"It is of no matter," said André in a low whisper from the back of his carriage heading into Fort-de-France. "The time will come when I shall be rid of the old bastard and Yvette."

"Did you say something, sir?" asked the black driver nervously.

"Not to you."

The driver tightened his lips and focused his eyes on the road. He didn't want to encourage trouble from this crazy white man. André Chevalier's ill feelings toward people of color were legendary on the island. The only time André mingled with the *hommes de couleur* was to participate in illegal, back-alley cockfights—further proof that blood and gore awarded him gratification at any cost. The fact that he had purchased an isolated run-down house high on a grassy knoll in the section of town mostly inhabited by those of color made no sense. Why, wondered so many islanders, did he want to live so close to the humans he blatantly detested?

"Monsieur Chevalier, we are at the governor's residency," announced the driver with trepidation quavering his voice.

"Wait here and don't leave until I return," ordered André, grabbing an attaché case.

19

St. Pierre, Martinique
December 19, 1901
David and Indigo

David continued south on Rue Bouillé until he reached the Mouillage Quartier and his hotel. It was a grand three-story structure. For nearly a hundred years, the antiquated building had belonged to an enterprising family of prosperous French merchants. No other house in all of St. Pierre could match its opulence. Intricate ironwork surrounded the building. Impressive fluted columns supported the front porch. Real glass graced the windows. Unfortunately, as rich as they were, all the money in the world could not protect this prominent family from the deadly smallpox epidemic that hit the island in the late 1800s. Every family member died—young and old alike. The stately mansion was sold at public auction and transformed into a fancy hotel called Hôtel Indigo. David paused at the entrance of the establishment recalling the first time he had been brought there two years earlier on a gray, rainy afternoon.

*   *   *

The *Silver Eagle* finally dropped anchor on September 3, 1899, in the height of the hurricane season, subsequent to hours of battling high winds, pounding rains, and rough seas between Dominica and Martinique. After meeting David on the pier, Marcel escorted him by buggy to the customhouse to meet with Laurant Montour to secure the unloading of mail and several tons of cargo. Agent Montour was advised that a doctor would also be needed for five seasick passengers confined to their cabins. With business matters completed, David assumed they would head straightaway for his customary lodge along the waterfront.

"You just passed my hotel," commented David.

"I know," replied Marcel. "I have a surprise for you. You will be staying at a newly opened lodge owned by a friend of mine. See, we are coming to it now."

The two men made a mad dash from the carriage through the rain into the hotel's teak paneled entry hall. An elegant doorman in an evening suit and white gloves took their wet rain gear. Gold-plated cherub statues guarded the front entrance. An oval ceiling enclave painted with naked women provided an interesting backdrop for a resplendent six-foot Waterford chandelier that cascaded in dazzling tiers. An exquisite tomato red Persian prayer rug partially concealed what appeared to be a jade-marble floor. Opulence of decor was an understatement.

Near the front off the hallway, happy customers were experiencing the finest of the island's cuisine in a crowded dining room surrounded by black marble mantels trimmed in gold and bronze chandeliers adding elegance to their dining pleasure. The new restaurant had become an instant hit and was one of the most popular in the city. In an adjacent saloon, two men in top hats and a trim, fashionable lady in an expensive lilac organza dress exchanged pleasantries at the polished oak bar. Their animated conversation and laughter carried into the hallway as they shared their third bottle of red wine and snacked on bits of toasted coconut.

"Marc," beckoned Marcel, approaching a man standing behind the registration desk located on the right side of the foyer opposite the bar, "this is Captain Cabot. I believe you have a room for him." The desk clerk nodded politely. Turning to a wall of small wooden slots, the clerk selected a room key. A bellhop was then summoned to take David's baggage to room 3C on the third floor. "I'd like to see Mademoiselle Indigo," requested Marcel.

Marc knocked on the office door behind the desk.

"Oui," answered a sweet voice.

"Monsieur Chevalier is here and wishes to see you."

An attractive mulatto woman walked out. David recognized her as an older and more dignified version of the frightened teenager who had, six years ago, been lying cut and battered in the plantation house of Marcel Chevalier.

Indigo wore a floor-length quilted lamé dress and matching topcoat loosely covering her petite frame. The elaborate costume enhanced, rather than overpowered, her beauty. Upon her head was a corresponding lamé turban patterned in royal blue stripes. A string of hammered gold beads encircled her delicate neck. She carried an air of nobility.

"Parlez-vous français?" asked Indigo.

David shook his head. "Très mal."

Indigo laughed. "Very well, in that case, Captain Cabot, we shall speak English."

An unexplainable bond instantly formed between the two. It was as if they had known each other all their lives. Indigo invited David and Marcel to join her for dinner at the hotel dining room. Marcel declined, but David eagerly accepted. After a marvelous meal, David followed Indigo to her private quarters, where they sipped cognac on her balcony, watching the falling rain and the bobbing ships in the bay. They chatted into the wee hours of the morning.

After listening to David talk about the wonders of his ship and the sea, Indigo slyly commented. "Have you not wished to have a wife and children?"

"I am not sure how to answer that. Someday I would like to have a family, but if it means giving up my current lifestyle, perhaps not."

"You love the sea that much?"

"I love the sea that much."

"What about women?" Too much cognac had flushed her cheeks.

"What about them?"

"You know . . . your ship . . . is she not made of steel? No matter how much you love her there are things she cannot offer like . . ."

"Like sex?"

"Oui!"

"I have met many fine women from all over the world. Women I've had the satisfaction of enjoying in many ways."

"And your favorite lady is?"

David tapped his chin and sipped his cognac. "Ginger."

"Ah. Tell me about Ginger."

"Not what you would call pretty. Her laugh is infectious. Her comely face is most expressive. Her long, curly hair is the color of sunset. She knows how to nurture. She makes me laugh until I beg for mercy. I remember getting drunk once and trying to count all of her freckles—it was impossible."

"And where is this Ginger of yours?"

"She is a singer from Liverpool. I do miss Ginger. I miss her caring ways. I miss her cooking. I miss her roast beef and Yorkshire pudding—they were sinful."

"This Ginger you are describing sounds more like your mother than your English tart," grinned Indigo with an arched eyebrow, "which makes me realize that you have not mentioned your mother. Is she not alive?"

David snipped the end off a cigar and dipped it in the cognac before lighting it. He was not one to disclose personal feelings on such sensitive matters. But there had been something so trusting about Indigo that he felt compelled to tell her his innermost thoughts.

"My mother is very much alive. I didn't spend much time with her when I was a young boy growing up in Boston. It seemed that I was either in the care of a nanny, going to school, playing football with my cousins, hanging out with my grandfather at his shipyard or my father at his shipping brokerage office. My mother is a woman devoted to opera, luncheons, and afternoon bridge games. She had no time for the needs of an active boy."

Indigo jumped up from her chair, went to her chambers, and retrieved a hand mirror from her dressing table. She returned to the terrace, knelt on the floor by his side, and held up the mirror so that it reflected both of their images. "Do you not think, my American brother, how truly remarkable it is that we nearly have the same color of eyes?"

"Quite remarkable," he expressed amusement.

In the warm glow of a kerosene lamp, inebriated Indigo made a declaration that she would henceforth refer to David as her *Américain frère*—American brother.

*   *   *

Now, two years later, as David stood before the yellow facade of the hotel, he found it hard to believe that time had gone by so fast since that first meeting with Indigo in 1899. The world was a few weeks away from celebrating the second year of the twentieth century. It was December of 1901 and it was hot. Damn hot.

David went to the registration desk. "Hello, Marc, is Mademoiselle Indigo in?"

"No, sir," said Marc, pushing up his pince-nez glasses. "However, she did ask me to deliver this note to you as soon as you arrived."

David went to room 3C on the third floor reserved year-round just for his use. It was a room where he kept many personal items. He pulled off his soiled shirt and read the note.

> *Dearest David.*
>
> *I will not be around this afternoon as I have a very important mission to fulfill. I shall be most anxious to know how the party went at the Chevaliers'. I regret I will not be able to attend. I do look forward to seeing you tomorrow.*
>
> *All my love, Indigo*

David felt he knew just about all there was to know about Indigo; however, there were times when he found her to be overtly mysterious and secretive. He was fully aware of her love for the opera, theater, and ballet, Shakespeare, Chaucer, and Keats. He enjoyed listening to her recite gentle poetry penned by her hand. Her unquenchable thirst for stories of his world travels flattered his ego. He was familiar with her desire to travel the world and live in Paris. Despite their closeness, he sensed that certain aspects of her life had been left unexplained.

David stopped by the hotel's busy bar for a quick beer before going downtown to shop for Yvette's gift. The beer was served warm. As he downed the drink, his ears picked up bits and pieces of conversation and gossip from whispering patrons.

"Do you think that André Chevalier will be there tonight?"

"I wonder what Yvette Chevalier looks like now."

"How long has it been?"

"Six years."

"Has it really been that long?"

"Perhaps there will be trouble again?"

"Are you going to the party?"

"Oh my, yes," cried the voices in unison. "It is all so terribly exciting."

David swallowed the last of his beer and made his way to Rue Victor Hugo. The avenue was mobbed. He found a gift and perfume shop specializing in expensive items imported from Paris and Milan. The proprietor recommended a lap *secretaire* that included an inkwell, a packet of parchment paper, and a nice variety of feather pens. It seemed a safe gift to give to someone he did not really know. He paid the woman in francs. David was looking forward to meeting, once again, the girl with the apple green eyes.

20

St. Pierre, Martinique
December 19, 1901
Indigo All Grown Up

Twenty-two-year-old Indigo adjusted the angle of her parasol and settled into the backseat of her buggy. Not only was the light of the sun blistering to the skin, but its bright glare was also hurtful to the eyes. She nodded to her personal driver and the buggy moved forward.

Indigo was a successful businesswoman. By the law of the land, women were not permitted to vote; nevertheless, nothing had been legislated to prevent them from operating a trade of their choice if financial and legal proprieties were in order. Oddly enough on this tiny French Caribbean island where white males ruled, it was the white males who acknowledged Indigo's uncanny business sense. Her rare combination of beauty and brains captivated them.

Due to the way she had obtained her equities, some would say that Indigo was no better than a whore. Others would fiercely disagree. How Indigo acquired her hotel was no secret among the islanders. What about her involvement in the Chevalier scandal? It hadn't harmed her in the least. Most of the people of color and the white men, for the most part, gave nary a glance to infidelities and scandals. Indigo knew that her high standing with the white men caused great suffering to the dignity of the white women. These ladies of special upbringing were forced to conduct themselves in a perfunctory manner, unfairly isolating them from any private or business involvements outside of their own homes or select social circles. Most were trapped in a chauvinistic world limiting their intellectual expression or demonstration.

These white women represented about 2 percent of a population made up of blacks, Indians, and mulattoes. Many white men in power kept two families on the island—one with white wives and children and the other with secret mulatto women and offspring. The wives of these men seldom complained. It was an understood island tradition that a white woman of social prominence practice the conservative Frenchman's conception of a perfect Christian wife and mother. Never was she to question her husband's private life away from the home.

Two or three times a week, she was left alone with their sleeping children for company. When the man did return, she did not dare inquire where he had been. She could tell by the smell lingering on his person. The powerful garlic and spice aroma of her husband's quadroon woman reeked spitefully from his clothes, clinging tenaciously to every fiber. How she must have hated that deplorable scent, thought Indigo. Come morning she most likely would have preferred to burn his trousers than to have them laundered.

"The white woman is not as grand as she seems," snickered Indigo as her driver pushed the horse down Rue Victor Hugo toward the Fort District. "She has no chance against les fille-des-couleurs on this island of Martinique."

Indigo was fully aware of the attractions of a pretty mulatto girl. For centuries, the dark-skinned women of Martinique were touted as being among the most beautiful of women in the world. Satin skin and jeweled eyes had brought many a steadfast man to his knees. Outwardly, these subservient but proud women portrayed themselves in the image of innocence and naïveté; inwardly, they hid an immeasurable depth of wisdom and cunningness. Their masters and lovers were kept fast alert. Mulatto women could be impish one minute, melancholy another, and erotic the next. They were perceptive, calculating, and bright. They knew how to extract a high price for their devotion, kindness, and love. It was not unusual to see the fille-de-couleur raising multicolored bastard children in nice little houses owned by married men. These mistresses of plantation barons and wealthy merchants were well clothed and well moneyed, and their children went to good schools. They had just about everything materialistic in life they could ever want; however, public recognition and a proper title seemed beyond reach—even for those like Indigo, who were independent, powerful, and wealthy. A fille-de-couleur, rich or poor, is a natural enemy for the white woman. Indigo struggled daily to overcome sensitivities to this intolerance.

Indigo gestured to her driver to pull onto the side of the road just before reaching the stone bridge overlooking the Roxelane River. Standing up on the floorboard of the buggy, she searched the linen-covered riverbanks for the ghost of her mother. It did not matter to Indigo that Honorine's illness had nearly caused the sacrifice of her daughter's future; Indigo still missed her. Indigo knew all too well that when her mother died three months after the shooting at Les Chats, her death resulted in part from river disease and in part from shame.

"Please continue on to the park, Samuel," said Indigo to the driver.

Samuel lightly jerked the reins and coaxed the horse across the bridge. They passed by a group of hormone-charged white teen males who were leaning over the waist-high stone wall of the bridge, taunting the younger and prettier of the laundresses. It was a game they delighted in, and their wild laughter denoted their folly.

"Fools," clucked Indigo. She resented the lack of appreciation and understanding of the great physical pain that these women of the river endured just to survive. She had no patience for these brainless whooping and whistling boys in their fancy breeches and frilly shirts, who had no idea of what it was like for the washerwomen to awake before dawn, quiet and somber, with the sleep of the night still heavy in their eyes; or how before the first light of day reflected the river's rippling surface, they would have to place large hats called *chapeau bacoués* upon their heads to protect them from the tropical sun; or how they had to stand knee-deep in the icy waters of the river for twelve hours or more each day smacking laundry against the surface of the river and nearby boulders; or how this backbreaking practice called *fesseé* required timing, patience, strength, and agility even though it appeared to be choreographed in smooth deliberate dancelike movements; or how a common river disease would slowly deteriorate the flesh of their legs and kill them soon enough.

Down in the river, Indigo spotted a withered old woman in her late thirties whose spine was locked in an arch from years of river work. The weary laundress began to sing an ancient Creole song. She was soon joined by another and another until the chorus of their honey-smooth voices reached a high-pitched crescendo that lifted up and over the currents enwrapping Indigo into a warm cocoon of familiarity.

A mile out of St. Pierre, Indigo and her driver stopped at the entrance to the botanical gardens. As soon as Indigo walked through the main entry gate, the sun disappeared behind a ceiling of cocoa palms. Giant ferns with fans stretching six feet in width fought one another for what precious space was available. Vines, thick as ropes, twisted wickedly around everything in sight. There was a fascinating array of foliage—some native, some imported. Indigo marveled at the varying shades of luminous green leaves in calming hues of chartreuse, shamrock, emerald, apple, forest, and olive.

Two paths emerged. Indigo took the one to her left as it provided the best views and was the shortest route to her final destination. She remembered the stories and had seen the paintings of how the garden once looked over a hundred years ago at the height of its beauty when these stone walkways and bridges were dutifully swept clean of leaves and debris, the marble terraces were carefully polished to a high sheen, and the pristine fountains were well tended and kept in good repair at all times. Now the botanical garden was decomposing from age and neglect, entwined with creepers, and everything coated with a thin layer of soft green moss. The jungle was reclaiming its territory. Maintaining such a large park proved expensive. Paris had long ago lost interest in supporting its upkeep. Current elected officials were hesitant to utilize public monies to sustain the vast park. Times were tough; and taxes were needed for more important concerns like schools, hospitals, and the military.

Indigo lifted her taffeta skirts and followed the overgrown pathway. She had chosen yellow to wear on this special day. Yellow was a happy color, and it suited her mood. It had been six years since she had seen Yvette. She was both excited and nervous. There was one thing that could ruin their reunion—the revelation of Indigo's unthinkable sin. Would Yvette ever be able forgive the betrayal of their friendship and trust? Indigo wondered as she took a deep breath, tilted her chin up, and headed toward unknown answers.

21

St. Pierre, Martinique
December 19, 1901
Bargaining with the Governor

"Mon Dieu, André, please discontinue that doodling," complained the governor.

André Chevalier ever so slightly lifted his head and narrowed his dark eyes. He did not like to be told what to do or what not to do. The piece of coal in his hand stopped upon the open page of the sketchpad. With a bang, he slammed the cover down over the none-too-flattering cartoon of the portly man sitting across from him.

"As you wish, Governor," said André.

Forty-five-year-old Louis Mouttet shifted the bulk of his huge body uneasily in his chair at the Fort-de-France governor's residency, where flags of Martinique and France flanked a custom-made office desk and an imposing colonial seal hung on the wall. The newly appointed governor of Martinique was in an irritable mood. The room's ceiling fan provided little relief from the unseasonably hot December. Perspiration trickled down a bulbous nose. He loosened his tie. When he spoke, it was more of a bark.

"What have you learned?"

"Plenty," answered André.

Mouttet did not particularly like nor trust this arrogant young man, yet the governor put up with him nevertheless. André was quite useful in digging up inside information on the liberal Radical Party. This strange young man knew the ins and outs of island politics like no one else.

"I'm waiting for your report," said Mouttet impatiently.

André enjoyed his position as the governor's unofficial right-hand man. It allowed him to use his connections with the Progressive Party to voice his own hard-line views against people of color, especially those who were demanding equal rights. André's prejudicial views were fanatical. So fanatical, in fact, that even the staunchest of white conservatives were taken aback by his prowhite political convictions. Martinique's conservatives wanted to keep their rightful control over the dark-skinned islanders, but not at the risk of a civil war.

"Amédee Knight is busy reorganizing the Radical Party and formulating a new plan of attack against the Progressive Party. I am sad to report that some of this black bastard's ideas are receiving a nod of approval by some of the white moderates."

Mouttet removed a monogrammed handkerchief from his breast pocket and blew his nose. He had been living in Martinique less than a month. He didn't expect much out of the island people. He would let them live and do as they pleased as long as they respected him and their mother country. He did not want to change the island. He wanted peace. He was looking forward to an easy governorship supported nicely by the Progressive Party leaders, the newspapers, and the banks. That was all. A tinge of apprehension ran down his spine. No one in Paris had informed him before he took this position that there was unrest on the island. He mentally scolded himself as he tried to shake off his latest bout of nerves. He had to remind himself that he had not achieved this level of position by being timid. Louis Mouttet stopped at nothing to obtain the comforts of an easy life. His quest for political power was legendary throughout France. He had ruined many a man who had tried to block his aspirations.

"Come, André, let's have some afternoon nourishment."

André followed the governor out onto a wrought iron balcony overlooking the port of Fort-de-France. A servant trailed behind them, carrying a tray of tiny French pastries and a pot of tea. André studied the man across from him as the servant poured the tea. *So,* he thought, *this must be the terrace where the gluttonous governor spends his time with his wife, Maria, dining on the balcony, indulging in tremendous quantities of rich French food and strong spirits.* André recalled photos of the highly honored Mouttet when he was young, vibrant, and handsome, and now a disfigured face from malaria and a bloated body from excess of food.

"Really, Governor," said André dryly, "you want me to drink tea?"

"Just try it."

Mouttet watched his guest swallow the tea heavily spiked with rum.

André didn't comment on the beverage. "Governor, you must realize that the Radicals are gaining confidence. They feel that the upcoming May elections will bring them not only victory but total power and control over the island. By tomorrow, I should know the details to their plan of action. I have my *boys* working on it."

"Frankly, André, I don't understand how one Negro can be of any threat to us. As far as I'm concerned, all this fuss is nothing about nothing. A lot of hot air coming from an individual who thinks he can conquer the French government. How silly when you think about it."

André banged his teacup.

"You don't get it, do you? Knight is gaining popularity not only with the people of color but with some of the liberal whites as well. This is no ordinary nigger. He was an honored graduate of the École Centrale in Paris. Almost as soon as he returned to Martinique, he got himself elected as assistant mayor. Shortly after that, he was elected secretary of the Chamber of Commerce, only to be appointed president of the town council. In 1899, he won the post of island senator. And now, Amadée Knight and his pack of liberal dogs have their eyes set on the deputy seat up for grabs in the northern *arondissement*. Do you have any idea what that means?"

Mouttet kept his eyes trained on a newly arrived cargo ship setting anchor in the Fort-de-France harbor. Even though André's condescending attitude was beginning to rile him, he kept his temper in check. At this early stage of indoctrination to Martinique, Mouttet could ill afford to lose André's vital underground connections. "Even though I have been in Martinique for only two weeks," he said, "I am not entirely ignorant of what was going on and who was doing what to whom. What are you trying to tell me?"

"Don't you understand that you may end up facing an uprising during your first year in office? If Knight gets a position as powerful as the deputy of the northern arondissement, he will seek more equal rights for his kind. If we don't win the election in May, we are dead."

"Then he must be stopped."

"Just give me the word, Governor, and I will see to it that our Radical Party friend is permanently removed from the race."

"No! I'll have none of that," growled Mouttet. "The Progressive Party has been in control of this island for decades. I have to protect its good name while at the same time deal with this Negro in a civilized fashion. I never heard what you just said. Keep feeding me with the information I seek. That is all I ask of you. Do nothing illegal."

It disgusted André to see what the ravages of soft living had done to this once vital and *débonnaire* Legion of Honor winner. Mouttet was legendary in France. André had read background documents and newspaper articles about this ambitious son of a farm laborer from Marseilles. Mouttet's political climb began in Paris back in 1883. He worked as a proofreader for the conservative newspaper *La Patrie*. For a brief time, he held the position of secretary of the Historical Society of Paris. Then he entered the French Colonial Service in 1886 as personal secretary to the governor of Indo-China. There seemed no stopping Mouttet's ascent to power as he continued to connive his way up the ranks. One of his smartest career moves, mused André, was the convenient marriage to socialite Maria Coppet, whose powerful uncle worked as a high-ranking French official. As a result of this union, Mouttet enjoyed several impressive colonial governorships in Africa.

In 1899, Mouttet became governor of French Guinea. During this time, he gained brief notoriety as the man who persuaded Dreyfus, the French officer who was unjustly accused of being a spy and traitor, to return to Paris to stand trial. This public notoriety led to Mouttet's appointment to governor second class that lasted until November of 1901, when the French government reassigned him to Martinique. At first, André had been delighted with the news that Mouttet was taking over the governorship, but now he was fostering doubts that this man would be capable of handling the delicate affairs of the island and its diversified people.

"If that is how you feel, Governor, then our salvation rests with Fernand Clerc. He is the only one who can run against Knight and have a winning chance. To our advantage, he is also an influential force with the colored masses."

"I do not like this man," said Mouttet. "Apparently, most members of the Progressive Party endorse him as their candidate. Therefore, I have no choice but to go along."

André shrugged his shoulders. "I too do not care for the likes of Fernand Clerc. From the very beginning, I have been against his nomination. His leniency toward his laborers is totally unacceptable. It makes it harder for the other plantation owners to control their people of color. He constantly voices his displeasure with the town's lax prostitution laws. The majority of the men of St. Pierre would pick up arms and go into battle to keep their whores. Fernand is a problem. His advantage to us is that he is one of the few white men trusted by both sides. I hate to admit it, but Clerc is the perfect candidate to represent the Progressive Party in the upcoming elections. If we can control his platform, then, perhaps, in four months we shall be the victors."

Mouttet yawned. It was time for his afternoon nap. "All I care about is keeping the Progressive Party in control."

22

St. Pierre, Martinique
December 19, 1901
The Transgressions of Indigo

Near the end of the path was a stunning waterfall. It was a familiar sight that Indigo acknowledged with a courteous nod of her head. As the thunderous water tumbled down from one swirling basin into another, Indigo took a seat on a nearby crumbling stone bench. Indigo recalled that Josephine, the wife of Napoléon Bonaparte and a Martinique native, used to steal away to the Jardin des Plantes when she was a teen to meditate on this very same bench. Indigo wondered what kind of dreams Josephine had dreamed as a young girl.

Indigo reflected on her own dreams. Her dream to become one of the most respected businesswomen on the island had been fulfilled. Her dream to live in Paris and write poetry had yet to be fulfilled. She was determined to make this aspiration happen in six months' time.

Indigo nervously intertwined, relaxed, and intertwined her hands. Expensive gold rings with dazzling sapphires sparkled from every finger. She reached up to fidget with the sapphire brooch fastened to the front of her yellow turban. Waiting was not easy. She closed her eyes and tried to relax. A lavender frog croaked shrilly at the same time a greeting voice rang out.

"Hello, dear Indigo."

A knowing smile touched Indigo's lip. She opened her eyes. Yvette stood before her. Gone was the little girl with short curls, the tomboy expression, and oversized clothing. Gone was the little girl. Yvette's copper hair was in a bun at the nape of her neck. A black riding hat stylishly topped her head. She wore a crisp white linen shirt and a pair of tight fitting English riding britches. Knee-high boots made of black Italian leather adorned her feet.

There was only one thing that had not changed—the green eyes.

"Yvette! You are so beautiful. So grown up."

"And you look like a princess, my lovely Indigo."

They hugged and took a seat together on the bench.

A little brown bird pecked at the ground near their feet, chirping a pretty song.

"Sounds as if the *siffleur-de-montagne* is announcing your arrival," said Indigo, not letting go of her friend's hand.

Yvette glanced at the bird. "It has been so long since I have heard the sweet melody of the mountain whistler. I have missed you so. Your wonderful letters and poems helped me keep in touch with Martinique. I never want to leave my home again. Never! Jamais!"

In the distance, a woman and a small child could be seen walking up the path toward them. Indigo hadn't expected them to arrive so soon. She wasn't quite ready to make known her secret. What would this revelation do to their friendship? She owed Yvette so much. If not for Yvette and her daring rescue at the brothel six years ago, none of Indigo's dreams would have been realized. Indigo sighed once again. Life was never meant to be easy.

Yvette recognized Aza. The old voodoo woman was holding a little girl protectively by the hand. Yvette watched in amazement as the youngster broke from Aza's grasp and ran to Indigo with outstretched arms.

"Maman!"

Mother and daughter rubbed noses and giggled.

Meanwhile, Aza pulled Yvette to her feet and hugged her with all of her might.

"Yvette, my dearest, you may not be the daughter of my loins, but you *be* the daughter of my heart. I missed you. Now you *be* back—a woman. You do these old eyes good."

"*Merci,* Aza."

Focusing her attention on the girl, Yvette was amazed that the youngster had copper hair and green eyes. Yvette sucked in her breath, realizing that she was looking at a carbon copy of herself when she had been that age.

"This is my daughter, Cyrillia," said Indigo.

"What do you mean that this is your daughter?"

"Aza, please take Cyrillia to see the waterfall," said Indigo.

"You have a lot of explaining to do," said Yvette.

"I know I do, dear friend." Indigo took Yvette's hands in her own. "Soon after you left for Europe, your father, feeling much guilt over what had happened between us and your step-brother, sent me to stay with your cousins, Roger and Caroline, at their hotel in Fort-de-France."

"I know that, Indigo."

"They were very kind and loving. It was all so perfect. For seven months, I was allowed to continue my studies at a good school. No one ever questioned my background. I was instantly accepted as a member of the Chevalier family. I even got to work at the hotel and the restaurant after school. The atmosphere was electrifying, and the foreign guests fascinated me. I absorbed the working mechanics of the business like a sponge. Before long, Roger allowed me to operate the front desk by myself. I loved the hotel business. I loved my new family. I was very happy and content. The crimes of the past were fading."

"Again," said Yvette, "all this I know. You were very detailed in your letters."

"I didn't tell you about my feelings for your father," continued Indigo. "About twice a month, he would come into Fort-de-France for a few days to pay us a visit. He was very kind to me. He brought flowers and gifts and a miniature black poodle. Every time I looked into my puppy's sweet brown eyes, I saw nothing but unconditional devotion. The poodle gave me a great sense of hope. That is why I named him Espérer. All these gifts and attention from Marcel made me feel very special. It reached a point where I couldn't wait for your father's visits. I thought I was in love."

"In love with my father?" asked Yvette incredulously.

"Yes. Remember, I was only sixteen at the time and very impressionable. At first he was doing these things out of guilt. His kind intentions were innocent. He treated me like a daughter with the highest respect. It was I who began to conjure up romantic fantasies about him. It was wrong, but I couldn't help myself. And as the months went on, my adolescent feelings grew deeper and deeper."

"I can't believe this," said Yvette.

"A party was planned in September for my seventeenth birthday, and your father sent us money to pay for the costs, including a new dress for me to wear. I was allowed to choose the dress myself. I wanted to look grown-up and beautiful. Caroline thought the blue dress was far too mature for a young lady of my age. But I insisted. A blue satin band for my hair perfectly matched my eyes. I put rouge on my lips. Caroline let me borrow some of her perfume."

"Why are you telling me this?" asked Yvette.

"I need you to understand and forgive me for what I am about to confess. It was a rather small birthday party, mostly Chevalier family members and a few of my friends. When your father arrived, I could tell by the expression on his face that I made an impact. He asked me for the first dance and for practically every one he could get after that. The boys my age didn't have a chance. I could tell when he held me in his arms that he was holding a woman."

Yvette abruptly stood up. "I don't want to hear any more."

"You must, Yvette. You must. Now sit down. Please. I have to tell you everything that happened. Then you can decide what you will do about it. Please hear me out."

Yvette sat back down and covered her face with her hands. She trembled slightly. She had already guessed the outcome of the story before it had been told.

"Your father's visits were more frequent during the weeks following the party," said Indigo. "It was obvious he was physically attracted to me. Nevertheless, he continued to be the perfect gentleman. One Sunday we decided to go for a buggy ride along route Le Trace from Fort-de-France to Morne Rouge. We chose a secluded place in the woods to have our picnic lunch. It was a glorious afternoon in March. I read him a poem I had written about a handsome Frenchman and the poor mulatto girl who loved him. Marcel had clapped his hands over my silly words and rewarded me with a light kiss on the lips. Once he had done this . . . we just couldn't stop. We just couldn't."

"How could you?" whimpered Yvette.

"It was one of those crazy moments of passion that got out of hand. We saw one another as much as possible for about two months until I discovered that our passion for one another had disappeared. Suddenly we became awkward in each other's company. It felt like the whole affair had been incestuous. It was awful. I could not write to you with such news. That is why I am telling you this story now."

Yvette squared her shoulders. "You might as well tell me the rest."

"I stayed with Roger and Caroline until the baby was born. Even though they were very supportive and helpful, it wasn't fair to burden them. I was in a dilemma as to what to do. It was Marcel who came up with the idea of relocating Cyrillia, a nanny, and me to the cottage he still owned in Morne Rouge. It was the same one where you and your mother lived. I agreed to this at once. Immediately I set out to convince Aza to come live with me and help take care of the baby. I didn't know who else to trust or turn to at the time."

"Aza agreed?"

"It was like she had known in advance what she would be doing. As you well might remember, she is a bit unnerving when it comes to knowing when something is going to happen before it happens. I have come to respect Aza's magical powers. Maxi went to fetch Aza from her mountain home, and she has been with me ever since. It has been so natural and right having her by my side. Dear Maxi has involved himself as much as he could. His stamina isn't what it used to be since the bite of the snake. I don't know what I would have done without Aza and Maxi. They are my family. All that was missing was you."

Yvette sighed.

"Your poor father truly did not know how to handle the situation with the baby. After Cyrillia was born and he saw how much she looked like you, he was a changed man. He was attentive and caring, but more like a dutiful parent than my lover. We developed a new kind of relationship because of our baby."

"What about Cyrillia?"

"When my darling Cyrillia was born, suddenly nothing else in life mattered. I knew what I wanted for her. And I knew how to get it. On my terms."

"What are you talking about?"

Indigo rolled her eyes upward toward a patch of blue sky and allowed the sounds of the cascading waterfall to sooth the moment. She had to be careful as to how she would tell this part of the story. She didn't want Yvette to get the wrong idea.

"Cyrillia was three months old when your father came to Morne Rouge to pay us his first visit. I remember how handsome he was that day in his pin-striped breeches, black waistcoat, white high-collar shirt, red silk bow tie, and his velvet bowler. A diamond stud had been fastened through the knot of his tie. He made a striking figure."

Yvette smiled for the first time.

"He found me in the nursery with the baby at my breast. The sight unnerved him. Later he explained that for one brief moment he thought time had reversed and it was Nicole with you, Yvette. Your father began to weep uncontrollably. I realized then and there the extent of his profound love for you and your mother. I pleaded with him to stop crying."

Tears bubbled in Yvette's eyes.

"Marcel knelt down before us and apologized profusely for his undignified outburst. It seemed that history was repeating itself. He said he could not marry me. It would not be right because of my friendship with you. Yet he did not want me to end up raising Cyrillia under an assumed name. He didn't know what to do. I told him I had no desire to marry. But there were some future considerations that I wanted for both myself and for my child."

Yvette cocked her head.

"Your father followed me outside into my garden of tea roses and Indian reeds. It was the same garden where I spent many happy hours singing lullabies to my newborn and making plans for our future under the shade of the banana tree. I remember the cool breeze that blew in from the north, and it was chilly. I told Marcel that I wanted him to give our daughter his name legally. I wanted her to grow up with the name Chevalier. I wanted to own my own hotel in St. Pierre. I had heard about this old house on Rue Bouillé that had belonged to the Chantel family who died of smallpox. I wanted it for my hotel. Marcel could not believe his ears. He said that people go to school for such things. I reminded him that Roger and Caroline had taught me everything I needed to know about the hotel business. I talked your father into buying the house in my name, help me refurbish it, and advance a six-month allotment. I would handle the rest. My goal was to vindicate my name and earn independence before moving to France."

"France?"

"Yes. I want to raise my daughter in Paris. If all goes well, this will happen in May."

"You will leave?"

"Yes."

"How do you run this hotel and raise the little girl at the same time?"

"I decided that she could be raised by Aza at the cottage until we were ready to move to Europe. I visit her as often as I can."

"These are very brave and ambitious things you have accomplished," said Yvette.

Indigo leaned back on the bench. "My drive and ambition have helped me accomplish a great deal, but it was the financial help and support of your father that lay the foundation for it all. I am very thankful that he decided to go along with my wishes. I have paid him back tenfold as the hotel has been very successful. It is considered the pride of St. Pierre."

Yvette was amazed by her friend's wondrous complexities and intensities.

"I just want you to know," said Indigo, "there are absolutely no romantic connections between your father and myself. We are friends who share a child. Don't hate me. I couldn't bear it. I couldn't."

Yvette rose. She did not know what to think or to say. It was all so confusing. She felt a hand touch hers, and when her eyes lowered, she was peering into the inquisitive, impetuous face of her half sister. Cyrillia knitted her brows. "Quel est votre nom?"

Yvette got down on one knee eye level to the child. "My name is Yvette Chevalier. I am your . . . I am your Aunt Yvette. Perhaps someday when we have more time, you can meet me here in the gardens or come to my house, and I will teach you some of the pretty songs I learned when I was living in Paris."

"Quand?"

"How about going the day after tomorrow?"

"Qui! Can we, Maman?"

Indigo smiled at her daughter. "Of course we can, my darling. If Aunt Yvette thinks it is an acceptable idea then we will gladly see her again."

The two childhood friends locked eyes. Words were unnecessary.

23

St. Pierre, Martinique
December 20, 1901
The Color of White

André left the governor's residency and headed south by foot for the Fort-de-France park called the Savane. Once there, he would seek out the statue of Empress Josephine protectively encircled by seven palm trees. The grand edifice was one of several places on the island André liked to visit whenever he had a lot of thinking to do.

"Monsieur," said an approaching street vendor holding up a box of Cuban cigars. "Is it not the most beautiful day in our capitol for only the best of smokes?"

André roughly shoved the black man. "Leave me be."

He made his way down a narrow street toward the city park, pushing through a dense crowd of colored people in town for market day. They curiously eyed the skinny white man whose one leg twisted and rocked outwardly with each step.

André finally reached the statue.

"Bonsoir, Madame Josephine."

Sculpted bronze robes draped the body of Josephine's likeness, leaving the arms and shoulders bare. A delicate hand rested upon a medallion carved with Napoléon Bonaparte's face upon its surface. Josephine's doelike eyes stared transfixed directly across the bay from Fort-de-France in the direction of her tiny childhood village of Trois-Îlets.

André reverently removed his hat. Josephine was the only woman other than his mother whom he truly admired and respected. She had been the young and beautiful white woman from Martinique with the good fortune of marrying his idol, Napoléon.

"*Ma chèrie* Josephine," said André, "why do I have to deal with such idiots? The old men in office are too soft. They aren't as strong and forthright as your gallant husband. I fear the proper colonial way of running the island shall be lost because of their complacency. The moment has arrived for me to start doing things my way. Au revoir, madame."

After leaving the city park, André followed a dirt road down past a group of ramshackle shacks not far from the docking area. He approached a small run-down structure near the end of the road and knocked three times. A white boy of about eighteen opened the door.

Kerosene lamps flickered on a far table. The windows were tightly sealed and covered with oilcloth. There was no fan to circulate the stagnant air. The temperature in the room registered over a hundred degrees. The stifling interior was as oppressive as the moods of the stoic white boys who sat in obedient attendance upon a line of old wooden chairs.

André raised his left arm high above his head and tightened his fingers into a fist.

The boys stood and did the same.

"Who are we?" demanded André in French.

The boys cried back in unison.

"Blancs pour blancs! Whites for whites!"

"What do we stand for?"

"Blancs pour blancs! Whites for whites!"

"Why?"

"Purity! Justice! Control!"

André brought his fist down hard against the tabletop, leaned forward, and burrowed his eyes at the group of impressionable young ten—to eighteen-year-olds. He fondly referred to them as his sewer rats. Troubled, confused, and easily impressed, the boys he had drafted hailed from a variety of economic backgrounds. André's steady process of brainwashing had proven effective. Unifying these waifs who shared abuse and neglect was a snap.

"Sit."

The boys followed his command and wiggled nervously in their seats. They dared not say a word. They dared not breathe without the permission of this crazy, wild-eyed man who paid them handsomely.

André was in total control. Finally, their master spoke. His sharp words cut through the air with a biting force. Although the boys recoiled in terror, they surrendered to his pied piper influence.

"We are losing. We are losing to the blacks. What is going on here? Where have we failed? Would someone please tell me?"

Fright stole their voices.

"I will tell you. Numéros! Where are the numbers?"

Again his fist hit the table. His eyes burned like eyes of Satan. He pulled out a knife from a leather thong. It was a special souvenir he had purchased while on a visit to America. He explained to his troops that the knife was called a bowie and that it had been very popular with the American frontiersmen. He held the knife out for them to see. An elk horn handle supported the strong fifteen-inch single-edged blade that curved slightly at the tip. There was much fear in the eyes of the boys as they viewed the weapon. André knew that with fear came respect.

"Manuel," commanded André.

"Yes, sir," answered Manuel, jumping to his feet and raising his left arm.

"As head of the recruiting committee, tell us about the numbers."

The boy lowered his arm. "We have three prospective new members. Louis is setting up the initiation to see if they can pass the grade. Some of the lads agree with our views, but aren't brave enough to join the cause." Louis was André's trusted childhood friend from school. The two buddies were reflections of one another in their like-minded viewpoints and prejudices.

André dug the knife into the table before him. He was clearly upset.

"We must have numbers. Get me the numbers. Now then, I have a job for you. I want all ears to the ground for more information on the Radicals. Nothing is too insignificant. And keep your mouths shut. There is to be no bragging or boosting to nonmembers of our private organization. Need I remind you little bastards what happens to traitors," he said, scraping the edge of the blade along the table.

Their eyes widened.

"Michael. Did you get your tattoo?"

Michael stepped forward and proudly rolled up his left sleeve. The thin biceps of the thirteen-year-old displayed a recent tattoo of a white dove in flight and the initials B.P.B. The initials represented the motto of André's supremacy organization: *Blancs pour blancs*.

André nodded.

They all stood.

"Who are we?"

"Blancs pour blancs!"

"Why?"

"Purity! Justice! Control!"

The boys quietly filed out of the shack. André sat down. He was bone tired. How he longed for the savoir faire of Paris. Someday he would return to Paris to live. But first he had to eradicate the sins of Martinique. He held up the blade of the knife and studied his reflection in the highly polished steel. He winced. The face was as ugly as ever. Thoughts of Yvette invaded his mind. He pondered her homecoming party scheduled for that evening. Marcel had politely requested that he stay away from the celebration fearing another incident.

"You are a stupid fool, Father," said André. "Don't you know by now I do what I want whenever I want? No one tells me otherwise."

André vowed that his father's mulatto offspring would inherit nary a spit of dirt from the land that he felt rightfully belonged to him. He smiled a rare smile as he envisioned how he would use his bowie on them all. The thought of their bloodshed excited him. As his smile grew, so did his erection.

24

Yvette's quarter horse pawed at the ground near the entrance of the Chevalier plantation as he awaited her next command. He liked this human. She was light in the saddle and gentle in moves. Yvette had received the animal as a welcome-home gift from her father. Marcel paid over fifty thousand in U.S. dollars and another five thousand just to ship the famous Kentucky champion to Martinique. Yvette decided to keep its American name—Inspiration.

"It is so good to be home again," said Yvette. She reached forward and ran her hand down the side of his sleek chestnut brown neck. "I hope you will like it here as much as I do, Inspiration. I think that racing butterflies and seagulls down dirt roads through banana and sugarcane fields is going to be a lot different than racing around those fancy racetracks you are accustomed to. I'll make you happy, I promise. We'll have great fun together."

Yvette sat up tall in the saddle. She sighed contently as her eyes drifted beyond the gate and across hundreds of acres of banana fields that rolled like green waves up a steep hillside to a clearing where the main house, the storage sheds, the great stables, and the labor camps nestled in the shadow of a tall mountain peak.

This peaceful viewing was interrupted by sounds of singing and laughter. Yvette spotted a group of carrier women walking down the main road toward St. Pierre. Unexpectedly, one of them tripped and fell into a shallow trench. Not once did the woman's perfectly balanced basket leave her erect head. Two of her younger companions carefully helped her to her feet in such a way as to not disturb their own head-top burdens.

Yvette marveled at their dexterity and strength.

Again Yvette spoke to her horse. "My Maman was a carrier woman until Papa came into her life and changed things. Just like he came into Indigo's life and changed things. And now there is another quadroon child growing up in the same cottage that Papa had set up for my Maman and me. Inspiration, my friend, history has indeed repeated itself."

The horse nodded its head up and down as if it understood every word.

"Let's race the wind," declared Yvette, removing her riding hat and undoing her bun.

Inspiration broke into a full run. His muscular legs and strong hoofs kicked up clouds of dust as they galloped along the drive and up the hill toward the stables. The two made a beautiful sight with Yvette's copper hair bouncing against her back and Inspiration's long chestnut mane blowing in the breeze. Animal and woman were one.

"Whoa," said the stable master when Inspiration galloped into the yard.

"Hello, Stefan," said Yvette sweetly, her heart skipping a beat at the sight of him.

The stable master dropped his mucking rake and approached the horse and rider. Yvette placed her hands on Stefan's bare, muscular shoulders as he grabbed her tiny waist and gently lifted her down. This was the fifth time they had come into contact with each other since her arrival from Europe two days earlier. There had been a strong attraction from the start.

Yvette removed an embroidered hanky from her breast pocket and wiped dust from her face. She could not believe that this was the stowaway boy called Stefan who had been adopted into the Chevalier household. She remembered meeting the shy boy in the dark warmth of the plantation kitchen a few nights after the brothel shooting. He had taken little notice of her, as he had been more interested in his sweet cakes and warm goat milk.

And now, Yvette observed, he had grown into a beautiful young man with long black hair, tied back with a strip of cured leather; skin the color of polished lava; a nose long and narrow; and thick blue-black eyelashes framing cocoa brown eyes.

"*Merci*, Stefan," said Yvette. His hands had not yet left her waist. For the moment, she allowed this. It amazed her how much her father had taken to Stefan after the boy's arrival to the plantation six years prior. Through Marcel's letters to her in Paris, she had followed Stefan's rapid advancements. Marcel wrote as if he were writing about a favorite son. And now Stefan was in total command of the stables. Yvette realized that the job of stable master was a respectable position for a young black man.

Stefan reluctantly released Yvette and took charge of the horse. His eyes followed her as she made her way to the plantation house. As she walked, her riding breeches showed every curve of her gorgeous figure. His throat went dry. He was hopelessly in love. Stefan led Inspiration to the stables, where preparations were being made for the evening event. Two stable attendants were busy making sure that the forty-plus stalls and adjacent corral were clean and enough hay available to keep the horses of the arriving guests happy during their stay.

Stefan paused before the stable doors to admire the grand structure with its grayish blue stones covering the outer walls and its rust-colored gables adorning the roof. Stefan gave thanks, for he never took his good fortune for granted. He loved his job, he loved his life, and he loved the land beneath his feet. After tending to the needs of Yvette's horse, Stefan made his way to his quarters located in the north corner of the building. His room contained a plump feather bed, a chest of drawers, a framed dressing mirror, an oak trunk, a pine desk, and a small table and two chairs. On one wall was a rendering of his mother duplicated from a faded photo given to him the last time he had seen her. André, hired by Marcel, had skillfully turned the tin image into an exquisite oil painting for Stefan's sixteenth birthday. The painting was Stefan's most prized possession. Stefan appreciated the talent of the artist, but abhorred the artist. He retrieved a pair of freshly laundered trousers and a white shirt. Tonight was an important night, and he had to look his best. He poured water from a red ceramic pitcher into a matching bowl and splashed his face. Grabbing a towel, he stood at a tiny window facing the main house. His eyes pivoted on the second-floor balcony. Behind those walls lay her living quarters. He wildly fantasized what Yvette was doing in the private confines of her chambers—his forbidden fruit.

25

December 19, 1901
St. Pierre, Martinique
Papa's Guilt

Yvette knelt on the floor of her room sorting through an opened steamer trunk. There were the photos of her mother, father, Indigo, and her cousin Paul. Paul had turned out to be not only a supportive relative in Paris, but a good friend as well. He was now apprenticing in his father's bank as a clerk. It was a job befitting him—metropolis affluent, society approved, high class, and in the safe confines of a cement city. A perfect environment for the once scrawny teenager who experienced a harrowing hunting excursion on Mont Pelée during his first hunt all those years ago, only to confront mutant spiders, deadly snakes, a voodoo woman, and his cousin Yvette's near-fatal shooting of his cousin André. After his nightmare summer vacation, he swore he would never return to the exotic, perilous island of the Chevaliers. Paul had been Yvette's anchor and safe haven while she attended school in Europe. Yvette smiled at the photo of the freckle-faced young man whom she adored. She would miss him.

She still wore her riding habit minus the hat and boots as she sat cross-legged near the foot of her canopy bed. In her hand was a bundle of tattered letters tied together by a pink ribbon. Letters she had saved over the years of news from her father and Indigo. Letters void of information about a new Chevalier child—especially one with copper hair and green eyes.

Yvette fanned the letters. One after another, they hit the palm of her hand, causing a slight breeze against her face. She was still having a hard time coping with the news of Cyrillia. Life had a funny way of handing out unexpected situations. Yvette set the letters aside and focused on framed photographs of her father, mother, and Indigo on a table next to her. She had kept them with her the entire time abroad. Yvette shook off her thoughts of family and the odd twists of life and went back about her task. She removed a pair of bloomers from the trunk. A tattered piece of paper slipped out of the folds and dropped into her lap. She smoothed the paper out on the floor. Sitting back, she gazed in puzzlement at the portrait etched upon its surface.

She didn't know the name of the man in the drawing; however, she vaguely remembered seeing him in the dining room of her home the night she shot her half brother. Yvette had no way of knowing that the sketch was of David Cabot drawn by André at Les Chats in 1896. It had fallen out of David's pocket to be discovered by Yvette near a chair just before her departure for France a few weeks later. Without unfolding the piece of paper and looking at its contents at that time, she had slipped it into her handbag. It wasn't until she was on board the ocean liner did she finally open the folded note. Yvette remembered sitting on the bed in her berth and curiously studying the sketch of the handsome man she had briefly encountered the night of the shooting. She didn't remember much about him, only that he was pleasant looking with blond hair and kind eyes. On the long ocean voyage, her youthful imagination conjured up romantic encounters with the handsome nameless stranger.

Someone knocked on Yvette's bedroom door. She quickly refolded the portrait.

"Qui?"

"May I come in?" asked Marcel.

"Of course, Papa. Entrez!"

Marcel sat down on the edge of the bed and smiled sheepishly at his daughter.

No wonder he stole the hearts of women, thought Yvette. Years in the sun had enhanced his noble yet rugged appearance. Back from an afternoon inspection of the east fields, his khaki shirt was spotted with rings of sweat, and his boots were coated with dust. He had grown a mustache in her absence, and she liked it. His green eyes danced at the sight of her.

"I want you to realize," he said as he picked up the photograph of Nicole, "that your mother was the love of my life."

"I know."

Marcel was drowning in a sea of guilt. He didn't quite know how to act around his daughter or what to say. He was aware that she had met Indigo and must know about Cyrillia.

"I'm sorry for so much."

"I know."

"I can't change things."

"No."

"What can I do to make it up to you?"

"What is done is done. I met with Indigo today and I saw the child. I have but one request. I want Aza and Cyrillia to come here to live."

Marcel was taken aback.

"You want what?"

"You heard me right, Papa."

Marcel raised his hands in surrender. He wasn't about to question Yvette. Besides, he too would like to have Cyrillia closer to him. He adored the child.

"I want to be involved with the business of the banana plantation. I want to put my agriculture studies to good use. I feel I can be of great help to you. I have some ideas that might help increase production. Oh, Papa, dear Papa, it has been my dream since I was a little girl to work the land alongside of you. Nothing would make me happier. Please don't let the fact that I am a daughter and not a son factor into your decision. I am more than qualified."

Marcel laughed with relief.

"My darling Yvette, I would like nothing better than to have you join the family plantation business. God knows I could use the help." He lifted a black velvet pouch from his pocket and handed it to Yvette. "This belonged to your mother. I know she would have wanted you to have it now."

Yvette pulled out a three-strand pearl choker to which a large marquis diamond had been attached. She gasped at the rich luster of the pearls and the high brilliance of the diamond.

"Papa, it is beautiful."

"I gave it to your mother the day you were born."

Yvette fastened it around her neck.

"I love you, Papa."

"I love you, my darling girl."

Henrillia marched into the room with fists firmly embedded into her plump hips. Maxi's wife, Coralline, was standing beside her. Even though it was Coralline's job to help Yvette dress, Henrillia held on to her role of the mother hen of the family.

"Mon Dieu," she said in scolding tones while shaking a finger at them, "do you not realize that we have the party in two hours? Coralline needs to get you washed and dressed, Yvette. Monsieur Chevalier, please leave so we might attend the preparations."

Marcel laughed. "Dear Henrillia, after twenty-five years of loyal service to this family, I wonder, which one of us is in charge here—you or me? Don't you have some cooking to do?"

Henrillia tapped the toe of her shoe against the floorboards. "I have the kitchen under control. The extra hired help *be* knowing exactly what to do. It all *be* done, and it all *be* done properly. Now . . . shoo!"

"Okay. I am on my way."

Before departing, he turned to his daughter. "Remember, Yvette, do not make your appearance until after eight o'clock. We want our curious guests in anticipation of your arrival."

26

December 19, 1901
St. Pierre, Martinique
The Celebration

As the sun disappeared in the horizon, a startling display of purple and red streaked across the early-evening skies. Twenty-eight buggies lined the torch-lit road leading to the front veranda of the Chevalier estate. Additional torches illuminated the circular driveway, the side galleries, and the rose gardens. Servants in formal waistcoats and white gloves greeted the guests and escorted them into the festive house.

Partygoers traveled in from as far away as Le Diamant to the south, Basse-Pointe and Macouba to the north, Ste-Marie and Trinité to the east, and Le Robert, Le Francois, and Le Vauclin to the southeast. Those in attendance included relatives of Marcel Chevalier, friends, foes, and curiosity seekers, members of the rival Progressive and Radical parties, and those who chose not to affiliate with either organization. Tonight they all stood on neutral ground.

David Cabot arrived in a hired buggy. Attired in captain's formal dress whites, he cut a striking figure as evidenced by admiring glances from the ladies.

"Captain Cabot, how are you, sir?" asked Stefan in perfect English. Marcel had provided not only a home for Stefan over the years but also a fine education at a private island school until he had reached the age of sixteen.

"Stefan, dear boy, how good it is to see you," said David, extending a gloved hand.

"And you, sir."

Stefan had barely enough time to return the handshake before making haste to attend to another newly arrived carriage. David beamed with pride. It had been rewarding to watch the one-time stowaway mature into an admirable young man.

Once inside the house, David turned over his gift for Yvette to one of the servants. It was placed on a table piled with other presents. David was ushered down a long, narrow hallway into a large room where elegantly dressed guests admired the decorations and each other. Every wall had been draped in garland. From the center ceiling hung a twelve-tier crystal chandelier, ten feet in width. Tiny reflections sparkled like diamonds over the crowd below. Elaborate ice carvings in shapes of swans and dolphins stood sentry over tantalizing foods lining the buffet table. From behind an oval alabaster bar, gloved bartenders in white shirts and straw hats were kept busy serving champagne and cocktails.

David ordered a drink. With scotch in hand, he quietly observed the scene.

A fifteen-piece orchestra stationed under a trellis of green fern and pink bougainvillea played a lively waltz. The musicians had been brought in from Fort-de-France. It was still too early for anyone to be eating or dancing; the diversified guests were more interested in sizing up new arrivals. Most of the gentlemen wore dove gray evening tails with matching bowties, white ruffled dress shirts, and top hats. Representative of the latest fashion statement, a few of the younger males showed off stickpins designed with their initials embossed with diamonds, rubies, or black jade. Women of all ages modeled extravagant ball gowns with tight waists, some with perilously low bodices. Imported fabrics dyed in fashion-popular hues of grape, violet, mulberry, lavender, and orchid brightened the room. Italian lace, intricate pearl beading, and priceless jewels added pretentious accenting to their splendid costumes.

Lovely dark-skinned servants attended the individual needs of the guests. The prettier of the females worked the party room. One of these exotics caught David's attention. A red satin petticoat seductively peeked below her rainbow-colored calf-length skirt. She moved barefoot through the crowd. Upon her silver serving tray were offerings of fancy hors d'oeuvres.

"Hello, David," said a familiar voice. "I see you are admiring one of our local beauties."

"Marcel," said David, "it is so good to see you, my friend. She's quite lovely. With that healthy cache of gold beads about her neck, it certainly makes one wonder which of us truly carries the power and wealth here tonight."

Father Roche joined David and Marcel.

"How is that sleeping mountain of yours doing these days?" asked David.

"Pelée has given me cause to worry," answered the Jesuit priest. "There have been a series of mild tremors of late. I consider that a bad sign."

"Mon Dieu, Father," said Marcel. "You are beginning to sound as superstitious as your parish members. Don't voice your opinions so freely. You will only stir up false alarms. The mountain is dormant and will likely remain that way."

"I hope you are right, Marcel," said the priest. "Now then, if you gentlemen will excuse me, I need to get myself a drink."

"Poor fellow," said Marcel as soon as Father Roche was out of hearing range. "Sometimes I think he hopes the mountain will spew to life just to prove his theories."

"What about these earthquakes?" David inquired.

"They are insignificant," said Marcel, dismissing the topic. "Say, will you look at this fine trio coming our way."

The British consul general, James Japp, along with the American consul, Thomas Prentiss and his wife, Clara, exchanged pleasantries with David and Marcel. During the past half-dozen years, David had become good friends with this group, spending many evenings at the Prentiss home in St. Pierre. It was a cheery safe haven for the foreigners to meet and converse while enjoying Clara's excellent home-style American meals.

"Clara, you look lovely," stated David.

"And you give a dashing impression in your white uniform," winked Clara.

"Excuse me, folks, I don't seem to be hearing any flattery coming my way," complained James Japp. The British consul general was bombarded with compliments along with hardy laughter at his expense. His friends could not remember a time when James wasn't in formal attire no matter the occasion. They often teased him that he probably wore his top hat and white gloves to bed. His dapperness was taken for granted. James was typically British with proper protocol, precise speech, decisive statements, and a die-hard loyalist to the British Crown. He generally kept to himself and his family, with the exception of the intimate dinner parties given by Thomas and Clara, as well as those times he had to entertain foreign dignitaries.

"I see our conservative buddies are here," said James, wrinkling his nose as if smelling a big stink. The island's most influential Progressive Party members gathering in a huddle nearby included the Progressive Party candidate, Fernand Clerc; the newspaper editor, Andreus Hurand; the owner of the Bank of Martinique, M. Saint-Cyr; the general manager of the English Colonial Bank, Emile Le Cure; the mayor of St. Pierre, Roger Fouché; a powerful ship builder, Alfred Decailles; the town notary, Georges Madeneux; the wealthy casket makers, Pierre and Joseph Theroset; and the world botanist and local professor, Theodore Landes.

"I overheard them talking about the upcoming elections in May," said Clara. "It seems that Senator Amadée Knight has gathered quite a force around him. He has the old guard quite worried. I'm glad. I know I should not be speaking my mind, but it makes me fume when I see what has been happening to the colored population on the island. Something has to be done and done soon. Thank God the Progressives had the sense to select Fernand as their candidate. He is the only one of them who has any genuine concern for the population at large."

"Clara, please," said Thomas with an air of caution in his voice, "we must be careful of what we say. Remember our place here. We must not state our personal opinions in public. It is our job to be here as observers and nothing more."

"And observe is what I have done," declared Clara, folding her arms in defiance. "I love this island and her people. There is much suffering going on because of a few stuffy men and their relentless quest for power. Do you think for one minute they really care anything about the people? All they care about is their money." Nothing was going to keep her quiet.

Marcel changed the subject. "Quite a turnout, don't you think?"

The tiny group surveyed the room. Six families from elite Families of Ten represented the most powerful dynasties on the island. There were the Guerins, the Hayots, the de Jaunvilles, the Aubreys, the Jannes, and the Cottrells. Even Fernand Clerc and Marcel Chevalier, for all of their power and wealth, did not belong to this tight-knit blue-blood society. The Families of Ten were extraordinarily rich. They socialized with only their kind, kept their aristocratic noses out of politics, and ruled their vast fortunes and grand estates as individual fiefdoms by the puritanical guidelines long ago established by ancestral rulings.

A young man left the click of Families of Ten to join David and the others.

"Good evening," he said with a bow.

Clara greeted René Cottrell with an air kiss on each cheek. René resided at his uncle's estate at the edge of town. Once in a while, he enjoyed stepping out of bounds to socialize with the so-called outsiders. Often René dined with Marcel, James, Thomas, and Clara. He enjoyed their honesty, and the expanse of their evening fireside conversations greatly enriched him.

"Who is that pretty girl I saw you with?" asked Clara.

"Ah," said René, "Ms. Colette de Jaunville, a bit young, only sixteen. She is bright and extremely willful with a mind of her own, which is what I like most about her. My parents are happy. She is one of the Families of Ten. Perhaps one day soon I shall get brave enough and ask for her hand in marriage. Say, it got terribly quiet in here all of a sudden."

The orchestra stopped playing, and the room fell silent. All eyes zeroed in on the elegant figure of a woman dramatically perched at the top of a mahogany staircase gently curving down from the second-story landing. Her loveliness was spellbinding. Gasps broke the silence. Her hair had been combed to one side of her head, allowing luminous copper curls to drop over a honey-colored shoulder. Her Parisian gown fashioned from cocoa brown velvet showed off ecru ostrich feathers along a low-cut neckline. Yards of shimmering velvet flowed from her tiny waist like swirls of melting chocolate. Her mother's pearl-and-diamond choker dazzled. Marcel climbed the stairs and offered his arm.

"Ladies and gentlemen," announced Marcel in a voice swollen with pride, "please allow me to present my daughter, who has just returned from school in Paris where she received her degree in agricultural science. I am proud to announce that Yvette will join me in my banana business at the Chevalier plantation."

A buzz generated the room. "A woman in such a position?" they questioned. "A mulatto woman?" they quizzed. "How could it be?" they wondered. Polite applause erupted. The more secure ladies greeted Yvette with genuine warmth. Others acknowledged with a subdued nod as proper etiquette warranted. There were several whose prejudices and jealousies toward those of mixed blood overrode their good manners and upbringing. These were the women who stepped back and watched the proceedings with detached hostility. Within minutes, the room was back to normal buzzing with social chatter and gossip.

David approached the debutante.

"The man in my sketch," she whispered.

"I beg your pardon," said David, a bit bewildered. It was hard to believe that this stunning creature was the same blood—and mud-covered child from so long ago.

"Yvette, dear," said Marcel, "allow me to introduce Captain David Cabot, of the United States of America."

The orchestra played a popular musical arrangement by the French composer Hector Berlioz. David asked Yvette to dance, and she graciously accepted. They waltzed to a chorus of *ohlalas* echoing through the room. His light complexion and flaxen hair dramatically offset her honey-colored skin and copper curls. Others joined the waltz. Long flowing gowns brushed along the marble floor in rhythmic patterns. Excitement and energy crackled through the room.

"You have grown up to be an exceptionally beautiful woman, Yvette."

"I fear that we first met under very bad circumstances. What an awful memory you must have carried with you all of these years."

"I only remembered your eyes . . . and they have not changed. What is this about a sketch?"

"After the *accident*, I found a piece of folded paper on the floor. Once on board the ship heading for France, I opened it, and there was this sketch of a man—it was you."

"Ah, now I remember. It was the drawing that André made of me that day when you, eh, well, shot him. It must have fallen out of my pocket that night." David flashed a wicked grin and winked. "I don't blame you, whatever the reason."

He held her out and twirled her around.

Once she was back in his arms again, he asked, "Are you glad to return to your island?"

"Oh yes. Yes. Now I know I could never be happy living anywhere else. I love the land of Martinique. I love the soil of our plantation. This island brings me much pleasure."

"I think I can understand your passion for the land. That is exactly how I feel about the sea. I too could not imagine being anywhere else. It brings me much pleasure."

Yvette laughed. "Oh my, such opposing passions we have. Shall we ever meet on equal ground or, should I say, water?"

David twirled her out and around and brought her back to him. Yvette's heart was beating fast, and she was having a difficult time catching her breath.

"I have to admit," said David, "that this island of yours is one of the most interesting places I have ever experienced in all of my world travels. I can't blame you for loving it so."

"There is a place that I think you should visit, if you have not seen it already."

"And where might that be?"

"The botanical gardens," she smiled.

"Oh yes. I have driven by the park many times on the way here, but I've never had the opportunity to visit it."

"Oh, but you must. It is rated one of the best in the world for its bountiful selection of exotic plants. There are waterfalls, fishing streams, and two little lakes with floating man-made islands that are the exact replicas of Martinique, Guadeloupe, and Dominica."

"Could there possibly be an inland paradise with land, water, and islands? I do believe this is where we should go. I shall have my water, and you shall have your land. How about tomorrow in the late afternoon after I have finished at the docks? Perhaps later we could have dinner—with your father's permission, of course. Will you join me?"

Her green eyes sparkled. "Yes, Captain. I would like that very much. Now then, I really should mingle with the other guests. Papa is giving me such a look."

"Yvette Chevalier, I am reluctantly releasing you. Just know, I shall return."

As soon as David stepped away, several anxious men, waiting in the wings, approached Yvette to ask her to dance with them. David reluctantly rejoined Marcel.

"You have a charming daughter, Marcel."

"Yvette has given me much joy. I can't tell you how happy I am to have her back."

Fernand Clerc approached the men.

"Marcel, my friend, you must be so proud of our sweet Yvette."

"Thank you, Fernand. I am."

"You are looking fit, Monsieur Clerc," commented David.

"As well as can be expected, Captain Cabot. As you have probably heard, things are in an uproar around here. This election business is beginning to take its toll on me. Trying to keep everyone happy is impossible. I truly want what is best for all of us. I am the first to admit that I am not a great politician. It is not my natural arena. I am more comfortable as a planter and a businessman. Such is the fate of life."

"Fernand," interrupted Father Roche, "finally I have found you in this mob."

"Father Roche," acknowledged Fernand, "if it isn't my volcanologist and partner in crime. The old goddess is doing a bit more grumbling than usual, wouldn't you say? Even though each ground trembling is slight, they are becoming more frequent. Every morning I go out to my bedroom terrace and check my wall barometer without fail."

"Thank God in heaven for you, Fernand," said the priest. "We must be the only two souls on the island who are interested in the mountain's disposition. When can we get together and compare notes on this disturbing subject?"

"How about meeting this Wednesday at my house for lunch? Veronique would also enjoy your company. Let's say around one o'clock?

"One o'clock it is then."

Yvette began to tire from the never-ending attention of her male suitors. She had been dancing for two hours straight. The best moments of the night were spent dancing and talking with the American. She found David Cabot fascinating, physically and intellectually. Their next day's tour of the Jardin des Plantes would not come soon enough.

Yvette escaped to the outside terrace for fresh air. A bright golden moon illuminated the outlying grounds and gardens in a wash of white light. In the distance, about five miles away, stood Mont Pelée, silhouetting sharply against the blue-black sky. To Yvette, everything seemed brighter and grander this evening. She felt ethereal and mystical. It was as if she could reach up and stroke each and every celestial body in the heavens.

The night-blooming jasmine bushes loaded with delicate white blossoms overwhelmed the air with a sticky-sweet fragrance. As the evening breezes chilled her flushed skin, Yvette wrapped the matching cocoa brown velvet shawl to her dress tightly around her bare shoulders and sighed with contentment. It was good to be home.

"Bonsoir, dear Yvette," greeted her uncle.

"Uncle Gregoire!"

"Oh my, but you make this old heart proud," said Marcel's brother. "Just you remember if there is ever anything you need, don't hesitate to call."

She gave her uncle a playful tug on his reddish brown beard. Although she adored both of her father's brothers, Gregoire was her favorite. The trips to his villa in Basse-Pointe during her childhood had provided her with cherished memories.

Yvette's second cousins from Fort-de-France joined them. Caroline planted a feather kiss on each one of Yvette's cheeks. "It is good to have you back home, cousin."

"Thank you. I want to also thank you for what you did for Indigo."

Roger waved his hand. "Don't think anything of it. Indigo is like the daughter we never had. We love her dearly. It was a gift to us to be able to help her."

"This news of Cyrillia must have been shocking for you," said her uncle.

"I was surprised, but now I am trying to be understanding about what happened. What is done is done. When a situation involves loved ones, what else can you do? I forgive them."

"Good for you," said Roger.

Caroline took Yvette's hand. "Sometimes good comes out of what we may perceive as bad. Cyrillia has been a blessing to Indigo. Indigo's entire being revolves around that child. As you must now know, it is Indigo's plan to move to France next year. During our last trip to Versailles, we made an investment for her. She entrusted us with the responsibility of purchasing an estate for her, the child, and Aza. We found an enchanting ivy-covered manor. I hope she will like it. It is called Chaumiere de Paix. It is over a hundred and fifty years old."

"Cottage of Peace—how lovely and how appropriate," said Yvette.

Caroline nodded. "One more thing before we go, Yvette. None of us in the family trust nor like André. He is very sick—both in heart and head. It grieves us that Marcel still refuses to recognize the danger of his son's mental illness. Know that you can come to us at any time if things here get too difficult."

"Thank you, dear ones. I feel so lucky to have you nearby. I want you all to know that no one is ever going to drive me away from my home again."

As soon as Yvette's relatives left, clapping echoed from the depth of the shadows behind her. André moved out into the moonlight from his hiding place. He was dressed head to toe in black, allowing him to blend in perfectly with the darkness of the night.

"Bravo, little sister. Bravo. You have such conviction. I didn't know you had it in you."

"How long have you been there?"

"I have been here most of the evening. I could not believe my good fortune when you came out alone. It seems our meeting tonight was meant to be, wouldn't you say?" He took a few more steps toward her. Yvette moved back until she reached the waist-level brick wall of the terrace and could go no farther.

"You weren't supposed to come here tonight. Father told me you weren't to be here."

"I don't take orders from anyone. This is my home."

"Go now or I shall call for help."

"Save your breath, little sister. You need not fear. I am not going to disrupt your debut here tonight. For now I shall let you play mistress of the manor. Just know that the day will come, and it will all end. I shall see to it. Our father won't be around forever, and when he is gone, you will be too. Mark my words."

"Go away, you beast."

"Yes, I am the beast. Just as you are the beauty. Look at us, Yvette—the Tragedy Duo of Martinique. What a ghastly bedtime story we have created for the children of our island."

"Go!"

"As you wish," he bowed. He roughly pinched her cheek between his gloved thumb and index finger. "Watch your step, sister dear. You may not always see me; however, like the stink of the skunk, you'll know that I am around."

André wobbled as he turned away. His right foot dragged slightly behind the left. He had a difficult time easing himself up and over the balcony to the ground below. Yvette leaned over the wall to see if she could spot him. She could not. He had disappeared like a spiteful spirit into the night. She realized that she had been holding her breath during their brief and unfortunate encounter. Now more than ever, she had no remorse about shooting him six years ago. She wouldn't hesitate to it do all over again, with one exception—she would not miss her mark. This was her home. She would fight to the death to keep it.

PART IV
Six Months Later

27

St. Pierre, Martinique
Thursday, May 1, 1902
The Beginning of the End

It was five in the morning.

Indigo went directly to her bedroom window to behold and embrace what was normally a picture-postcard view of St. Pierre's sun-kissed harbor. There was nothing, however, picturesque to behold or embrace. The entire coastal and inland area around St. Pierre had fallen prey to a blight that had cruelly robbed the legendary port town of its famed loveliness and color. For the past three months, Mont Pelée had polluted the northern point of the island with foul-smelling sulfurous gases and daily fallout of gray powder.

Indigo counted eight foreign vessels anchored out in the roadstead. Like everything else in St. Pierre, the ships were covered in a thick coat of ash. "Mon Dieu," she said, applying a wet handkerchief to her face, "my pretty little city is soiled."

Indigo prayed that Mont Pelée's activities would remain mild and not worsen. For in eight days' time, on Friday the ninth of May, she would embark with Cyrillia, Aza, a pony, and a poodle aboard the SS *Romaima*, a Quebec ocean liner bound for France.

After several months of interviewing qualified applicants, Indigo had chosen University of Paris business graduate Charlene Julie to take over the hotel as a working partner. For her small investment, twenty-five-year-old Charlene would be awarded 50 percent of the hotel's profits and full control of hotel operations during Indigo's absence.

Indigo felt that Charlene was the ideal choice to run the hotel. Charlene's white mother descended from an affluent Parisian family and her black father from one of the few wealthy Negro families who operated plantations near Le Diamant, Martinique. It impressed Indigo that for a short while after graduating from the university, Charlene stayed in Paris, where she worked as a concierge for one of the finest hotels on the right bank. To Indigo's delight, the savvy young woman understood Indigo's unique business style.

Charlene wasn't a good-looking girl; however, her European ways and outgoing personality made her quite appealing. After twelve weeks of indoctrination, Charlene had less than a week to test out how she would do on her own before Indigo's scheduled departure. In five days, they would meet with their lawyers at the hotel and sign the final paperwork.

"Oh, volcano," said Indigo as she continued to scan the dismal waterfront, "please be good and go back to sleep. You wouldn't want to make me miss my boat to Paris, would you? I only ask for eight more days. Just eight days."

Three steamer trunks were already packed and ready for Indigo to set forth on her way to France and closer to those grand homes, grand carriages, grand museums, grand literary minds, and the grand people of Paris. In her new country, she would be free of her mulatto label and no longer considered a second-class citizen. Until the departure of the ship to France, Indigo would spend her last days at the Chevalier plantation, where Aza and six-year-old Cyrillia had been living happily for the past five months. It had been a good experience for the child, as well as for Marcel and Yvette.

The thought of Cyrillia brought about a smile.

"Ah, my *bebé*," said Indigo while closing the shutters and searching the room for any personal item she may have missed. "I will take you to a lovely place where everything is very magnificent. Trés magnifique."

Indigo fretted. How would her daughter handle leaving the plantation and those she loved? Often Cyrillia asked her mother if Yvette, Maxi, Stefan, and Marcel would be coming with them to this faraway land called France. Indigo realized that Cyrillia's attachment to the Chevaliers was powerful. The child loved and idolized Yvette to such a point that she mimicked Yvette's every move and facial expression. As he had done with Yvette, Maxi had taught Cyrillia how to climb trees, fish in the rivers, and hunt small game in the fields. Stefan had given her riding lessons on a miniature black-and-white pony named Sucre. And Marcel read Cyrillia adventure stories before rocking her to sleep each night.

"Okay, Espérer, let's go," she said, sliding her handbag under one arm and scooping up her black poodle under the other. Indigo found Charlene downstairs in the hotel's front office buried nose deep in accounting books.

"Are you leaving now, Indigo?"

Indigo sat down in a chair across from the desk with the feisty poodle in her lap. "Yes, I am, with many thanks to you. If you have any questions this week, don't hesitate to contact me at the Chevalier plantation. If not, I will be back here on Monday to finalize our contract."

Charlene escorted Indigo to the front lobby doors.

"I won't let you down, Indigo, I can promise you that much."

Maxi was waiting for indigo in a buggy parked alongside the ash-covered avenue. He helped his friend, her little dog, and carpetbags into the back seat.

Maxi removed the protective head sack from the head of the horse. It sneezed. Over the course of the last few days, the animal had begun to realize how much comfort and protection the bag provided against the biting effects of volcanic vapors and dust.

*   *   *

"Mon Dieu," bellowed André, brushing away a skiff of ash from his bed covers. He yawned widely. "I cannot tolerate much more of this filth." He yawned once again as he stumbled through his darkened St. Pierre cottage and into its small kitchen, where he grabbed a bottle of rum and gulped down what was now becoming a routine morning eye-opener. Standing before the dressing mirror next to his bed, he winced. His image was repulsive. Cotton long johns hung loosely against his bone-thin frame. His skin and the whites of his eyes had taken on a yellow hue. The palms of his hands were red. A newly grown goatee covered a pink spot that had appeared on his chin. His doctor warned him that alcohol poisoning was slowly destroying his liver. André wouldn't quit drinking. Liquor fortified his nerves. He had to have it.

André grabbed his middle. It was as if a knife were cutting away at his insides. As he did just about every morning, he stumbled through the house and out into his front yard, where he vomited up the contents of his stomach. Dropping weakly to his knees, he gasped for breath as ash blew up little flurries of gray particles around him. For a minute, he felt as if he were going to choke to death.

"Oh, vile place of my birth," he hissed with fists locked tightly to his head, "I cannot tolerate your mean-spiritedness much longer."

He dragged himself back inside and closed the door.

*　　*　　*

With Maxi positioned in the driver's seat and Indigo and Espérer settled in the back, the horse reluctantly pulled the buggy down the narrow ash-covered Rue Victor Hugo. Clouds of ash swirled with the turn of each wooden wheel over the cobblestone avenue. Indigo and Maxi noted that people were trying to go about their business as normal. It was impossible, however, to ignore the dirty mess that had been caused by the volcano.

The banana merchant did not have much of a lilt to her step this day. She did not like the feel of the talclike substance that pushed up and between her calloused toes. Her calico skirt dragged through the thick ash, making it difficult to balance her heavy load.

Securing a rag around his nose and mouth, the basket vendor coughed. The rag did little to filter out the vapors that burned his lungs. It felt as if shards of glass raked his raw throat. He was old and tired, and the foul conditions were not helping his disposition.

A group of soldiers stood in line before the orange merchant. Soon the juice from her fresh oranges would satisfy the wicked dryness of their mouths. The orange vendor could not help but giggle over her good fortune. As long as her sweet fruits were selling, she didn't care if the volcano puked ink or belched acid. She turned in the direction of the great mountain and blew it an appreciative kiss.

The upbeat pastry seller had lost his zeal. He had no use for the filth that had invaded his pretty avenue. His bright smile disappeared behind a soured expression, clearly showing the contempt that he felt for Mont Pelée. For the fifth time that morning, he removed his tall white hat to shake out clumps of fine powdery ash gathered in its pleats. Another hour of this misery and he was calling it quits.

As soon as Indigo's buggy reached the outskirts of town, Maxi stopped the horse. The tortured animal tossed back its head and snorted as the fumes irritated its sensitive nostrils. Maxi and Indigo viewed the destruction of the land in disbelief. Four miles away loomed Mont Pelée in a coat of fresh ash. The lush tropical land was no longer green, the crystal clear waterways were no longer blue, and the red gabled roofs of the pale yellow buildings had lost their charm and luster. All color in northern Martinique had vanished into a brindled monotone.

There were no signs of the washerwomen as the buggy crossed the stone bridge at the Roxelane River. For the first time in her life, Indigo saw the river void of its white patchwork of garments and linen. In disbelief, she watched as the flooded, fast-moving Roxelane overflowed its banks. Within the force of its currents were many dead animals.

"Oh, Maxi," said Indigo, dismayed, "I fear that St. Pierre will never be the same."

About a quarter of a mile from the Chevalier plantation, the path of the horse was blocked by hundreds of mountain crabs desperately seeking refuge. The horse reared on his hind legs, causing the buggy to twist dangerously to the right. Maxi somehow managed to control it.

"What do we do?" cried Indigo, trying to calm her barking dog. "Do you remember stories about crabs attacking a group of sick pioneers back in the mid–sixteen hundreds? According to legend, the bones of these poor souls were picked clean within an hour."

Another buggy pulled up behind them. Maxi handed the reins to Indigo and asked the stranger if he could be of assistance. The two men used dead tree branches to clear a wide path through the flanks of marching pinchers.

Stefan greeted Maxi and Indigo at the plantation stables. Hearing the arrival of her mother, Cyrillia dashed out of the house. Yvette was not far behind. Indigo released her squirming, yipping poodle and kissed her child about the cheeks many times.

"Stop that, Maman, stop that. Yucky kisses."

Cyrillia wiggled out of Indigo's arms and dashed over to the panting horse.

"He sounds awful."

Maxi bent down to her level; his eyes were wide, and his face very serious. "Why, that horse and us almost got eaten up by monster crabs!"

It took all of Maxi's willpower to keep a straight face.

"Really, Uncle Maxi," she squealed. "Maman, were there truly monster crabs?"

"I don't know about the monster part, but there were a lot of crabs."

"Don't worry, Maman," said Cyrillia bravely, "I'll go get my *bam bams*. I promise to protect us if those bad monsters dare come here."

Maxi maintained his seriousness. "We all feel so much safer, now, missy. Most certainly we do."

"Maxi, please don't encourage her in these silly warrior games of yours," begged Indigo.

Cyrillia tugged at Indigo's dress. "Maman, you can go now," she said, dismissing her mother before turning back to Maxi.

"Uncle Maxi, tell me more about the monster crabs."

Maxi got down on one knee in front of her and lowered his voice menacingly. "Well, the mighty Crab Emperor had the biggest claws of them all. It is as big as my foot." Cyrillia's eyes widened as Maxi lifted his bare foot to demonstrate his point. "And you know what the favorite food of the Crab Emperor *be*?" Cyrillia shook her head. "It prefers tiny little girls with red hair and green eyes and ponies by the name of Sucre." He jumped both feet forward pretending he was the Crab Emperor, grabbed Cyrillia's waist, and began tickling her on the ribs. Cyrillia giggled with glee.

Exasperated, Indigo threw up her hands. "Mon Dieu. I give up." She knew that if there was to be any hope of her daughter growing up to be a fine lady, this was not the place.

Cyrillia stayed with Maxi as Yvette and Indigo headed for the house with Espérer barking at their heels. They stopped for a brief moment in the front garden. A small skiff of ash covered the ground, but the fallout was not nearly as bad as it had been in town.

"What will happen when you, Cyrillia, and Aza have gone?" said Yvette sadly.

"I wish you would go with us, but you would never leave here, would you?" said Indigo, putting an arm around Yvette.

"Oh, Indigo, I can't tell you how much at peace I am working the land side by side with Papa. It is a dream that has come true. The volcano will go back to sleep, just as it has done before. Someday I will come visit you and Cyrillia and Aza in France, but I would never go there to live."

"I know. You are this island, dear friend. I swear that the waters of Martinique's rivers run through your veins, the soil of its earth fills your heart, the scents of its wild flowers are the perfumes of your pores, and the rains from its sky are the tears in your eyes. You are one with nature, Yvette Chevalier. Yes, you do belong here. I just hope that André discontinues his fanatic involvement with the current politics and leaves you alone. I hope that nasty mountain goes back to its place of rest. Perhaps then, your harmony here on the island will continue."

"My goodness, Indigo, you certainly have a poetic way with words."

Indigo laughed. "So I've been told. Who knows, maybe someday in France I shall be a great poet . . . or writer. Say, look at all these other buggies, who do they belong to?"

"Fernand Clerc, Father Roche, and René Cottrell are meeting with Papa to discuss the activities of the volcano. Come, let's join them."

On the way to Marcel's office, Indigo and Yvette came upon Aza fast asleep on the divan in the dining wing. The two childhood friends quietly tiptoed by, glad that she was resting. Her voodoo warnings of doom and disaster had kept her restless for months now.

Yvette and Indigo entered Marcel's office. Oak bookcases, framed maps upon the walls, and an impressive pipe and gun collection in display cabinets shared the room with the stone-faced men standing solemnly around Marcel's desk. Pipe and cigar smoke cloaked the air.

"What has happened?" asked Yvette.

"We are debating whether plans should be put into action for an emergency evacuation of all residential areas within a five-mile radius of the mountain," said René Cottrell.

"That's a lot of people to move," said Indigo.

"Nearly thirty thousand men, women, and children," answered Fernand. "A few weeks ago, I sent a note to Governor Mouttet expressing my concerns. He sent word back to me by messenger that he appreciated my amateur observations and to please keep him posted of any further changes in the mountain. He clearly did not want to be bothered with the subject."

"And now this," exclaimed Father Roche, waving the latest copy of the island newspaper *Les Colonies*. "There's barely a mention of Mont Pelée in today's issue."

"Two days ago I called the newspaper's editor, Hurard," interjected Fernand, "to ask him to please run a story advising the people of St. Pierre of a possible eruption. He accused me as an alarmist. He had the nerve to ask if I had forgotten about the elections next week. As a responsible citizen, he could not possibly do anything that might interfere. He demanded to know why I, the Progressive Party candidate, dared to make such an absurd suggestion that would most certainly affect the continuity of our political progress. I shouted at him that we are talking about peoples' lives on the line. He dismissed me rather rudely."

Father Roche held up a dog-eared volcanology journal. "The facts in this notebook clearly detail the activities of Mont Pelée over the last four months. In my opinion, all indications point to an imminent eruption."

Marcel lit a pipe and drew in long and hard. "I don't know what to say. The same thing happened with the volcano fifty years ago, and nothing came of it. Just a few spits of ash and some rumblings. I am not worried about the elections. Damn the elections. Although I'm not as yet convinced that this is the right time to sound the alarm. We really should summon the town's civic leaders to jointly decide what to do."

Yvette retrieved a spyglass from one of the cabinets and stood by the French doors facing the ash-covered volcano. Long streamers of white smoke trailed up into the air from the crater lake, forming interesting patterns against the blue background of the sky.

"Look at Mont Pelée," she called out.

The rest of the group joined her.

"Mon Dieu," whispered Father Roche, "the mountain of fire is showing us a new trick."

28

St. Pierre, Martinique
Friday, May 2, 1902
The Lies

Stretching down the street for more than two blocks was a line of grumbling people anxious to get into St. Pierre's telegraph office. The operators were having a hard time keeping up with the influx of urgent messages that trumpeted the news of Mont Pelée's recent tremors and ash storms. Telegrams sent directly out of St. Pierre were generally first relayed by ocean cable to Martinique's neighbor to the north, the island of Dominica and then from there bounced back and forth to various receiving stations at points all over the globe; however, in the wee hours of this Friday morning, the volcano had produced underwater earthquakes severe enough to cause major damage to the thirty-one-year-old cable that linked St. Pierre to Dominica. All outgoing telegrams would now have to be transferred by overground wire to the telegraph office in Fort-de-France and from there to the island of St. Lucia via ocean cable. Another force, more human in nature, was also preventing news of the eruption from reaching the ears of the world, for earlier that morning, the new governor of Martinique had issued secret orders to intercept and censor any telegram containing information about the volcano.

"How much longer is the wait?" asked Yvette to the manager of the telegraph office, who walked down the line to check its length. He shrugged his shoulders as he passed her.

After waiting in line for over an hour, Yvette reached the telegraph counter. She presented the operator a prepared message to be sent to David Cabot on board the USS *Silver Eagle* located somewhere in the Caribbean. Yvette knew that David was to have departed New York's pier

49 on the East River on April 30 and was due to arrive in Martinique sometime on Thursday, May 8. She wanted to alert him to the threat.

Yvette's message read:

> DEAR DAVID. STOP.
>
> PELÉE AWAKE. STOP. NOT BAD AS YET. STOP. ASH ONLY. STOP. I AM OKAY. STOP. FATHER SAYS WE ARE SAFE DISTANCE. STOP. IF SITUATION WORSENS WE WILL GO TO MY COUSIN'S IN FORT-DE-FRANCE. STOP. FIND ME THERE IF NOT AT HOME. STOP. SEE YOU NEXT THURSDAY. STOP.
>
> ALL MY LOVE. STOP. YVETTE. STOP.

Yvette paid the frazzled telegraph operator and left the building. She glanced at her timepiece and realized that she was running late for a meeting at the Regency of the American Consul with Thomas Prentiss and his wife, Clara. Thomas had sent the Chevaliers an urgent message that morning to meet with him. René Cottrell and Fernand Clerc had also been summoned to this meeting. Yvette and her father decided to arrive separately as Yvette had to post her telegram and Marcel had to make his usual morning inspection of the plantation.

Inspiration pawed the ground as soon as he spotted his mistress heading his way. Yvette patted his cheek, took the reins, and led him by foot toward Le Place Bertin. Mounds of ash, fine as powdered snow, towered seven feet or more in great drifts against the buildings.

Not sure of his footing, Inspiration hesitated in the ankle-deep ash. "Come on, boy, you will be okay," coaxed Yvette.

The avenue was quiet. People were staying indoors as much as possible. Yvette pressed a handkerchief to her face to combat the fumes. She thought of David. Since her homecoming party in December, he had made four stopovers in St. Pierre during the last five months. They saw each other as much as possible during these visits, delighting in each other's company. The more time she spent with David, the more she found him to be a splendid man. She knew that David had fallen in love with her. His eyes betrayed his emotions. She was flattered. During their last picnic at the botanical gardens near the waterfall, he kissed her for the first time. His touch had been gentle and his lips delicious, so much so that for days afterward, she could still taste his flavor in her mouth. Yvette wasn't quite sure if her yearnings for David represented romantic love or a lingering infatuation still associated with the fantasy man in the drawing.

* * *

Fearful that news of the volcano would leak to the foreign press, Governor Louis Mouttet took matters into his own hands by planting a watchdog at the Fort-de-France telegraph office to screen and censor all related outgoing messages. He nervously tugged on one of his triple chins while envisioning an onslaught of snooping reporters digging and probing for news, eager scientists expounding on volcanic dangers, and sightseeing doomsday wishers proclaiming all sorts of dire events. He knew the island would be turned into a three-ring circus, and along the way, the elections would be pushed aside. By Mouttet's official degree as governor, no one on the island was exempted from this censorship.

As far as Mouttet was concerned, it was an inconvenient time for the volcano to rear its ugly head. Any election delay at this point was unthinkable. The Conservative Party had not fared well in recent voting polls. A postponement could mean an election loss. Mouttet was, by law, supposed to maintain a neutral interest in local politics; but that line of thinking would not benefit his personal cause and goals. No matter the risk and cost, he would continue to keep the world ignorant of Pelée's awakening.

The governor stuffed a creamy éclair into his mouth, licked the sugar off his fat lips, leaned back in his chair, and put his feet up on his desk. Damn it! All he ever wanted was a quiet, easy existence. If only Mont Pelée would go back to sleep and leave him the hell alone.

* * *

Mont Pelée had no intention of going back to sleep nor leaving anyone alone. Drawing a deep breath, it belched up tons of vile dust from the pit of its churning stomach. The giant ball of ash temporarily eclipsed the sun before swirling like a blizzard over St. Pierre. The roar of the volcano was so deafening, herds of terrorized animals began neighing and bleating in alarm. The people of the land covered their ears, fearful of the sound. When it was all over, they giggled like silly schoolchildren, embarrassed by their unfounded fright.

*   *   *

Fernand Clerc had just finished his breakfast when the mountain across the valley from his home began to rumble. He nearly tripped over his chair in the rush to get to the barometer hanging on his terrace wall. Fernand frowned. The needle jumped back and forth in wild reaction to the forceful blast. His frown deepened.

*   *   *

Father Roche was perched cross-legged on a grassy knoll atop a high peak in the Pitons de Carbet. This natural observatory faced the southern slopes of Mont Pelée. Nestled in between these two mountains was a narrow four-mile-wide valley. The priest had been studying the volcano for about an hour now. As he entered his latest notation of observation into his journal, the mountain across from him began to hum shrilly. In all of his years of study as an amateur volcanologist, none of his books had documented anything about volcanoes behaving in this erratic manner. What could this queer activity mean? The priest rose to his feet. It was time to return to St. Pierre, where his parishioners awaited his sermon. He allowed one last deep breath of the sweet, fresh mountain air before making his way back to the stench and filth of the valley below. More than anything, he wanted to stay on Morne Vert and continue his vigilant watch.

*   *   *

Yvette tied her horse to a hitching post at the American Regency. Clara greeted her young friend at the door. Unkempt, the wife of the American diplomat explained that she had just returned from a futile attempt to attend morning mass. On the way to church, blowing ash had soiled her good clothes. Embarrassed by her untidy appearance, she made a hasty retreat back to the Regency. Yvette took note of Clara's ruined bonnet and silk gloves tossed in abandonment upon the foyer table.

"I wish I could get away dressing in casual clothes like you," confessed Clara in French, pointing to Yvette who was comfortably clad in a dusty, but fetching, riding habit. "But as the dutiful wife of a senior foreign diplomat, it would not represent proper attire. This damn ash destroys everything. Silk doesn't have a chance."

"I dare say there isn't a surface within a ten-mile radius that hasn't felt the ill effects of the fallout," agreed Yvette, rubbing her burning eyes.

Clara took Yvette's arm and guided her toward the Regency library. "I hope the volcano settles down before our anniversary party on the tenth of this month."

"How many years has it been?"

"Thomas and I will be celebrating our fourth year representing America here. It doesn't seem as if it has been that long since we first came to live on this magnificent island. Although it isn't so magnificent anymore, is it, dear Yvette?"

In the library, they found Thomas Prentiss, René Cottrell, and Fernand Clerc lounging in overstuffed chairs by the fireplace.

"Where is my father?" asked Yvette, noting his absence.

"Hasn't arrived yet," answered Thomas.

"I don't understand. He should have been here by now."

"Don't worry. I am sure he will arrive shortly," said Thomas. He picked up the latest copy of the local newspaper *Les Colonies*. "This periodical is an abomination."

The periodical was passed around. The front page carried a brief testimony from an unnamed person only described as a leading authority on volcanoes who maintained that the stirrings of Mont Pelée should not be taken seriously. The newspaper's editor, Andreus Hurard, assured his subscribers that there was no cause for alarm. The volcano would be back to normal soon. So much so that the community's leading citizens, convinced of the volcano's harmless nature, were planning a public picnic on Mont Pelée's summit.

"May we remind our readers," wrote the editor, "that the grand excursion organized by the Gymnastic and Shooting Club will take place next Sunday, May 4 as scheduled. Weather permitting, excursionists will experience a day they will long keep in pleasant remembrance."

René Cottrell toyed with a button on his jacket. "Hurard is a fool and a fraud. I'd be willing to bet that he fabricated this so-called leading authority. No such person exists except in his mind. This editorial is a manipulation of facts, and I wouldn't be surprised to find out that Governor Mouttet is also behind these charades. Mouttet and the Conservatives know they can't afford to have the town evacuated as it could possibly mean the loss of precious votes. I am speaking both as a friend and a concerned citizen. It is time to put politics aside. Fernand, you are the only one here who might be able to get the newspaper or government to listen."

Fernand agreed.

A hard knock hit the front door. Clara sent a servant to answer it. Marcel rushed in breathlessly. Sadness filled his eyes. He sat down wearily and buried his head in his hands.

"Why, Papa, what in the world is wrong?" asked Yvette.

"Pierre Laveniére and seven of his men were out on a morning inspection at one of Laveniére's sugarcane fields when a flow of mud trapped them like quicksand. All eight were sucked under and drowned. Pierre's daughter, Suzette, witnessed her father's death from a safety point about a half a mile away. She is being treated for shock. Lava flows are blocking several valley service roads and destroying many of the villages on the mountain's northern slope, including the town of Le Prêcheur. A priest from Le Prêcheur was seen leading an exodus of villagers away from the volcano toward St. Pierre."

No sooner had the words left his mouth the earth at their feet began to shake.

*   *   *

It was high noon. The south collar of Mont Pelée's summit was bright and warm. Maxi and his team of hunters had spent the morning tracking and killing dozens of frightened boar trying to escape lava flows from the north. As soon as the men had collected more carcasses than they could handle, they started a bonfire in a clearing. The meat would be lightly roasted, carved into chunks, and wrapped in palm leaves for easy transport. Maxi would then take his share to the Chevalier plantation. As the meat crackled over the open fire, Maxi marveled at the transformation of the valley below. A winter wonderland blanketed the land inland all the way to the bay, where the ships appeared to be encased in a lake of ice. At three o'clock, the meat was ready for transport. The men uttered a prayer of thanks for they would be glad to return to the safety of their homes and away from the mountain that hummed louder than ever.

Maxi and two of his men were ahead of the others by about twenty yards when the ground collapsed from beneath their feet into a bottomless pit of molten lava. One of the men was tossed like a rag doll over the edge into the thick bubbling mass. Another man clung helplessly to a large rock just inside the tiny crater until the pain of his burning flesh and the fright of his ordeal was too much to bear. He dropped to his death into the fiery pit. Maxi was thrown near the edge of the opening where tongues of flames licked out from its depths. Braving the scorching inferno, Maxi's surviving hunting companions rushed to his side and quickly dragged him a safe distance away to a cool patch of moss. The intensity of the heat radiating from the fissure had melted the skin from his face, arms, and legs. Maxi was dead.

* * *

André sat in the office of the governor, where he eavesdropped on an angry phone conversation between Mouttet and the editor of *Les Colonies*. After five minutes, Mouttet slammed down the receiver and blotted away a film of perspiration heavily coating his pockmarked face with the sleeve of his linen jacket.

"According to Hurard, our candidate, Fernand Clerc, stormed into the newspaper this morning and demanded that a story be published in tomorrow's edition advising the entire population of St. Pierre to prepare for an evacuation. Hurard told Clerc that he did not have the authority to print such a thing without the direct authorization of government officials."

André bit a piece of a thumbnail and gritted it between his teeth. "Where the hell is his loyalty? Doesn't Clerc know it is critical to keep everyone quiet for a few more weeks? Doesn't he realize that this kind of move could crucify us at the polls?"

"Wait! Wait! I'm not finished. There's more. Right on the heels of Clerc, Thomas Prentiss arrived with reports that two of the American captains have set anchor a good distance away from St. Pierre and the volcano. They refuse to come into port."

"Who cares about that?" said André, uninterested. "I just want to know how Hurard is handling this crisis."

"He promised he would do whatever it would take to assure the people of St. Pierre that they are in no danger from the volcano," said the governor. "He said he would even go so far as to print misrepresentations of the truth. I told him that he would be greatly rewarded if he could manage to keep the population unafraid and calm and sway the voters back to the conventional wisdom of the Progressive Party."

André snickered. Any thread of hope he had in the island's leader had completely vanished. Words! Words were useless, no matter how cleverly they were used. If only Mouttet would allow him to carry out the assassination of Senator Knight, Thomas Prentiss, Father Roche, René Cottrell, and any other nigger lover or troublemaker including his father, Marcel Chevalier. But André knew that Mouttet would not incorporate murder in his agenda. Mouttet's hands had been tainted in the past, but as yet, they had never been bloodied.

A paid spy from the Fort-de-France telegraph office entered the room. "Excuse me, sir, but this just came in, and I thought you should see it at once. It was penned by the American Consul to the president of the United States in regard to the eruption of the volcano. We didn't think you would want the message to go through at this time."

"Not one telegram is to leave this island if it mentions Mont Pelée."

*   *   *

The Chevalier plantation house was cast in a solemn din that evening. Maxi's body was ceremoniously wrapped in a white cotton sheet and placed in the funeral parlor. Father Roche agreed to conduct services for burial in the family cemetery the next morning. Supper that night was a quiet, self-reflective affair with few words spoken. Upon completion of the light meal of soup and bread, solemn members of the household retired to their quarters to privately mourn the loss of the man they dearly loved.

*   *   *

It was midnight when Stefan stepped out of the stables. The mountain air felt crisp and cold. He was naked save for a pair of knee-length thermal shorts. He had not been able to sleep although he knew he should be resting when the volcano was silent. No one could predict what it was going to do next. The nighttime sky glowed from the bright luminescence of the crater's bubbling lava lake. Stefan shivered and went back inside the stables to check on his horses.

The stallions and mares snorted nervously. They were none too pleased with the shaking ground beneath their hooves. Stefan gave each one a reassuring pat. His touch calmed them.

Yvette entered the stables. At first, she did not see Stefan. Overcome with grief, she had been unable to fall asleep that night. Maxi's death left her with a tremendous void. Not wanting to be alone with her sad thoughts, she felt compelled to be with her horse. Inspiration neighed happily upon seeing his mistress. Yvette embraced his warm chestnut head in her arms.

"Bonsoir," said Stefan softly.

Yvette continued to nuzzle her horse. "Stefan, I didn't expect you to be up at this hour."

When Stefan realized that Yvette was wearing a thin gown that barely concealed her slender frame, he did not know what to say or do. He was sure that Marcel Chevalier would disapprove of his daughter parading in inappropriate state of dress around a single male.

Yvette was unaware of her allurement or of how vulnerable she appeared as tears of sorrow splashed from her sorrowful green eyes onto her honey-colored cheeks. Stefan could hardly breathe. She was more than a woman—she was a goddess. And if it happened that he was destined to serve her as her stable groom, he would ask for nothing more the rest of his life. She left Inspiration and moved toward Stefan; a sweet-sad smile settled upon her face. Stefan hung on tightly to the neck of the distressed horse he had been comforting. Did Yvette not see that he too was scantily dressed in nightwear? His heart was pounding.

"Oh, Stefan . . . my dear, dear Stefan," she whispered.

His stomach fluttered as her angelic voice caressed his ears. She had called him her "dear" Stefan. It was as if she had bestowed a thousand kisses upon his brow. No sooner had these words passed through his mind when, of all things, Yvette actually did plant a light kiss upon his brow; and while doing so, her corset-free breasts, with only the sheer cotton of her gown acting as an invisible buffer, briefly brushed against his bare chest. For an instant, he felt hard nipples press against his skin. Consumed with uncontrolled fire in his loins, he desperately fought the passionate urge to take her into his arms and smother her with his love.

"Thank you so much for taking such good care of us," she said.

Yvette returned to the house. Stefan's hand went to the spot on his forehead where she had touched him with her lips. He placed his other hand to his chest where she had touched him with her breasts. A residual wave of excitement rocked his body. His yearning for Yvette was as hot as the lava bubbling inside Mont Pelée's throat.

*   *   *

Yvette slipped back into the house and out to the west veranda.

"What have I just done?" she scolded herself.

The kiss had been meant as a simple gesture of appreciation. She must be careful around Stefan. He was no longer a boy. As a nineteen-year-old, he could get the wrong idea, especially since they had been spending so much time together during the last few months. Yvette and Stefan had discovered shared interests. Their conversations centered on land or animals. Like a sponge, Stefan absorbed everything Yvette taught him in regard to the latest growing techniques in agriculture learned at the University of Paris about fertilizers, planting times, plowing times and harvesting times, the effect of the sun and the moon on the seasons, and how to deal with local pests and weather problems. She found herself often spying on Stefan from behind the French doors of her bedroom balcony. His taunt muscles rippled with each move of the mucking rake, or each stroke of the grooming brush, or each swing of an ax stole her breath. She couldn't help the attraction she was feeling. Every time Stefan lifted her with ease off her horse or out of a buggy, her heart leaped. There was no mistaking his attraction for her. She could tell. And as hard as she tried not to be, she was fonder of him than she should allow.

"Oh, dear God, what am I thinking?" she asked the heavens.

Her emotions and hormones swirled in turmoil. She was charmed by two men widely divergent: one white, one black; one cultured from the teachings of books, one educated from the teachings of nature; one of expensive cologne, one of horses and sweat; one of the sea, one of the land. And she cared equally and deeply for them both.

"Want some company?" asked Indigo.

"Of course," answered Yvette.

Indigo grasped the edge of the brick wall in the glow of the volcano. "Next Friday cannot come soon enough when I am on board the ship and on my way to France. Aza predicts sometime terrible is going to take place with the mountain. I'm not so sure that it will return to its slumber like it did fifty years ago."

"Aza and her witchcraft, it can be silly at times."

"Aza has an amazing gift," said Indigo. "She has been right many a time about the outcome of the future. I have learned to trust her powers. They are very strong."

"I know they are. But if we get caught up in fear, then what will happen? Fear is weakness. Weakness is lifelessness. I have to rely on hope. And I won't be driven away from my home by anything, including threats from André or the volcano."

Indigo grinned at her friend's tenacity and decided to change the subject. "I must go into town this Sunday as I have an early morning meeting on Monday with my business partner, Charlene, and our two attorneys. Come with me, please. We should be back by Monday night. Aza will take care of Cyrillia for me."

"Of course I'll go with you." Yvette was quiet for a few seconds. "Things are never going to be the same here again, are they, Indigo?"

"No, my dear friend, I fear not. Things are never going to be the same."

A thunderous explosion tore through the stillness. Indigo and Yvette watched a safe distance away as fire-covered boulders shot out from the mouth of the crater like minicomets to drop like lava bombs over the countryside and St. Pierre. There would be no sleep that night.

29

St. Pierre, Martinique
Saturday, May 3, 1902
The Bones Never Lie

The tropical sunrise over Martinique was exceptional. The flawless beauty of the sky offered the only source of normality now left to the exhausted people of St. Pierre; however, as soon as their eyes dropped back to earth, disbelief and despair tore at their hearts. Mont Pelée had vomited up enough ash the night before to bring the town to a near halt. Most of the schools and shops were closed. Toxic fumes and firebombs had claimed the lives of many. The death toll on northern Martinique was rising.

*   *   *

Maxi had been buried at sunrise in the family cemetery at the base of a small knoll about an eighth of a mile behind the plantation house. No fresh flowers had been placed upon his grave as there were no fresh flowers to be found. All about the burial mound were dozens of crucifixes and tiny statutes representing Christ and the Madonna. A crudely carved headstone was surrounded by a bevy of handmade wax candles and oil lamps. As soon as Father Roche conducted his Christian "ashes to ashes" eulogy, the plantation voodooist, Yébé, performed a voodoo burial rite. Nothing was left to chance in Martinique.

*   *   *

Marcel Chevalier wheedled the carriage horse down the Morne Rouge dirt highway toward St. Pierre. The road sounds of the wheels and hoofbeats had been muffled in the depth of the gray ash. Father Roche sat in glum silence next to Marcel. They had just left Maxi's funeral and were on their way to a meeting with Fernand Clerc and a number of influential men at Clerc's office on Rue Victor Hugo.

The buggy came to a halt near the Roxelane River. Its banks overflowed in a collection of rushing water, debris, and dead bodies of humans and animals. In the center of this river was the island upon which the residence of the British Consul had been built. Two bridges to the castlelike structure had been washed away. Anyone caught inside the residence was trapped.

The British consul, James Japp, could be seen eating breakfast upon his dusty rooftop terrace. Japp's devoted servant, Boverat, poured his master a cup of tea. Marcel cupped his hands and yelled over the roar of the swiftly moving currents.

James went to the balcony railing. "Fine pickle I am in, wouldn't you say?"

"Oui!" said Marcel. "Is there anything we can do?"

"Nothing can be done here until the water recedes," shrugged James. "No need to worry about us. All is fine. We have plenty of food. Say, I am terribly sorry about the loss of your meat purveyor. Maxi was a decent chap. These are terrible times."

*   *   *

After the funeral, Yvette changed into work clothes. She and Stefan would assess the eastern fields and the workers' compound; and the plantation overseer, Félecien, would take two of his men to inspect the western banana fields for crop damage while Marcel attended his meeting in town.

Yvette came down the stairs from her bedroom just in time to overhear Aza pleading with Indigo in the dining room parlor. There was high-pitched urgency knitted into the old woman's voice. "We must leave now, Missy Indigo. I fear the devil *be* loose and time *be* precious. The signs say this *be* the place of death. We must leave."

"Aza, darling, we are leaving," said Indigo calmly. "In six days we shall be on our way to France, then all will be well. Nothing is going to happen to us before then. I promise."

Cyrillia had been playing nearby with Espérer. The six-year-old was not at all interested in her mother and Aza's conversation for she was too busy tormenting a terrified *mabouha* lizard trapped in the corner of the room by the end of a broomstick. The lizard stretched out about seven inches long, gray in color, and was none too happy at its unfortunate predicament.

"You had better surrender, great dragon," commanded the child.

Espérer joined in the fun with high-pitched yips. Not able to take any more abuse, the lizard leaped three feet up in the air up and over them. Before Cyrillia could react, it scurried across the floor and down the hall where it found sanctuary in a closet. Cyrillia squealed in delight at the mastery and agility of her prey. Indigo shook her head wearily at the antics of her tomboy daughter. Aza could not help but grin despite her gloomy mood.

"I'll be back for lunch," said Yvette.

"Be careful," warned Indigo.

"Not to worry."

Yvette went to the stables. Stefan was waiting with their saddled horses. Little was said as they made their way to the east field. Surreptitiously, each caught an admiring glimpse of the other. Yvette forced herself to concentrate on the task at hand as she surveyed the ash damage to the plants. Though most of the leaves were wilted, the green banana fruit was healthy enough; however, if the fallout continued for another few weeks, the entire harvest would be lost. The Chevaliers would have no choice but to sell what they could as soon as possible and be satisfied with whatever revenues they received as a result. Yvette had seen enough. She kicked her horse and headed for the worker's compound. Stefan was close behind.

Stefan remained with the horses at the edge of the compound while Yvette made her way by foot to Yébé's dwelling. The only sounds in the compound were a few chickens clucking, a hunting dog barking at a rabbit, and a baby crying out for its midmorning feeding. Yvette ducked inside Yébé's hut and found him sitting cross-legged on the floor before a pile of sun-bleached chicken bones. He had wrapped a red cotton sarong around his narrow waist. Several loops of hand-carved wooden beads dropped across his collarbone. The hair on his chest and his beard were the same pale gray color of the volcanic ash. Two of his front teeth were missing, and the rest were yellow. Cataracts clouded his once keen vision. He looked so old. Had he always been that way? She couldn't remember.

Yébé finished a voodoo reading of the bones. Worry lines were etched deeply into his wrinkled black face. He motioned for her to sit. She did.

"The bones never lie," he leaned forward and whispered. "They warn that evil spirits of the dead be askin' Mont Pelée to provide them with fresh souls. Accordin' to the bones, Mont Pelée be more than willin' to do so."

"How are your people, Yébé?" asked Yvette. "Papa and I heard rumors that some of them are thinking about leaving. We hope that you will use your influence to persuade them to remain here. Papa promises that we are a safe distance away from the mountain and that no harm will come to us here on the plantation."

"You and your father *be* very good to us. I cannot in my good mind tell my people to go the direction that is the wrong direction to go. I think maybe that it be me beggin' you to go away with us rather than you beggin' us to stay."

Yvette departed from Yébé's dwelling and found Stefan waiting with their horses. She took the reins of Inspiration and mounted. Yvette yawned. She was exhausted. The uncertainty of the volcano, the condition of the crops, the unrest of the workers, and the strain of Maxi's death were taking a toll. She closed her eyes and pressed the sides of her temples with shaky fingers.

"Come with me," said Stefan. "You need a little break from all of this. I want to take you to a special place where I go as often as I can to get away and think."

He led her along a narrow path that twisted up and behind a tall mountain a few miles south of the plantation. The morning sun was penetrating and hot. Stefan removed his shirt and tied it to his saddle. Yvette's eyes rested upon the muscles that seemed to rival the quivering flanks of his stallion. He sat straight and proud—an ebony prince upon the back of a white horse.

After the riders rounded a wide bend, they came upon a forest liberated from the gray and ugliness of Pelée's wrath. A lush hidden world of healthy plants, trees, and flowers unfolded before them. Yvette was taken aback by the splendor.

"Oh, Stefan," she cried happily.

*   *   *

Marcel Chevalier and Father Roche stopped by the American Regency before heading to Fernand Clerc's office. Clara escorted the men onto the second-story balcony with a view that faced the back of the lighthouse and the bay beyond. Thomas leaned against the railing with the morning copy of *Les Colonies* clutched tightly in his fist. His eyes were bloodshot. He had not slept in several nights. He shook hands with his guests and invited them to sit down at a patio table. Clara had made sure that everything on the terrace had been cleared of ash.

"Hurard is not only an abominable newspaper editor," his voice quivered with anger, "but has about as much common sense as a gnat. Now I ask you, what the hell does this mean?"

Marcel read the front-page story of the newspaper out loud to the others.

"On to Mount Pelée," the article headlined. "The excursion to the volcano still takes place on Sunday as planned. Those who have never enjoyed the astonishing panorama offered at a height of more than four thousand feet and those who desire to see close at hand the yawning hole of the crater, should indeed profit by this fine opportunity and register their names this very evening at the latest. The grand excursion will start at three-thirty precisely from Marche du Fort. Those who do not care to trouble themselves with food should pay an assessment of three francs. They will not regret being relieved of the trouble of procuring food. To judge from the list of those who are going, the company will be numerous, and, if the weather is fine, the excursionists will pass a day that they will long keep in pleasant memory."

Marcel was stunned. "I cannot understand this insanity."

"There's more," said Thomas pointing to another section of the front page. "It pokes fun at Americans who have fled the island. And look here, Hurard had the nerve to crucify me in print for spreading unnecessary bad news."

"This is an outrage," said Father Roche.

"Have you heard about that Negro who is to be hanged?" asked Thomas. "He killed a Frenchman."

Marcel and Father Roche nodded.

"It appears that the Progressive Party is using this man as an example of what could happen to other whites if the blacks come into political power. Hurard is portraying the Radical Party as an out-of-control group of activists who spread false panic among the islanders in order to gain power of office."

Father Roche picked up the newspaper and read Hurard's editorial. "So when you hear tales of panic and impending doom to St. Pierre because of Mont Pelée's little ash fallout, weigh those tales carefully. They may have been spread by Radicals eager to drive you away from your duty to oppose them at the polls."

Thomas shook his head. "I doubt that Fernand will be able to convince anyone at the meeting today that an evacuation of the town and countryside is of the essence. Not after these printed lies. Also, if Fernand goes against the thinking of *Les Colonies*, he automatically goes against the thinking of the Progressive Party. It could mean the end of his political career."

Marcel agreed. "Especially since the conservatives have all of France backing them. The power behind the throne, so to speak, is invincible. I have to admit, however, that at this point in time, I too am not totally convinced that an evacuation of the area is necessary. Yes, I believe the villages and towns around the base of the volcano should be cleared. But the entire population of St. Pierre? Think of what that would mean."

"My dear Marcel," said Thomas, pointing to the volcano. "Look for yourself. The mountain is in full eruption, for the love of God. I don't care that we seem a safe four miles away, Mont Pelée posts a grave danger. We have to do something now before it is too late."

Father Roche held out his hands to Thomas. "Dear man, please come to the meeting with us today. Your presence would be a big help."

"They won't listen to an outsider. This has got to be handled through local officials."

Marcel and Father Roche left the American Regency by foot and headed for Fernand Clerc's office. On the way through town, they found the Le Prêcheur priest, along with his entire village of refugees, heading back north, returning to their village near the base of the volcano.

"Qu'est-ce qui est arrivé?" asked Father Roche.

The priest from Le Prêcheur raised his hand and his progression of followers dutifully stopped. He tried brushing off his filthy frock as he answered. "I have decided to take my people back home. Yesterday we were herded like animals and imprisoned by the governor's garrisons inside the town hall complex. My people are a proud people. We'd rather take our chances in our tiny fishing village with the threat of the mountain than with Governor Mouttet's men. I know what you must be thinking, but this is our decision. Au revoir!"

*   *   *

Shortly before noon, the northern portion of the tiny island convulsed. Two mighty earthquakes at the base of the volcano hit seconds apart. Many of the town's citizens were thrown to the ground. Others grabbed the nearest person to them. Some screamed. When the tremors finally stopped, the people either laughed wildly or wept hysterically.

Luci Lucien, the prostitute who had befriended Indigo at Les Chats six years earlier, had just finished a rowdy lovemaking session with a French sailor when the earthquakes knocked the frolicking couple off the bed and onto the floor.

"*Mais oui*," laughed Luci, patting the bare buttocks of the shocked sailor, "did I not tell you that I was the best."

*   *   *

Nineteen-year-old Auguste Ciparis cautiously peered out from behind the tiny ground-level window of the solitary cell where he had been observing the construction of the hanging platform. This was the same platform where he would die in five days' time. Suddenly the ground shook so violently that the platform collapsed and crushed the gallows into a pile of useless wood. Ciparis fell to his knees onto the dirt floor of his thimble-sized underground cell and held up his powerful black hands in a thankful prayer to whatever god wanted to hear him. The same black hands had strangled the white man who had treated him no better than a dog.

*   *   *

It had been weeks since Yvette had observed the radiant tropical colors normally found in the jungles and plantation fields around St. Pierre and Morne Rouge. Plant life had either wilted or turned brown. But now, here in this mountain enclave, in this hidden eden, this isolated oasis, this paradise lost, was life. How glorious it was to behold the healthy greens of the ferns, the bamboo, the *balistiers* and the palms, to take in the patches of wild red and yellow roses, the ground cover of pink and white begonias, the sweeping lines of scarlet passionflowers, and the delicate purple veils of bougainvilleas. A mountain brook with pristine waters cascaded past moss-carpeted rocks and waving reeds of fish grass.

Heaven had been found in hell.

"Oh, Stefan," rejoiced Yvette, taking in a deep breath of unpolluted mountain air. She dismounted and ran to the bubbling stream. Scooping up water into the cup of her hands, she splashed it on her face. The liquid felt cool and refreshing. It energized her senses.

The first earthquake struck with a jolt. Yvette tumbled backward into the shallow of the stream. Sitting waist deep, she didn't move as the ground continued to rock. Stefan calmed the horses until the shaking stopped. Yvette was soaking wet. Her naked breasts plainly displayed through the transparency of the wet material of her white shirt. She undid her braid, shook her head back and forth, allowing a shower of water to spray into the air around her.

"I must say," giggled Yvette, "that was a bit more than I bargained for."

Stefan was speechless. He dared not move. Yvette smiled. He smiled back. Still he could not speak. As she walked toward him, he couldn't help but focus on her glorious breasts bouncing up and down with each step. He could see that she was tipsy with the sudden pleasure of the moment. Her green eyes sparkled with newfound life. Droplets of water beaded around her lips. Stefan took a step back. He had to remember his place and keep himself in check. He had to remember who he was and who she was. Damn conventions of society. The laws were severe on the island. If a black man dared touch a light-skinned woman without her consent, it was a crime punishable by death. Only murder was more heinous in the white man's society.

Yvette placed a friendly hand upon his bare shoulder. He stiffened.

"Thank you so very much for bringing me here. Thank you for giving me a few minutes of escape from that dreadfulness. This can't be real. It must be a dream. Thank you."

Stefan was giddy with desire. Every nerve pulsated. He could no longer withstand the temptation of this female. One hand reached out and touched her cheek. *God forgive me*, he mentally declared, *if, as a result of what I am about to do, condemns me to death, then this criminal act will have been well worth my life in return*. His other hand scooped the back of her head. Firmly, he brought her lips to his. To his surprise, Yvette didn't resist.

The moment was electrifying.

"You could hang for this," threatened Yvette when the kiss was over.

"Then I shall die a happy man. I won't apologize to you. I had to know what it was like to hold and kiss you. I won't apologize. I won't."

Yvette was thunderstruck by her unbridled passion for this boy.

"I think we should go home at once," announced Yvette in the most proper-sounding voice she could muster. She thought she was going to faint; so dizzy was she from the kiss.

*   *   *

Only a handful of the island's prominent businessmen felt the situation serious enough to attend the emergency meeting at Fernand Clerc's office. Assembled round a large table in the conference room were seven prominent island leaders: M. Saint-Cyr, the owner of the Bank of Martinique; Emile Le Cure, the general manager of the English Colonial Bank; Alfred Decailles, shipping baron; Pierre and Joseph Theroset, casket makers; Georges Madeneus, the town's leading notary; and Roger Fouché, the mayor of St. Pierre. Marcel Chevalier and Father Alte Roche stood in the back of the room. They would watch the proceedings as neutral observers.

At the head of the table was Fernand Clerc, a man fully aware of his strengths and weaknesses. He was an astute businessman. Brilliant shipping decisions brought rewards to all those connected with him. He settled employee problems with ease. He was also aware of his shortcomings. He hated politics. He hated representing the Progressive Party. Most of all, he hated public speaking. A great wave of responsibility rolled over him. It was quite possible that the entire future of St. Pierre rested in his hands. The speech he was about to present was of momentous importance. His words must be delivered with conviction and skill.

"Gentlemen, I want to thank you for coming here on such short notice. I cannot express strongly enough the gravity of the situation. Many claim that Mont Pelée is behaving the same as she did in 1851. They say that there is nothing to fear, as all she is doing is letting off a little steam and will soon settle back down. I beg to differ. Today alone, over twenty bodies have been spotted in the Roxelane River along with numerous animals. The earthquakes, like the ones we experienced just a few minutes ago, have interrupted the telephone service in town. I have recently learned that we are without telegraph services. There is a mass exodus of people from the countryside. Housing and food supplies in St. Pierre are running short. If we don't find a solution to this problem soon, we shall have rioting in our streets. Our twenty-two rivers are flooding. Lava flows have been sighted at various points around the foot of Mont Pelée. An uncountable number of humans and livestock have lost their lives from sulfuric poisoning inhalation. Something has to be done about the situation and done now."

The room was quiet as each man wrestled with his own moral choices.

Mayor Fouché, close friend and puppet of Governor Mouttet, spoke first.

"It is my understanding that medical evidence proves that sulfuric fumes can be extremely good for those suffering with lung complaints."

Joseph Theroset agreed. "Why, yes. As a matter of fact, since the ash fallout, I have actually found that I can breathe easier. The fumes seem to rid the air of humidity. The reason the animals are dying is because they have a breathing system much different from ours."

M. Saint-Cyr tugged nervously at his beard.

"Are you saying, Clerc, that we here, in St. Pierre, are in mortal danger?"

Fernand leaned forward and slapped his hands on top of the table. "Yes."

Pierre Theroset turned to his brother, winked, and turned back to Fernand.

"Well then, dear Fernand, would you then have us evacuate the entire population?"

Fernand Clerc ignored the obvious tone of ridicule in Pierre's voice. "Yes, Pierre, I would."

Stunned silence enveloped the room. Then a roar of protest erupted from the men. In the midst of their objections, the conference table was nearly overturned. The men stared at Fernand in disbelief. There was no doubt that Fernand Clerc had completely lost all of his senses. Such foolishness, some yelled. One of the men exclaimed, "An evacuation of that magnitude would destroy the economic and social lining of the town."

"Where in God's good name," asked the mayor, "would the population go?"

"Mes amis," said Father Roche, addressing the group, "perhaps, yes, it is too premature to evacuate the city at this moment, but does it not stand to reason that there should at least be an evacuation of those living near the base of Mont Pelée in dire danger from lava flows. Qu'en dites vous? What do you say about that? Perhaps we can at least agree on this?"

Again the men were silent. Each waited for the other to speak first. One of the men sheepishly asked the others what harm would it do to evacuate the countryside; after all, it could force more plantation owners to come into town to vote. An action committee was formed, and Saint-Cyr elected to head it. Mayor Fouché was appointed to inform Governor Mouttet of the formation of this committee. It was also agreed that they would all meet again within the next few days to formulate and present an evacuation plan for the people near the mountain. The meeting then came to an abrupt end. Fernand dropped his head in defeat. Greed won out over reasoning. Greed was too powerful to fight. There was little more that he felt he could do for the citizens of St. Pierre. Fernand Clerc left the meeting a broken man.

*   *   *

Governor Mouttet's day was having its ups and downs. The highlight was Hurard's clever editorial in the morning edition of *Les Colonies*. Brilliant writing, Mouttet praised. It was a masterful manipulation of the people. Mouttet read a telegram relaying bad news. Fernand Clerc was insisting on a complete and immediate evacuation of St. Pierre. The Progressive Party candidate now bore the scarlet letter T—a traitor to his political peers and to France.

This bad news was followed by more bad news from André Chevalier who had attended a rally at the Radical Party headquarters earlier that morning. The impressive showing of whites in the audience alarmed André. Senator Knight was encouraging his followers to unite as there was a split within the Radical Party between two battling candidates: Percin and Lagrosillere.

If all of this unwanted news was irritating enough, a messenger arrived from St. Pierre with a propaganda flyer—one of dozens given out at the Radical Party rally. It had also been nailed to trees and plastered on walls all over the town. It read:

PELÉE DEMANDS ALL WHITES LEAVE ST. PIERRE
OR DEATH FOR US ALL!

Mouttet swatted the paper off his desk as if it was something vile and alive. He yanked out his gold pocket watch and nodded approvingly. By now his telegram sent to Paris earlier in the day should have been received by Pierre Louis Decrais, the Minister of Colonies. The upbeat telegram contained basic information on the elections, but said nothing about the erupting volcano. Why alarm Paris about the temporary sound off of Mont Pelée, figured Mouttet. Tomorrow, the preliminaries were scheduled to take place, and the following week, on Thursday, the eighth of May, the main elections would finally be held. Perhaps by then, the volcano would be calm and the island back to normal.

*   *   *

That night, Les Chats was in full swing. Madame Rose was elated. Never had her bar and brothel been so busy. Foreign sailors and the locals stood shoulder to shoulder in her establishment as well as dozens of young countrymen driven to the safety of the city from lava-destroyed homes. It was a place to escape the reality of the volcano. It was a place to forget. It was a place to dive into drink, music, sex, and pleasure.

André Chevalier did not like this crowd. He did not like these small-time sharecroppers from the valley—nothing but white trash. And he especially did not like all these high-rolling niggers. André stewed at his table by the stairs and tossed back his fifth glass of rum. The warm liquid provided temporary comfort. He was there to seek the company of a special whore. His squad of little boys was entertaining, but voluptuous Tattoo was who he needed this night. He beckoned Madame Rose.

"Is Tattoo ready?"

"Tattoo is always ready for you, *chèri*. Remember you paid good money to have her saved exclusively for yourself."

He smiled a rare smile for he liked Tattoo. She had been working at Les Chats for only three months. Tattoo was Caucasian, dirty blonde, twenty-seven, and accomplished at odd lovemaking techniques. Best of all, she did not seem to mind his rough and sadistic behavior. Her parents had been poor merchants who died in a mysterious fire at their business in Fort-de-France. She was just thirteen at the time. Immediately following the fire, she sought work at one of the local brothels. She loved her occupation. It was tawdry, but filled with excitement. She liked life on the edge. In January of 1902, she moved to St. Pierre. Her first night there she met André, and he was so taken with her that he literally purchased her full-time from Madam Rose.

A collection of tattoos covered practically every inch of his whore's backside like a canvas of skillfully drawn figures in the shapes of roses, snakes, ships, tigers, spiders, birds, and hearts. André loved tracing the lines of the drawings upon her naked skin with the tips of his fingers. His favorite artwork was that of a knife depicting an exact replica of his bowie with his name tattooed in the handle. Blood dripped from its blade. Tattoo had presented the image on her right buttock to him for his birthday. It was a wonderful gift, and he adored her for it.

Tattoo reminded him of Paris, France. She had a sharp sense of humor, a brawny laugh, and could tell wicked tales of lust and murder. His drunken breath and unkempt appearance never seemed to offend her. Not since Daniel had he been so happy and content with another human being. Could he possibly be falling in love with this woman?

Madame Rose gave him a nod. He went to Tattoo's room. They spent two hours romping in her featherbed. It had been the best session with her yet. Afterward, they walked arm in arm out onto the upper landing of the stairs. Tattoo kissed his hawklike nose, pinched him on his protruding cheekbone, and slapped his skinny backside. He, in turn, did the same to her—perhaps with a little more force—but she didn't seem to mind. André had stopped at the bottom of the stairs to wave good-bye when a major earthquake struck. Bottles from the bar crashed onto the floor, dancers toppled into the bandstand, paintings fell from the wall, and Tattoo pitched headfirst down the stairs. André rushed to her side, dropped to his knees, and held her lifeless body in his arms. Like a wounded animal, he howled in misery.

30

St. Pierre, Martinique
Sunday, May 4, 1902
The Exodus

Mont Pelée exhibited a spectacular show before sunrise on Sunday morning. Atmospheric energy turned lines of white lightening into wild shapes above the crater. Surrounding these sky drawings were smaller starbursts exploding like tiny clusters of fireworks. This powerful display of nature ended with a showering of red-hot pumice stones over the countryside.

* * *

"I don't like it," said Marcel, pacing back and forth in the kitchen of the main house that Sunday morning. "The town is overburdened with homeless people who are desperate from hunger and thirst. Bloating carcasses of dead animals on the streets carry god knows what kind of diseases. Countless people have died from gas fumes. Senator Knight is stirring up the black population into believing that the mountain will never go back to sleep until the whites have been driven out. It is far too dangerous for you to go into St. Pierre today. I forbid it."

Yvette reached up from the table and took her father's hand.

"Papa, *s'il vous plait!* Sit down. You are wearing a trench through the floor tiles. It will be for only one night. Indigo and I will dress in trousers and wear hats. With all the commotion, no one will pay any attention to us. Let's face it, you have to stay here and begin the harvesting of the crops while I meet with our shipping broker to see if we can get our produce on board one of the ships currently anchored in the roadstead.

You have no choice. Aza will watch Cyrillia in our absence. That is it, Papa. End of discussion."

Marcel looked up at the ceiling and beckoned to the ghost of his late wife. "My dear, lovely Nicole, where are you when I need you? And where, for the love of God, did our daughter get her tenaciousness?"

Yvette threw her arms around her father and grinned.

"Okay. You may go," he said. "But I insist you take Stefan with you . . . I—"

"No!" Yvette bolted out of her chair. "He would draw too much attention to us. It is best that Indigo and I travel alone. My goodness, you make it sound as if we are going on a long journey. The town is only a few miles away."

"Very well," he declared. "Don't get so excited. Make sure you are inside the hotel and off the streets before dark. Now leave me be. You are giving me gray hairs."

*   *   *

Stefan was tired and grumpy. He expected military police to come and haul him away for molesting Yvette, but they never showed up. It was most apparent that Marcel had not been told of Stefan's insolent advances toward Yvette. This was a good sign. Perhaps Yvette had not been offended by their passionate kiss. Ah, what he wouldn't give to taste those sweet lips again. Between the never-ending thoughts of his tongue locked in Yvette's mouth and the antics of the volcano, Stefan had suffered a sleepless night.

Dutifully, he readied Inspiration for Yvette and a gentle mare named Callé for Indigo. He placed side blinders on the animals; the less they saw, the safer for their riders. Indigo requested a horse with very little spirit. She was not happy with the idea of riding. Although a fairly good equestrian, she still preferred the comforts of her buggy.

*   *   *

Indigo knelt on the wooden floor of the private guest quarters in the Chevalier plantation house and put her arms around her daughter. "I want you to behave yourself and mind Aza while I am away. Remember she is an old lady and can't move as fast as you. Please be a good girl and do what you are told. I shall bring you back a grand surprise as a reward."

Cyrillia's narrowed her bright green eyes and surveyed the room. She didn't seem a bit concerned about her mother's leaving. She was perfectly content to be on her own. She could take care of herself. *Now then*, she thought, *what can I get into?* Indigo groaned, knowing full well that her daughter was seizing the moment to plan some kind of mischief.

"Oui, Maman," said Cyrillia, sensing her mother's suspicions.

The capricious six-year-old, with favorite doll in hand, climbed onto a wicker rocking chair and, like an angel, began humming a sweet island song while innocently rocking back and forth. Espérer sat nearby, wagging his stub of a tail. He liked the pretty music of the child.

"Bye-bye, mommy," said the child sweetly.

"You don't fool me for a moment," said Indigo, shaking a mistrustful finger.

"Are you ready?" asked Yvette coming into the room.

Indigo patted her poodle on its curly head. "Watch out for the baby, Espérer."

In order to not draw attention, Yvette and Indigo had dressed in khaki pants, plaid shirts, and brown fedoras. Yvette felt quite comfortable and at home in the clothes, while Indigo felt underdressed without her traditional *jupe* costume. She did not like wearing the trousers of men.

* * *

Governor Mouttet addressed the seven men standing before him in the office of the Governor's Regency. "I apologize for having called you on the Sabbath, but the urgency of the situation in regards to Mont Pelée and St. Pierre leaves me no choice."

The man standing closest to the governor, Andreus Hurard, owner/editor of *Les Colonies*, was mesmerized by anything the great Louis Mouttet had to say or do. The rest of Mouttet's team included deputy governor Lieutenant-Colonel Jules Gerbault; head chemist of the colonial troops Paul Alphonse; assistant civil engineer William Leonce;

and professors of science at the Lycee of St. Pierre Eugene Jean Doze and Gaston Jean-Marie Theodore Landes.

Governor Mouttet scarcely spoke above a whisper. "I am appointing you men as part of my new Governor's Commission. Because of the emergency at hand, the normal protocol for forming such a commission, including ratification clearance of appointees from Paris, will be bypassed. Your main objective on this mission is to visit the volcano and come back with a report verifying that Mont Pelée does *not* represent a threat to St. Pierre. You have two days in which to complete your investigations and your pre-scripted findings."

The men knew exactly what he meant. If downplaying the threat of the erupting mountain and falsifying scientific reports insured extra incentive payments, then so be it.

Mouttet continued. "Deputy Gerbault will head this special commission. I am sick and tired of these doomsday criers and their ideas of mass evacuations. It must be stopped. And it must be stopped at once. Mon Dieu! A little shortage of food and accommodations is not a sensible reason for needless panic. Thank God the voting booths in St. Pierre are reportedly open and the primaries are proceeding as planned. The main elections will be held on Thursday no matter what. There will be no postponements. In order to demonstrate a show of confidence in the situation, I shall announce that my wife and I plan to attend the Ascension Day festivities in St. Pierre scheduled on Thursday. We will also be present at Mayor Fouché's annual Governor's Ball the night before. This act of confidence should show the alarmists how foolish they are."

He received a brief applause of approval.

Each man bowed in respect before filing out of the office.

Deputy Governor Jules Gerbault and Andreus Hurard stayed behind.

"I have made another decision that will help ensure a Progressive Party victory," said the governor. "I have decided to reprieve the Negro, Ciparis, from his date with the gallows as soon as the scientific report by the Governor's Commission is revealed in Wednesday's newspapers. The timing will be perfect. Hopefully this will come across as an act of mercy that will sway some of the undecided voters to our side. If we play our cards right, we can use Mont Pelée's awakening to our advantage at the polls."

A messenger handed the governor a letter just received from St. Pierre.

"Listen to this, Jules and Hurard. Here is another example of needless hysteria and foolishness," said the governor. "The mayor of Ajopa-Boullion took it upon himself to call off an evacuation of his village. The damn fool succeeded in convincing the people to stay. It says here in the report that the earth cracked open beneath the village and released a vat of hot steam and mud. As a result, over one hundred and fifty people were instantly cooked to death."

The two men reacted appropriately at the bad news. They were totally unaware that they were just about to commit the same crime.

"Hurard," said Mouttet, "I do not want you to curtail the details of this terrible episode. How could that idiot have kept those people there at the foot of the volcano? I suppose that his cacao plantation operations were more important than his responsibility as a mayor. Most of the men in the village worked for him."

Deputy Governor Gerbault mused silently. Mouttet was such a hypocrite. What the governor had just accused the Ajopa-Boullion's mayor of was precisely what he himself was guilty of, only on a grander scale. Gerbault shrugged his shoulders. What did he care? This wouldn't affect his life one way or another. So what if the governor wanted a falsified report on the volcano? Gerbault could care less.

*   *   *

Clara and Thomas Prentiss sat on the balcony of their home. Both husband and wife were exhausted. They had been arguing for hours. Thomas insisted Clara leave the island with the children at once. Clara stood her ground. She would not go without Thomas and refused to leave his side. He pleaded with his stubborn wife. She insisted that if they were to depart this world, then, by heavens, it would be together. Thomas had little else to say to her.

*　*　*

André followed Madame Rose into Les Chats. Their faces were sorrowful. They had just returned from Tattoo's memorial service. Madame Rose worried about André. Over the years, she had seen the worst of his volatile nature and bizarre mood swings. Yet, she had never seen him as demented as he did on this gloomy Sunday morning. She sensed that he was on the verge of a complete breakdown.

"Is your phone working, Rose?"

"As far as I know, we still have communications."

André helped himself to a bottle of rum from behind the bar, pulled the cork out with his teeth, and went into the private office of Madame Rose. He placed a call to the governor.

"André here," he announced.

"I have been trying to find you," scolded the Governor from his desk. "Is there any more on the Radicals? The primaries are today and I need to know what is going on in that camp."

André stared at the phone vacantly a few seconds before he finally answered. "The polls opened at eight o'clock. Thus far, there has been a good turnout of voters. Clerc voted and went to mass at the Cathedral of St. Pierre. He will need all the prayer and help from his god that he can muster. The booths will close at two o'clock this afternoon. Mayor Fouché is scheduled to announce the results this evening on the steps of the town hall."

"Damn it, boy, you are not telling me a thing that I don't already know!" Cold silence greeted Governor Mouttet on the other end. "André, I hope you aren't planning to do anything foolish. You better not. Do you hear me? Answer me!"

"Of course not, Governor," André muttered. He hung up the receiver, took another swig from the bottle of rum, and pondered Mouttet's words of warning. No one told him what to do.

*　*　*

Yvette and Indigo trotted their horses down a side road toward the harbor, avoiding Rue Victor Hugo on the north end of town. The overwhelming number of refugees weaving back and forth across the crowded cobblestones astounded the two women. Nearing one of St. Pierre's more popular restaurants, they witnessed a hungry and homeless black man grab a platter of freshly steamed fish from one of the tables. He ran away with what would be his first meal in days. Along with the restaurant owner and the customer, an angry mob quickly formed and took off after the thief with shaking fists. Locals had reached the end of their rope with outsiders taking up space, water, food, and whatever else rightfully belonged to the good citizens of St. Pierre. The homeless man and his platter of fish were cornered at the back of an alley. He was so weak from hunger and numb from fear, he dropped to the ground on his knees. Seconds later, the man was dead. The crazed mob had clubbed him to death.

Yvette and Indigo kicked their horses into a light gallop and headed through the crowds toward La Place Bertin and Hôtel Indigo. The worried eyes of the hotel's doorman cautiously peered out of the peephole in response to their knock on the locked front doors.

"Ms. Indigo!"

As soon as the women were inside, the door was locked again. With the exception of a light coating of dust, the interior of the bustling hotel had been kept surprisingly clean.

Charlene Julie came into the lobby aglow. "Indigo! Thank goodness you are here, I have been so worried. How nice to see you, Ms. Chevalier. Isn't this something? We are so busy we are turning people away. I am asking triple the usual rental amount for our best rooms. The front door is locked to keep the refugees away."

"You have things well under control," observed Indigo. "How are your supplies?"

"Thanks to your good planning, our storage room has enough food and emergency supplies to last a month if need be. There is very little fresh food to be found in St. Pierre, so I have been sending my porters into Fort-de-France every morning to bring back what produce is available. Our chef has been creating miracles out of the tinned goods."

Charlene received a hug of gratitude from Indigo.

"Good for you! Good for you!"

Indigo escorted Yvette up the stairs to the third-floor landing. Halfway down the long hallway, Indigo stopped, paused at a door, and smiled mischievously. "This is David's room."

"David's room," said Yvette curiously as she ran her fingers over the brass letter on the door. "You never volunteer much information about him. Why?"

"Why should I?" answered Indigo as she opened the door of her private three-room suite directly across the way. "We are good friends. We have been for many years."

Yvette removed her hat and sat upon a divan covered in an exquisite needlepoint design. "I have been afraid to express my feelings about David to you. I wasn't sure how close you two were. Frankly, I don't understand your relationship. He has told me time and time again how much he has enjoyed your companionship. I can't tell if he is talking about his lover or his sister."

"I see," Indigo smiled. She picked up the phone and ordered up a pitcher of lemonade and a platter of tea sandwiches for their lunch.

"Let me reassure you that David and I are truly the best of friends and nothing more. It is a very difficult relationship to explain, but yes, we *are* like sister and brother. We are very close and will always be. Do you know he is in love with you?"

"I know."

"You don't sound too happy. I was under the impression that you liked him."

Yvette kicked off her riding boots, brought her feet up, and wrapped her arms around her legs. "I care for David in a certain way. Probably more than I care to admit. He is the perfect gentleman. His funny American accent makes me laugh. Never have I met a white man, other than my father, with as much charm, sophistication, and wit. His stories of the sea, Boston, and travel greatly fascinate me. I have found that his is a world opposite mine."

Their lunch arrived. The claret of lemon was served warm out of a silver pitcher. Tiny sandwiches made from biscuits and dried beef lined the matching platter. A small tin of ginger cookies imported from England had been sent along as well.

"I wonder," said Indigo while taking a bite out of her sandwich, "if that stable boy of yours may not be distracting you a bit."

"Why, what do you mean?"

"Yvette, anyone with eyes in their head can see there is an attraction between you two."

"I won't deny it," said Yvette, rolling her eyes. "My emotions are in a terrible state of confusion. I may be fond of both men. Is that possible?"

Indigo laughed. "Anything of the heart is possible. You will know sooner or later what is best for you. Many will try to convince you that neither one is the right choice. An American captain? A black stable boy? Scandalous! Don't be alarmed over the shouts of protest. Do what you want. You have always been strong in spirit. Be just as strong with your emotions."

Yvette went to the window, opened the shutters, and leaned out the opening to view the activities of the town and the volcano to her right. "Indigo! Come! Look!"

A thick black mass spreading across the sky a mile wide in girth billowed out from the crater's top and floated over the mountain like a swarm of locusts. It withdrew within itself and expanded back out again as if it were taking a long deep breath. The imposing apparition moved down the mountainside toward town. Once over the city, the black cloud broke apart into a rainstorm of tiny hot pumice. People ran for cover as burning stones and cinders pelted the ground. Indigo closed the shutters. She wanted no more of this world for today.

*   *   *

Hearing the commotion, Andreus Hurard jumped up from his desk and ran to his office window. He watched the phenomenon with detached interest before returning to the preparation of the Monday edition of *Les Colonies*. He would use this theatrical black cloud as an example of the harmless and awe-inspiring wonders of their magical volcano. The editor also planned to print convincing testimonies from experts verifying that there was absolutely *nothing* to fear—even though those "experts" were imaginary. Hurard liked playing God. He loved creating fiction as fast as his pen could write—fiction that the public would enthusiastically accept as fact.

*   *   *

The hands of the Chamber of Commerce clock were minutes away from signaling eight o'clock. Mayor Fouché left his town hall office to announce the polling results to the hundreds of anxious townspeople waiting in silence at the bottom of the stairs. Mayor Fouché walked out onto the upper landing of the cement steps with a piece of paper held tightly in his hands. He didn't look happy as he read its contents out loud to the crowd.

Fernand Clerc had received 2,367 of the votes while the combined votes of his Radical competitors were 3,170. If one of the Radical candidates withdrew and pledged his votes to the other—it would mean an assured victory on Thursday for the Radical Party. Only 800 votes were needed to overtake and win the final election four days away.

André slammed his fist against a nearby stone wall. Licking the blood from his abraded hand, he angrily studied the political jesters on the town hall steps. Clerc's weakness infuriated him. That cocky smile upon Knight's mud-colored face sent him into a rage. It was now time to take matters into his hands. Mouttet's conventional ways were not working. There was only one solution to this problem—kill them all. One pierce of a bullet or one slit of a throat would solve the matter in an instant. André kicked a stray cat and set it flying against a crate of boxes. The cat, like many of St. Pierre's abused inhabitants, was not only hungry and homeless, but now beaten up as well.

31

St. Pierre, Martinique
Monday, May 5, 1902
The Calm Before the Storm

An eerie calm greeted the people of St. Pierre at sunrise Monday morning. The volcano was quiet. Only a few puffs of smoke signaled her presence. Did the people dare hope that this was a promising indication of submission? Could this mean the end of Mont Pelée's violent awakening? Was the mountain finally going back to sleep, or was it taking a rest to recharge for yet another murderous assault?

*   *   *

Aza, snuggled in her bed sheets, opened her eyes with a start. She thought it was another earthquake, but soon found that it was only Cyrillia jumping up and down on the bed trying to get the old woman's attention. "May you turn into a toad," snapped Aza. She rubbed her sleepy eyes and stretched her arthritic bones before playfully pushing her young charge out of the way.

Cyrillia giggled madly. The little girl was a boundless source of energy. She couldn't sit still for a minute. Much like Yvette, she hated to be cooped up inside and was happiest playing out of doors, especially in the fields and woods. She adored adventure and fantasy stories from her books. Nothing seemed to frighten her.

"Let's play warrior and hunter," suggested Cyrillia, her eyes bright and alert. It was her favorite game. Most often, Cyrillia managed to get Aza to pretend to be the enemy or prey while the six-year-old took the part of the mighty warrior or champion hunter, gallantly saving the day or freeing the world with her imaginary bow and arrow.

Aza groaned. "I *be* too old for this! First I *be* gettin' dressed and then we will have our breakfast. And then we shall play. How about a nice tea party? That *be* soundin' like fun?"

"No!"

"Well, tea party it be, young lady. Like it or not!"

Cyrillia stuck her tongue out just as soon as Aza turned around to open up the shutters of her bedroom window. The sky was blue, and the volcano looked harmless. Aza froze. It was too quiet and too peaceful. Foreboding feelings gripped her body. She instinctively reached for the protective pumice fetish she wore around her neck. If only she had time to work her magic and read the signs.

"Would you like to talk with God, the Gran Mèt, creator of heaven and earth? Or perhaps we *be* callin' upon the loa spirits to help keep us from the dangers of the volcano. What be you *be* sayin' to this? That *be* fun things to do?"

Cyrillia shrugged. She'd rather be outside chasing imaginary enemies. "I'm hungry."

"Go on down the stairs. Henrillia *be* preparin' your breakfast. I *be* comin' directly."

Before Cyrillia could skip off downstairs, Aza removed the well-worn pumice fetish and tied it around the child's neck. Cyrillia was pleased with her new gift. It made her look like a warrior. Aza went to a large trunk that held her personal possessions. Once the lid of the trunk was opened, she sighed. All her jars and potions had been carefully wrapped and packed for the journey to France. It would be too much trouble to take them out and set them up for the proper ceremony. She carefully dropped to her knees and prayed. It was the only magic she had left.

Fifteen minutes later, Aza went down to the plantation kitchen. There was no sign of Cyrillia anywhere. Espérer chewed on a lamb bone in the corner of the room. Aza asked Henerillia if she had seen the little girl. Henrillia, busy wiping down the countertops, shook her head. She wasn't interested in a missing child. The ash had made a mess of her spotless kitchen, and she was none too happy about it.

"How am I suppose to cook with all this soot about?" complained Henrillia, stomping her feet in the annoying powder.

Aza combed the second floor of the house without luck. She knew that Cyrillia could not possibly be with Marcel for he left before dawn to tend to the harvesting. Aza found Maxi's wife, Coralline, sitting quietly out on her third-floor veranda. She was wearing widow's black and reading a Bible. No, she had not seen Cyrillia. Another servant thought she had just seen the little girl playing in the front gardens.

Aza hurried outside. Cyrillia was not out front. Aza went to the stables and found Stefan grooming a horse. He had not seen Cyrillia, but promised that as soon as he returned the horse to its stall, he would join in the search.

"Don't worry about her, Aza, "said Stefan, "you know Cyrillia likes to explore. There's not too much trouble she can get into around here. I'll be with you soon."

*   *   *

Cyrillia squealed with joy. The tall banana plants provided a perfect forest setting for her game of stalking the wicked fire-spitting dragon that threatened the mighty castle of the Chevaliers. Cyrillia peeked out from her hiding place behind a banana tree and pointed her stick at the imaginary beast. *Swish!* She made the sounds of an arrow flying to its target. Darn, the cunning creature got away. Moving farther into the row of banana plants, she crouched low and took aim once more. That bad old dragon won't get away this time. She sneezed. The ash was tickling her nose. Cyrillia was probably the only one in all of Martinique who actually enjoyed the ash, for it made the countryside near her home look very much like the winter snow scenes in her fairy tale books of Merlin and King Arthur—adding even more realism to her game.

"Old dragon, you had better come out now. Or else!"

Cyrillia held her breath. All was quiet. Where is that ornery dragon? Tiny red eyebrows knitted up into a curious frown. What was that noise? Was it the dragon? No. The noise was more like logs popping in a crackling fire. No. The noise was much more like the crunching of dead leaves. Whatever was making this terrible racket, the thing was loud and big and was heading directly for her. Cyrillia realized that the noise she was hearing was real and not caused by the made-up dragon in her mind. Her natural instincts of survival took over, and without a second thought, she whirled around on her toes and started running toward the main house. It was then when she heard Aza calling out her name.

The noise grew louder behind her. It sounded vicious. Near the edge of the banana field, Cyrillia tripped and fell. As she was getting up, she glanced over her left shoulder to be greeted by a scene more terrifying than any dragon—real or imaginary.

*   *   *

Aza was gone when Stefan exited the stables to offer his help. In the distance, he could hear Aza frantically calling for Cyrillia. Then he heard a child scream. Stefan followed the sounds to a clearing just outside the last row of banana plants. It took his brain a few seconds to comprehend what his eyes were seeing. Marching across the fields, climbing up and over the banana plants were hundreds of thousands of deadly three-inch ants and foot-long centipedes.

Aza scooped Cyrillia up into her arms and started walking as fast as she could on her arthritic legs. Aza was all too familiar with the force and destruction of these creatures. In 1851, during the last eruption, ants and centipedes trying to escape the wrath of the volcano had been driven from the upper jungles down onto the floor of the valley.

As Aza fled the advancing armies of the *fourmis-fous* and *betes-a-mille-pattes* with the screaming child locked tightly in her arms, she remembered that awful time. The giant ants had inflicted painful, burning stings. The jaws of the centipedes were so powerful, they could rip through shoe leather. Helpless babies had been eaten alive in their cribs. Defenseless animals were turned into skeletons within minutes. Adults suffered horrendous injuries.

Aza could go no farther. Her strength was gone. Her knees had given out. There was no way she could keep ahead of the ants and centipedes. Just as the first ant had reached her foot she saw Stefan just a few yards away and gave immediate thanks to the Gran Mèt. She handed Cyrillia over to Stefan and ordered him to flee with the child as fast as he could. He knew there was no time to argue. He would not be able to save them both. Looking back over his shoulder as he ran for the plantation house,

Stefan could see, with horror, that Aza was completely coated with the ants. She never uttered a sound. She did not want her screams of pain to linger in the mind of the child. Death was quick.

Seeing the flood of insects, Marcel emerged from the east fields upon the back of his galloping horse just as Stefan had reached the front door of the plantation house and threw Cyrillia into the arms of Coralline. Marcel organized a defense force. The workers were divided into three groups and instructed to saturate the outside of the barrier wall with tar and set it on fire to form a protective ring of flames around the perimeter of the estate. Before the tar had a chance to be fully ignited, hundreds of ants and centipedes managed to scurry over the wall and push forward toward the house and stables. The ones trapped in the fire crackled and popped from the blast of the heat.

Henrillia was in the process of removing two of her prized sweet cakes from a hot brick oven in the kitchen when she heard a scampering noise on the counter top behind her. Quite used to unexpected surprises from unwelcome vermin, the cook took a deep breath, expecting to find a mouse or a rat, but instead she came face to face with a fourteen-inch-long centipede. It was revolting. Half of its long, flat body swayed in the air, with hundreds of little feet waving back and forth while its lower half anchored to the counter. It had eyes—intelligent eyes. And they were seriously focused on the plump human. Henrillia, void of all patience, unleashed a cry of declaration of war. The startled centipede lost its opportunity of a surprised attack. Instead, the mesmerized creature found itself looking at the underside of a heavy cast-iron skillet. Its blood sprayed against the kitchen walls.

The house echoed with shrieks as servants battled the invaders with brooms, irons, umbrellas, and shoes. The exceptionally aggressive and determined centipedes seemed to sense that they were in a battle with the humans. Armies of ants attacked the horses and cows in the stables and the pastures. Stefan and his coworkers first tossed buckets of hot water on the stinging hides of the animals to wash off the ants; the centipedes were finished with the back of a shovel or the head of a hoe.

The battle lasted for an hour.

Marcel rushed into the house to search for Cyrillia. It was Coralline who led her master to a trunk where she had hidden the wide-eyed, whimpering child. Marcel gathered his daughter up into his arms and kissed her curly redhead. What a relief that she was safe. Cyrillia stopped her crying and studied him curiously. Love and comfort was found in the safety of this man's arms. With tears of joy, Marcel steadily rocked his little girl.

*   *   *

While Indigo met with Charlene and the lawyers finalizing the partnership agreement of Hôtel Indigo, Yvette traveled by foot to the office of the shipping broker about six blocks away from the hotel. The early morning sun basked St. Pierre in a flood of warmth as Yvette pushed her way down the crowded Rue Bouillé. During the night, hundreds of additional refugees had moved into the town. Yvette winced at their helplessness. Despair hung on the faces of men who were once proud farmers, fishermen, or merchants from the villages that surrounded the belching mountain. They had spent several days and nights spent in the open. Volcanic ash rudely soiled their hair, clothes, and spirits. Torment weighed heavily in their hearts as they beheld the impoverished conditions of their suffering loved ones. Vomit and human waste ran thick in the water of the gutters, upon the streets, and the sand of the beaches. Public latrines could not keep up with the sanitary demands of the homeless. Human hygiene was at its worse.

Refugees frantically hung on to what few possessions they gathered before abandoning their country homes. Entire villages of people had sought refuge. St. Pierre was bursting at its seams. Food, water, and medical care could not be properly administered to so many humans in need. The weak and sick lay crumpled against walls and lampposts, fountains and park benches, and alongside alleyways, bridges, and sidewalks. Outstretched arms begged for compassion, begged for mercy. They reached out pitifully for food and water for themselves and their children suffering from malnutrition. Babies and the children could be heard above the church bells, wailing in anguish from the pain of their empty bellies. Abandoned dogs and cats had long been captured, butchered, and cooked on spits over makeshift fires.

Some of the homeless gathered in tight, protective packs forming a natural barrier against common street muggers and against those who preyed on others in such plight. The older of the refugees spent their time daydreaming of what had long been the comfort and safety of their homes and, most of all, the independence and privacy they had all once enjoyed. Having been raised on rich farmland where wholesome food and fresh water was in abundance, these hardworking people of the country were unaccustomed to the feeling of hunger and thirst. It hurt their pride—hurt it real bad.

Cheers of hope cascaded down the street just as Yvette was about to enter the office of her shipping agent. An escaped bull, delirious from starvation, was on the loose. It was a few yards away from Yvette when it was shot and killed by municipal soldiers. As soon as the bull hit the ground, a stampede of knife-wielding men, women, and children attacked the carcass. The crazed humans tore away at the flesh like starved wolves. Yvette was stunned at the sight. The butchering of this five-hundred-pound animal had been completed in minutes. The crowd backed away with chunks of meat dripping with the warm blood of the beast. All that remained were its glistening bones and streaming entrails. The people were so hungry, they ate the meat raw.

Yvette hurried inside.

"Mon Dieu! What are you doing here, Yvette?" asked Laurent as he pulled her in through the door and away from the madness. He led her to a chair by his desk. "It is insane out there. No one is safe on the streets—especially a pretty girl."

"I have come to arrange for the immediate purchase and shipping of our crops—or what is left of them."

Laurent sat down at his desk. "We are in the middle of a crisis. You aren't the only planters trying to get rid of produce. I don't have enough ships or the buyers to take it all."

"Please, Laurent, you must help us."

"Okay, Yvette, there is one Italian captain who has been taking on extra cargo, but at a fraction of the market value." Laurent pulled out a file and read over a list. "I see that your cargo was scheduled to go out at the beginning of next week."

"We can't wait that long. We have to sell what we have been forced to harvest early."

Laurent placed a friendly hand on Yvette's back. "I'll do everything in my power to help you and your father, Yvette. Give me a day to see what I can do. In the meanwhile, please get off these streets and go home. I will send a messenger as soon as I have made arrangements. Do you realize, Yvette, that you could face serious legal problems by breaking your original contractual agreements with the commissioned ships?"

"Force Majeure!"

"Act of God or not, there is still going to be trouble."

Heading back into the hotel, Yvette could hear a chorus of grumbling female voices some distance away. Now what? Yvette wondered. It sounded like a riot brewing.

*   *   *

The angry voices belonged to a group of carrier women gathered in La Place Bertin. They cried out against the sugar planter Dr. Eugené Guérin. It was unforgivable that he had made his workers cut cane on the previous day, Sunday, the day of Sabbath. Guérin, like so many other plantation owners, had been trying anything to salvage his crops. He knew the decision to finish up as much of the work as possible on Sunday would be unpopular and against the wishes of his highly religious employees.

On Sunday, reluctantly the field men had wielded their machetes. As the cane fell, as usual, it was the task of the *ammareuses*, the field women, to gather and bind the stalks. Guérin and his workers had just finished loading cane onto the third ox cart when a high-pitched whistle rose up from the depths of hell, cracking the earth open like an egg and swallowing twenty men and their women in a blink of an eye. Just as fast, the fissure closed in one murderous solitary clap, crushing to death all who were trapped and screaming inside the instant tomb.

Julie Gabou, the leader of the carrier women or porteuses, had lost her husband in this Sunday morning disaster; and she was none too happy about it. Julie was a formidable young woman with the athletic build of a man: strong, agile, and tall. With much anger, she led her team of women through the town and toward the waterfront warehouses utilized by local sugar and banana planters. The women were tired of being made to work fourteen hours a day, seven days a week. Julie and her strikers were not unreasonable women as they easily understood the concerns and worries of their rich masters. Why, they could even go so far as being sympathetic toward their masters' current economic predicament. Their livelihoods and the livelihoods of hundreds of islanders were at stake. But forcing people to work on the day of the Sabbath was a mortal sin against God. There must be restitution. Julie was not going to tolerate blasphemy.

A long, thin cigar hung from the corner of Julie's mouth as she announced that the carrier women were on strike. This was unhappy news for those who relied on the help of these women of invaluable commodity. Julie knew it. She enjoyed her power. The thought of driving these greedy white men to their knees was exhilarating. The women began singing songs of protest.

*   *   *

All morning, disturbing news poured into Governor Louis Mouttet's office from St. Pierre with reports of retreating passenger and cargo ships, ant and centipede invasions, lava flows, displaced villagers, and food shortages. Governor Mouttet summoned his principal secretary, Edouard L'Heurre, to his office. L'Heurre had just arrived from his annual vacation from the south side of the island. Upon his return, the principal secretary was surprised to learn of St. Pierre's chaos. Postings he had received from Mouttet during his absence had led him to believe that all was well up north and that the volcano was presenting only minor problems to the area. L'Heurre was not fond of his new boss. It had been seven months of questionable behavior. He felt that Mouttet lacked the diplomatic skills necessary to handle the sensitive problems on Martinique. He believed that the governor was too self-indulgent.

"Edouard, take a look at this report from the prison governor of St. Pierre. A riot took place there yesterday. Fortunately, it didn't take long for the prison guards to get the situation under control. Those prisoners responsible for this uprising are to be issued no less than fifty lashes of the *bastonnade*. Ciparis must be kept safe from harm's way. That Negro is still my ace in the hole for the election. It is your duty to travel to St.

Pierre. Please make clear to the prison governor that Ciparis is to be kept under close guard."

"Yes, sir."

Thirty-year-old L'Heurre saluted his superior and clicked the heels of his highly polished shoes. He was a man fiercely dedicated to his mother country and an officer who made wise use of protocol. As a result, he was trusted by both the Progressives and the Radicals.

Mouttet knew about L'Heurre's righteous qualities and was careful as to what was said and done around his principal secretary. The governor's political schemes, especially those involving André, would have been considered too unethical for L'Heurre.

"Before you leave, L'Heurre, I want you to take this message right away to our telegraph office. Make sure it gets off immediately."

As soon as L'Heurre was in the privacy of his own office, he took the liberty of opening the sealed message addressed to the minister of colonies, Pierre Louis Decrais, at the government office in Paris, to review its contents. Mouttet's vague telegram read,

> ERUPTION OF MONT PELÉE HAS TAKEN PLACE. STOP. LARGE
> QUANTITIES OF ASH SHOWERED NEIGHBORING COUNTRYSIDE.
> STOP. INHABITANTS ABANDON DWELLINGS PRECIPITATELY AND
> SEEK REFUGE IN ST. PIERRE. STOP. ERUPTION APPEARS TO BE ON
> THE WANE. STOP. YOURS TRULY. STOP GOVERNOR LOUIS MOUTTET

This would be the first official statement regarding the eruption. The message omitted any mention of the true crisis; any mention of the unofficial Governor's Commission; any mention of loss of life; any mention of the primary results; any mention of the rioting, looting, and hunger; any mention of the devastation of the crops and the villagers; any mention of the floods, fires, and lava flows.

*   *   *

"Since the volcano has been quiet for the past few hours, it is evident that the crater is behaving as it did in 1851," said Louis Mouttet, verbalizing what he was recording by ink and quill in his private diaries.

He tapped a fountain pen against the side of his head in a moment of indecision. To validate his lies, Mouttet wrote more distortions of the truth. He felt confident that somehow his current troubles would soon end and everything would be normal again, the volcano to be damned.

*   *   *

Realizing that their animals could be in jeopardy with so many hunger-crazed people around, Yvette and Indigo hired two soldiers to escort them and their horses out of town as far as the Roxelane River. They were right. The refugees stared wistfully at the mare and stallion; horsemeat was considered a delicacy. Inspiration pulled his ears back, sensing danger. Yvette tried to reassure him, but the reassurance did little good as menace was in the air.

The soldiers accompanied Yvette and Indigo along a little used route near a poor section of town. They had stopped briefly to rest on top of a small knoll when they heard desperate cries for help. Much to their horror, dozens of poisonous snakes slithered down the street just below them. No different from onslaught of the ants and centipedes, these reptiles had been driven from their sheltered jungle homes by the heat of the lava flow at the base of the mountain. The fer-de-lances stretched five to six feet in length from the tip of their heads to the tip of their tails. They moved quickly, intertwining and crawling over one another in a frantic attempt to get to safety. The unfamiliarity of the town caused the agitated reptiles to strike and bite anything unfortunate to be in their way. A deadly situation was just about to unfold.

The first victim was a three-year-old mulatto boy. Seven of the snakes plunged their fangs into his thighs and buttocks. It took only seconds for the icy poisons to burn through his veins, dissolving the flesh from his bones. Several soldiers shot at the coiling, wiggling, and twisting invaders. Gunfire echoed throughout the district. As soon as the soldiers took control of the situation, a crowd gathered and curiously watched the ensuing battle between the flicking tongues of the fer-de-lances and the rounds of ammunition hailing from the military muskets. It seemed that every time the soldiers fired upon the front ranks of the red-eyed vipers, twice as many more slithered in from behind. The parade of snakes seemed endless.

Then the feral cats arrived.

There is no greater enemy of the fer-de-lance than that of the cat. The soldiers stepped back and smiled. The people stepped forward and smiled. What was about to happen would be more fun than witnessing a cockfight. Yvette and Indigo watched in morbid fascination.

Each cat selected its quarry and crouched down just short of striking range. Ears pushed back and eyes narrowed. The felines began to hop, bob, and prance like a synchronized dance team around the snakes. This comical ballet stopped as fast as it started. For a few seconds, nothing moved—animal, reptile, or human. Soon the snakes grew weary of the taunting and hissed in protest. Sensing imminent danger, each snake wrapped its lower body into a coil with the upper portion pushed up and ready in striking position. The cats—leaping in acrobatic unison and crying out in a high-pitched symphony of meows—landed on the startled reptiles.

The first stage of the battle had been completed.

Tails switching, the cats backed away and studied their battered trophies. Replacing the snake's clawed-out eyes were bloodied holes. The reptiles were blind and confused. A few minutes of motionless silence passed before the agile cats pounced once again. Sharp teeth sunk deeply into the soft vertebras of the fer-de-lances. The reptile invasion was over. All the snakes were dead, along with fifty people, two hundred horses, and numerous goats and dogs.

*   *   *

Aroused from his drunken stupor by gunfire and screams, André stumbled away from his feather-tick mattress and out the door of his St. Pierre dwelling. His head hurt, and his stomach churned from all the rum he had downed the night before. He couldn't believe his eyes. Was that Yvette and Indigo standing less than two hundred feet in front of him? Yes, and it appeared that they were with two soldiers. André had carried his bowie outside with him during the commotion; as he studied the two quadroon women whom he hated to the depth of his immoral soul, he caressed the knife's finely honed steel edge.

"Hey, what is going on?" asked a young voice behind André.

"Nothing," said André, turning to a sleepy-eyed boy of sixteen. "Hurry up, *mon chér*. I want you to start rounding up our lads in St. Pierre. Notify Louis to reach as many members as possible in Fort-de-France, Le Lamentin, St. Joseph, Trois-Îlets, and Gros Morne. Spread the word that we will gather here tomorrow at two o'clock sharp. Our time has come."

With undying love in his light blue eyes, the boy responded with a raised left arm and the flash of a smile. André bent down and gave a more-than-friendly pat to the boy's naked backside and more than a brotherly kiss to the boy's lips.

*   *   *

The suffering of St. Pierre's people was taking a toll on Father Roche. Thirty of his beloved parishioners had expired within the last forty-eight hours and were now being prepared for burial. The fer-de-lances killed eighteen of his followers, sulfuric vapors suffocated eleven, and *la vérette* took the life of a sweet fifteen-year-old girl by the name of Sylvie.

Father Roche greatly feared la vérette.

He remembered during the late 1800s, when smallpox hit the island with such force, many of his followers died horrible deaths. Then the white population seemed immune from the deadly disease. Now, because of the unsanitary conditions brought about by the overcrowded town, a perfect breeding ground had been established; and no one was immune, including sweet Sylvie.

Sylvie's death especially grieved the priest. He had performed her baptism only fifteen years before. Had it been that long? How could it be possible that he was about to officiate at her funeral? Sylvie had been full of life and promise, a free-spirited soul, as lovely on the inside as on the outside, a good girl, a thoughtful girl. It pained him to cover her face and body with lime to prevent further spreading of the disease. After fighting the pox for three days, her flawless beauty had been scarred with blisters and pockmarks. Father Roche wrapped the body in banana leaves. Sylvie was ready to meet her maker.

An old mulatto woman, draped in veils of black, rocked back and forth upon a bench outside the church's preparation room. She wrung her hands and stomped her feet, protesting to her god for taking away her precious granddaughter. She wailed plaintively. It wasn't fair at all; why not her? She had lived a long life. Sylvie's grandmother began singing a song of heartache and hopelessness. Its sorrowful tune echoed sadly through the rafters of the church.

"Toutt bel bouis toutt bel moune ka alle!"

"All the beautiful trees are passing away!"

*   *   *

After the burials, Father Roche headed for his mountaintop observatory away from the chaotic climate of St. Pierre. No sooner had he reached the summit than the most startling event began to take place on Mont Pelée across the valley. The priest opened and closed and reopened his disbelieving eyes. For a second, he thought that they were playing tricks on him. In a state of wonder, he watched as the side of the mountain, at about the two-thousand-foot level, split open as high and as wide as a three-story building. Tons of lava mud burst from giant fissure at an alarming rate of speed. Hot steam bellowed from its bubbling surface. The thick waterfall of mud cascaded down the side of the vibrating volcano into the river below. It took only seconds for the molten flow to build up layer after layer until it rose above the earth one hundred feet in height and nearly a quarter of a mile in width. Roche's hand went to his chest in a hopeless move to calm his pounding heart. The monster forming in front of his eyes gently broke away in a sucking sound from the mountain. Pushing, buckling, rising up and over, folding and refolding, this mobile molten tower built up enough momentum to propel itself forward at an unbelievable pace of five miles per hour. It appeared alive as it headed west along the course of the river toward the coastline.

Father Roche splayed his hands as if to tell this thing of horror to stop. It didn't heed his pleas. Picking up velocity, the wall of lava mud rolled over rivers, jungles, and fields with the greatest of ease. Four miles away, dead center in its path of destruction stood the cliff-side sugar plantation, refinery, and villa belonging to the powerful Guerin family. It only took fifteen minutes for the wall of mud to reach the properties. Once there, it only hesitated a moment before it enveloped all that lay within its path. The top portion of the refinery chimney peeped up at an angle through the surface of the clay tomb. The lava flow continued its journey over the cliffs down onto the beach and into the sea, where it violently shoved the waters back from the coastline. The swiftness and completeness of the obliteration forced Father Roche to his knees. Two hundred people worked and lived at the Guerin properties, including refinery workers, field hands, servants, and fifty family members. Not one of them could have survived this holocaust, reasoned the priest. The family had to be at home making final preparations for their traditional holiday cruise to the Gare del' Est resort in Paris the very next day.

The priest crossed himself and wept.

* * *

Fernand Clerc was in a foul mood. The results of Sunday's primaries greatly offended and disappointed him. Along with the stupidity of the government, dealing with the carrier strike reportedly taking place in the area of his waterfront warehouses and docks was too much to bear in one day. He had no choice but to see if he could reason with this Julie Gabou. By the time he reached the harbor, the women were nowhere to be found. Clerc's dock foreman reported that the porteuse women had left more than an hour ago heading for the Guerin plantation, where they planned to continue their protests.

* * *

Julie Gavou was in her glory. Her brilliant speech at the Guerin plantation had inspired more workers to join her. Her talk of God's wrath against those who would dare work on the Sabbath was making an impact. Doom was imminent. She was right. For at that very moment the wall of lava mud swooped down upon Julie, her strikers, and their employers alike.

* * *

Fernand Clerc, exhausted and unaware of the tragedy at the Guerin plantation, walked from his office through throngs of unruly people to a bench beneath a palm tree. He had to sit and calm his nerves. The warehouse area was conspicuously quiet. Other than a few displaced strangers and disgruntled dockworkers, no one was about. St. Pierre had always been such an idyllic port town; not anymore, Fernand concluded. He surveyed the ash-covered ships bobbing in the bay and wondered which was the worst cause of the ruination, the ravages of the volcano or the ravages of man?

A large wave hit the shore. It startled him. Another wave, larger and more powerful, followed the first. Fernand found this odd. The weather was void of wind. Curious, he walked to the water's edge. Without additional warning, the waves rolled in with such fury, causing the ships in the roadstead to violently pitch back and forth. Fernand stumbled backward after spotting a fifty-foot tidal wave rolling down the coastline from the north.

The elevated wall of water rode the curve of the shore, tearing apart everything it touched. By the time it reached the waterfront district, it had lost some momentum but still packed enough power to lift the wooden Italian *barques* up and out of their moorings and smash them like toy boats against the first row of harbor side buildings. Piers, warehouses, repair shops, and barrels of cargo exploded into unrecognizable piles of kindling.

*   *   *

Madam Rose was counting her take from Sunday. The daily deposit to the Bank of Martinique scheduled for Monday afternoon should be respectable. "Bless that damn old volcano," she chuckled as she sorted the paper money into three piles upon her desk. Business had never been this brisk. She looked up startled. The floorboards quivered beneath her feet, and the rum bottles on a cabinet shelf next to her desk rattled. "What now?" she mumbled. "Pray tell, is that noise thunder or another earthquake?" After a few seconds, she decided to ignore the distraction and continued counting her precious francs. It was probably another false alarm.

The prostitutes were fast asleep, exhausted from their sexual marathon of sixteen-hour days, seven days a week, for the last two weeks. Madame Rose had awarded all of them with Monday morning off, promising the girls undisturbed rest until three o'clock.

The noise grew louder, and the vibration stronger. The wall lamps in the office fell to the floor and shattered. More disturbed than alarmed, Madame Rose stowed her cash box in the safe, walked through the bar, and pushed open the front door of the saloon. She glanced outside to the left. All appeared normal. She looked to the right and her jaw dropped. Twenty feet away, a wall of water, as tall as her building, moved toward her. The unexpected magnificence and hypnotic effect of the wave was paralyzing. Her brain had no time to comprehend that she was experiencing her last breathing moments on earth as she desperately searched for a glimpse of the sky above the peak of the wave. The approaching horizontal panel of the water wall was flat and smooth, like that of a window. The blues and greens teased, pleased, and calmed the senses. This pleasurable sensation changed in a flash. Behind the crystal beauty of the fish-tank facade, Madame Rose could see a severed head, a donkey cartwheel, a splintered rum barrel, a black girl with red ribbons in her braids, a yellow cat with no tail, and the fifty-year-old blue sign from the local mercantile store. As the mass of water engulfed the brothel owner, as well as her establishment, Madame Rose's mind registered one last thought—her life was coming to an end.

*   *   *

Fernand Clerc was paying the price for his poor physical condition. Years of little exercise had made him soft. He wheezed, huffed, and puffed in an attempt to outrun the tidal wave rushing up behind him. By the time he reached the end of La Place Bertin, the majority of the people fleeing the water monster were well ahead of him. Unable to continue, Fernand fell to his knees and braced for certain death when he could not take the physical strain any longer.

Wails of hopelessness echoed along the shoreline from the workers.

"Nou ka mo toutt d'leua," they cried out in Creole. "We will all die of the water."

The waning tidal wave finally reached Fernand. It was only a few inches high as it gently swept around his wide girth and retreated, its fury spent. The planter uttered a prayer of thanks as he struggled to his feet. He faced the sea and searched the northern shoreline. The extent of the damage to the waterfront left him in shock. Boats lay splintered on the beach, masts ragged and torn, hulls cracked in half, crews from ships washed ashore drowned or critically injured, warehouses reduced to kindling wood.

Unknown to Fernand, Emile Le Curé, general manager of the English Colonial Bank, and two of his employees had drowned. Along the northern portion of Rue Victor Hugo markets, shops, and restaurants were underwater. Streets littered with dead bodies. In the poor section of town near the bay, shanties of tin shacks, banana and mango groves, ox carts, tethered goats and horses, coops of chickens, and plots of wilted gardens had completely washed away as if nothing had ever existed. All that remained was barren earth devoid of life.

*   *   *

Lunch at the Governor's Regency in Fort-de-France was taking place at approximately the same time the tidal wave hit St. Pierre. Around the table sat Mouttet's team of conspirators comprising the Governor's Commission. The members had just returned from the "discovery" trip and were reporting their observations of Mont Pelée. They, of course, never went to Mont Pelée for scientific evaluations; instead, the group had taken the easy and safe way out by going only as far as the botanical gardens to determine the effect of the ash on plant life. An eighteen-page report turned over to Mouttet was based on fabricated findings.

"It is of our opinion," said Deputy Governor Jules Gerbault, "that the current fallout of ash created by Mont Pelée is indeed toxic to plant life. However, it presents no more a threat to humans than the previous emissions of 1851. We cannot see where an evacuation of St. Pierre is warranted. The positioning of the volcano in relationship to the valley is such that the complete safety of the town is absolutely assured."

"Thank you, gentlemen," said Mouttet, winking in approval with food spilling out of the side of his mouth. "This is exactly what I wanted to hear. It should quench any cowardly cries for an evacuation." In between chews, he thanked the men for their good work.

Later that day, Governor Mouttet received a message of great urgency from the garrison commander of St. Pierre detailing the occurrence of the morning. He read the news of attacking snakes, mud avalanches, tidal waves, and mass destruction and death with minimal emotion.

"Another example of exaggerated hysteria," muttered Mouttet. "I shall have the garrison commander flogged for insubordination and needless dramatics. He has to be mistaken about the severity of the situation. Tomorrow I shall see for myself what is going on."

*   *   *

Andreus Hurard, in his newspaper office, dropped into his desk chair and buried his head in his arms. He had just returned from viewing the aftermath of the Guerin disaster and was still mulling over the magnitude of destruction he had just witnessed—the ruins of the waterfront, the exodus of the townspeople leaving the city with mattresses upon their heads, pots and valuables under their arms, and panic written upon their stunned faces. Guilt weighed heavily upon him as he reviewed the lies he had penned in the last few editions of *Les Colonies*. For the first time since the volcano stirred to life, the remorseful editor wrote objectively from his heart.

"As far as the eye can see it meets with nothing but a sea of motionless mud," he wrote to his readers for the next edition. "Nothing is left. Yes, over there is the chimney of the factory, slightly inclined. The refinery and outbuildings have gone down under the lava bed. It was but a moment ago, where a center existed of prosperity and activity for a world of workers. All gone now, swept out of life or into misery and ruin. Over this scene hangs the silence of annihilation broken only by muffled sounds of breaking puffs of steam. The spectators cannot shake off an indescribable feeling of anguish. How many human lives have been wiped out? How many fathers of families have gone forever? Will the exact number ever be known? The reality is far more terrible than anything imagined."

Hurard placed his pen down and pondered the eyewitness account given by Dr. Guerin's head overseer, Joseph de Quesne, who had been on a hill near the Guerin compound just seconds before the wall of lava mud appeared. He reported seeing Dr. Guerin and his wife at their estate trying to convince their son to evacuate the premises and join the family friends, the Moreguts, on their yacht in the bay below the cliff-side estate. No sooner had Mrs. Guerin won her argument with her son when the crest of the wall plopped down on top of them. As everyone around Dr. Guerin ran for their lives, he stood frozen in place, transfixed by the big bubbling brown giant gobbling up his land and his family. Moments later, he realized that his wife, Josephine; his sons, Eugene and Joseph; his daughter-in-law, Sarah; his English nurse, Mary Goodchild, from Lowestoft; two housemaids, Marie and CeCe from Dijon; and even the family cook, Georgette, had been buried alive in the boiling mire. The Moreguts and their fancy yacht also disappeared beneath tons of mud and debris. Miraculously the mud stopped short a few feet from where Dr. Guerin was standing. He was the only member of his family to survive. Dr. Guerin lapsed into a state of shock. The complete destruction of his life and loved ones was too much to bear. The mighty plantation owner, deep in shock, was carried into town by Joseph du Quesne and his first superintendent, Louis Clemencin.

That night, in the comfort of his brass bed, guilt-riddled Hurard continued to agonize over his false reporting in his newspaper. The nameless faces of Mont Pelée's most recent victims haunted him. There seemed to be a ghost to haunt him for each lie he had written in the past few weeks. These spirits of sorrowful souls would never allow him to be at peace in life or death.

32

St. Pierre, Martinique
Tuesday, May 6, 1902
Voodoo Revenge

Mont Pelée spewed up swirls of crimson fire from her glowing cone hundreds of feet into the nighttime skies shortly after midnight in the wee hours of Tuesday morning. It was just the prelude to a spectacular firework show of burning cinders that shot up into the heavens, only to be pulled down into a downpour over St. Pierre. Anything made of wood was torched. The citizens and soldiers of the town had grown so used to these nightly displays that they calmly doused the insignificant blazes, admired the brilliant light show, and went back to bed. A few hours later, the people were once again awakened, but this time to the eerie pounding of drums reverberating over the hills, across the valleys, and throughout the towns. The ominous sound signaled incoming quimboiseur sorcerers forewarning suffering, death, and the afterlife. For many who were undecided to stay or not to stay, this was the last straw; the continued activity of the volcano, along with the threat of hostile sorcerers, triggered a mass exodus out of St. Pierre.

* * *

Aza was buried next to Maxi in the family cemetery shortly before nine that morning; two fresh graves side by side for two dear friends. Father Roche was swamped with the illnesses and the deaths of his parishioners and therefore could not leave his church. It was up to Yébé to officiate. Marcel, Yvette, Indigo, Cyrillia, Stefan, Coralline, Henrillia attended at the graveside services. Yébé wove a tapestry of haunting

Creole words and Christian prayers over Aza's plain coffin. The hearts of those present were as gray as the ankle-deep ash on the ground.

*　　*　　*

Yébé returned to his hut. The tin of chicken bones was removed from a shelf holding a variety of voodoo paraphernalia. He knelt down upon a mat made of goat hair, dyed red from wild berries, and scattered the chicken bones. Yébé called forth the spirit of Mont Pelée. A blast of hot air swept into the hut. The spirit voice inside his head spoke in a stern, hollow voice. It told Yébé that for too long the people of the island had taken Pelée's gifts of bounty for granted, and now, the time had come to take that bounty away. The spirit cared deeply for the people who lived within its umbra; however, it was confused by their lackadaisical behavior by not heeding its warnings. Why did the people stay? Why was there still praying in the churches, gaiety in the bars, and business in the streets? It was only a matter of time before its final assault upon the island. Yébé gathered the bones and muttered a prayer. The spirit disappeared.

*　　*　　*

At 10:00 AM, the family gathered to exchange fond anecdotes about Aza. A comforting fire crackled in the fireplace, warming the nip from the crisp mountain air. In the midst of their eulogizing, they were interrupted by pounding against the front door. A travel-worn messenger boy from St. Pierre arrived with two handwritten notes. One was from Thomas Prentiss, and the other from Laurent Montour. Marcel tipped the boy five sou. Feeling grandly rich, the young messenger greedily seized his coins and galloped away.

"What is it, Papa?" asked Yvette.

"There is news about our shipment. Laurent has located an American captain who is willing to take on our cargo at a loss of 40 percent. We can't quarrel with that."

"Quand?"

"Tomorrow."

"So soon?"

"Yes. I will go into town today to make the necessary arrangements. Yvette, I need you to alert Félecien that as soon as the harvesting is completed, the crops must be crated and ready for transport into St. Pierre first thing tomorrow morning. This leaves him little time to prepare, but he should be able to handle it."

"What's the other message?" asked Indigo.

"According to Thomas, Governor Mouttet has issued orders that by four o'clock this afternoon, every route leaving St. Pierre will be blocked by soldiers. No one will be allowed to leave or enter St. Pierre. The soldiers have orders to shoot those who try. Several ships have pulled anchor. Many captains have left without their quota of cargo or scheduled passengers."

Indigo panicked. "How will this affect the arrival of my ship? Will it come in on Thursday morning as planned? Marcel, I won't stay here a minute past the time I am due to depart on Friday. If I have to climb the *mornes* by foot or steal a boat, I will."

"Indigo, dear girl, if for some reason the ship is unable to enter St. Pierre's roadstead, you will make your way to Fort-de-France and stay with Caroline and Roger until passage can be booked on another ship at a later date." He raised his hand up for everyone to be quiet. "Those voodoo drums could mean trouble. I'm posting armed guards around the property."

*   *   *

Upon arrival to St. Pierre, Marcel discovered a few brave ships still weighing anchor, much to his relief. Sitting grand and mighty in the ash-covered waters were the *Topaz, Orsolina, Pouyer-Quertier, Grappler, Biscaye, Tamaya, Quora Maria de Pompeii, Diamant, Bell Dawn, Fusee,* and the *R. J. Morse.* In the din of his office, Laurent Montour introduced Marcel to a stocky man with a thick curly black beard. The man was agitated and seemed in no mood to do business under the threat of an active island volcano.

"Marcel," said Laurent, "this is Captain Jeb Stewart of the American steamer, *Bell Dawn,* who is leaving port on Thursday morning. He has agreed to take on your cargo."

The American captain gnawed at a thumbnail. "We must have your product loaded onto the ship by tomorrow evening. I will not stay a minute past six o'clock in morning on Thursday in this godforsaken place. Is that perfectly clear?"

"Parfaitement."

A contract was signed and the American left.

Laurent pulled out a flask of whiskey and poured a generous amount into his coffee.

"I can't tell you what a pitiful mess it is around here, Marcel. The situation along the waterfront is grave. Many ships set sail at dawn with empty cargo hulls and staterooms. Their fears for the safety of their crews and the few passengers who somehow managed to get on board in time were greater than the risk of breaching their contracts and breaking maritime laws. We could get into legal trouble by loading your cargo early and negating the contracts already negotiated and signed with other shipping companies. I hope it is worth the risk."

Marcel made assurances and left for the American Regency. Once there, a servant escorted Marcel to the library, where Thomas, Clara, and René Cottrell were discussing matters at hand. Marcel was immediately concerned by Clara's unhealthy appearance.

René waved his hands after listening to Marcel rant. "You think you have problems with exporting your crops, Marcel? They are nothing compared to what I have to face."

Clara laughed at René's dramatics. "What is the matter, dear René?"

"It is in great fear that I must go to the de Jaunville estate this afternoon to convince my fiancé and the rest of her family to cancel plans to attend the Ascension Day ball tomorrow night. We are to publicly announce our engagement. I cannot allow us to go as it is not safe."

"So what is the problem?" asked Marcel.

"The de Jaunvilles are a very stubborn family. I dare say my suggestion will be met with an unwelcome response, especially from Colette." René placed his hand to his heart. "My darling will interpret my suggestions as selfish and mean. Of this I can assure you."

"Poor René," chided Thomas. "Colette's obstinacy is known far and wide. Are you sure you want to go through with this engagement thing? It's not too late, you know."

"It is true that Colette can be a handful. But I fear, I am hopelessly in love."

"René," asked Thomas with much seriousness, "as a member of the Families of Ten, is there anything you can to do to help persuade our government to evacuate those in danger?"

"I have tried. They refuse to address the subject. My people are set in their ways. The homeless are not included in their list of priorities. Such matters are an inconvenience. The Ten refuse to recognize the dangers at hand."

Clara spoke. "Father Roche is facing the same difficulties with the church. His pleas to the vicar-general have fallen upon deaf ears. The vicar-general does not want to supersede the state in these matters. If the situation worsens, the vicar-general may address the issue after the Ascension Day celebrations on Thursday as he feels that by that time, the people may be more responsive to an evacuation. It seems that no one really wants to take responsibility for the town and its people. And of course, God forbid, if the elections get postponed, it could spell political tragedy for both parties. I am afraid nothing can be done."

Marcel shrugged. "I have to admit that I too am not so sure that it is time to evacuate the town. I was under the impression that St. Pierre is a safe distance from Mont Pelée. Isn't that what Father Roche had been maintaining all along?"

"Father Roche has changed his mind," answered René. "The intense activities of the volcano during the last twenty-four hours indicate that a major eruption is imminent, and Fernand Clerc agreed."

Thomas took Clara's hand. "Listen to me very carefully, my dear. I must call upon you to take an urgent message to President Roosevelt. I cannot trust communications by any other means. Please. It is your duty, darling. There is no room for argument now."

Clara was quiet for a few seconds. "Very well, Thomas, when do I leave?"

"Don't be mad at me, but I have taken the liberty to book passage for you on the *Orsolina* bound for the United States on Thursday morning. Thank you for going." He kissed her hand.

Clara dabbed her eyes.

"Has anyone heard from James Japp?" asked Marcel. "I didn't see any activity at the British residence on my way into town. The Roxelane

River is overflowing its riverbanks, and flooding is worsening. Any way we can get to the poor man? He is a prisoner in his own home."

"Boverate stopped by earlier this morning with a satchel of documents earmarked for the British government," said Thomas. "His master has given up all hope for escape and forced the servant to save himself by swimming across the swollen river. There is no way a man of Japp's weight and age could endure those treacherous waters. Boverate was devastated to take leave of his master. He loves Japp like a father."

*　*　*

Around noon, Marcel and René bade good-bye to the Americans and headed by foot for the Cercle de St. Pierre, where they hoped to find Mayor Fouché and convince him to cancel Wednesday and Thursday's Ascension Day celebrations. A river of sludge flowed down every street and alleyway and made walking difficult. Searching for the source of the muck, Marcel spotted workmen washing off days of ash from the tops of the tile roofs with buckets of water.

"Hey," yelled Marcel to the workmen, "what the hell is going on up there?"

One of the men stopped mopping, pulled off his cap, and whacked it against the side of his leg. "The mayor has decreed that all rooftops in the city be washed off and readied for the holiday," he shouted back. He was having a hard time seeing through the bright sunlight and was getting tired of the same question being asked over and over again.

"You must stop this at once," ordered René. "Can't you see the mess you are making down here? The mayor may be getting clean rooftops, but the streets are impassable."

The workman walked to the edge of the roof. With a dirty hand shielding his eyes, he scanned the view below and was startled by clogged streets. Little did he realize that as soon as the ash mixed with the water, it turned into a thick paste running down the side of the building out onto the sidewalks, avenues, and gutters, gathering up disease-infested excrement, decayed corpses, and rotted garbage along the way. The sludge dried like plaster and stank of animal dung. Those who fell into the foul-smelling quagmire could not help but vomit.

"Je regrette, monsieur, une ordonnance de maire," shrugged the workman.

A few minutes later, Marcel and René joined a group of curious citizens reading a large poster. The ink was still wet. It was a public proclamation from the mayor, and it read,

EXTRAORDINARY PROCLAMATION TO MY FELLOW CITIZENS OF ST. PIERRE! THE OCCURRENCE OF THE ERUPTION OF MONT PELÉE HAS THROWN THE WHOLE ISLAND INTO COMPLETE CONSTERNATION. BUT, AIDED BY THE EXALTED INTERVENTION OF GOVERNOR MOUTTET AND OF SUPERIOR AUTHORITY, THE MUNICIPAL ADMINISTRATION HAS PROVIDED, IN SO FAR AS IT HAS BEEN ABLE, FOR DISTRIBUTION OF ESSENTIAL FOOD AND SUPPLIES. THE CALMNESS AND WISDOM OF WHICH YOU HAVE PROVED YOURSELVES CAPABLE IN THESE RECENT ANGUISHED DAYS ALLOW US TO HOPE THAT YOU WILL NOT REMAIN DEAF TO OUR APPEALS. IN ACCORDANCE WITH THE GOVERNOR, WHOSE DEVOTION IS EVER IN COMMAND OF CIRCUMSTANCES, WE BELIEVE OURSELVES ABLE TO ASSURE YOU THAT, IN VIEW OF THE IMMENSE VALLEYS, WHICH SEPARATE US FROM THE CRATER, WE HAVE NO IMMEDIATE DANGER TO FEAR. ANY FURTHER MANIFESTATION WILL BE RESTRICTED TO THOSE PLACES ALREADY AFFECTED. DO NOT, THEREFORE, ALLOW YOURSELVES TO FALL VICTIM TO GROUNDLESS PANIC. PLEASE ALLOW US TO ADVISE YOU TO RETURN TO YOUR NORMAL OCCUPATION, SETTING THE NECESSARY EXAMPLES OF COURAGE AND STRENGTH DURING THIS TIME OF PUBLIC CALAMITY.
MAYOR R. FOUCHÉ

René ripped the poster from the wall and tore it to shreds.

"What kind of madness is this? Has the mayor of St. Pierre lost his mind? There is no way I am going to allow Colette and her family to make a mockery of this tragic situation by partying like fools in the wake of death. This is one pomp and circumstance that will be losing its pomp. Colette will return to Fort-de-France with me tomorrow until things in St. Pierre are back to normal again. My decision is final."

"I think everyone has taken leave of their senses, my friend," said Marcel.

By the time Marcel and René reached the Cercle de St. Pierre, Mayor Fouché had returned to this office busily working on the final preparations for Wednesday's ball.

"I don't get it, Marcel," said René. "What is going on? It seems all that is on the minds of the town's politicians, socialites, and businessmen are celebrations, balls, and elections. Why aren't we getting disaster relief? Why isn't the government of France or the governments of other nations intervening? We are desperately in need of housing, food, medicine, and clothing for the homeless and sick. I don't get it. Is the world not aware of what is happening here?"

*   *   *

The world was *not* aware. Governor Mouttet had seen to it that Martinique had been cut off from all outgoing communications. How could aid and help be offered when no one knew what was going on? Governor Mouttet wasn't the only culprit masking the truth about Mont Pelée. A short fifty miles away from Martinique, the volcano Soufrière on the island of St. Vincent had gone into full eruption. An immediate evacuation of the area had been carried out with daily reports sent to news agencies through Europe and the United States. Ironically, none of these agencies had been notified of Martinique's catastrophe. Soufrière's ash fallout spanned out over a three-hundred-mile radius around St. Vincent, thus camouflaging Mont Pelée's ash fallout. While the eyes of the world were focused on the events at Soufrière on St. Vincent, the events at Mont Pelée on Martinique went unnoticed.

*   *   *

Yvette spent the balance of Tuesday morning helping harvest the bananas in the east field. The hard labor helped keep her troubled mind occupied. By two o'clock, most of the partially ruined crops had been harvested. Félecien assured her that he and his men would have the bananas crated, loaded, and ready on time. Yvette returned to the plantation house to change her clothes and wash up. She joined Indigo and Cyrillia in the kitchen. Henrillia served them hot homemade bread and a mutton soup called *pâte en pot*. After her traumatizing experience with the centipedes and ants, and the loss of her nanny, Cyrillia had been unusually quiet. She sighed a lot and toyed with her food.

"Maman, où est Aza?"

"Aza has gone to heaven."

"Où est ciel?"

"Heaven is not far away. Why, I bet Aza is watching over us right now as we speak."

Cyrillia craned her head toward the ceiling.

"Allô, Aza!"

Indigo and Yvette could not help but grin at the innocence of the child.

Indigo rose from the table. "I think it is time for a nap. How about you, Yvette?"

"In a little bit. You two go on up and get some rest."

Sounds of drums and intonations of singing echoed from the direction of the workers' compound. Although the Chevalier workers weren't as radical in their voodoo practices as some of those in town, they were, however, a superstitious lot easily spooked. Yvette decided to pay them a visit to comfort their fears.

"Where are you going?" asked Stefan.

"To the workers' compound," she answered while saddling up Inspiration.

Stefan saddled up a horse for himself.

"What are you doing?"

"I'm going with you."

"That isn't necessary."

"Of that, I know, Mademoiselle Chevalier. I cannot allow you to go alone."

* * *

There was an eager turnout of white boys. On short notice, André's trusted friend, Louis, managed to round up and deliver twenty-five of the organization's fifty members to the St. Pierre headquarters. The boys, along with Louis, were mesmerized by André's every move.

André toyed with his bowie.

"Who are we?"

"Whites for whites!"

"Why whites for whites?"

"Purity! Justice! Control!"

André held out the palm of his hand. The tip of his knife was dragged along the skin from his thumb to his little finger. The boys gasped. At first nothing happened. Then slowly, very slowly, blood seeped out of the self-inflicted wound. The boys whispered in disbelief as a tiny pool of blood formed on the floor by their leader's feet. Louis grinned.

"Can you believe it?"

"He didn't flinch."

"Didn't it hurt? It had to hurt. Didn't it?"

André broke into a rare smile.

He handed the boy nearest him the bloodstained knife and nodded. The twelve-year-old looked at the knife and then looked at André. Did he really expect him to do that too? Surely not. André nodded again. The boy turned to his comrades for support. He was met with expressions of disbelief. André was becoming impatient. The boy with the knife knew he had better do something—and do it fast. He held his breath and gritted his teeth as the knife teased through his flesh. It wasn't a deep cut, but it did bleed. And gosh, it didn't even hurt that much.

In unison the others shouted, "Victory to you, brother."

A few of the recruits ran away in a panic. They wanted no part of this.

"Let them go," ordered André. "To hell with them all, I say. Now, lads, show me your courage. Show me your blood. Show me your courage."

The remaining boys made cuts and displayed them with manly pride. André handed out a roll of gauze. The boys wrapped their wounds. "Tonight we strike. With so much confusion going on in the streets, no one will ever realize what is happening. Our targets are the blacks and mulattoes. The women of color are the most important. These are the witches who can birth more niggers. One hundred francs for every ten of these roaches will be rewarded.

The boys let out a war whoop. One hundred francs! Why, they would kill their own mothers for less. And André knew it.

*   *   *

Marcel had little knowledge of his son's underground political activities other than rumored involvements with the Progressive Party. He truly did not care what André did or did not do. As far as he was concerned, his son was no longer his responsibility. Marcel was glad that André spent the majority of this time in St. Pierre and away from the plantation and Yvette.

About five minutes outside of the St. Pierre city limits, Marcel approached a barricade in the road where Fernand Clerc and an unhappy group of citizens waved fists at unflinching border soldiers standing guard at the blockade.

"You have no cause to stop us."

"Allow us through."

"We have rights."

Marcel brought his horse alongside Fernand's carriage.

"Qu'est-ce qui c'est?"

"The governor has issued an order that no one is allowed to leave St. Pierre. He is afraid that if too many leave the town, it will, in turn, cause mass hysteria; and everyone else will want to evacuate. That would spoil the elections."

At that moment, a thunder of galloping hoofs and squeaking wheels, government horses and carriages, approached from behind them. The excited driver of the first carriage shouted, "Please make way . . . for officials." The soldiers on guard pulled aside the barricade in great haste and saluted as the entourage of carriage horses kicked up clouds of ash and dust in passing.

"You people are more like clowns than government representatives," shouted Fernand, agitated. He turned to Marcel. "I want you to know that Father Roche and I are in complete agreement that it is only a matter of time before the mountain erupts. A slow and deliberate evacuation of people into safety camps needs to be implemented immediately."

"You are the Progressive Party's candidate, Fernand, can't you do something? Won't you do something?"

"I tried. Believe me I have tried. This morning I pleaded with Hurard to print the truth and warn the people of the dangers of the volcano—especially after yesterday's disasters and loss of lives. He interpreted my actions as a concession to the Radicals. He reminded

me that my foremost duty was to promote the elections. I left him in
the middle of his lecture and slammed the door shut on my way out. I
then made my way to Mayor Fouché's office hoping to reason with him.
The mayor said that he had no time to discuss such trivia. He was too
occupied with the seating arrangements of his guests at tomorrow's
banquet. Can you believe it?"

"So what do we do, Fernand?" asked Marcel.

"I for one am going home. I shall prepare my family to be ready to
leave at a moment's notice. All I care about now is the safety of Veronique
and the children. When my barometer tells me we are in imminent
danger, I shall depart at once for our plantation in Vivé on the east coast.
There is nothing more I can do for the people of St. Pierre—nothing. It
is time for me to think of my family."

Marcel and Fernand confronted the soldiers who refused to allow
them to pass through the barrier. The plantation owners were warned
that they would be shot if they tried. Marcel and Fernand ignored the
commands and broke through. The stunned soldiers did nothing.

*   *   *

Yvette and Stefan tethered their horses at the workers' compound.
They were amazed at what they found within the perimeter. Standing
on a chair at the end of an elongated circle was Yébé. His spindly legs
worked hard to keep him in balance. Inside the circle, three women
bounced up and down, twisting and turning, reaching and pulling to
the sounds of the drums. Yébé stretched his hands out over the heads
of his people and cried out to the voodoo spirits.

"The great mountain has taken away the crops," he groaned. "The
Zaka Mede, loa of the seeds that grow, please help us in our time of
need."

One woman tore off her blouse and flung herself to the ground while
a junior voodoo priest held a live chicken by its legs and whacked off its
head with a machete. Yvette rushed into the circle just as the gyrating
woman was being anointed with the blood of the chicken.

"Stop!"

Yébé stepped down. The worshipers froze.

"Don't you fret, Missy Yvette. It *be* a good thing we do to protect us all from the mountain and from de voodoo quimboiseurs. We fear they come for the child with the hair of red. The quimboiseurs want her as the sacrifice for the mountain. We must stop them with our good voodoo."

The men and women and children who worked the fields at the Chevalier plantation politely smiled at their pretty mistress. They understood that she had their best interests at heart, but they also knew that she did not understand the power of the spirit of the great mountain. An old lady began singing a Creole song. The melody was rich in hope.

Yvette apologized for interrupting their private religious ceremony.

"Let's go," said Stefan, guiding her back to where their horses awaited.

He helped her onto Inspiration's back, grabbed the reins, and led her up the path toward their secret place. Yvette didn't protest, and for the life of her, she didn't know why. Fifteen minutes later, they were surrounded by the unmarred brilliance of a healthy tropical forest. Yvette curiously watched as Stefan jumped off his horse and began gathering armfuls of delicate yellow *alamandas* and pink hibiscus creating a floral mattress by the edge of brook.

"What are you doing?" she asked.

He said not a word as he lifted her off Inspiration and placed her upon the cushion of freshly picked blossoms. The aromatic sweetness of the fragrances was dizzying. Stefan removed his clothes and knelt naked beside her. He placed a calloused hand upon her cheek.

"Under normal circumstances, I wouldn't dream of touching you, but these are not normal circumstances. We may all die soon. We may not. I will be damned if I pass up the chance of going to my grave without having loved you. I want you. You need only to say no, and it shall end here and now. I promise to honor your wishes."

She tried to think. She tried to reason. The power of desire was overriding the ethical and moral codes of society. Stephan's hand had not left her cheek. His black eyes watched intently as she tried to make up her mind. She knew he was waiting for her to surrender to the lust that had been building up for months. Yvette placed her hand on top of his, and they fell back together against the bed of flowers. He unbuttoned her top. He kissed her lips. She closed her eyes. She heard the birds singing, the wind blowing through the trees, and the water running through the brook. She ran her hands over his muscular arms down the crevice of his back and over his tight buttocks. His kisses moved down her neck and to her golden breasts.

"Oh my sweetness," he sang out.

*   *   *

René Cottrell was a broken man. Nothing was going right, and he didn't know what to do. It was late as he made his way back to his uncle's villa after spending hours arguing with Colette's parents about postponing the engagement. Their protests still hammered in his head.

"It is protocol, René."

"This is not how things are done, René."

"There are the Families of Ten rules to be followed."

"Involve ourselves with the government? It's outrageous!"

"The volcano is not our problem, René."

"Evacuation or not, we must do things in order."

"Your engagement is a major social event, René."

"It is one that takes precedence over all other concerns."

"Invitations have already been sent and acknowledged."

"Are you an expert on volcanoes, René?"

"Did not the mayor and governor endorse the people's safety?"

"Postpone the engagement party? No!"

Colette had stomped out of the room yelling something about how René was spoiling all her fun and plans. And because of him, she would not get to wear her new party gown. Under the burning eyes of her parents, he was asked to leave.

*   *   *

Most everyone at the government building had left for home with the exception of the principal secretary, Edouard L'Heurre, who remained behind to work in his office. He just left a heated meeting with the governor. Mouttet had been in a terrible rage over a telegram posted by Senator Amédee Knight in care of Minister of Colonies Pierre Albert

Decrais. Somehow, the telegram had slipped by the Fort-de-France telegraph watchdogs and had found its way to Paris.

VOLCANIC ERUPTION DESTROYED LIVELIHOOD OF PRECHÊUR POPULATION. STOP. EXCLUSIVE COMPOSED OF SMALL HOLDERS. STOP. CROPS AND LIVESTOCK DESTROYED ALONG WITH FACTORY. STOP. OVERSEAS ACT OF HUMANITARIAN HELP WOULD PRODUCE DESIRABLE RESULTS FOR ENTIRE POPULATION. STOP. I REQUEST YOU MENTION MY INTERVENTION IN CABLE REPLY. STOP.

SENATOR AMÉDEE KNIGHT

L'Heurre pitied the naïveté of Senator Knight. It was obvious that Knight felt by sending this urgent telegram for humanitarian reasons, he would then be ingratiating his position not only with the good people of Martinique, but the leaders in Paris as well. It was well-known within the tight political circles of the whites that Minister of Colonies Pierre Albert Decrais was a racist who decreed his dislike for Negroes. Amédee mistakenly brought his humanitarian pleas to the wrong man. Decrais did not respond to Knight; however, he did very quickly respond to Governor Mouttet.

KINDLY KEEP ME INFORMED OF ERUPTION. STOP. PARTICULARLY LET ME KNOW NAMES OF VICTIMS HAVING RELATIVES IN FRANCE. STOP. WILL CABLE HELP AS SOON AS RESOLUTION CARRIED. STOP. YOU AND SENATOR KNIGHT CONVEY TO POPULATION SYMPATHY OF GOVERNMENT. STOP. NOT HAVING ANY CREDIT FOR AID PURPOSES AT MY DISPOSAL. STOP. SEEK INTERVENTION INTERIOR AND AGRICULTURE FOR REFUGEES OF MONT PELÉE. STOP. I HAVE PARTICULARLY PRESSED MY COLLEAGUES FOR ALLOCATION FUNDS. STOP. I WILL CABLE WHEN DECISION IS TAKEN. STOP.

PIERRE LOUIS ALBERT DECRAIS

Shortly after receiving this telegram, Governor Mouttet departed by carriage to St. Pierre to see for himself that his orders blocking anyone from leaving the town were executed. No one was to leave without his permission. Upon his return from St. Pierre, a meeting was called with the principal secretary. The governor could not understand why everyone was in such a panic in St. Pierre. Yes, it had been tragic that the Guerins and others had lost their lives in the tidal wave, but it could have been worse—much worse. He handed L'Heurre a reply telegram to be sent to Minister of Colonies Pierre Albert Decrais in Paris. Mouttet explained in his telegram that his Governor's Commission concluded that the lava-mud wall responsible for destroying the Guerin plantation had released enough pressure to render Mont Pelée harmless. To prove the validity of this report and the safety of the situation, the governor would fearlessly attend the annual Ascension Day celebrations in St. Pierre.

Edouard L'Heurre was convinced of Mouttet's lunacy. The telegraph from the governor to the minister of colonies had no sooner reached Paris than an earthquake destroyed the major telegraph link with St. Lucia. There were no telegraph services on the island. Martinique was completely isolated. Governor Mouttet didn't care.

"I have all the proof I need to show the people of St. Pierre that they are safe from the volcano," insisted Mouttet, waving the Governor's Commission report in L'Heurre's face.

"But, sir, how can you make such guarantees?"

"I have it on good authority."

"On whose authority?" L'Heurre challenged.

"Professor Landes."

"Professor Landes is not an expert on volcanoes."

"I'll hear no more. I intend to send a copy of this report to Hurard at *Les Colonies*. It will be rewritten as a personal interview with Landes. No one will know the difference."

"Is Landes aware of your plans?"

"He won't care."

"But it is a lie."

"It is the truth."

"But Professor Landes did not give such an interview."

"He contributed to the report. Why should he mind if we turn his findings into an interview? You worry too much. Now please leave me be."

An hour later, Edouard L'Heurre continued to stew in his office. He was miserable. He poured himself a shot from a bottle of whiskey he had taken from the bar cabinet in the Regency lounge. The principal secretary was not one to indulge, but Mouttet was driving him to drink.

*   *   *

Close to midnight, St. Pierre resembled a battlefield more than a pretty Caribbean port city. Driven by starvation, the homeless had gone to extremes to survive. Mothers prostituted their daughters for food. The municipal police and soldiers were ill equipped to handle the high volume of violent crimes. Smallpox was spreading. Hospitals, doctors, nurses, soldiers, and the clergy could not keep up with medical needs. Burning cauldrons of smoking tar lined the town and waterfront areas in a futile attempt to purify the air of plague.

*   *   *

The prisoner, Ciparis, blessed his great fortune. It was unheard of for a man of color to be granted an order of protection by the governor of the island. Ciparis did not know why he received this pardon, nor did he care. No more gallows to worry about. He praised God, shouted halleluiahs, and chuckled so hard he strained his stomach muscles. His elation ended when the whistling from the mountain began. He covered his ears with his big hands and looked out of the tiny barred window of his solitary cell as the volume of the noise increase. The sky was on fire; even the clouds were ablaze. He stumbled backward to the corner of the underground holding pen and began to pray. Ciparis had escaped the death sentence of man, but he wasn't certain that he would escape the death sentence of Mont Pelée.

*   *   *

André and his boys left headquarters at one o'clock in the morning. Armed with knives, clubs, and ropes, they followed the sounds of drums coming from the direction of Pont Basin.

"It is the quimboiseurs," said André. "These are very bad human beings, for the quimboiseurs refuse to recognize the leadership and the rules of the French whites, let alone those of their own race. Wait until they are below us and then surround them. You must be quiet and you must be fast. They must not realize what is happening until it is too late. I will stay here and watch. I want to determine your worthiness. Don't let me down."

What André did not realize was many sorcerers had lost family and friends over the past few days. They were crazed with grief, blaming the white man and his church for the awakening of the volcano. Like André, they were on a rampage seeking revenge.

The quimboiseurs hesitated in a cross section of two side streets. Their torches cast a yellow glow against the walls of the stone buildings. Silhouetted in this glow were elongated shadows jumping, dancing, twirling, and swaying. The pounding of the drums was feverish, loud, and rash. Angry chants increased the cacophony. They beckoned the dead to rise from their graves and bring harm to those who had caused Mont Pelée's discontent.

The women removed their clothes indicating the discarding of bad luck. They began to mimic the movements of animals: swaying, crawling, prancing, barking, stretching, flapping, and slithering. Overtaken by an invisible spirit, one woman screamed, grabbed her sweat-drenched breasts, and threw herself facedown to the ground. Pounding her pelvis hard against the ash-covered cobblestone street, she mumbled incomprehensible words and moaned with sexual pleasure.

Ah," said the grand wizard of the group, "loa Danbala Wedo, the spirit snake, rides her."

The quimboiseurs watched with excitement as the spirit snake took over her gyrating body; this was a good sign. She sang out a high-pitched note of ecstasy, relaxed, rolled onto her back, and spread her legs. Cheers of approval resounded. The voodooist's prayers had been answered.

A live baby goat was brought forth. Earlier in the day, the animal had been bathed and perfumed and readied to be accepted as an honorable sacrifice to the Gran Mèt. The goat bleated in a hopeless effort to free itself from its captors. In an instant, a chorus of knives plunged into its throat. Tin cups caught the warm blood. The sorcerers drank the liquid with much eagerness. Once the sacrifice was completed, they continued with to their macabre march.

André sent his boys to circle and attack. The people of the town would later thank him.

The older boys, armed with knives, singled out their victims with nary a sound. Throats were slashed, bellies gutted, and necks strangled. One boy snatched an attractive black girl and dragged her into the shadows. With the commotion of the singers, drums, and the shrill whistling of Mont Pelée, her screams went unnoticed as he brutally raped her. When the boy finished his criminal act, he picked up a brick and smashed her head.

It didn't take long for the quimboiseurs to realize what was happening. One of them snatched a white boy and dangled him in the air for a few seconds before snapping his neck as if he were snapping the neck of a chicken. André's recruits, outnumbered and no match against the strength and agility of the sorcerers, were rounded up and savagely executed. The boy who had raped and killed the girl was castrated and left to die.

Frenzied by the vicious attacks upon them by the white boys, the quimboiseurs went completely out of control with rage and headed toward the Cathedral of St. Pierre. Once there, they desecrated the doors of the church with blood. They then made their way to the Mouillage Cemetery, where they used their voodoo to call upon the dead to rise and join the fight.

André collapsed to his knees and pounded the ground with his fists in defeat. His boys were either dead, dying, or in hiding. Wisps of ash flew about his head. He was alone. All was lost, his little army destroyed. There was nothing more for him to do now except go home to the Chevalier plantation and finally take care of the demons of his past. He raised his left arm high in the air as he mourned the butchered boys lying in the street below.

"Whites for whites," he said for one last time.

33

St. Pierre, Martinique
Wednesday, May 7, 1902
Tongues Licking the Sky

It was two o'clock Wednesday morning. The terrified citizens and the homeless of St. Pierre hid from the quimboiseurs behind locked doors, under benches and blankets, on top of roofs, in between boxes and crates. There would be no rest. The timbre of a city locked in desperation included many elements. Echoing through the roadways and alleyways were plaintive howls of strays, whimpering of hungry children, and an occasional terrifying shriek from a victim of rape or murder. Most annoying was the deep sucking sound created by people and horses fighting the quicksand grip of the knee-high sludge clogging the streets.

André whipped the neck of his frightened horse and kicked its sides with the heels of his boots. The animal, uneasy with the thick mud, shied as a myriad of hidden objects nicked its legs. By the time André and his steed had reached the outskirts of town, they were covered from head to toe in muck. Silhouetted in the glow of the flames licking the sky, the ghostly horse and rider created a supernatural sight.

The people of the land knew that zombies worshipped volcanic fires called *mauvais difé* or evil flames. They also knew that the zombies existed as the fires. Cries of zombie warnings tore through the already noise-cluttered air of St. Pierre. Do not look at the fires; they will lure you, they will make you follow, and they will lead you to the zombies. No one knows what the zombie is. It can take many forms. It can fool you. It can be a sweet little old lady. It can be a cute puppy. It can be a pretty girl. It can be a harmless moth. Beware . . . take no chance, for if you wander within its reach, no power can save you. All is lost. Your soul is gone. You will no longer be of this earth. You will be of the walking dead.

Sunrise was three hours away. Other than the skies illuminating a blackish red above the road to Morne Rouge, the night was pitch-black save for a sliver of light from the waning moon and the light of the torches from those few who were brave enough, or fraught enough, to flee the city. André edged around a group of weary foot travelers on their way to Fort-de-France. They held up their torches curious to see who was passing by on horseback and were taken aback by the ghastly sight that loomed over them. Dropping their eyes to the road, they quickly crossed themselves. This stranger of the night upon a horse of clay must surely be the father of all zombies—a life-size version of one of their carnival papier-mâché evil spirits called *bois*.

The people talked in dreaded whispers.

"It is the zombie."

"Its eyes are glowing."

"Do they not light up like the embers of fire?"

"Yes! Yes, they are glowing."

"Hush now."

"Stop that nonsense."

"It is only your imagination."

"It is only a man."

"I believe it is the son of Marcel Chevalier."

"It is! It is!"

"No, it cannot be André Chevalier."

"A zombie has stolen his form to fool us."

"Something that hideous cannot be made of flesh and blood."

"Turn away! Do not look into the eyes of the devil."

*   *   *

Andreus Hurard completed the finishing touches on the most brilliant newspaper work of his entire life. It was a masterpiece of creative writing as well as a masterpiece of word magic, sleight of hand, yellow journalism, and blatant propaganda. The moment Governor

Mouttet promised vast financial rewards and favors for publishing a fake interview with Professor Landes in the next issue of *Les Colonies*, Hurard's remorse over Monday's fatal lava mudflow and tidal wave vanished. Hurard was given implicit instructions by the governor to make Wednesday's issue of the paper sound as if the volcano was on the wane and not a threat to the people of St. Pierre. It was hoped that the feigned article would create a public calmness to last through Sunday, May 11, when the final elections were scheduled to be held. The interview read:

> *M. Landes, the distinguished professor at the Lycee, was kind enough to give us an interview yesterday on the subject of the volcanic eruption of Mont Pelée and of the phenomena, which preceded the catastrophe at the Guerin factory.*
>
> *At five o'clock in the morning, M. Landes saw torrents of smoke escaping from the upper section of the mountain at the spot known as Terre Fendue. He noticed that the Blanche River was swelling to a volume five times greater than that of its greatest known rising . . . M. Landes, who was then in the Perrinelle settlement, went to Etang Sec at ten minutes before one o'clock . . . Later on, it appeared to M. Landes that a new opening existed at the foot of Morne Lenard . . .*

The article charted the fictitious route used by Professor Landes. It reported that the professor had climbed all the way up the side of the volcano to peer into its crater. In actuality, it would have been impossible for any living soul to make their way across rivers of molten lava, through clouds of poisonous gases, enduring temperatures hot enough to instantly set human hair on fire. Professor Landes ventured no farther than the botanical gardens the morning of his supposed expedition to Mont Pelée. And by early afternoon, he was lunching in comfort with the governor back in Fort-de-France.

The Landes interview wrapped up as follows:

> *In conclusion, Mont Pelée is no more to be feared by St. Pierre than Vesuvius is feared by Naples.*

Andreus Hurard ran a separate editorial to guarantee Governor Mouttet's insane propaganda that would put the lives of thirty thousand trusting citizens at stake. Satan himself could not have done a better job. It read,

> We confess that we cannot understand the panic. Where could one be better off than in St. Pierre? Do those who are invading Fort-de-France imagine that they would be safer there than here in case of an earthquake? This is a foolish mistake. It is necessary to put the people on their guard against it. We hope the opinion expressed by M. Landes in the interview we published will be convincing to those who are most afraid.

*   *   *

André slipped by the soldiers and made his way to the Chevalier plantation, where he cut across the west fields toward his cottage. By doing this, he avoided the guards posted at the entrance to the main driveway. A month had passed since he had last seen his cottage. As soon as he lit the wick of the lantern, rats and mice scurried out of sight. Nothing had been touched: his bed was still unmade, dirty dishes were still piled in the basin, cigarette butts and ashes still marred the table, and empty rum bottles still cluttered the floor.

Five easels, each with a work in progress, faced a large window to the north. Although disturbing in subject, the canvasses displayed an accomplishment of technique and color. André gathered a palette of oils, a can of clean brushes, and a stool. Pushing away an old painting from one of the easels, he added a fresh canvas. He was fitful with nervous energy. He would pass away the night by painting for his mother.

As sunrise neared, the painting came to life. His art style was softer, the colors more gentle, and the theme tamer than he had undertaken before. André studied the painting and likened himself to van Gogh—a madman and a genius. His mother sat on a park bench in the Public Garden of Arles along the Boulevard des Lices. The park brimmed with cobblestone pathways, stretches of well-manicured lawns, and beds of colorful flowers. It was rich with majestic pines—teal in color and towering in stature. The delicate leaves of the maple trees were changing from their summer greens into resplendent shades of yellow and orange. Eveline loved the colors of autumn and the coolness of the air in Arles. And now, there she was, duplicated in oils on her son's canvas, sitting on her park bench, pretty as a picture with a cloudless sky above her, happy people strolling by her, and a favorite book upon her lap. He captured his mother's dream. The dream his father had stolen from her. Rare tears left wet paths upon the dried clay that masked his face.

"I'm sorry, Mother. I'm sorry you were never happy here. I'm sorry you never got back to Arles. You will be revenged. I shall see to it." André studied the finished painting, and for a brief moment, he allowed himself to get lost in its conventional charm. With misery weighing his icy heart, he raised his bowie high above the masterpiece and destroyed the only thing of beauty he had ever created. His mother died a second death.

*   *   *

At the break of dawn, Mt. Pelée exploded with the force of a thousand cannons. The blast propelled chunks of rocks as big as carts toward the town. Two fresh openings in the crater released flames hundreds of feet high into the darkened skies. Thunder roared. Explosion after explosion jarred the island. The mountain coughed up a geyser of white lava showering the remains of Le Prêcheur, the Guerin factory, and the northern edge of the city. Dozens of residences and businesses were ignited. Military police tossed sticks of dynamite into the burning buildings to blow out the flames.

*   *   *

After the quimboiseurs desecrated the doors of the church, they vandalized coffins in the cemetery. Finished with the city, they departed for the outskirts making their way along the road where soldiers stood post at the barricades. At the first light of day, the quimboiseurs fell upon two of the soldiers asleep on the job. Cords of cured intestines coiled around necks. The men were lifeless in a flash, and the quimboiseurs vanished before the rest of the soldiers could react.

*   *   *

Captain Marino Leboffe of the *Orsolina*, bound for the United States, warily watched and scrutinized the volcano during the night. At dawn, he made the decision to set sail from St. Pierre sooner than scheduled void of booked cargo, mail, and passengers. First mate, Luigi Contoni, was sent to shore in a longboat to collect whatever passengers and mail he could gather in two hours. If Luigi did not receive official clearance from port authorities, then the hell with them.

Two hours later, Luigi, one lucky passenger, and a solitary bag of mail in his longboat fled St. Pierre with two shipping agents in hot pursuit. Luigi glanced over his shoulder and flashed a boyish smile as his oars madly scooped through the surf. The cursing agents scrambled on board the ship long after Luigi had successfully boarded the passenger and unloaded the mailbag. Captain Leboffe politely listened to the agent's pleas to stay in port for one more day as there were eighteen additional passengers holding tickets for passage to America, most especially, the wife of the American consul. Captain Leboffe expressed his regrets, but stood his ground. He politely ordered the shipping agents off the *Orsolina*. At nine o'clock that morning, the ship steamed out of port and headed for New York.

Clara Prentiss had missed her only chance of escape.

*   *   *

André left the cottage after Mont Pelée's bombardment and stole through the darkness toward the main house. He made nary a sound as he eased his light frame over the terrace wall and inched his way to the French doors of his father's study. The light of a candle flickered inside. André crouched low and positioned himself flat against the outside wall before carefully peering inside. His father rested his head on his desk. A cigar was smoldering in an ashtray near a half-empty glass of cognac. André slid back down into a sitting position next to the doorway. He would take his time. He would not be rash. No room for mistakes. Listen and wait.

*   *   *

Marcel squinted as the morning sun filtered into the study. He had been up most of the night sifting through legal documents. The smell of brewed coffee drifted in from the kitchen, an indication that Henrillia was preparing the family's breakfast. Marcel put the documents in three separate folders and returned them to the safe. He went to the kitchen.

"Bonjour, Henrillia."

"Bonjour, Monsieur Chevalier," she greeted. "Vous désirez?"

"Jevoudrais une tasse de café, s'il vous plait!"

Marcel took his cup of coffee and stepped out into the side yard containing the garden of vegetables for Henrillia's cooking. He watched in fascination as red rivers of lava flowed out of Mont Pelée's crater toward the valley. Five minutes later, he heard Indigo and Yvette talking in the kitchen. He found the women deep in conversation at the table. Cyrillia was still asleep.

"Please, ladies, bring your coffee and come with me," invited Marcel. Yvette and Indigo followed him to his office and sat down in two leather chairs before his desk. "The activities of the volcano over the last twenty-four hours have given me great pause. I concede that the lives and properties in St. Pierre and the surrounding valleys and mountains are in grave danger. With the exception of the ash fallout, I feel confident that we are a safe distance from the volcano on the plantation as most of the lava activity is taking place on the northwest side facing St. Pierre and the sea. If, at any time, you feel your safety is in jeopardy, don't hesitate to head straight for the summit of Morne Parnasse. I have instructed Stefan to keep five horses saddled and readied at a moment's notice. I will issue the same instructions to our workers and their families."

"Are you still taking cargo into town this morning, Papa?" asked Yvette.

"Yes, I am." He removed the three packets from the safe. "I want you to keep these with you on your person at all times." He gave Yvette and Indigo one packet each and opened up the third. "Everything I am about to show you has been duplicated. My attorney, Léon Douvres, is in charge of the originals. This first piece of paper is my Last Will and Testament. It assures that the plantation will be left to Yvette. There is a provision that if anything happens to her, the property will automatically transfer to Cyrillia, with Indigo as the executor. Years ago, Indigo and I worked out a trust for Cyrillia. My money will be divided equally between my three children. There is one stipulation. André will not receive his share unless he agrees to move away from the island and never return. I do not like the person he has become, and I don't want him here near any of you. Also in your packets I have information about our bank accounts in Fort-de-France and Paris, along with copies of the deeds to all of our properties and holdings."

* * *

Governor Mouttet was having a hard time keeping up with the reports of death and destruction in St. Pierre; even with all this information at hand, he still refused to open his eyes to the urgency of the situation, even though he had been advised that law and order in the town had basically ceased to exist. The governor was also having a hard time dealing with his renegade principal secretary, L'Heurre. Since sunrise, the two men had been engaged in a heated debate over several issues. L'Heurre insisted that the governor cancel St. Pierre's social festivities. It was of his opinion that the continuation of the mayor's silly ball would create an impression that the Progressive Party was more concerned with celebrations and food than of the welfare of the people. L'Heurre pointed out that notes of "regrets" arrived from Fernand Clerc, the vicar-general, Senator Knight, and even a few members of the mayor's action committee.

"You win, Edouard. You win! Send out an official proclamation postponing all of the celebrations, banquets, and balls. There. Does that make you happy?"

"It is not a matter of making me happy, sir," answered L'Huerre dryly. "One more thing, Governor, it is important that you and Mrs. Mouttet make your trip into St. Pierre, anyway."

"In the name of God, what for?" Mouttet questioned.

"Don't you want to keep the people calm? Your appearance there will assure them that there is nothing to fear. Just think of the political field day the Radicals would have if you did not show up as planned. Also, the presence of Mrs. Mouttet is most critical. The whole of Martinique is aware of how easily unnerved she can become. It will be accepted as a noble act of encouragement."

"You had better be right, Edouard."

Edouard L'Huerre knew he was taking a big gamble with the use of reverse psychology on Governor Mouttet. The principal secretary hoped that as soon as Mouttet got to St. Pierre and saw for himself the deplorable chaos, he would issue an immediate evacuation of the city.

*   *   *

André etched designs in the terrace tile with the tip of his bowie near the door of his father's den. His face twisted in savage anger. His father was handing over the land to his bastard mulatto children. There was no doubt in André's mind what had to be done. By the time he was through, there wouldn't be an heir left, but for him. He would make his first move as soon as his father departed for St. Pierre. He estimated that it would take Marcel a good part of the day to direct the loading of the produce crates onto the ship. He mentally calculated how many would be left at the plantation after his father's departure: the hired guards, two servants, the cook, Stefan, two stable boys, Yvette, Indigo, and the child.

*   *   *

Everything Father Roche had ever loved was dying: the town, the people, and the beauty of the island. Never had he seen so much death and destruction. He knew it was only a matter of time before Mont Pelée's finale. The priest had hoped that the government would listen to the church if it knew that the church supported an evacuation. But the church wanted nothing to do with government decisions. It had its hands full attending to those in need. It insisted that Father Roche quit playing scientist and return to his religious duties. God would take care of the rest.

*   *   *

Smoke and fog blanketed the town to such a degree, it was impossible to see one's hand before one's face. All was quiet. The good citizens of

St. Pierre tried to ignore the cast of doom hanging over them as they conducted business as usual that Wednesday morning. The homeless, still traumatized from the evils of the night before, were afraid to make a move. They did not care to bother anyone or be bothered. The decency of their idyllic country life seemed like a faraway dream. The city was a vulgar and dangerous place. If only they had the strength, they would leave. But where would they go? Most of their homelands had been destroyed. They had no choice but to stay where they were and pray that the mountain would take pity.

Marcel and his men had been at the dockyards for nearly an hour awaiting the loading of the first transfer lighter. No one was in a good mood, and work was moving at a snail's pace.

"Hurry up. Dépéchez!" shouted Marcel, pacing back and forth on the beach. It was hot and sticky. The air stank of sulfur. He was ill at ease. He was edgy. He should be at home with his family, not here. He sensed that something was amiss at the plantation.

Felecien approached his master. "Je vous demande pardon."

"Qui, Felecien, what is it?"

"That I ask of you, sir."

"What do you mean?"

"You are not acting like yourself."

"Felecien, I want you to stay here. Make sure the cargo is loaded. I am going home."

"Comment?"

"I am going home."

With alarm in his heart, Marcel collected his horse and galloped away from the beach.

*   *   *

The attention of the workers guarding the plantation entrance was trained on the rumbling volcano. André was swift in his attack. The guards had little time to cry out as the blade of the knife cut a smooth path across their throats. Next, he moved around the side of the house just in time to see Yvette walking toward the stables. He stopped and crouched. Where was Yvette going? He hoped she wasn't leaving the compound.

Stefan emerged from the stables and gathered Yvette into his arms. They kissed long and hard. André shuddered. There was nothing more repugnant to him than seeing a dark-skinned male with a light-skinned female. It wasn't right. It was disgusting. André spat.

The sound of a little girl's laughter coming from an outside terrace toward the rear of the house momentarily distracted André from Yvette and Stefan. He followed the noise and found Cyrillia sitting upon her mother's lap playing a hand game. He would deal with them later.

André slipped into the house. Henrillia was preparing lunch in the kitchen. He checked the rest of the main floor. No one was in the dining parlor. No one was in the library. The housemaids must be upstairs. Good. He came across the first maid sweeping the hallway carpet on the second floor. She didn't hear him steal up behind her. The knife found its way into an area just below her narrow waist, rupturing her left kidney. She died instantly. The broom fell out of her lifeless hand before she dropped to the floor. He stuffed the body and the broom in a linen closet. Maxi's widow, Coralline, was in her third-floor quarters singing an island tune and working on household mending. Her song was the same one Maxi sang when he courted her so many years ago. How she missed his sweet baritone voice.

"Ti fenm lá doux—li doux."

"Sweeter than syrup the little woman is!"

Coralline choked back tears of grief for her man. The floorboard creaked behind her. She twisted around in her rocking chair just in time to see a heavy piece of pottery hovering above her. Coralline had no time to respond. She died uttering Maxi's name as André crushed her skull.

"Now you can be with Maxi," laughed André over his deed.

Henrillia prepared two chickens for the family's favorite meal, *poule épi dire,* and a side dish of rice and white beans and vinegar. Henrillia heard footsteps. She clapped her hands when she saw him. "André, my boy, come give your old Henrillia the big hug. You be gone a long time. Come. Come, boy. Let us have a big hug just like you got when you were a wee one."

André approached the cook. He hesitated. Had she not been a nurturing mother figure over the years? Had she not been good and kind to him no matter what? Some feelings of love did stir within his cold heart. As she placed her hefty arms around his slender body, he entered a familiar zone of comfort and safety. For a moment, he *was* a small boy again. Henrillia grabbed at a sudden hurt in her side. Surprised, she pushed him away. A sticky substance covered her probing hand. Was that chicken blood? No. The blood was hers.

"André! Pourquoi?"

The knife came down again. This time it punctured the right side of her chest. The pain was unbearable. She stumbled across the kitchen tiles and collapsed. It wasn't easy, but André managed to drag her huge body into the kitchen pantry. He grabbed a rag and wiped up as much of the blood as he could. He was out of breath and tired.

The front door opened and closed. He peered around the corner. It was Yvette. He heard her go up the stairs. He followed her. She went to her chambers. Peeking through the keyhole, he could see her on her bed. He tried the door. Locked? Very well, he could wait.

*   *   *

Yvette rolled onto her stomach and buried her face deep into her feather pillow. Earlier that morning, the bed linen had been sprinkled with rose water to take away the scorch aroma that permeated everything. The soothing scent of the fragrance carried her through a dream of forests and fields of flowers, over clear rivers and ponds, up and through cloudless skies of blue.

David entered her dream. They were in the lush surroundings. They embraced by the waterfall near Josephine's bench in the botanical gardens. A light breeze toyed with his flaxen hair. He was the mystery man of her adolescent fantasies. She could smell cologne upon his clean-shaven skin and the musk of the sea that marked the fabric of his white uniform. His hands, as smooth as the polished teak of the pilot wheel that steered his ship, cupped her face.

"Stop!"

It was Stefan invading her slumber. He yanked her away from the American captain.

"Not him. It is me you want."

What was that smell? Manure? Soil? Sweat?

He was of the earth. He was of Martinique.

Stefan's held her at arm's length. His black-burgundy skin stretched over hills and valleys of well-defined muscles. Passionate dark eyes held her captive as the calloused fingers touched her lips.

"Stop!"

David pulled her back. "You belong to me."

Stefan held on to the other arm. "No. You belong to me."

In her sleep, she twisted and turned with outstretched arms for both to leave her alone.

*　　*　　*

André left the house and stole to the stables. The first attendant was stabbed in his neck while grooming a horse, and the other took a hard blow to the head with the edge of a mucking shovel. Stefan heard the commotion and came running from his quarters. André bent his right arm back and smoothly pitched his bowie. As the knife spun through the air, the light of the sun streaming in from the cracks in the roof rafters bounced off the glistening steel of the twirling blade. Upon hitting its target, a burst of heat tore through Stefan's chest.

*　　*　　*

Indigo left Cyrillia playing on the terrace to go inside to ask Henrillia for lemonade. The housekeeper was nowhere to be found. Indigo searched the main floor of the house. Empty. In the foyer, by the stairs, she thought she recognized a familiar voice. Shivers ran down her spine as she turned around expecting the worst. An angry fist slammed into the side of her jaw.

*　　*　　*

Yvette bolted from her bed and raced down the stairs, where she found Indigo in a heap upon the tile floor. She placed her hand over her friend's nose. Thank God, Indigo was still breathing. Yvette looked around; no one was in sight. Who did this? In her heart, she knew.

*   *   *

Cyrillia had been drawing pictures of flowers and hearts with her finger in the ash that coated the terrace. The makeshift grime provided a good canvas for her creativity. She looked up. Was that her mother crying out? The child ran inside the house. Yvette kneeled on the floor, holding Cyrillia's sleeping mother. Cyrillia recoiled in horror when the clay man come into view behind Yvette like a gray ghost. He pressed the tip of a big knife against Aunt Yvette's back. By instinct, Cyrillia retreated, took silent steps backward, tiptoed quietly up the rear stairway, and hid under the bed in her mother's chambers, where she found Espérer trembling in the corner.

*   *   *

André forced Yvette to stand up and face him. His mouth was inches away. A strong whiff of stomach decay reeked from his breath. She braced herself.

"What do you want?"

"What is rightfully mine, you mulatto bitch."

"You don't want what you think is rightfully yours, André. You only want to have your own way. You have no interest in life here on Martinique. We all know that you would rather be in France. I know the rotten depths of your soul, brother. I know you are here only because you want what you cannot have, and that is this plantation. As soon as you have it, you'd either leave it or destroy it. It is not us who made you this way. It was your mentally ill mother who killed herself before you. I am sorry about that. You are blaming the wrong people. Go away. Leave us alone in peace. Father has never denied you anything. Why do you continue to hate?"

"This plantation was forged by my white French ancestors. White! My mother was white. My mother was good. And she was wronged. This was *my* mother's home. Then Nicole came along and stole it all away with black witchery. If my mother was insane, it was because she was driven there by our father and Nicole. And now my nigger-loving father wants the land willed to the half breeds he has sired. Does the idiot really believe he is going to force me away from here? Yes, Yvette, I hate this land. I hate it as much as my mother did. But it still belongs to me. It is mine by legal birthright. Not yours and not your miniature look-alike."

"André, don't harm Indigo and Cyrillia. Do what you want with me."

Indigo moaned and reached for her jaw. "Where's Cyrillia?"

"Yes," said André, looking around, "where is she, anyway?"

"If you hurt my child I will kill—"

André dug the point of the knife into Yvette's neck. "One more move and I shall thrust this into her and she'll be dead in seconds."

Indigo froze. His cold eyes told her that he would carry out his threat.

André pushed Yvette down to the floor and straddled her. "I think it is time to find out what kind of treasures your black buck has discovered."

She did not fight him. If she could keep him occupied long enough, perhaps it would buy the time needed to keep them alive until help came. Yvette fought off the sickness lurching in her belly and rising to her throat as she felt his free hand unbuttoning her breeches.

* * *

From her hiding place underneath the bed, Cyrillia sensed her mother and aunt in danger, and it was up to her to help them. She needed a weapon—a real weapon—not her pretend *bam bam*. You can't be a soldier without one. Then she remembered the small pistol her mother kept in her purse. Time and time again, Indigo warned her daughter to never touch it. That it could hurt and it could kill for real. Cyrillia retrieved the pistol. She whispered, "*Bam . . . bam . . . bam.*"

* * *

Marcel stood in the doorway of the front parlor, his rifle aimed at his son's head. "One more move and I will end your miserable life right here and now." Marcel clicked the weapon.

André pressed the knife deeper into Yvette's chest. "Go ahead, Father. She will be dead before you fire the first bullet. Go ahead. I suggest you drop your rifle."

The rifle fell out of Marcel's hands.

Cyrillia made nary a sound as she came up behind André. She didn't understand what was going on, but she intuitively knew that the situation posed danger to her family and that the clay man was the cause of all the jeopardy. She sucked in her breath when Marcel dropped his weapon and André threw his knife. The bowie landed dead center in Marcel's throat.

"Bad man," said Cyrillia. "You hurt my papa." She managed to pull the trigger of the pistol and shouted, "Bam . . . bam . . . bam." Only this time, the bullets were not imaginary.

André growled like a wounded animal from the pain, dropped to his knees, and reached for his buttocks, where three small caliber bullets had entered.

Yvette rushed to her dying father's side. "Oh, Papa, dear Papa . . ."

"Watch out behind you," warned Indigo.

Out of the corner of her eye, Yvette saw André struggling to his feet. She picked up her father's rifle and fired off one round. The force of the blast flattened André against the wall. He grabbed the gaping hole in his chest and dropped down to the floor, leaving a skid mark of blood down the wall. "I'll see you in hell, you black she-devils," he uttered with his last breath.

*   *   *

The principal secretary accompanied the governor and Mrs. Mouttet to St. Pierre that gloomy afternoon. Unimaginable ruin from the relentless attacks of the volcano and the looting of the people greeted them. Mouttet kept a poker face, covering up his true feelings. Mrs. Mouttet placed a lace handkerchief to her fashionably made-up face and coughed. The stench was deplorable. She latched on to her husband's arm for support. Mouttet knew by her dilated eyes that she was traumatized by the devastation around her.

"It truly isn't as bad as it seems, my darling. Trust me."

The governor's buggy had a hard time rolling through the sludge on the way to St. Pierre's town hall, where they were to meet with the mayor, Professor Landes, and what was left of the Action and Governor's Committees. The governor waved to his subjects. Excited crowds normally surrounded the entourage of government vehicles wanting to get a glimpse of their appointed leader, but on this day, no one was interested. Mouttet's arrival held no meaning. His heart sank. A shouting match between Mayor Fouché and Professor Landes was taking place on the steps of the town hall. No one noticed the arrival of the governor.

"I demand a retraction in tomorrow's paper," screeched the professor. "I will not be held accountable for what was written in the newspaper. I did not give an interview. Those were not my words. It has always been of my opinion that the town be evacuated. Lies! Lies! You wrote lies and used my name."

The cancellation of his ball, the anger of Professor Landes, and the chaos of his town had Mayor Fouché on the verge of a nervous breakdown. His world was falling apart. "What about my preparations?" he whimpered. "Do you not realize the enormous amount of work that goes into organizing a ball of that magnitude? Everything is ready. The food for the banquet is being prepared as we speak. The tablecloths and china are in place. The orchestra is tuning up and rehearsing. I have a staff ready to clear the air and linens of any ash that tries to make its way into the hall. Why cancel it? Look! The governor is here. There is no need for a cancellation."

The mayor was greeted by stunned silence.

Even Mouttet realized the futility of the situation. Pelée had won, and that was the end of it. He greeted the mayor with a weak smile. "Dear man, the annual celebrations and festivities, including the elections, will have to be postponed and rescheduled. No one in their right mind is going to venture out on these streets to attend a party or cast a vote."

Mayor Fouché dropped his head and walked away in defeat.

Professor Landes continued his tirade running after the mayor. "I shall sue the newspaper for this. I shall sue everyone involved in this lie." He too left.

"L'Heurre," ordered Governor Mouttet to his deputy, "you must return to Fort-de-France. If the telegraph cable has been repaired, get word to the minister of colonies about the situation here. My wife and I will spend the night here at the Hotel de L'Independance. Tomorrow morning we will attend mass at the St. Pierre Cathedral before returning home. Then I'll decide what to do about the evacuation of this town."

*   *   *

The Chevalier plantation was in turmoil. Yébé had been fetched from the workers' compound. He wasn't a doctor, but he was the best thing they had. A makeshift infirmary was erected in the parlor for Henrillia and Stefan. Henrillia's tremendous bulk had been her saving grace, and Stefan's youth and muscle mass had been his. As Yébé cleaned, stitched, and wrapped their knife wounds, he sang a healing song.

The bodies of the guards, the maids, the stable boys, and Marcel were laid to rest in the parlor on the main floor and covered with white sheets. The door was locked. André's body was unceremoniously thrown in the barn like unwanted garbage. A roaring fire warmed the sitting room. Yvette and Indigo cuddled on the divan and watched the flames in the fireplace. Cyrillia fell asleep in her mother's lap. Yébé's wife brewed a pot of coffee.

Indigo broke the silence. "Come with us to France, Yvette. There is nothing left here for you anymore. We are all that you have now."

Yvette took a sip of her coffee. "You know I can't do that."

*   *   *

René Cottrell tried once more to convince the de Jaunvilles to leave. Their answer was a slammed door in his face. He went straight to his uncle's villa where he collected his things and returned to Fort-de-France minus the girl he loved.

*   *   *

Fernand Clerc studied the barometer on his terrace. The oscillating needle indicated renewed ground activity. In his heart, he knew the mountain was about to blow. This put Fernand on the alert. He was ready to depart with his family at a moment's notice.

*   *   *

Thomas Prentiss poured Clara and himself their customary nightcap. They toasted each other silently, sensing it would be for the last time.

*   *   *

Governor Mouttet sat on the bed of his St. Pierre hotel and loosened his tie. It had been a long day, and he was bone tired. He was soulfully aware that he had made a grave error in placing comforts and politics before the powers of the volcano.

*   *   *

Father Roche observed the smoking volcano from the rectory tower. Its cone shone hotter than ever. The priest paced back and forth before the window as heavy storm clouds rolled over the hills toward St. Pierre. The moon was closing its monthly cycle and had been reduced to a tiny shaft of brilliance. He fell to his knees in prayer as he watched the remaining thread of lunar light disappear. "Heavenly Father," he wept with the cross of his rosary beads pressed tightly to his lips, "I greatly fear that this shall be the *last moon* for my St. Pierre."

34

St. Pierre, Martinique
Thursday, May 8, 1902
Farewell, Pretty Town

As the sun broke into a new day, it brought with it a most glorious morning. The rains of the night had not only cleansed the air and washed away the ash, but they had brought renewed hope to the people of St. Pierre. For the first time in weeks, the air did not reek of fumes. The mountain was quiet. No explosions. No quaking. No smoke. No lava.

* * *

Thomas and Clara greeted the bright morning with relief. There was a knock at their door. Who could that be at this early hour? It was a messenger with a note from Governor Mouttet and Mayor Fouché. In the wee hours of Thursday morning, the two leaders had decided to evacuate the town as soon as possible. An official announcement would be presented to the public after high mass at the cathedral. The American consul and his wife hugged each other.

* * *

Regardless of the warm, cheery sunrise, Fernand Clerc could not allow himself to be optimistic. His wife, Veronique, and their children were stationed at the front of the house in the family carriage. While they waited, Fernand was compelled to go back to his balcony, where he kept one wary eye on the mountain and one on the barometer. The erratic needle told him it was time to leave his beloved home and flee to a place of safety with his family. His heart sank.

*   *   *

St. Pierre's tranquility was short lived. At 5:00 AM, a shrill trumpeting and violent quaking shattered the peace. Hundreds of locals and homeless fled to the cathedral, cramming the pews and the aisle to pray for their lives. Others were forced to crowd shoulder to shoulder in the front courtyard. Huge billows of menacing dusty red smoke broke out of the volcano's mouth, blanketing the blue sky. Cries of anguish resonated across the town. It was as if the people knew that they were doomed as the oppressed air closed in around them. For those not frightened by this colorful display, it was actually captivating. Five minutes later, a total eclipse pitched the town into blackness. The timorous braced themselves.

*   *   *

Father Roche wasted no time gathering his many journals of record and rushed by horseback to his observatory high upon a mountain a safe distance across the valley where he scrutinized Mont Pelee. He would have plenty of time to study the mountain's latest antics before Thursday morning mass. He had just dismounted his steed and was halfway up Morne Vert when red ash swathed the sky. He knew from his volcanic studies that Mont Pelée was reaching dangerous levels of combustion. At 6:00 AM, the volcano coughed up immeasurable amounts of boulders from its throat. Powerful blasts, detonating deep within its belly, exploded with unbridled fury. Once he reached his observatory on top of the peak, a trembling Father Roche braced himself for the damnation that he knew must soon be coming.

*   *   *

Yvette had spent most of the night alone out on the side terrace listening to the rain; and now, in the early morning light, she viewed Pelée's spectacular fireworks show. The tragedies from the day before had failed to destroy her inner strength. She made up her mind to fight with her life to preserve the integrity of the Chevalier name and the Chevalier plantation. The land, her land, was all that mattered. Indigo joined Yvette. Neither one spoke. They held hands.

Mont Pelée

*   *   *

Regional shipping agents had convinced the captains of those ships still anchored in the harbor that they were not in danger from the erupting volcano. Passengers on board the vessels were assured they had nothing to fear. Under the guise of false guarantees, two more foreign ships, the *Roddam* and the *Romaima*, entered the port. A total of eighteen ships were anchored in St. Pierre's waters. Not knowing any better, trusting crews and passengers assumed a holiday attitude, collecting souvenir vials of volcanic sand that had rained upon the decks. The visitors to St. Pierre's gateway were excited to be given the rare opportunity of witnessing a volcano in full eruption. They frolicked, laughed, and squealed as they played like children within the gray shadow of the pulsating red beast looming nearby. The baritone clanging from the colossal cathedral bell intermingled with the delicate chimes of bells from the smaller churches masked the ignorant sounds of gaiety from the harbor and the plaintive screams of panic from the city.

*   *   *

At eight minutes to eight, Mont Pelée exploded with unbridled force. Two ill-omened pillars of lethal gas and incandescent particles punched up out of the top of the pressure-stressed crater. The heat radiating from these mammoth clouds of energy mass reached temperatures as high as 1800°F. A blast from the south face of the mountain opened up a gaping hole where a third fume emerged. As soon as the three clouds combined, they created a monster cyclone that shot up twelve thousand feet above the crater and stretched out nearly a quarter of a mile in width, measuring in height taller than the mountain that bore it. So voluminous was this phenomenon, its density blocked visibility as far away as Fort-de-France. Scorching windstorms fanned out several miles.

A portion of the dense cloud, pulled down by gravity, toppled from its own weight of pumice stones and searing gas bubbles. It adhered itself like packed snow to the slope of Mont Pelée. Propelled by an underskirt of molten sea of fire, the scarlet avalanche of red-hot sand, gravel, and rocks tumbled down the side of the volcano and rolled toward the town of St. Pierre at speeds up to ninety miles an hour. In less than four minutes, the firestorm twisted, pushed, and somersaulted over morns, forests, valleys, rivers, plantations, towns, and all eighteen ships in the bay. In less than four minutes, St. Pierre ceased to be. All forms of plant and animal life had been annihilated, and thirty thousand people lay dead or dying in its wake.

*   *   *

Cyrillia kept escaping her mother's grasp to run out of the plantation house to watch the eruption taking place. Indigo was desperately trying to prevent her daughter from viewing such a malevolent sight, but Cyrillia would have no part of it. "I've got to see, Maman."

Despite Indigo's pleas, the stubborn child finally ran into the arms of Yvette. "Cyrillia is okay, Indigo" said Yvette, hooking the child to her hip and carrying her to the top of a small hill next to the stables where they would get a better sighting of St. Pierre. "I'll take care of her."

*   *   *

Father Roche had expected a major volcanic eruption, but nothing of this magnitude. From his vantage point, his eyes followed the course of the rolling avalanche as it ate its way from north to south. Churches, hospitals, schools, bars, parks, shops, and homes were incinerated instantaneously under its blazing bulk as if they were made out of papier-mâché. Father Roche calculated that the volcanic squall from the time it started to move to the time it disappeared into the sea beyond the bay took only three to four minutes. Before long, strong island breezes lifted the dense fog of choking smoke to reveal a most curious line of destruction that cut a precise eight-square-mile charred path leading from the top of the volcano across hills and valleys through St. Pierre and out and over the ships in the roadstead. Deep in his heart, Father Roche knew that there would be little or nothing left to save. This fatalistic realization struck a hard blow to his faith. How could his god have allowed such a terrible cataclysm to happen?

*   *   *

It took the *Silver Eagle* four hours to reach the island of Martinique. The steamer had experienced much difficulty pushing a path through dead bodies and scorched debris. Many of the passengers who were squeamish retreated to the confines of their cabins while the curious remained at the port side, where they held respectful silence. Normally this part of the journey provided travelers with tranquil scenes of lush vegetation clinging to the steep incline of a dormant island volcano. Snuggled at the base of this volcano, sandwiched between the outer edge of the jade-colored forests and the turquoise-colored coastline should have been the sleepy hamlet of Le Prêcheur appearing peaceful with glistening fishing nests drying on a hot sandy beach.

On this eighth day of May in the year 1902, however, those on board the *Silver Eagle* steamship were not to be greeted with the usual vistas. Nothing resembling topical splendor was within sight, only burnt forests, flaming villages, and impenetrable rivers of lava. The dwellings of Le Prêcheur, including its quaint little church, had been reduced to rubble by daily showers of hot pumice and mudflows. Romantic palm trees once lining the main street in majestic ambiance now appeared bent in a subservient curtsy toward the volcano with their once-glorious fan leaves dangling from seared crowns like pieces of wilted lettuce.

Nothing but ruin welcomed the disbelieving viewers. Those familiar with Martinique's northernmost topography searched for common landmarks. Where the infinite forests shaded the mountain, now only stumps of broken trees and smoldering embers remained. Where the prodigious Guerin plantation and refinery spread out topside over a gallant cliff, now a steaming waterfall of lava camouflaged any trace of the mighty compound. Where the dazzling coastline sparkled with pristine beaches, now a thicket of ash and unsightly piles of debris spoiled the splendor. The northern tip of Martinique was a barren moonscape, void of color, void of life.

* * *

Roger Arnoux, a member of the Royal Society of France, was one of hundreds of spectators gathered on Mont Parnasse. Having just completed the last of his vacation in south Martinique, he decided to get a quick glimpse of the rumored eruption taking place on Mont Pelée before sailing home to France. He would have quite a story to tell. "We've got to get down there and help the injured," he said to the teary-eyed man standing next to him.

Fernand Clerc sighed and nodded.

They joined an assembly of men who were forming a search party. As he made his way down the mountain, Fernand could see in the distance that his sister's plantation had been wiped off the face of the earth. Not long after entering the south end of St. Pierre, the rescue team found what remained of Fernand's hillside villa. Only the foundation stood firm. Farther down the road, they came upon dozens of collapsed pedestrians. A few were still alive, but severely burned with no chance for survival. The victims would suffer indescribable pain for agonizing hours before gratefully succumbing to the relief of death. Fernand identified a close friend by the man's partially melted ring upon his scalded finger. Unable to handle any more sights of horror and desolation, Fernand retreated up the hill to his waiting family. He would take them to their country home in Vivé on the east side of the island and then, perhaps tomorrow, he would come back to offer help. For now, he wanted no more of this nightmare.

*   *   *

Morbid silence gripped both horrified passengers and crew alike as David slowly guided the steamer around a bend and into the harbor of St. Pierre. Hundreds of gallons of alcohol from ruptured rum barrels had spilled into the water, setting the surface of the bay on fire. Several foreign vessels had caught fire and sunk with only the tops of their masts showing above the surface of the water. Six ships, the *Roraima*, *Roddam*, *Teresa Lo Vico*, *Korona*, *Maria de Pompeii*, and *Gabrielle* were still afloat, their giant hulls reduced to skeletons. Desperate cries of anguish echoed across the bay from dozens of severely burned passengers who had been caught in the eye of the fire cloud. Along with the *Silver Eagle*, more incoming ships cautiously approached the scene to offer help, including the Danish cruiser, *Valkyrien*, and the interisland cable repair ship *Pouyer-Quertier.*

*   *   *

Yvette left Cyrillia alone on the hillside. The child refused to take her eyes away from the ruins of the valley and the city beyond. "I'm going to check on Henrillia and Stefan," said Yvette to Indigo, who was helping Felician load the carriage with travel trunks. Not wanting any more to do with this island, Indigo was determined to depart for Fort-de-France first thing in the morning to catch the next ship leaving for France. "Cyrillia will be fine," assured Yvette.

Indigo nodded.

Yvette stopped short before the hallway mirror. She looked a mess. Her clothes were soiled from soot and dried blood. Her mane of copper hair fell in a mass of tangles. Her green eyes were puffy and red from lack of sleep and strain. Her reflection revealed an adult version of the thirteen-year-old girl who had shot and wounded her half brother years earlier. The only difference now is that she had hit her target right on the mark. André's demise fortified her.

Stefan, who was weak from loss of blood, rested in a chair in front of the fireplace. The advantage of his youth and his love for the mistress of the plantation provided him the will to recover. Nearby, Henrillia was stretched out sound asleep on the divan. Yvette checked the housekeeper's pulse and smiled faintly. The old woman would outlive them all.

"How are you doing, Stefan?" asked Yvette wearily sitting down in the adjoining chair.

"I'll survive this. With you by my side, Yvette, how could I not? The sight of you gives me life." Stephan frowned when saw that her eyes were void of emotion.

"Much has happened in the last few days, Stefan," she answered in a hollow voice. "I have lost many who are dear to me. With Indigo and Cyrillia departing, no one will be left."

"But you will have me, my sweet."

Yvette dropped her eyes. "What happened between us was very special. I have no regrets. However, things are different now. The salvation of this plantation solely rests upon my shoulders. I have a job to do. I have the responsibility to rebuild not only the banana fields, but the Chevalier reputation as well."

"I can help you do that."

"No, Stefan, you cannot. I will need all the support I can get from the white men who run the laws, who run the banks, and who run the businesses. They could easily boycott me if they so choose. I can't afford our relationship. I do care deeply for you. But I love my home more and will do anything to keep it safe and flourishing."

The pain from his wounds was nothing compared to the pain in his heart. "Believe it or not, Yvette, I do understand your position, but I don't like it. My love for you is forever. I will never love another. I am very patient and will wait a lifetime for you to change your mind. I believe deep in my soul that that time will come one day."

"I too hope it will. Meanwhile, I am sorry, but I cannot have you living here. My uncle in Le Robert has been in need of an assistant overseer. As you know, Uncle Bernard is very fond of you and, I am sure, will be thrilled to hire you for that position."

"As you wish," said Stefan resigned.

*   *   *

Tears of anguish washed down Father Roche's face as he prayed over a stack of charred bodies. It was hard to tell whether they had once been men or women, white skinned or black skinned. Their scorched flesh had created an unidentifiable unity. There was a comedic sense of irony that the unrelenting political division between the blacks and the whites on the island had ultimately led to the cause of their combined deaths. It was, indeed, poetic justice, mused the priest, that Mont Pelée had cast the deciding ballot to determine the inane winner of the inane election. Neither side had won in the end.

St. Pierre lay in ruins. Gone were the pretty yellow buildings. Gone were the foreign ships anchored in her colorful port. Gone were the shops with imported French goods. Gone were the street vendors, carrier women, dockworkers, laundresses, and whores. Gone were the mulatto children with their jewel-colored eyes and bright wide smiles. Gone were the Creole voices, high and poetic, like notes of a song upon the wind. Gone were the pungent smells of garlic and burnt sugar. Gone were the perfumes of passionflowers and bougainvilleas. Gone were the heart, soul, and life of one of the most exciting little towns to ever grace the planet.

Father Roche vowed he would never live in the shadow of the mountain again. As soon as possible, he would depart this city of ghosts to live the rest of his life in Fort-de-France. The priest pressed a silver cross to his lips in the memory of the place he fervently treasured.

"*DouDou,* my sweet St. Pierre," he whispered. "*DouDou.*"

* * *

David focused his spyglass on Mont Pelée. Like an old lady stripped of her fineries, she was gray and ugly. He shifted his scope to catch sight of the French warship *Suchet* emerging out of the smoky haze near the outer edge of the bay. David turned control of the helm over to first mate, Nathan Smith, and went portside with a bullhorn to communicate with its captain.

"Ahoy there, *Suchet!*"

"Ahoy there, *Eagle!*"

Captain Pierre de Bries stood near the aft of the warship with his bullhorn. His slumped shoulders indicated signs of hopelessness. His face and clothes were dirtied with soot and wet with sweat. Fatigue weighed heavily in his eyes. "All is gone, Captain Cabot. The volcano has snatched away the town's life. The entire city of St. Pierre has all but vanished. I fear we have lost thousands of civilians."

"When did this happen?" asked David.

"Around eight o'clock in the morning."

"What about survivors?"

"The temperatures closer into the roadstead and shore are over one hundred forty degrees, making it too damn hot to venture a transporter to the waterfront region. I braved it around two o'clock this afternoon just long enough to pick up thirty critically injured passengers and crew from the *Roraima*. I'll be surprised if half of them survive. Men, women, and children were caught out on the deck of the ship during the firestorm. Several have severe burns to the inside of their mouths and throats from breathing scalding air from the death cloud that exploded out the mountain. They can't even swallow to drink water. We've been feeding them ice chips to suck on. Others were caught in a downpour of blistering mud that coated their heads with the consistency of boiling glue. When cooled, the gook hardened like concrete. We haven't been able to pry off the castings for fear of ripping away their scalps."

"Dear God."

"Governor Mouttet was in town at the time. We fear he is dead. Hell, no one could have survived the inferno. I fear nothing is left of St. Pierre."

"I am heading for shore first thing in the morning," declared David.

"You can't do that. It's suicide. There is nothing more that can be done until the fires have burned themselves out. The fumes alone will kill you, Captain. I repeat—you can't do it."

David dropped the bullhorn listlessly to his side as he watched the luminescence of the inferno raging throughout the town and hillsides. He grimly thought of Yvette and Indigo. The anguish of not knowing what had happened to these women sickened him. He issued orders to his first mate. "Nathan, have the ship's doctor prepare for possible burn victims. Poll the passengers to find out if any will volunteer to help nurse the injured. And, Nathan . . ."

"Yes, sir."

"I will need six crew members to head to shore with me first thing in the morning. Tell these men that the mission is extremely dangerous. See to it that our transport boat is equipped with ample medical supplies, food, water, and firearms. You will be put in command."

David was not a religious man; however, as he scrutinized the dim outer waters of St. Pierre's lifeless bay, he grasped the rail and bowed his head.

35

St. Pierre, Martinique
Friday, May 9, 1902
Ruins

Against the advice of Captain Pierre de Bries, David Cabot and six of his crew boarded a longboat and headed toward the blackened shore. Left behind was First Mate Nathan Smith, the rest of the crew, and frightened passengers. The *Silver Eagle*, under the control of Smith, would soon be joining the Danish cruiser *Valkyrien*, the interisland cable repair ship *Pouter-Carder*, and the French battleship *Sachet* on a search-and-rescue mission that would take the four ships around the northern coastline of the island.

The crew from the *Silver Eagle* struggled to pull their boat through a veil of haze onto an ash-covered beach near the former dock area. Ash and cinders dirtied the sugar white sands of St. Pierre's waterfront. Once he stepped on land, David could feel the ground baking through the leather soles of his shoes. He had to relieve himself, and where his urine hit the ash, the ground sizzled and steamed. The gagging stench of decomposing flesh and acrid volcanic fumes forced the men to tie wet handkerchiefs around the lower half of their faces. David could not tell if his men were weeping from their stinging eyes or from the wrenching sights.

Bodies littered the dock area for as far as the eye could see. Hundreds of unidentifiable human beings curled upon the ground in twisted positions of torture, their clothing burned off, their flesh peeled away, and their bellies distended. They suffered appalling demise—tongues and throats burned to charcoal, eyelids and eyeballs vaporized. These poor creatures, roasted alive where they stood or ran in terror, displayed yards of hissing intestines, pressurized by volcanic heat, spilling out of their ruptured guts like links of cooked sausage.

"Stay close together, lads, we don't know what dangers lie ahead," warned David.

The crew gathered their supply packs and headed for La Place Bertin. All that remained of the stunning landmark Fountaine Agnés was its blackened basin. Nearby, a few mango trees poked out of the ground like black skeletons. The three-ton statue of the Virgin Mary, which had stood watch over the roadside for more than a century, had been blown forty feet away from its pedestal. Dozens of heavy cannons were ripped from their bases and scattered about the hillside as if weighing no more than wooden toy pegs. Thick iron rods that used to support buildings and ships twisted around one another with the ease and flexibility of a shoelace. Heavy sheets of roofing wrapped around what remained of lampposts. The pale yellow walls belonging to the magnificent estates, eateries, manors, saloons, businesses, and government offices once gracing the crescent of the beach had been reduced to mounds of nondescript ruble.

David and his men on their way to Rue Victor Hugo met another group also searching the ruins for survivors. Expressions of despair upon their grim faces reflected the bleak horror of the situations encountered during their findings. Dialogue was unnecessary. Their pitiful mission proved futile. There was no one to save. There was nothing to salvage. The Cathedral of St. Pierre stood gallantly with only a few of its walls and arches, along with a portion of one of its towers, surviving the blast. Hundreds of parishioners were found trapped, mangled, and buried within the pews and isles of the great hall, along with a silver chalice containing perfect white wafers queerly intact, as if protected and preserved by divine intervention. The majestic theater of St. Pierre had lost it grandeur. All that remained of this formidable gothic architecture were two vague flights of broken stairs curving up the hillside to an unsightly stage of broken tile and wreckage. The elegant support wall holding up the opposing staircases from underneath endured the catastrophe quite well, save for its portico of peeling plaster and smoke-damaged appearance.

One of the men from the other rescue group, still dressed in business clothes from the day before, wrinkled his nose and spit out saliva and grit. "No use going towards town," he advised. "There isn't anyone or anything left to save. We have been here since last night and are heading to Fort-de-France until the air clears, then we'll return. You should do the same."

Three of David's crew, wheezing and coughing, developed respiratory problems from gas vapors and smoke inhalation; three more suffered emotional trauma—not able to cope with the annihilation. David ordered all six of his men to take the transporter back to the *Silver Eagle* with instructions to set sail for the port of Fort-de-France. He would make his way on foot.

Striking out alone, David entered Rue Victor Hugo and dropped to his knees. The sight of this once-beloved thoroughfare was more than he could stand. The pretty buildings flanking either side were now a facade of collapsed roofs and broken walls. Tons of masonry blocks inundated the cobblestone street, forming minibarricades down the corridor. It appeared as if a tornado had battered the quarter with a mighty punch. He got to his feet. With the weight of grief upon his shoulders and in his heart, David climbed over heaps of debris, stopping now and then to dry-vomit after discovering a familiar person lying dead or an abandoned object incinerated along the avenue. He wept when coming across a pile of wicker baskets smoldering on the basket seller's corner. David marveled to locate several lion fountainheads still spewing ice-cold water as if nothing had happened. Destruction stretched down the length of Rue Victor Hugo, up the lower foothills void of vegetation, save for a few seared trees, all the way to the top of the bald smoldering peak of the rumbling and still unstable volcano. David stepped in the doorways of the few standing buildings to find gory scenarios of families still positioned around their breakfast tables. They had been caught in midaction eating, drinking, or talking when the fire cloud hit, instantly solidifying them into inanimate blackened statues.

*   *   *

Yvette and Indigo walked to the awaiting buggy that would take Indigo and Cyrillia into Fort-de-France. Indigo pointed to a knoll where her daughter stood motionless. The arms of the girl were folded, her eyes steadfast upon the burning town of St. Pierre. She refused to leave.

"She is so much like you."

"I know," said Yvette.

"Too much like you. I have to take her away. She must see that there is another way of living. I want her to taste Paris and the freedom it can give her. When she turns sixteen, I will then give her the choice to come back to you or stay in France—but not before. And please don't try to influence her otherwise. I hope you understand."

"I do."

"I love you, Yvette."

They hugged. They cried. They laughed. Theirs was a friendship stronger than the spiritual bond between parent and child, between siblings, between husband and wife, between lovers. There were no rules. There were no conditions. It was a sweet relationship built on an everlasting thread of mutual trust, respect, and love.

Cyrillia knew that soon she would have to leave with her mother. During the events of the past week, she had been shocked by catastrophe after catastrophe and wizened beyond her years by experience. In spite of her ordeals, she studied the aftermath of the volcanic explosion with calm eyes. She sensed that the land would survive—just as she had survived. She sensed that the people would never be quite the same again—just as she would never be the same again. But somehow, deep in her soul, she sensed that both the land and the people would continue and flourish—just as she would continue and flourish. She wished she could stay and help the land on its path to recovery. Yet she was most anxious to explore new horizons and see the foreign places of her storybooks. She knew that one day she would return to this place of wonder, back to her home, to the land, to Martinique. It was where she belonged. For the magic of this island had been indelibly burned into her soul. Cyrillia sighed heavily and marched down the hill to join her family. Indigo was waiting in the buggy in quiet tears. Felecien held the reins with the little dog, Espérer, wagging its tail at his side. Yvette gathered Cyrillia in her arms, kissed her cheeks, and handed her over to Indigo. As the buggy pulled away, the copper-haired child turned in her seat and waved to the woman she had only known as Aunt Yvette. Their mutual green eyes locked in understanding; instinctively, each one knew her future and the future of the other.

*   *   *

At the outskirts of town, David ventured upon an abandoned horse and buggy along the road to Morne Rouge. No one was in sight. The fallen horse had been burned to a crisp from the tip of its nose to where the outer line of volcanic cloud had pared the animal's midsection with such precision that not a hair of its cream-colored backside had been scorched. It amazed David that the maroon surrey had also been left undamaged. There were no occupants around. Farther along, he came upon an exodus of refugees who had survived the edge of the inferno. David gratefully accepted the fresh water and food they graciously offered him. He was warned to be on the lookout for looters preying upon the disadvantaged. Many plantation homes had been brutally plundered by these hungry and crazed men who had nothing to lose.

*   *   *

Yvette was awakened from a nap in the sitting room by gunfire erupting outside the main house. Earlier in the day, those field workers who had not fled the plantation had sought refuge in the front gardens of the circular drive. She ran to the terrace to see a band of a dozen looters attacking her people with bullets and machetes. Two of her field supervisors were doing a gallant job of keeping the attackers at bay. A handful of the workers ran into the house, not knowing what to do. Yvette broke the glass to her father's gun cabinet and began passing out weapons and ammunition.

"Tuto and CeCe, head to the back of the house," she commanded. "Charles, Yé, and Bon Dié, go upstairs and take positions at windows facing the north and south. Franck and Jerome, you two come along with me. There is no time to be afraid. These scavengers won't hesitate a second to kill us. Now fight for your lives."

She grabbed her boar rifle and headed for the front door.

*   *   *

David could hear the sound of gunfire from the dirt road leading to the Chevalier plantation. By the time he reached the main compound, all was quiet. In the yard lay the bodies of nine bandits, along with four dead Chevalier field workers. Three other bandits had been captured by workers.

"Hello there in the house," hollered David. "Is everyone okay?"

The bullet-shattered door opened.

Out stepped Yvette, stalwart despite her apparent exhaustion. She lowered her smoking rifle to the ground when she saw him. "Mon Dieu, David, is it really you? My dear Papa, Aza, Maxi, and so many more are dead, hurt, or gone. It's unbearable. And the land—the beautiful land and its bounty—has vanished," she said, pointing to wilted fields, barren mountains, and the billowing volcano. Overwhelmed by grief and devastation, she wept.

David embraced her trembling body. His intensity offered protection. She pressed a cheek against his chest and, for a moment, surrendered to his strength. The sobs gradually subsided into deep gulps of breaths; and then, finally, quiet resonation calmed her. As soon as she regained control over her raw emotions, she eased herself away from David and squared her shoulders. This was not the time to show weakness. There was too much to be done, and she had to be resilient. She would not let sorrow defeat her.

"I'll be okay now," she proclaimed with steel in her voice.

David knew where Yvette's heart truly belonged. As he would always be one with the sea, she would always be one with the land. And yes, he also knew that she would be okay for those eyes, those beautiful apple green eyes, burned with determination.

THE END

EPILOGUE

One year later
1903
Paris

Indigo relaxed in her lounge chair, taking in the delicate beauty of her rose garden. She was most happy. Her life was complete now that she had fulfilled her dream. She lived in a splendid home with servants of her own. Two of her poems had been published, and she was working on memoirs of her life and times in Martinique. The owner of a publishing house was one of her many male suitors, as well as Yvette's cousin, Paul, who was now a vice president of his father's bank. Paul, smitten years ago when he had visited Martinique as a teenager, had set in mind an image of Indigo that was short of divinity. Now, he was certain of that vision. Over the last twelve months, they had spent hours exploring the exciting Parisian attractions with Cyrillia. Indigo found him endearing, honest, and intelligent. Cyrillia found him silly and fun. It was, in reality, a perfect blend of needs for both mother and daughter.

Today, Indigo had received a letter from Yvette.

Dearest Indigo,

I hope this letter finds you well and happy. How is darling Cyrillia? Mont Pelée is finally quieting down a bit, but the area around here is not. You wouldn't believe the endless traffic of scientists, volcanologists, geologists, reporters, and curiosity seekers poking about the ruins. There are so many conflicting theories and reports. The May 8, 1902, eruption has been declared one of the most catastrophic in history, killing more than 30,000; however, the May 20, 1902, secondary eruption annihilated what was left of St. Pierre and flattened what stood to bare ground. On

August 30, when she erupted yet a third time, as you know from my prior writings, the mountain destroyed out our pretty village of Morne Rouge, killing 2,000 people. The latest scientific report released states that our eruptions are of an unusual volcanic nature not ever seen or recorded before in history. This is what I have learned and will account to you accordingly. Apparently, solidified lava plugged the crater vent, thus creating a powerful buildup of pressure. So when the mountain blew, it blew fragments of the inside of the crater as tiny as dust and as big as houses from a lateral blast from its side, and not from the mouth of the volcano. The molten rock particles glowing at the base of the pent-up matter fueled a fire avalanche. This new type of volcanic eruption, now being referred to as a glowing cloud, has been given the name of nuée ardente. Oh my, this must be boring you. But please, read this part to Cyrillia, as I am sure it will fascinate her.

Again, as you know, the British and American regencies were completely demolished in the May 8 disaster. The bodies of Thomas Prentiss and his family received full military honors in Fort-de-France. I was told that another smaller eruption was taking place about the same time that James Japp's body was being removed by soldiers. They abandoned him. It is most likely that his body will never be recovered. It is assumed that Governor Mouttet and his wife perished in their hotel. Professor Landes was found barely alive at the botanical gardens; his injuries were awful. He died a painful death, I fear.

Father Roche is living in Fort-de-France. He leads a quiet existence. I see him periodically. He is a broken man with broken spirits. Fernand Clerc is residing at his plantation on the east coast of the island. I go there when I can to visit him and his family as they will not venture this way. I am delighted to report that he has become involved, once again, in island politics. Imagine that!

Quite astounding, the two men in St. Pierre who survived the eruption have become quite famous. One of the men was the local cobbler, Léon Compére-Léandre, who was barely alive when found in the cellar of his home. The other survivor was a black prisoner by the name of Auguste Ciparis. He was discovered after surviving in his underground solitary confinement cell for three or four days suffering with second—and third-degree burns. He received a pardon and will be traveling to America to become a sideshow act with the Barnum and Bailey Circus.

Last week, David was here on his stopover in Fort-de-France, his sixth or seventh since the eruption. I daresay he greatly misses the scenic roadstead of St. Pierre. He told me to send you his best. Our friendship has enriched my life, and I treasure it. I care deeply for him, and I know he does as well for me. I feel very comfortable at the present time with the arrangement of our brief encounters. It is a situation that works for us both.

What about Stefan? I know that you are most curious about his role in my life. He is still at my uncle Bernard's plantation in Le Robert and doing quite well as an assistant overseer—as I knew he would. I was there for a visit about two months ago. Stefan is being groomed to become the head field supervisor. I understand from my uncle that he is very ambitious. It wouldn't surprise me if one day he will own his own plantation. He is a remarkable young man and irresistible in so many ways. He continues to profess his undying love and swears that one day he would make himself worthy of me. I told him that he was already worthy of me. It was our society that thought not. I sometimes wished that we lived in a more tolerant world. If this were so, I am sure our relationship would have taken a different turn. Who knows?

The plantation has kept me very busy. Even though the crops were destroyed and all of the following eruptions prevented the planting of new fields, now that the mountain has settled down and has gone back to sleep a few months ago, we begin again seeding the earth. The ash that had fallen upon the soil was rich in minerals and once again, the land will flourish. It is ever so exciting to witness this astonishing rebirth.

I truly enjoyed your latest poem and look forward to your book. Now be kind to the facts, dear friend. Please send my regard to my darling cousin Paul. He writes to me about you, and I think, you might have stolen his heart. Yes?

Stay happy and please give Cyrillia a kiss for me.

All my love, Yvette

Indigo folded the letter, placed it in her bodice, and went to search for her daughter, who was playing hunter in a maze of sculptured dragon-shaped evergreens at the border of the estate.

"Maman," shouted Cyrillia, hiding behind one of the dragons.

"Hello, my darling," answered Indigo.

Indigo beamed. She knew that her child was very special and exceedingly bright for a seven-year-old. People often commented how poised she was for such a young girl. Few knew what she had experienced. Cyrillia wore a golden chain around her neck, and attached to this chain was the pumice stone that Aza had given her the day of the centipede and ant attack. Also attached to the chain was a gold locket—a recent gift from Yvette. Indigo often found Cyrillia opening the locket and staring in wonder at its contents. On one side was a picture of Yvette, and on the other a miniature painting of idyllic St. Pierre the way it looked before its destruction.

Indigo sighed. As passionately as she had dreamed of going to France, she knew her daughter, just as passionately, now dreamed of returning to Martinique. Back to a land blessed with rich volcanic soil and soft tropical breezes.

It was only a matter of time.

*   *   *

INDEX

NOV 1 5 2021